BOOK 1 OF THE "BLOOD & HEARTS DUOLOGY"

A.E. COSBY

BLOOD SEX AND VIOLENCE

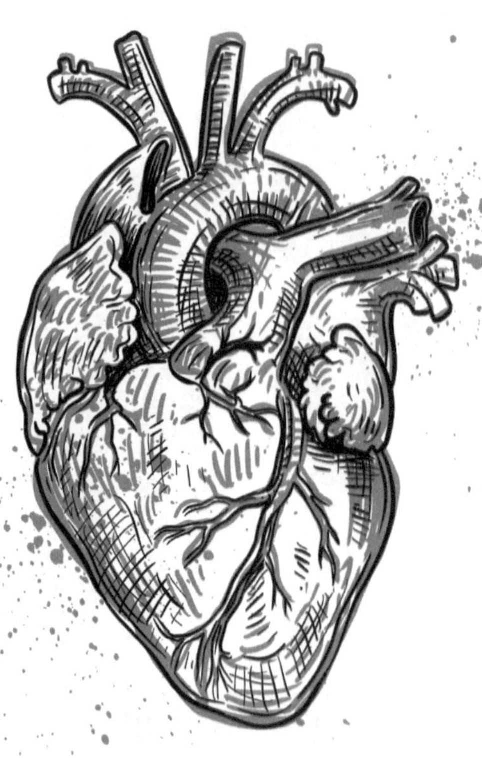

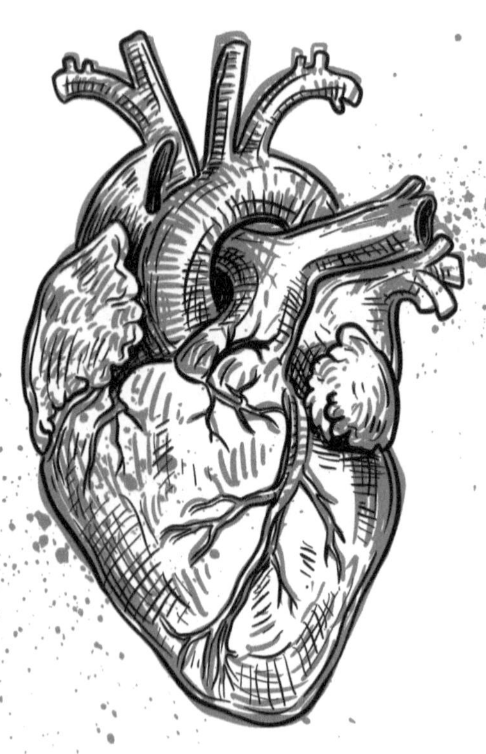

*For those who have loved and lost
but found the strength to keep moving on.
I'm really glad you're still here.*

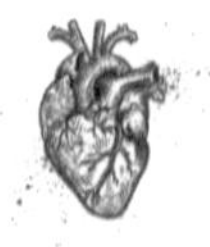

"CYRUS" SOUNDTRACK

(Can be found on Spotify)

Music. I see the world through music. Notes fly through the air, creating song and sound for everything I see. Everything has a song. Everything has a theme. Music has always been a part of my soul. It's how I associate with life.

It was crucial for me to create a soundtrack for every book. Every major scene has a song. Every main character has a song. To add an interactive piece to the novel, when there's a scene with a song, you'll find * with a footnote with the name of the song to listen to.

- Book Theme Song – "Suck It" by Orgy
- Cyrus' Song – "Broken Heart Collector" by Ekoh, Arankai
- Bex's Song – "American Horror Show" by Snow Wife
- Killian's song – "Bad Things" by I Prevail
- Aida – "Daisy" by Ashnikko

SCENE SONGS:
- "Like That" by Sleep Token
- "Mount Everest" by Labrinth
- "Moonlight Sonata – Epic Trailer Version" by Hidden Citizens
- "Descending" by Sleep Token
- "wRoNg (feat. Kehlani)" by ZAYN, Kehlani
- "Jaws" by Sleep Token
- "Slumber Party (feat. Princess Nokia)" by Ashnikko, Princess Nokia
- "Who Do You Want" by Ex Habit
- "CHIHIRO" by Billie Eilish

- "Closer" by Palaye Royale
- "RUNRUNRUN" by Dutch Melrose
- "Desire" by MEG MYERS
- "Go Fuck Yourself" by Two Feet
- "MAKE ME CUM" by Witchz, a calmer place., Erika Sirola
- "Gorilla" by Bruno Mars
- "Please" by Omido, Ex Habit
- "Change (In the House of Flies)" by Deftones
- "Yen" by Slipknot
- "on your knees" by Ex Habit
- "EAT SPIT! (feat Royal & the Serpent) – By Slush Puppy, Royal & the Serpent
- "I'm The Sinner" by Jared Benjamin
- "RAGDOLL" by Vana
- "Aphrodite" by Sam Short
- "No High" by David Kushner
- "Lose Control" by Teddy Swims
- "Skin and Bones – MEDUZA REMIX" by David Kushner, MEDUZA
- "Love Is Going To Kill Us" by David Kushner
- "Dark Signs" by Sleep Token
- "When the Bough Breaks" by Sleep Token
- "DAMAGED (feat Spencer Charnas)" by In This Moment, Ice Nine Kills, Spencer Charnas
- "Bones" by Jared Benjamin
- "when the party's over" by Billie Eilish
- "The Night Does Not Belong To God" by Sleep Token
- "Popular Monster" by Falling in Reverse

AUTHOR'S NOTE

Thank you for deciding to read "Cyrus"!

This is book two of the "Blood & Hearts Duology" and a separate story from book 2. "Cyrus" is a tragic love story with **NO** HEA.

<u>It is not a romance!</u>

If you're familiar with Tristan Aries from "Wrath's Daughter", you will find him as a side character in this book. Please note that this is **before** he's met Styx. You will find a very different Tristan than you're used to.

In this book, you will find two primary languages: Trezoran and Potroyan. They will be reflected in the dialogue as English and Spanish.

Please do not use this book as a guide for romance, BDSM, or coping with mental health disorders. This is a work of fiction and not meant to be used as a guide.

There is a portrayal of suicidal ideations and a suicide attempt.

There is a portrayal of addiction and overdosing.

If you are considering suicide or self-harm, please get help now by contacting the Substance Abuse and Mental Health Administration at: **https://www.samhsa.gov/** or my dialing 988 (for the USA).

CONTENTS INCLUDE

General:
experimentation, eye trauma, gore, graphic violence, graphic language, heavy drug use via snorting, kidnapping, mentions of drug use via needles, mentions of sexual assault due to forced drug use (non-graphic), multiple sex partners not included in the main love interests, sex work, stalking, torture, using sex as a coping mechanism, vampirism and blood feeding

Psychological:
addiction, addiction recovery, anti-social personality disorder, anxiety, depression, graphic attempted suicide, graphic self-harm via cutting, mentions of attempted suicide, mentions of overdosing, mentions of rehab, scarring due to cutting, negative self-talk, overdose, suicidal ideations

Sexual:
anal, bondage, brat taming, cum worship, cock warming, collaring, consensual non-consent, Daddy kink, deep throating, degradation, dom/sub, dubious consent, exhibitionism, free use, fisting, frotting, graphic sex, instances of anal without proper prep (with consent), masochism, orgasm denial, orgies, praise kink, ruined orgasm, sadism, sex against a near dead body, slapping, snowballing, spanking, spitting, spit roast, voyeurism

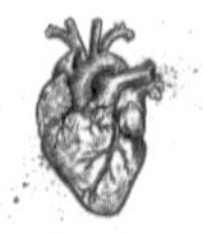

PRONUNCIATION GUIDE & GLOSSARY

Characters

- Aida (a-da)
- Bex
- Cyrus (sigh-rus)
- Jacinto (yah-sin-though)
- Cin (ss-in)
- Killian (Kill-ee-an)
- Tristan Aries (tris-ten) (air-ees)
- Rizor (rye-zor)

Locations

- Euhaven (you-hey-vin) – planet
- Trezora (trey-soar-ah) – Bright Continent
  - Asherai (ash-er-eye) - Country
  - Calñar (cal-knee-ar) - City
  - Melhold (mel-hold) - City
  - Dolsano (dole-sah-no) - Landmark
  - Shayce (shay-ss) - Country
  - Adventus (ad-vent-us) - City
  - Mutuba (moo-too-bah) – City in South Asherai
  - Jilbori Jungle (jill-bar-ee)
- Potroya (poe-troy-ah) – Dark Continent
  - Ayobaí (a-oh-bye) - Country
  - Aludam (al-u-dom)
  - Malagado (mal-ah-gah-though) – City
  - Milagros (me-lah-grows) – City
  - Seeker's Pointe
  - Vascaria (vah-scare-e-ah) – Country
  - Faysos (fay-so-s) – City
- Gailux (gay-lucks) – Northern Continent

- o Tuthia (too-thee-ah) - Country
  - o Ethnies (et-n-eyes) – City
  - o Trustek Slopes (trues-tek) – Mountain region
  - o Grenivik (gren-eh-vick) – Country
  - o Lundr (lun-der) – City
- Temisraine Ocean (tem-is-rain)
- Isla del Cuervo (ee-s-la) (d-el) (kwehr-vo) – Island of Crows

Other

- Anima (an-ee-mah) - Soul
- Orcus (awr-kuhs) - underworld
- Cassus (cass-yus) - the in-between, anima rehabilitation
- Pax (packs) – the afterlife and peace, reincarnation
- Mordax (more-ducks) – punishment for evil/criminal animas

EUHAVEN
Potroya
Faysos
Vascaria
Loquiza Peaks
Seeker's Pointe
Jacar Volcano
Ayobaí
Potroyan Lighthouse
Malagado
Milagros
Aludam
Isla Del Cuer
Temisraine
Horizon Line
Capital
Harbor
Riptide
Melvina's Sacrifice
Silvermoon Biome
Aeshma's Impact
Temple of the Tetrad

Gailux
...hia
Grenivik
Lundr
Ethnies
Trustek Slopes
Trezora
Mt. Vancarres
Crystal Lake
Alburg
Othea
Asherai
Trevern Mesas
...rmoon ...arbor
The Badlands
Shayce
Dolsano Wood
Melhold
Adventus
r
Mt. Chimazi
Shayian Desert
Jilrobi Jungle
...uth Asherai
Mutuba

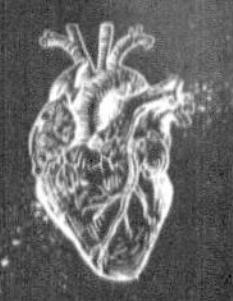

CHAPTER 1

BLOOD & SEX MAKE FOR AN INTERESTING COCKTAIL

I *AM GOING TO MURDER* this motherfucker and make it look like *a fucking accident.*

Cyrus groaned as the thought crossed his mind, making his dick twitch inside the hot wet mouth of the woman who was currently sucking him off. Rolling his hips, she took him further, her tongue expertly working around the head of his cock. He gripped her blonde hair, pale blue eyes staring at him as tears streamed down her face.

"Fuck, okay, stop. Keep it warm," he growled, and the woman blinked twice in acknowledgment.

Cyrus sighed, stretching his arms wide over the back of the couch. Music played in the background, the loud bass thrumming through his body. The Den was alive tonight, people enjoying themselves on the various floors of the club. Resting his head back, he gave the man beside a deadpan look.

"So basically, you're telling me you don't know where the incubus is?" Cyrus' jaw clenched when he nodded. "Erick, what use are you if you can't give me this information?"

"He's a spy. You really expect me to find him?" Erick scoffed, the sound becoming a cry when Cyrus grabbed his hair.

"I expect you to keep an eye on your Governor. It's what I pay you for," Cyrus growled. "Your Governor is Westly's mate. And you are the Governor's fuck toy."

"I'm sorry, I should've tried harder," he whimpered.

"You should've *fucked* harder is more like it," Cyrus snapped.

A server passing behind the couch startled at his tone, dropping their head in a bow as they continued walking. He took a deep breath, pushing it out through his nose, and let his gaze glance around the Exhibition Hall. Smirking, he watched as a man in a muzzle attached to a leash crawled next to his leather-clad Mistress. She gave Cyrus a wink, pink succubus eyes glinting in the neon lights.

Cyrus turned his attention back onto Erick. "Look, just get me the information. If I start to get the sense that you're lying to me to protect them, I will not hesitate to hand you over to the Interrogator."

Erick paled, panic rising in his gaze, and the sound of his pounding heart made Cyrus' fangs drop. "I-I will, I promise. Give me another week or two, please," he begged.

Cyrus eyed the pulse at the man's neck, his vision tinting red as his bloodlust rose. Keeping his grip on Erick's hair, he pulled the man closer in to lick the sweet, throbbing vein.

"I know you're not working tonight," he purred, smirking when the incubus shivered.

"Go ahead. Please." He arched his chin to expose his throat further.

Cyrus didn't hesitate, fangs sinking deep. The sweet rush of blood filled his mouth as he greedily drank.

Cyrus grunted, gripping the woman keeping his dick warm with her hot mouth by the hair. Shifting his hips, he urged her to start bobbing, the sensation almost making his eyes roll.

Fuck. How long had she been sitting there? An hour? He mentally shrugged as he held her down so he could fuck between those plush lips.

The red haze clouding Cyrus' vision deepened as he continued to drink from Erick. The man's pulse turned thready, his life draining. Shit, that wouldn't be good. He needed him to find Westly, which couldn't happen if the incubus was dead.

"You taste fucking delicious. I'll give you that," Cyrus breathed as he managed to pull himself away.

Incubi always tasted like sex and sin and made him higher than a kite. He licked the puncture wounds, closing them with his saliva.

"Now, find out where Westly is hiding." He moved his hand

from the man's nape to his throat, digging his fingers in while continuing to buck up into the woman's mouth. "I don't want to ruin this pretty neck of yours."

"Yes, my lord. I'll make sure to do that. I promise I'll get the information you need," Erick said, standing once Cyrus let him go.

"Keep doing that," he groaned, driving into the woman's mouth deeper until her throat closed around him.

A pair of hazel eyes held him hostage, keeping him from being able to relax and enjoy the wet heat around his length.* Strands of short, wavy hair fell to their cheekbones. Those eyes flashed the neon green of a werewolf, their gaze holding his as they jerked off two men while straddling the face of another.

"Get off," he bit out to the human in his lap.

Disappointment covered her face as she parted from his dick so he could stand. He pulled her up to sink his fangs into her throat, her blood adding to his much-needed high. Passing her off to another vampire, he stalked toward the wolf. Those hazel eyes heated, tongue darting out to play with their lip ring.

"My lord," they moaned, their voice a husky alto with a slight feminine lilt. As they rocked their hips, their small breasts swayed. The o-ring collar clinked with each movement.

"You like being a little fuck toy, don't you," he observed, sinking a hand into their navy hair and using his free hand to stroke his dick.

The wolf was stunning. An amalgam of tattoos adorned one side of their lithe body. Their lips were swollen and pouting, evidence of how much they'd been putting them to use. This close, he could see their pupils were dilated, and not just from desire. They were high, likely on potions, but that was none of his business.

Stamped on their wrist was a golden stamp of a mouth with white droplets surrounding it, signaling that the wolf was into head and cum play only for the night.

"Yes," they panted, the men next to them groaning as the wolf stroked their dicks faster. "I have a hole you can fill," they

---

* "Like That" by Sleep Token

moaned as they opened their mouth.

"Yes, you fucking do," Cyrus growled, thrusting between their parted lips. "Does the filthy wolf enjoy being a cum slut?"

He held their head so he could use them as he pleased. Watering hazel eyes locked onto his in agreement. He grinned, running a fang over his lower lip. He briefly looked at the men on either side of the wolf, a vampire and Water Wielder, and his grin widened.

Placing his hands over the wolf's, he stilled their movement, ignoring the grunts from the men.

"Jerk yourselves off, gentlemen. Let's reward the slut with all the cum they want." Cyrus continued fucking the wolf's mouth, getting deep enough to feel their throat tighten around his dick. "Such a perfect fuck toy."

"Fuck, you're so wet, dripping all over me," the man moaned from under the wolf as he stroked himself faster, cock angled toward the wolf's back.

"All of you aren't to come until the toy does," Cyrus commanded.

The vampire and the Water Wielder knelt to take the wolf's breasts in hand, mouths latching onto each nipple.

"Oh fuck!" they moaned, momentarily pulling away from Cyrus.

He roughly grabbed their hair and thrust back in to gag them.

"No. Toys don't speak. They get fucked." He groaned when they whimpered around him and gripped his thighs, nails digging in. "That's right. The slut is ready to come in front of everyone."

They'd garnered an audience, a mix of people watching their orgy with hungry gazes. The wolf's eyes rolled as their orgasm rocked through their body.

"Coat their body. Only *I* get their mouth and face," Cyrus said as the three other men worked themselves higher.

One at a time, each of them—save for Cyrus—came, painting the wolf's back and chest with their release. Their light brown skin glistened under the neon lights, and he watched with fascination as the cum dripped down their heaving chest.

"Watch if you want but they're all mine now," he growled. No one argued as they moved away from the wolf, who was now on their knees before him. The wolf looked up at him with delight in their eyes, ready and willing for more.

With one hand under their chin and the other in their hair, he growled, "My turn."

Like the toy they were, he fucked their throat. He fucked it till he was confident they would be hoarse and sore when they tried to speak.

"Look at the mess everyone made of you," he groaned, encouraged further when they gripped his ass tightly.

"Fuck, keep your mouth open," he ordered as he pulled out.

Saliva poured from their mouth, mascara running down their cheeks. They were filthy. They were perfectly messy. He quickly stroked himself and shouted as he came, covering their face and mouth with his cum. The wolf grinned, elation clear on their face, as they dragged their fingers in his seed and sucked them off one by one.

"Thank you for your cum," they rasped, voice barely audible.

He pulled them up to stand by their collar, enjoying the whimpers that escaped them. "Be careful, little wolf. Keep talking like that, and I'm liable to keep you as my own personal toy," he chuckled. "And I don't share my toys without permission." He took their hand and spun them to get a good look at their cum covered body. "Fuck I want to clean you up just to dirty you all over again."

"Why don't you, my lord?" they whimpered when he dragged his fingers through the cum to rub across their face. He plunged the digits into their mouth, and they sucked, cleaning them off as he pumped.

"I have someplace to be," he said, continuing his shallow thrusts. "If I had the time, I'd fuck you until you were a sobbing, cum-covered mess and begging me to stop. You'd make the perfect little cum slut for me."

Dragging his fingers out, he gripped their chin roughly to keep their mouth open. "Until next time, fuck toy." He spat in their mouth and let them go.

"Sure thing, boss," the wolf said with a smirk, allowing a woman decked out in black leather to attach a leash to their collar and pull them away.

Boss? He shrugged off the thought, grabbed a rag to clean himself, fixed his clothing, and headed toward the Hall's exit. A set of ebony double doors separated the hall from the VIP lounge beyond it. No one was allowed in the hall without getting stamped. It was the verification necessary to make sure everyone who participated was there willingly and enthusiastically.

Music rapidly became louder as he moved through the smokey lounge area and down the stairs. As soon as he reached the first floor, he beelined it to the massive black marble bar. Shelves lined with glow lights were filled with an assortment of liquor selections.

Cyrus' gaze caught on the sexy as fuck bartender and owner of The Den, Royal. His warm, light tan skin was flushed as he hustled and made drinks. The playful smirk on his pouting lips was as if he had a secret to tell. Flawless black hair was smoothed back, and a graphic tee and blue jeans completed his look.

"Tequila," Cyrus said, getting the man's attention, calling emerald eyes to meet his yellow gaze.

"Single or double?" he asked, hopping onto the bar ladder.

"Double. Heading out." Cyrus' rings clinked as he drummed his fingers along the obsidian bar top.

"Ayobaí's best," Royal said with a grin as he jumped from the ladder to land on soft feet. After pouring the glass, he pushed the drink toward Cyrus. "Gotta go."

"You know, if you keep looking at my brother like that, his partner will definitely attempt to fuck you up," a smooth masculine voice garnered his attention.

Cyrus did a double take, looking at the man, then at Royal, and back.

"I didn't know Royal had a twin," he said, arching an eyebrow. They were nearly identical, except that the man before him was thick. He had a slightly rounded face and a soft stomach that Cyrus wanted to get his hands on. His hair was a ruffled mess, sticking up in a way that somehow worked for his grunge look.

"Yeah. Well. He doesn't talk to me much," the man said nonchalantly. "I'm the *bad* twin." He snorted, taking Cyrus' drink and downing it in one gulp. "I'm Killian."

"And that was my drink…" Cyrus grumbled with an annoyed huff.

Killian shrugged, clearly not giving a fuck.

"I'm—"

"I know the King's Cortesano when I see him."

"Naturally." Cyrus tapped his finger on the empty glass. "And what brings you here?"

"Family business. I own The Crow's Cauldron up the street but occasionally help around here. Royal needs to take some time off, so here I am," Killian said as he hopped his ass onto the bar. He twisted and landed on the other side. Taking a step onto the ladder, he gave Cyrus a wink. "Double pour of the best tequila, right?"

Cyrus had to give it to the man. He paid attention. Nodding, Cyrus took a good look at the man's plump ass as he climbed to the top shelf. The jeans he wore pulled tight around his thighs, a chain clinking as it hung from his front belt loop to his back pocket. Fuck, he was thick and soft in all the right places.

Killian jumped down, landing lightly, just like his twin. Cyrus didn't hide his obvious perusal of the human, starting with his tattooed hands and arms, to the way his clothes clung to his body, and up to those delicious, fuckable lips.

A blush crossed Killian's light tan cheeks, and he smirked.

"Enough," he said firmly, pushing the glass toward Cyrus.

"Can't help it if you look good enough to eat," he said with a wink.

"Oh, booooo," Killian taunted, nose scrunched up, his kohl-lined emerald eyes squinting.

Cyrus couldn't help but laugh at his attempt at a joke going horribly.

"I am not sure if that's the best thing for a vampire to say to a human." A tongue ring glinted in the neon lights while he spoke. A couple on the other end of the bar drew the man's attention. "Gotta go. Bro's getting swarmed, and he won't admit he needs help. Want me to close it out?" When Cyrus nodded, Killian left to help his other guests.

As he brought his drink to his lips, a woman bumped into his arm, almost spilling the precious liquor.

"Fuck!" she slurred, turning to look up at him with the most intense grey eyes he'd ever seen. The Storm Wielder's dark brown skin glimmered with a dusting of glitter and sweat.

"Damn, baby, gotta watch where you're going," the man behind her said, pulling her into him. "Sorry, man."

Cyrus nodded, downing his drink and placing the empty glass on the bar.

The woman licked her lower lip, swollen from obvious kissing, and turned to her partner. "Come on, let's go fuck," she said, grabbing his arm and leading them toward the second floor.

Cyrus watched them go with mild intrigue. He looked back up the bar once more in search of Killian, who paid him no mind. Smirking, he left a sizeable tip, heading toward the exit and the fresh, cool air.

Cyrus' overheated skin welcomed the breeze. Nights like this made Cyrus grateful for Potroya's perpetual darkness. The yellow crescent moon hung lazily in the sky, signifying it was true night and not just the planetary tilt. A deep inhale of the chilled air brought him some semblance of calm.

He had shit to do, and he needed to get it done before Ithea rose to signify a new night.

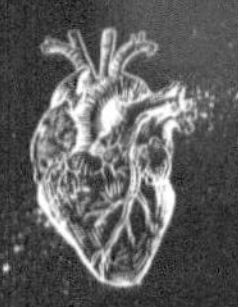

CHAPTER 2

NO ONE SAID BEING THE BOSS WOULD BE EASY

CYRUS WHISTLED AS HE carved into the screaming incubus currently hanging by his wrists in his interrogation cell. His white suit was coated in blood, and a grin split across his face as he finished the word 'TRAITOR' on his back.

A signature look, that.

Rounding the man, he dragged the tip of his serrated knife along his jawline.

"You've failed your kingdom, Westly. You were next in line to become Spymaster and threw it all away. For what? Money? Prestige? How stupid are you?" he mused, drawing the blade down the center of the incubus's chest, leaving a trail of blood in its wake as the skin split like butter.

"I'm sorry! I-I promise it won't happen again," the man sobbed through punched-swollen lips.

"Correct you are, little incubus. It won't happen because you'll be dead. Now, is there anyone I should notify? Let them know you've—"

"Wait! Wait, I have information," he screeched right as Cyrus inserted the knife above his navel.

He bit back a growl, wanting—no, needing—to pull the entrails out through the man's stomach. His madness had been on the edge of uncontrollable lately. As a berserker, his need to feed was already nearly insatiable compared to normal vampires. Add on the stress of all of these traitors threatening his King's rule, and it left an ache for violence. Cyrus wondered if the wolf he'd mouth-fucked at the Den added to the risk of his sanity. Or maybe it was

---

* "Mount Everest" by Labrinth

Killian? The two wouldn't leave his mind. Their faces on constant replay. Frustration at the distraction overtook him.

"And what information is that?"

"I-if you promise to make my death swift, I'll tell you."

"You're a bold motherfucker," Cyrus chuckled, twisting the knife slowly and grinning at the glorious scream that followed.

"Please!" the spy sagged in relief when he stopped.

"All right. Speak."

"D-defectors! I know someone who might know who some of them are."

Cyrus froze. "Might?"

"No, I mean he does for s-sure..." Westly breathed. "June Edwards, siren. He boasted about it. Being in the big leagues." Westly groaned in pain and coughed. "There's movement happening in Asherai. I don't know what. But June does."

"Is that all?" Cyrus asked gently, injecting a false sense of empathy into his tone.

"Y-yes. Please. Make it quick," he sobbed.

Cyrus' grip on the pommel tightened. "For a spy, you are terrible at your job," he said flatly, dragging the knife down.

Pure glee filled him as he dug his hands into the man's stomach, taking a fist full of his entrails and pulling them out. What a fucking sight! He clapped his hands, pleased with his work. Watching the bloodied organs slop to the ground, he sighed.

Cyrus resumed whistling as he exited the interrogation cell, leaving the screaming incubus behind to succumb to his wounds. Slow deaths were his favorite form of torture. Knowing they were filled with pain and thinking of their traitorous ways satisfied his need for bloodshed.

As he walked to his private changing room, he absentmindedly adjusted his blood-soaked white suit, taking a look at his watch. Fuck. He was running behind.

Managing to keep his handkerchief clean, he plucked it from his breast pocket and wiped his face. After shrugging out of his clothes, he dropped everything into an incinerator, having an endless supply of white suits available when needed. He wore them only for Interrogations, enjoying the way crimson looked splattered against them. He quickly washed his forearms and hands, wishing he had time for a shower.

"Cin is going to be pissed," he grumbled.

Cyrus was rarely, if ever, late to meetings. But the past two weeks had him on edge. Thoughts of the Den filtered through his mind. Between the sexy slut of a wolf and Killian's fine ass, he was pent up.

So what if his prisoners suffered for it?

After cleaning and dressing into a navy, double-breasted suit, he made his way to the conference room. He almost snorted when he found Jacinto lounging in jeans and a tee, sneaker-clad feet up on the table. He relayed the information he'd learned to the King, crossing his arms.

"Kayne has a recommendation for a new spy. One he trained to take his place as Spymaster one night," Jacinto said in greeting.

"I hope they're better than the last one," Cyrus grumbled.

"I am. Very much so," came a familiar, raspy voice.

Slowly, he turned toward the open door and froze. The werewolf from the Den leaned against the frame, wearing a leather one-piece that hugged every bit of their lithe and athletic body. Daggers were strapped to a belt around their waist, guns holstered on their thighs. A small tactical backpack completed their gear. The o-ring on their spiked collar dangled as they moved.

"You…"

Cyrus never felt the need to fill the silence. Over two hundred years, he'd learned to use his voice sparingly. Even so, it was rare for him to be rendered speechless. But looking at the wolf… he was at a loss for words, his silence their doing rather than his choice.

Fuck. How was it possible that someone this sexy existed?

"Hey, boss," they said, a smirk pulling up their pierced, lush lips.

Lips he remembered quite vividly being wrapped around his cock. Cyrus fought to calm the blood, trying to rush south.

"You two know each other?" Jacinto asked with amusement, drawing Cyrus' attention back to his King.

He and the wolf spoke at the same time.

"We've met."

"We've fucked."

He scowled at the spy, ignoring Jacinto's bark of laughter.

"I'm Bex," they said with a wink.

"¡Coño! You didn't even get their name?" the fucker of a King belted, laughing harder.

He narrowed his eyes at the vampire.

"Sue me. I was too busy making a—" Cyrus cut himself off with a clenched jaw. Now was not the time.

"What information do you have, Bex?" Jacinto asked when he got himself under control.

The wolf sauntered to the King, unsnapping their backpack to pull out a holoport. After tapping a few items, they handed it over.

"First, there's been movement in Othea. My sources say they're moving their navy into a protective position."

"How did you obtain this information?" Cyrus asked, suspicious.

"I am a spy?" they asked as if it were a question. "Want me to tell you all the trade secrets?"

Their sass made his dick twitch. He wondered how he could put that mouth to better use. See how much sass they'd have when they were choking on his dick.

Whoa now…

"Mira, focus," Jacinto snapped, drawing both of their attention.

"Sorry," Bex said with a bow of their head. At least they knew when to apologize. "Something is off overseas."

"Besides the fact they're trying to obtain our trade and military secrets?" Cyrus asked dryly.

"No, it's not all of them. I haven't received word that Adventus is making any moves. South Asherai, either. I think the Martyrs might be involved. Did the incubus give you any information about this?"

"Yes," Cyrus bit out. "We have a name. Tristan will be doing the pickup."

"All right, I can work with him." They shrugged. "Maybe—"

"Actually, you will work alongside me on a separate assignment," Cyrus interrupted, amused at their annoyed glance.

An idea struck him, and if it meant he could spend more time in their presence, he would do it. Why? He wasn't sure. All he knew was that he needed to.

"Sure. Fine."

He bit back a grin at their clipped words.

Jacinto looked between them with a raised eyebrow. "Am I going to regret having you two work together?" he asked seriously.

"Nope," Bex said, popping the P.

"Never," Cyrus said immediately after.

"Mhmm. All right, Bex, you're dismissed for now," Jacinto said, turning to get on his comm.

The wolf nodded, brushing past Cyrus on their way out. His eyes nearly rolled at their spiced apple scent. They stopped abruptly, staring at him with piercing hazel eyes.

"What were you going to say earlier?" they murmured soft enough that only he heard. Cyrus' brows furrowed in confusion. "When you were trying to reason why you never got my name." Bex stepped closer. Just a few inches shorter than his six-seven frame, their chest brushed against his.

For some reason, the proximity made his heart rate increase. Cyrus didn't stop himself from leaning in, subtly hooking his finger in their collar to pull them closer.

"I was going to say I was too busy making a cum slut out of you to get your name," he whispered, enjoying the shiver that shook their body.

His gaze flicked to Jacinto, whose back was still to them, and sucked on their earlobe, dragging a fang across the flesh. It was risky, but he did it anyway.

"Oh..." they breathed, gripping the lapels of his jacket.

He pulled back, smirking at the pout that formed on their lips.

"I was serious about working together. Meet me tomorrow, mid-Ithea, and we'll talk about it," he said abruptly, taking a step back as the King turned to face them with a questioning look.

"You got it, boss." They winked as they made their way down the hallway.

"Rizor needs an update on exports…" Jacinto grunted as he motioned for Cyrus to sit, pushing his hair into a messy bun. It made his features sharper, highlighting his smooth jaw and crisp cheekbones.

A glint passed Jacinto's eyes, and Cyrus sighed, dropping his head.

"Out with it."

"Seems I was right about going to The Den. Also, it seems like you need to go again."

"Is it that obvious?" Cyrus asked as he lifted his gaze to him.

"You forget, I made you. I am always aware of your needs." He held up a hand before Cyrus could retort. "You can't keep trying to go weeks without satiatioin."

"We just fed not too long ago," he pointed out.

"Sí, but don't act like you got your fill. You need blood more often than other vampires. You test yourself when you go more than three nights between feedings."

Cyrus hated to admit his friend was right. His focus had been much more sharp after feeding at the Den. But he hated how dependent he was on it. It was dangerous for a berserker like him to go too long between feeds, and yet he found himself tempting it each time, trying to see how far he could push his limits. It was painfully foolish, and his Sire saw straight through him.

"You let your internal chaos keep you from your needs," Jacinto said with concern, brows furrowing as he sat up. The King let his gaze rove over Cyrus' face, reading him clear as Ithea.

"Who's going to keep watch when your back is turned?" Cyrus asked softly, averting his gaze. "My purpose is to ensure that you, as my Sire, are always safe and protected."

"I've long since released you from that commitment. You are free to do what you want."

"You know I can't do that," he said sharply. "I need you to keep me controlled. I..." His nose flared as he closed his eyes, hating the show of vulnerability.

"Mirame," Jacinto commanded gently. Even if he wanted, Cyrus couldn't stop the compulsion to follow his Sire's order. "I am here. I will always be here. You can still serve yourself while doing your job as Cortesano. You've never broken my compulsion before. I trust you'll be fine as long as you keep up with your feedings. Just get out of that cabeza of yours."

"You're right," Cyrus said, hating it all the same.

There were nights where he just wished he was... what? Normal? He didn't know, just something other than a monster.

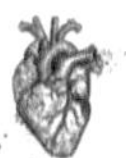

CYRUS GLARED AT THE holoscreens in front of him. He rubbed his temples as he read over the details of the current case he was working on. He spent overnight and part of early Ithea pouring over it all. The planet was now high in the sky at its zenith, aiding in how they told the time.

"Knock, knock."

Bex's sultry voice drew his attention from the screens, and he nearly growled as he took them in. A black mesh top showed their purple bra and tattooed-covered body. Their signature leather pants looked painted onto their lean legs. As they stepped into his office, the chains at their waist clinked along with the ones on their studded combat boots.

"Close the door," he said, voice gruffer than he intended. Bex did so without question, ruffling their short, navy hair that fell over their brows.

The wolf had an odd effect on him that he didn't understand. What words could be said about the way his heart raced when they were near? Or the way their scent was intoxicating? For some reason, from the moment they met, he felt a tether. A tether that was unwelcome because Cyrus did not do attachments.

"What's up?" they asked, playing with their lip ring.

"What do you know of the Carnicero Cerebral?" he asked as he pushed a holoport across the desk.

Bex raised a brow, sitting across from him and taking the device. After looking it over, they pursed their lips.

"They're a serial killer with a penchant for infecting the brains of their victims, leaving the brains with black markings. Considering the clean cut around the skull, they likely have a medical background." They placed the holoport back down. "Motive is still unclear, only that the numbers are increasing. Why is this serial killer important to the Cortesano of the King?"

"I need to find out what exactly they're doing to these brains," he said simply.

The pair stared at each other for a long moment.

"... And?" Bex finally asked.

"I have a special interest in understanding their findings. Why are they doing it? Why are all their victims people with a criminal history? It seems more than just vigilantism." Cyrus sighed. "And it is making the Governors weary. There is already dissent, and now we have the risk of defectors. It must be handled delicately, so I want to work on this with you."

Amongst other things.

Bex nodded in understanding. "All right. I'll gather the intel I have."

"Don't leave. I'm not done," he commanded when they rose from their seat.

Bex instantly complied, plopping back down.

"What else did you need?" Their knee bounced as they gazed around the room before settling back on him.

"Have somewhere to be?" he asked, adjusting his cuffs nonchalantly.

"Yes and no," they sighed.

"Come here," he said, watching their pupils dilate slowly.

Rising, they sauntered their way around the desk to stand

in front of him. Cyrus knew keeping things professional between them was the best route. Having sex once with someone he barely knew shouldn't have been taking over his impulses so much.

But … they were. So, he didn't stop himself from commanding, "On your knees."

Bex knelt without question. He leaned forward, hooking his finger in their hot pink and purple collar, and jerked them toward him. "I don't care that you're an addict. When you are here, you are not to be high. You deal with that shit outside of the Palacio, understood?"

"Y-yes, my Lord," they whispered, licking their lips.

Their tongue slid out to play with their piercing. How tempting it was to make a mess out of their mouth. Unable to resist, he used his free hand, dragging his fingers along their supple flesh, and plunged them in. They latched on to him, sucking on the digits.

Fuck.

"You know. I was going to try and keep this professional, but then I remembered how good you looked at my feet." His fingers slid in and out of their mouth as he spoke. "So, I still plan on making a cum slut out of you again," he growled.

"You're going to swallow and choke on my dick. Cry and beg for more." The grip on their collar moved to their throat, tightening slowly. "You will be my special toy to use and fuck."

Bex whimpered as he thrust his fingers deeper. Their tongue relaxed under his fingers, staving off their gag reflex like an expert.

"Such a filthy little wolf." He pulled his fingers out, cock straining against the front of his slacks as he smeared their saliva across their face. Gripping their chin, he forced their mouth open. "I will see you next week, and you better be sober," he said, spitting onto their eager tongue and making Bex moan.

"Yes, my Lord," they breathed when he let them go. Slowly, Bex rose to their feet, legs wobbling. Cyrus shot up to catch them when their knees buckled. The scent of apples and spice wafted from them, and he had to keep himself from groaning. "Sorry. I'm okay. I'm good," Bex said as they removed themself from his arms.

"Are you sure?" he asked, surprised at his sincerity.

They nodded as they maneuvered around the desk, chains swaying as they did so.

"Yep. See you next week, boss," they said, winking as they exited the office.

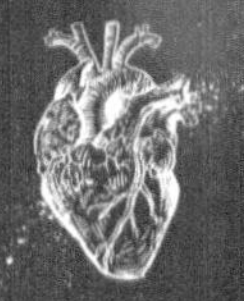

CHAPTER 3

LOOK WHAT THE STORM BLEW IN

"**'LL ADMIT THAT I** am surprised to see you here, Cyrus," Lyn said curiously from behind her face mask. The coroner rounded the autopsy table, humming as she took gentle care of holding the man's head up from the surface.

"I've been assigned to this case personally. The Governors are not too pleased a serial killer is galivanting around Malagado." Cyrus leaned in to take a look at the clean cut around the victim's head.

Hands gloved, he tugged the hair gently. The top of the skull popped off like a bottle cap, revealing what he already knew. "Black veins..." he mused, admiring the handiwork. If he could only get his hands on the killer ... Oh, the questions he'd ask while seeing how they held up under torture.

"There are electrode markings on the temples and chest," she stated.

"Did they all have these markings?" he raised an eyebrow.

"Not that we noticed unless Carnicero Cerebral got sloppy this time. I've seen a lot of shit over the decades, but this is a first, for sure."

"That's why we're bringing in a consultant," he said.

"Oh ... About her—" she started.

"Hmm, but why the brain?" he wondered out loud at the same time she spoke.

"For study," came a feminine soprano from the opposite side of the room.

He turned his gaze up to look at the woman who had just graced the doorway of their autopsy room. A woman he most certainly had seen previously.

Thick, tightly coiled, black hair rested on the head of a stunning Storm Wielder. Her silver eyes glowed in bright contrast against her dark brown skin. Those piercing eyes were the same as the night they'd passed each other in The Den. Her sneakers barely made a sound as she made her way inside. The glare she leveled at him was unwarranted, given that they'd never formally met. He doubted she remembered him from their brief passing, considering she was drunk as fuck.

"Oh boy…" Lyn mumbled with caution, sinking into her lab coat. "Just know I tried to warn you." Her voice was so soft only Cyrus could hear.

"And you are?" Cyrus asked the woman dryly as he removed his mask.

"Doctor Aida Broderick," she said smoothly. The woman somehow managed to look down her nose at him, being over a foot shorter. "If someone is infecting brains, it is to study them; that much should be obvious."

"You must be the neurosurgeon, then." He removed his gloves and extended a hand. "I'm Cyrus—"

"I know who you are." She looked up from his hand without taking it. He narrowed his eyes at her disrespect. "Cortesano to the great King." Sarcasm laced her tone.

Cyrus nodded to the body on the table. "Explain your reasoning."

She brushed past him, the scent of lilacs and petrichor following behind. He tried not to clench his jaw as she removed her plum leather jacket, revealing navy scrubs underneath. Storm Wieldermarks crawled up one of her arms in an array of lightning, storm clouds, and tornados. After washing her hands, she slapped on some gloves to inspect the brain. She hummed as she ran her thumb gently over the black veins.

"The brain is a fascinating specimen. It holds answers to how we live, breathe, think, and more. The decisions we make are all housed here," she said without looking at him. "Why else would someone infect it if not to study it? The electrode markings on the temples and chest indicate some form of medical testing was performed prior to their deaths. It's clear the Carnicero Cerebral is studying the victims. It might not even be an infection. Sounds more like experimentation."

"That makes a lot of sense," he murmured, reluctantly impressed.

The doctor straightened, leveling that glare at him again.

"Excuse me, is there a problem here?" He raised an eyebrow, wondering if he needed to consider a different consultant. Her attitude was lighting his own, and he wouldn't stand for it. Respect was something he worked for and demanded. He refused to accept otherwise.

"Yes. You." She pointed at him with a scalpel in hand.

He stepped up to her, noticing Lyn had made herself scarce. Probably to avoid what seemed to be an impending explosion. Smart woman.

"*Me?* Why? I don't even fucking know you," he bit out.

"You are in *my* space, possibly fucking things up." Doctor Broderick motioned to the gloves he discarded on a nearby counter and motioned to the trash bin to prove her point. "A politician has no place here. All you do is waste time asking questions about things you'll never understand."

"*I* am the one who brought you in," he growled as he snatched the gloves and deposited them like he would've had he not been distracted. "Your expertise is why you are here. But your disrespect will cost you your job if you keep it up."

"My *expertise* is exactly why you won't do that," she snapped. "You don't have anyone better than me who can explain what is wrong with the brains or the psychological aspects behind the serial killer's motive. Do you know any other double-board-certified physicians? Specifically in neurosurgery and—"

"Psychiatry. Yes, I know your credentials, doctor," he cut her off.

The need to sink his fangs in her throat came strong and fast. The more she pissed him off, the more he could imagine spilling her blood. Fuck. He would've found a way if they didn't need her.

"Smart as you may be, you will understand your place. You said it yourself; you know who I am. That means you know I can royally fuck up your life in an instant." He emphasized with a snap of his fingers. Cyrus took immense joy at the lightning flashing in her eyes, her jaw clenching tight. An evil smirk slowly pulled up his mouth. "Your nice little attitude earned you a new lab partner."

"What?" she hissed, nose flaring.

He saw it the moment she realized what he meant, and his grin grew. What better way to piss off an arrogant jerk than to add another to the mix?

"Oh, yes. You'll find I'm deeply invested in finding this murderer. Cortesano or not, I will be your partner."

"Absolutely, fucking, not," she seethed. "This is an already sensitive and difficult case. I do not need some politician to babysit while I work. I can do this myself."

Cyrus raised an eyebrow, fixing his cuffs while continuing to grin, knowing it pissed her off. "I'm sure with your *expertise*, you can explain as you show me."

It was his turn to brush past her. He held back a hiss when electricity skittered from her body to his. While Storm Wielders couldn't Wield their weather abilities indoors, electricity was the one thing they could use at a minimum capacity. Snatching her arm, he whirled her around to face him. Those silver eyes glowed, full of disdain.

"Try your Wielding on me again, and I will personally lock you. The fuck. Up."

"Let me go," she growled, though the lightning in her eyes dimmed slowly.

"I will be back in two nights. Bring your annotations and findings along with any pertinent research you have."

He dropped his hand before he risked piercing her flesh with his nails. He had to keep the doc intact until he could do what he really wanted.

"I have surgeries back-to-back that evening," Doctor Broderick said, stepping away from him.

Cyrus grinned at her again, flashing his fangs. "Make sure you have an energy drink then."

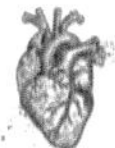

CYRUS FOUND HIMSELF AT Malagado University Medical Center's neurosurgery department, sitting comfortably in Doctor Broderick's office chair. He had one foot crossed over the opposite knee, ring-covered fingers tapping the desk lightly. He'd been patiently waiting for the good surgeon to finish up with her workload. The doorknob jiggled as he heard voices on the other side.

"Doctor Broderick! Wait, there's someone—"

"Not now, Poppy. I have to get ready for this asshole of a vampire, and I hate to admit that I *do* need that energy drink," she snapped, throwing the door open and stopping dead in her tracks when she saw him.

"Why the fuck are you in my office?" She stuck her head out of the door, presumably to yell at her assistant, "Why the *fuck* is he in my office!"

"I-I tried to tell you. He's the Cortesano. I can't exactly say n-no," the assistant whimpered.

"Now, now. Cut her some slack and get in here," Cyrus said, cutting off whatever Doctor Broderick was going to fire back.

Her jaw clenched as she turned slowly, stepped in, and snapped the door shut.

"This is an invasion of privacy and a risk to the confidentiality of my patients." She rounded the desk, motioning at him to move. "Get out of my chair."

"Only if you ask nicely," he snarked.

"Classic." She sneered, heading to her mini-fridge to pull out a can of buzz juice. Cracking it open, she guzzled it down. "I figured you had control issues wrapped up in your past," she grumbled as she tossed the can into a bin.

"Excuse me?" His grin dropped immediately, back stiffening at her assessment.

"What happened before you turned into a vampire? Back

in Mutuba?" Crossing her arms, her eyebrow lifted, eyes darkening to steel in ire.

He stood up slowly, anger filling him like lava in his veins.

A sick, sadistic smile perked up her full lips. "Yes, I can research too. I'd be stupid not to."

"Don't speak on things you don't know," he warned.

Visions of his past flashed through his mind: blood on his hands, the screams of his mother and sisters, and children crying. He had to avoid shaking his head lest he prove to her how much she rattled him. Fuck her for that.

"Funny, I think I was trying to tell you the same when I said I didn't want you as a partner." She hummed to herself as she looked him up and down. "Your shoulders tighten when you feel threatened or annoyed. You had a slight shift in your gait, which tells me one or both of your hips went taut. It's clear that disrespect is a slap to your face a bit more than it would be to anyone else."

She tilted her head, eerily reading him as if she'd known him forever. How the fuck did she know all of this from one meeting? The question played several times as he processed where she was coming from.

"So, what, you're trying to tell me that it's all because of trauma?" He took a threatening step forward, mildly impressed that she remained firm in place.

"Oh! Look at you," she said while clapping her hands. "I guess I don't have to explain everything after all."

"Question..." Cyrus looked at his cuffs, waiting for her reply. He tilted his head to the side, cracking his neck and doing the same on the other side.

"Ask it," she snapped after a few moments.

"Do. You. Have..." he started, taking a step with each word until he was practically touching her with his body. "A death wish?" he growled, finally meeting her unflinching gaze. "I've sliced throats for less."

His fangs crested at the thought, a low hum sounding from within his chest. Once more, he was envisioning what it would feel like to tear into her throat and gorge himself on her blood.

He internally groaned as Jacinto's voice echoed in his head, reminding him why it was essential to feed frequently.

"Have you ever asked yourself why your first response is violence?" Doctor Broderick tapped a finger on his chest, making his nose flare in irritation. "Someone hurt you or someone you loved. Badly. And that has made you a monster."

She scoffed and tried to turn away, but he caught her arm, gripping tight enough to bruise. She gasped, looking down at his hand and back up. Electricity skittered across her arms to his, and he grunted but didn't budge.

Anger fueled him, red tinting his vision as bloodlust rose quicker than he could temper. He shoved her against the wall, fangs fully descended.

"Call me a monster again, and I'll prove you right," he snarled as he got into her space. "You can try and psychoanalyze me, but you know *nothing* about my past." And there went any decorum he had left for the evening. "Expert or not, you will *not* continue to disrespect me."

"Guess you'll have to find another expert," she said boldly, gaze flicking to his sharp teeth briefly.

The woman did not have an ounce of fear in her, and he was unsure whether to be impressed or furious.

Rip into her throat. Make her pay. What would her heart feel like between my fingers? He shook his head and let her go abruptly. He didn't hide the satisfaction he felt about the bruises he left on her arm despite her dark complexion.

"Aida Broderick. Daughter of Uma, Jeska, and Lucious Broderick. And I know who your brother is, too." He didn't fight the manic grin that pulled at his face. A slight widening of her eyes told him enough. She wasn't afraid for herself, but she was for her family. "Cooperate. Or you'll find their heads at your doorstep."

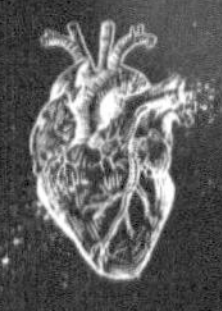

CHAPTER 4

WHOSE DUMB ASS IDEA WAS IT TO BECOME A VAMPIRE?

OVER TWO CENTURIES AGO

BLOOD. THERE WAS BLOOD everywhere. Sobs lodged in his throat as Cyrus tried to identify who it belonged to. His mimi, pa ... They were dead. His sisters. Dead. His people. Slaughtered. The sight of his mother being raped played in his mind on replay. The cries for help were sounds he would never forget.*

He couldn't get to them in time. What use was being a soldier if he couldn't protect his family? He stumbled out of the house to find the city of Mutuba ablaze.

They hadn't seen it coming. The Asherites attacked by sea in the south and managed to cut them off at the Jilbori. How had they made it through the jungle undetected?

Gunfire drew his attention, making him duck under a downed tree. A jeep whizzed by, its engine loud and smoke puffing out of its exhaust. With Mutuba in flames, Asherai had finally won the continental war and claimed his people's land.

Fury raged in his anima as he watched women get snatched up by soldiers and hauled off to be raped. Children wailed as they were ripped away from their parents. The little ones were being locked up. Men were killed, unable to protect them. Shouting from the east drew his attention to a small contingent of soldiers in black and red. They shot at the Asherites, working to keep them at bay.

Who were they?

Pain lanced through him, and he looked down. A bullet

---

* "Moonlight Sonata – Epic Trailer Version" by Hidden Citizens

nearby, and a large, imposing man knelt beside him. He pulled his tactical helmet off, ignoring the protests of his armed Guard. With his vision blackening, Cyrus could barely make out the towering soldier.

"Oye, stay with me," his bass voice said.

"W-what..." Cyrus coughed, spittle flying. Shivers wracked his body, his vision wholly black.

"Quick, do I have your permission to turn you into a vampire?" the man asked as gunfire rang in Cyrus' head. "¡Oye! Do you want revenge?" he snarled.

"Y-yes," Cyrus grunted, body going numb.

How he remained conscious, he didn't know. Maybe destiny was calling? Vampire? Did he want it?

"Do it!" he managed to bark out.

The coppery tang of blood poured onto his mouth. The man took Cyrus by the wrist and sank his fangs into the flesh, making Cyrus groan. More blood dripped onto his open wound before it found his mouth again.

The skin along his lips was soft, and with what little strength he had left, he held onto the hand and sucked. It was similar to rich wine, creating a hunger in his belly. He took and took until he suddenly broke away and passed out, drunk on the blood.

He jolted awake in a room he didn't recognize. The world went white, and his body raged with pain. He couldn't move, his body seizing from the onslaught of pure fire eating at his veins. Was he going to explode? Burn from the inside out?

"Calmáte, you will be all right. Breathe." The deep, familiar voice flowed through him, making his body slack in relief.

Cyrus panted, the pain still prevalent but somehow manageable. A scream crawled out of him, scraping his throat raw. His body expanded, muscles growing, bones cracking. An ache formed in his mouth, and an inhuman growl vibrated his chest.

"W-what..." he stuttered, his tongue cutting on something

sharp. Fangs! Pain blossomed in his gums as they descended.

"It's the virus. It is changing your genetic code. I promise it'll be over soon," the man said, yellow eyes flaring.

Clenching his eyes tight, tears streamed down his face as his body convulsed, sweat coating his body. With a gasp, the pain subsided. It was so abrupt that his body buzzed. He felt as if he was floating.

"Bring the human," the vampire said to someone in the room.

Cyrus shot up at the scent of blood, another growl escaping him.

"Fuck you! Let me go!" the man yelled as he was dragged in.

The Asherite bared his teeth at the Guard holding him by his hair. Cyrus recognized him as the one who took his mimi and raped her in front of him. The man balked when he saw Cyrus snarling.

"Oh shit, no!" He fought to break free to no avail.

"Feast," his maker said.

Unaware that he had even moved, Cyrus tore into the man's throat. Blood rushed into his mouth, and he drank it in gulps, unable to get enough. Flesh broke apart as he shook his head like a rabid dog, enjoying the squelch under his teeth. He kept going until he grabbed the man's hair and pulled his head from his shoulders.

"More," Cyrus growled, voice guttural. The vampire smirked, eyes bleeding red.

"Berserker…"

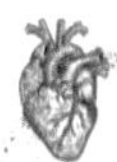

CYRUS WOKE WITH A shout, sweat covering his naked body. Fuck that fucking doctor for bringing up his past. It was the last thing he needed. His vision bled into crimson as he opened his eyes.

Taking several panting breaths, he managed to get his heart rate under control. It was like inhaling shards of ice, scraping and burning as it went down his throat. He preferred his past to be where he left it.

"I should find her and rip out her fucking throat," he growled to himself as he got out of bed. There was no use. Once he was awake, he was awake, and that pissed him off even more. "Would feel nice. Her blood on my hands."

He shook his head, realizing his spiral would soon take him to dark places. He hit his comm, placing it on the table as he pinged his Sire.

Monster. That was what she called him. He was every bit of one and more. It was something he had to live with every night. The constant urge to feed, the addiction to blood and violence. He tore through villages without bias. He knew he was a monster, and he hated it. No one needed to remind him of that.

"Dime, what's up?" Jacinto asked as his image appeared, pulling Cyrus out of his self-loathing.

The vampire's hair was tussled, and there was soft ruffling in the background. The sounds of moans traveled through the comm.

"I need you," he bit out. The King opened his mouth to make a witty remark until he took a good look at him.

"Coño ... I'll be right there." Cyrus watched as Jacinto turned to the people fucking in his bed. "Out!"

The comm went dark, and Cyrus paced for what felt like hours. His hands trembled, and the need for violence was an ache in his belly. He was fully dressed in white by the time his Sire showed up. He needed to hurt something, and he couldn't hurt the good doctor despite how badly he wanted to.

"What happened? What triggered you? I thought you've been feeding?" Jacinto asked, catching Cyrus by the shoulders and keeping him from leaving the suite.

"I have been. The fucking surgeon consulting on the serial killer case is a fucking fuck-head." He didn't understand his own words. They made no sense. *He* made no sense. "I need blood, 'Cin." He nearly begged despite knowing his Sire would give him what he asked for. Cyrus knocked his forehead several times with his knuckles. "Please..."

"Do I need to lock her up?" Jacinto's voice held no hint of humor, his eyes reddening at the pupils. The King wouldn't hesitate; Cyrus knew that.

"No ... No. I've got her. She'll learn," he growled. He would make her learn the hard way if he had to.

His Sire's warm hands gripped his shoulders, his compulsion flowing through his body.

"Lucky for you, we have someone in an interrogation room. Go get the blood that you need. As soon as you're done, head to The Den to unwind and feed."

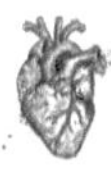

"HOLD ON A MINUTE. You and three others came on them?" Tristan gasped, straddling an office chair and spinning in a circle. "So, it was basically a baby shower?"

"Tristan..." Cyrus tried and failed to hide his humor.

They had a job to do, and this was not the time. A groan sounded, and Tristan popped out of his seat to straddle the siren strapped to a chair in the center of the interrogation room.

"Well, hello there, June-bug. Do you have a secret to spill?" Tristan asked brightly.

Cyrus grinned as he watched the Ice Wielder work. He enjoyed working with someone just as much off his rocker as himself. The Wielder asked no questions, and he was reliable. If Cyrus requested assistance with an Interrogation, the man wouldn't hesitate to join. He appreciated it. Tristan was one of the only people he could be himself around and one of the only people who knew he was a berserker.

"No!" June yelled, holding his head back, trying to escape the dirty tweezers that plucked at his eyelashes. The Ice Wielder laughed, tapping the siren's chin with a bloodied finger—*June's* cut-off finger, to be exact.

"Boss, I'm pretty sure he's lying. What do you think?"

"I believe you're right, Aries," Cyrus mused, standing behind June.

Tristan stood, and Cyrus pulled a nearby chain. The man's wrists strung up above him, leaving his naked back open for Cyrus. "Another traitor." He flipped the knife in his hand a few times and sliced deep into June's shoulder.

The man screamed as Cyrus worked the first T into his flesh. A full-body shudder wracked his body at the scent of fresh blood being spilled.

"Now there, buddy. Word on the street is that we have a couple of defectors. Why don't you let us know who they are, and we kill you ... gently?" Tristan looked at Cyrus in question and shrugged.

"Sure, we can try that," he responded, completing the letter R.

"Please! Wait!" Snot and spittle flew from the siren's mouth.

Cyrus licked the blood that poured down the man's back and winced. Siren blood was never his favorite. Add sweat and fear, and it made it sour. Oh well. He knew his tongue against the wound would make it hurt more.

"For the love of the Deities, please stop!"

"How's he taste?" Tristan asked, following Cyrus and licking up the man's face. "A bit sour..."

"That's exactly what I was thinking!" Cyrus barked a laugh as if the siren in between them wasn't sobbing in pain.

Tristan patted June's face, tossing the man's finger over his shoulder. "There, there. The time for crying will come later. Tell us what you know."

"I-it's Tyson! The werewolf ambassador. He's been talking about trading military secrets to the Martyrs." *Fuck.* Bex was right. "He didn't know I was there or that I heard," he whimpered.

"Tsk," Cyrus sucked his teeth. June screamed as he carved the letter A into his back. "I like it when they scream..." he remarked to himself.

"Now, June-bug, I don't take kindly to liars," the Ice Wielder snarled, grabbing the siren's chin. "The more you lie to us, the more you hurt. Do you want that, buddy?"

"I'm not lying!" he sobbed.

"This motherfucker is not very bright..." Cyrus scoffed, the red tinting his vision deepening. Rougher than earlier, he dug in an I. The squelching of his knife burying into the man's skin made a shiver ride up his spine.

"Oh! Can I do the T?" Tristan wriggled his eyebrows.

"By all means," he said casually as he chuckled.

The Ice Wielder skipped around June, grabbing some rubbing alcohol.

"Gotta make sure it's clean." The siren howled when Tristan poured it down his back. He plucked the knife from Cyrus and neatly carved in the letter. Before handing the blade back, he added a heart over the I. "Hearts over the I. Never forget the heart over the I."

"Fucking Deities, man. Give me that." Cyrus snatched the knife back, grinning as he did so. "Now, back to this asshole." He tapped the blade on June's shoulder. "Are you going to continue to lie? I still have two letters left."

"O-okay, okay," he panted.

Tristan rounded back to the front, pulling a gun from his vest.

"Where is Tyson?" the Ice Wielder asked, running the nozzle of the revolver down the man's jaw.

"Crystal Light district," he sobbed. "Please, just kill me."

"What do you think, boss? Want to finish up first?" Tristan inquired, tapping the gun on the siren's forehead now. June whimpered when he put more pressure on the gun. "Tsk. Open up, buddy. Look death in the eyes."

"And I thought I was crazy."

Cyrus couldn't keep the grin off his face as he worked on the final two letters, blood spraying and painting his suit crimson. His favorite color. As he finished the R, he dug deeper, opening the man's lower back by his kidneys. Cyrus worked his hand into the gaping wound, wrapping his hand around the organ.

"Louder?"

"Yes, louder," Tristan responded. June tried and failed to move his head back. "Keep those eyes on me, June-bug. I'll end it now. I promise."

"Now *this* I've gotta see," Cyrus said as he rounded the hanging man to stand behind the Ice Wielder. June's eyes fluttered open, meeting Cyrus' gaze before turning them to Tristan.

"That's a good boy," he purred, firing and blowing the man's brains out the back of his head. Tristan patted the dead man's shoulders and turned to look at Cyrus. "Wanna go get a drink?"

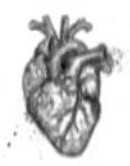

AFTER CLEANING UP, THE pair headed to The Den. The music blared, surrounding Cyrus with bass, the beat vibrating up his bones. Tristan's whistling was barely audible in the loud club, but Cyrus still heard him, nonetheless.

"It's packed tonight," the Ice Wielder observed as they sat at the bar.

Killian was on the other side, seeming haggard as he prepared drinks for several guests. Though that sexy grin never left his plush lips, it was apparent in the pinched corners of his eyes that he'd been at it all night.

"What can I get you fine gentlemen?" the man asked when it was finally their turn to order. He turned green eyes to Cyrus and winked. "I mean, other than myself."

"Double pour of bourbon for me," Tristan said, amusement in his expression.

Cyrus' gaze roved over Killian's body, not hiding his interest. He smirked when he noticed the man doing the same.

"Tequila, please."

"You've got it, sir." The human licked his lower lip, flashing a tongue ring. He hopped on the ladder to grab the top-shelf spirits.

Cyrus adjusted himself on the stool, keeping his gaze on the man who had sent his heart racing for reasons unknown.

He avoided humans for the most part unless he was feeding or fucking. Having a conversation with one? No, he preferred not. The number of humans that tried to garner his attention to get closer to the King reached the hundreds. He was protective of not only his peace but also his Sire.

"You think he's hot, don't you." Tristan nudged Cyrus, grabbing his attention and giving him a knowing look.

"Yeah, but I'm under orders to leave him alone," he almost groaned. "Jacinto seems to think I'll kill him. But I wouldn't. The man is too sexy to kill."

"Uh, do you always kill the people you fuck?" Tristan hedged, weariness now covering his amusement.

"No! That's the point," Cyrus huffed as he shook his head. "My bloodlust has been worse. I think that's where the worry comes from."

"Got it. That makes sense." Tristan thanked Killian as he slid their drinks over. "Can I ask you a question, and you not be mad at me?"

"Sure … you'll ask anyway," Cyrus groaned.

Tristan chuckled, sipping his drink. "Have you and Jacinto ever … ya know…" Tristan made a circle with his thumb and index finger while using the opposite finger to penetrate it.

"Ask me plainly, Aries," Cyrus grinned, loving to make the man squirm.

"Fine. Have you two ever fucked?" Tristan raised an eyebrow in obvious curiosity.

"Has anyone ever told you you're a nosy motherfucker?"

"All the time." The Ice Wielder's amusement was evident as he polished off his bourbon and raised his hand for another. "Also, that's not a 'no' so I'm guessing…"

"Yes, we have," Cyrus finally admitted. "We have hundreds of years of history. It was inevitable."

"Nice. Do you still fuck?" Tristan blurted, propping his elbow on the bar to rest his chin on his hand.

Cyrus had to fight the grin that the man often brought to his face.

"You're lucky I like you. Anyone else would've had their tongue ripped out."

"Oh, well, I'm honored, boss." He fluttered his eyelashes. "Now, are you gonna answer..."

"Occasionally." Cyrus shrugged. Lately, it'd been more than that, but that wasn't Tristan's business.

"How is it? Does he top? Or do you? Oh!" he gasped. "Y'all switch, don't you? I can see that actually. Man, ain't nothing wrong with a switch. I prefer a sub, but that's me, ya know? Gotta keep 'em coming all night."

"Tristan..." Cyrus started.

"But men can only come so many times. So, gotta make sure they have enough rest. Do you get enough rest? Tell me you get enough rest. And water! That's crucial. Especially so for vampires, right?"

"Tristan!" he laughed, stomach hurting from the force of it.

It'd been a long time since he laughed this hard. The Ice Wielder's eyes widened as if he just realized what he had done. Red flushed up to his ivory cheeks, darkening his freckles.

"Oh, well fuck. Sorry." He grimaced. "The mouth goes quicker than the brain, and the filter goes adios." He downed his second drink, tapping the holoport to transfer credits and a sizeable tip from what Cyrus could see. "Thanks for humoring me. I am going to game plan and grab Tyson. I'll let you know when I've got him."

He bowed his head slightly in clear embarrassment as he left. Cyrus made a mental note to get the man some pie the next time they saw each other. Poor thing.

Cyrus nursed his tequila, watching Killian hard at work behind the bar.

"As the co-owner of The Den, you'd think he would have employees to help," he said to himself as he stood and shrugged out of his coat.

Casually, he pushed his crimson henley sleeves up to his elbows and removed his comm watch, rings, and bracelet. Stuffing them into his jean pockets, he rounded the bar, startling

Killian.

"What are you doing?" he asked with a raised eyebrow. "I don't have the time for behind-the-bar entertainment, no matter how much I think I'd enjoy it."

"Relax. I'm going to help you." Cyrus grabbed a towel and flung it over his shoulder as he looked at the holoport, memorizing the drink orders.

"Do you even have experience with this sort of stuff?" Killian asked suspiciously while working on two cocktails.

His tattooed forearms flexed, veins showing as he set up the shaker tins. He flipped them upside down and shook one in each hand. That tongue ring flicked in and out of sight again as he licked his lips in concentration. He poured each into tall glasses, garnishing them with a cucumber slice and lime. Then, he pushed the glasses toward the guests in front of him.

"Watch me and find out. I'll take this side. You take the other."

"If you fuck this up…" Killian's words died out when Cyrus started making the drinks with expertise.

"Close your mouth unless you want it filled," he quipped without looking at the bartender.

Killian's surprised squeak made Cyrus grin. What other sounds could he drag out of the man? He ignored the guests' shocked looks at the fact that the Cortesano to the King was working behind the bar. He was a normal man, just like anyone else, and had time to kill.

Well, okay. Normal was not precisely the word he would use to describe himself. But being perceived as normal was vital to him, especially with Killian. He wasn't sure why it mattered more with the human. It likely had to do with the unusual fluttering in his chest that didn't subside as the night went on.

Cyrus felt thoroughly worn out by the night's end, and his head was clear. Maybe he should take up bartending as a side gig? He was helping Killian clean up when he felt the man's stare on him.

"Want to share with the class what's on your mind?" Cyrus

asked as he cleaned.

Killian leaned his elbows on the counter behind him.

"Where did you learn how to bartend?" he asked curiously.

Cyrus shrugged, trying not to think too hard about his past.

"I had a different life before I became a vampire," he said casually. "Why were you behind the bar alone?"

"Royal is on a trip with his partner. Two of my barbacks were sick. There's a bug going around. My other bartender was a no-show. I haven't been able to contact her, and I'll be honest, it's odd she didn't show up," he said more to himself.

"Tell me more." Cyrus moved for the mop simultaneously as Killian and the two men crashed into each other.

"Ah fuck!" Killian snapped.

"Damn it!" Cyrus responded, catching the human by the elbows to keep him from falling over.

They were suddenly close to each other, Cyrus towering over the shorter man. Their gazes locked briefly, and he allowed his to drift to Killian's lips.

"Were you just helping me to get into my pants?" The bartender smirked, emerald eyes dilating slowly.

"I promise you that was not the intent," Cyrus said as his hands trailed to Killian's hips. He had to actively keep his fingers from digging in. Those green eyes had him in a chokehold. "I have very strict orders to leave you alone."

"Me? Why?" he asked with raised eyebrows.

"The King favors you. The Den." Cyrus shrugged. "He thinks I'll ruin you."

"I think it would be the other way around, big guy," Killian snorted, patting Cyrus' chest, finally stepping out of his hold.

The emptiness Killian left behind was unwelcome. He could handle distance. He could handle not touching someone. Right? So why did it feel like winter swooped in and took away his only source of warmth and comfort?

Get it together…

"Are you sure about that?" He shook his head, grabbing the mop and getting to work. "I have a reputation, you know."

"Your reputation means nothing to me. A ruiner can still get ruined."

"That's not a word," he chuckled, intrigued by the man's perception.

When was the last time someone told him his reputation hadn't mattered? How long had it been since someone viewed him for him and not as a useful tool and weapon of the King?

"What? 'Ruined'?" Killian asked, scrunching his nose in thought.

"No! 'Ruiner'." Cyrus found himself enjoying his time with Killian a bit too much.

"Are you sure? I'm pretty sure it is." He pushed his messy black hair from his forehead, making it stick up all over. "I think the floor is clean enough, my dude."

Cyrus looked down to find that the floor—was, indeed—spotless. He was grateful for his dark skin. The heat creeping up to his face didn't show through his complexion. *What the fuck?*

"Here." Cyrus held out the mop awkwardly, which Killian took with a chuckle. Cyrus scratched the back of his head as he rocked from foot to foot. He had never behaved like this before, which struck him as odd and uncomfortable. "If you ever need help again and see me around, let me know."

He made to walk around the bar when Killian took hold of his elbow.

"I think I'll be fine. I appreciate it. But just so you know, I don't fuck my guests."

"I told you I wasn't helping you to get in your pants."

"Making sure you understood. You're sexy as fuck, I won't lie. But I have to keep business and pleasure separate," Killian murmured as he let him go.

"Is that a challenge?" he asked with a raised eyebrow.

Killian rolled his eyes with a shake of his head.

"I don't know. Is it?" the man smirked, nodding to the exit. "Thanks again. I can finish up here."

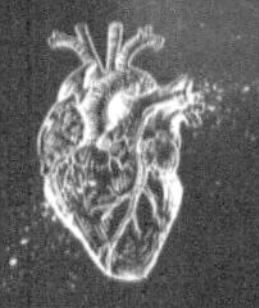

CHAPTER 5

WHEN MURDER SOUNDS TOO EASY

CYRUS BARELY REGISTERED THE words that came out of the coroner's mouth as they looked over the Carnicero's latest victims. The body laid out in front of them was the same as the others. But his focus was elsewhere, constantly flowing back toward Killian.

The man had infiltrated his mind, right next to Bex, making Cyrus uncomfortable. Who permitted them to worm their way in? His growing obsession with the two of them was dangerous. He knew he had to end it, but he was reluctant to do so.

He was breaking his number one rule: no attachments. To anyone. Period. The fact that even a small one had latched on was enough to wriggle its way into his brain as a problem.

"The killer has been hard at work. We're at ten deaths," Lyn said, pulling him out of his thoughts. Fuck. "All victims have been scumbags, and weirdly enough, three of them worked at The Den."

"Repeat that for me?" He examined the woman on the table.

The telltale signature of the Carnicero Cerebral crossed over her temple. When he pulled the skull, it popped open to reveal the damaged brain.

"She was a bartender. Helped drug people and pull them out of the club to traffickers." The coroner let out a growl, reminding Cyrus she was a werewolf. "It's fucking sick. I'm almost not mad at her demise."

"I understand that." A sick feeling twisted in his gut, and it was going to drive him insane. "Did any of the other victims have a tie to The Den? Either as a patron or employee?"

Lyn turned to her paperwork. "You know, I'm just the coroner," she said with a chuckle.

"Yes, but you're nosey and get the best intel." Cyrus looked at his watch comm.

The doctor was now a half hour late. For someone who seemed to be anal-retentive, he had to admit he was surprised at her tardiness. Although, part of him knew she was doing it on purpose.

"I don't know if I should be offended," she huffed, giving him a grim look. "Looks like the answer is mostly yes."

Cyrus swore he could feel his stomach leave his ass. This was what he was worried about. Sometimes being right was a bitch.

"Two bartenders, a dancer, a server. But that's not all," She trailed off, nibbling on her lower lip.

"What is it?" Anxiety built from his core, hoping what she said next didn't confirm the sick feeling.

"Two of them were baristas at the Crow's Cauldron."

"Fuck ... I think we have a suspect." And for some reason, it bothered the fuck out of him.

Killian didn't seem like the type. But then again, looks could be deceiving. This was why he didn't form attachments. When people showed him their true colors, Cyrus rarely liked what he saw.

"Who—" Lyn was cut off when the double doors swished open, and the good doctor walked through.

He had to fight the scarlet haze that threatened to encroach on his vision as he took in her arrogant presence.

"Look what the cat dragged in," he nearly growled. The pulse in her throat called to him, the vein pulsing loudly in his ears. Cyrus bit the inside of his cheek to keep his fangs from fully descending.

Doctor Broderick glared at him, threw her jacket onto a chair to wash her hands, and turned her focus to the body on the exam table.

"*You're* the one who is insisting on working with me," she

snapped as she pulled on gloves. "They've—"

"Been expertly cut around the skull. And yes, their brains have been experimented on. They have the electrode markings. Seems they all had a foot in criminal activity. Lastly, they have ties to the Den, so we have a potential suspect." Cyrus enjoyed the way her jaw clenched. "I mean, had you been here on time, we would've worked this out together."

"Have you forgotten I don't *want* to work with you?" She brushed past him, electricity skipping from her to him. Before he could retort, she held up a hand and palpitated the first dead woman's scalp.

"She has a deformity," the doctor stated. "How her head is positioned on the table is uneven." She said it as if it should be obvious, and it was Cyrus' turn to clench his jaw. "Details. Takes a surgeon to understand."

She turned her silver eyes up to him briefly, a fucking smug expression on her face. He clenched his hands to keep from wrapping them around her little neck.

"So, tell me, *surgeon*, why criminals? Just pure vigilantism or something more?"

After removing his gloves and tossing them—giving her a pointed glare as he did it—he crossed his arms, leaning against the counter. Doctor Broderick pursed her full lips, a dimple piercing one of her cheeks.

"If they're experimenting, like I think they are, they might be trying to understand something about the victims. The question is, what? What is so fascinating about them that they're worth studying?"

"Wouldn't that be more psychological?" Cyrus asked, genuinely curious, though he wouldn't show it to the she-demon.

"Did you know there are many serial killers who have had a seemingly normal childhood with no experience of trauma but still do what they do?" For once her tone was void of arrogance, turning into a teacher as she continued looking over the body.

Gently, she turned the head to the side, lifting the hair to show a flat spot at the base of the skull. "Minor deformity. Not likely to affect her brain," she whispered more to herself. "Psychology isn't the only answer to why people do what they do. The chemical reactions in our brains guide our decisions just as much as our consciousness."

"Like when someone kills in a crime of passion," Cyrus said in understanding.

"He *can* be taught," Doctor Broderick said, clapping her hands. He narrowed his eyes at her, annoyed. "Anyway, the killer is likely interested in understanding why people make bad decisions, considering they've all been criminals."

"I'll speak with Killian and see what he knows." Cyrus nodded to Lyn.

Would he have to bring him in for an interrogation? The thought made him wildly unreasonable. In no way would he bring that man into his darkness. Just considering it made Cyrus sick to his stomach. What the fuck?

He never hesitated to bring someone in until he got the answers he needed. And yet, here he was, allowing his personal shit to cloud his judgment.

"Why are you here?" Doctor Broderick asked, drawing his attention.

She had discarded her gloves, hands on her hips. The worst part about the doctor was that she was beautiful. Cyrus hated that tidbit the most. She grated his nerves, making them raw and frayed whenever she was around. Despite it all, he still wondered what her blood tasted like or what it would feel like to rip her head from her body.

"I've answered this question," Cyrus sighed as he thanked the coroner and took the holoport with the findings. He stopped shy of the doors when Broderick spoke.

"You're the Cortesano. You are supposed to be doing whatever it is that politicians do. Yet here you are. Either you're doing very badly at your job, or you're easily distracted. Neither are very good traits, not that you had any to begin with."

If audacity had an image reference, it would be this woman. A growl vibrated in his chest as he turned to her, a red veil rising in his vision. Something on his face must have changed because fear wafted over to him from Lyn, who mentioned she had to use the restroom, hoofing it from the room and leaving the two alone.

"You are seriously testing my patience, good doctor."

"Don't fucking call me that," she said, her piercing eyes never leaving his. "Why. Are. You. Here?" She approached him like he wasn't over a foot taller than her.

"*You're* the fucking head doctor. Why don't you tell me?"

It took all his energy to keep from strangling the Storm Wielder. The vision of her throat torn and her blood on his hands returned to the forefront of his mind and had him fighting a shiver from running up his spine.

"Probably has to do with figuring out more about yourself. There's more to you than meets the eye, but it's probably not that interesting. At least not to anyone but you."

"Do you enjoy pissing people the fuck off and testing your limits?" he snarled, his patience barely hanging on by a thread.

His hands flexed with the need to feel her heartbeat in his palms. This woman riled him up, and he hated to admit how much it bothered him.

"Only those who have no place in my space. You have no medical experience, ask questions that could be researched if you try hard enough, and are an unnecessary barrier to the work I have to do here." Pure electric fire lit up her eyes, ire radiating off her in waves. The Storm Wielder raised an arrogant brow, her defiance daring him to react.

"Is it me or the fact you're not the one in charge? Is it me or the fact that you have to do as you're told, like a *good doctor,* knowing your family is at risk if you don't?" They both seethed at each other, chests heaving as they stared each other down. "I think you enjoy working alone because you know people hate you."

"Fuck you!" she yelled, pushing at his chest. The woman had more of a punch than he expected. He grunted softly but did not budge.

"Never. Not my type," he snapped back. "Why are you so invested? Hmm? I know it's more than because it's in your area of expertise." He watched her eyes widen ever so slightly, cluing him in on his assumptions. "Knew it. You're hiding something, good doctor, and I will figure it out."

"You know nothing about me." She refused to back down. "I am invested because I want this serial killer off the streets. My patients are already scared enough as it is. They have been canceling their surgeries, afraid that the serial killer is a doctor at the medical center." Her nose flared as her ire grew. "Despite your assumptions, I'm very good at what I do, and I will not stop until I find this killer."

"Well, you're stuck with me because I won't either." He stepped into her space, making her eyes glow in disbelief. "You know why I am so invested?" He chuckled as he pushed a stray curl from her face and cupped the back of her neck. He leaned forward, knowing his grin was menacing. "I enjoy learning new ways to Interrogate people. Maybe I can reverse engineer the process."

"You're the..."

Something passed through her eyes, and it wasn't fear like he had hoped. It pissed him off, and he had the sudden urge to disorient her. Make her flustered. Anything to bring her down a notch.

"Bingo, doctor," he growled, gripping her chin. She gritted her teeth, the anger in her gaze flaring bright. "Keep disrespecting me." He brought his lips to her ear. "And I'll be sure to teach you all the ways I can Interrogate a person."

His sensual tone didn't match the threat of his statement, and he felt her sway. He slowly licked a line from her earlobe up to her temple, making the woman tremble. Pushing her back, he grinned as her eyes dilated in and out before focusing once more.

"You're disgusting," she bit out, grabbing a paper towel to rub his saliva off her face.

"That I am. Now, stop questioning me and get used to the fact that I will be here until we find the Carnicero Cerebral."

As he made his way out, she said to his back, "You will find that I'm quite persistent, Cortesano. And you won't like it."

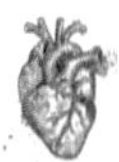

CYRUS WHISTLED AS HE walked down the city block to a quaint apartment complex. It had been an arduous night. Finding Tyson was proving difficult. He needed to discover what trade secrets he planned to sell to the Martyrs.

That, plus figuring out who the fucking Carnicero Cerebral was and why he couldn't get his hormones in check had him run down and exhausted. His thoughts often turned to Killian and Bex—the latter he hadn't seen in a week.

Cyrus crossed the soft navy grass to lean on the trunk of a thick willow tree. Ithea had long set and the yard was dark, lights having gone out as people went to bed. Long branches covered with teal and green leaves shrouded him, leaving him with enough space to look through. In the short distance was an apartment whose lights were still on. Curtainless glass double doors to the porch gave him a view of the interior. An eyebrow raised as he heard yelling and focused his hearing.

"You're fucking insane!" a man shouted at the good doctor, stumbling through the living room in just his boxers. He snatched his clothes from the floor, not bothering to put them on, and stormed toward the door.

"Are you serious?" she yelled back as she followed behind. "Come on, I kept them in my room!"

Cyrus was surprised to see her out of her scrubs, wearing an oversized shirt that fell to her mid-thighs. He tilted his head as he continued to watch the exchange.

"Nah. You got all them brains and shit. Like, who fucking does that?" the man shook his head, but before he could open the door, she caught up and slammed her hand against it.

"They're *specimens,* and they're in glass containers. They're for a case I've been consulting on. I *told* you we should've gone to your room. I didn't want to freak you out."

Despite being over a foot taller than her, Doctor Broderick held his stare, making him wither. The show of dominance from the Storm Wielder didn't come as a surprise. Though petite, she was still intimidating, and damn, did it do something to his dick.

Fuck. Focus, Cyrus.

"Too late! This isn't the first odd shit I've seen or found. I thought it was all in my head, but..." he sighed, rubbing his smooth jaw that housed lips swollen from rough kissing.

A flash of something carnal crossed her eyes as she licked her lower lip, dragging the man's attention to them, but he snapped them back up. *Well, well, this was interesting.*

"I can't. Let me go. I'll come back tomorrow with a truck to grab my things."

"Jay!" She let out an exasperated sigh. "So, after being roommates for three months, we finally fuck, and now you want to ghost. Is that what it is?" she growled, grabbing his shirt.

His hickey-covered throat bobbed, and Cyrus could see, even from his position, the way Jay's pulse fluttered in his neck. The sight painted Cyrus' vision red. He worked to keep a growl from vibrating in his chest.

"That's not it! I swear," he stammered out.

Cyrus moved closer while remaining under the cover of the large tree. He caught their scents, Doctor Broderick's lilac and petrichor mixed with the man's citrus and cinnamon. Underlying that was fear. Jay was scared of her. Whatever it was he saw freaked him the fuck out. Cyrus needed to find out what it was.

The man dropped his clothes to cup her face, hand trembling. "I promise you it wasn't because of that." He sighed, head drooping. "Let me go. Please?"

"Fine." She pushed him as she let him go, making him grunt as he hit the door. "I'll leave your shit in the front."

"But—"

"Nope. I don't need you coming back in here. It'll be out there when you're ready to get it." She opened the door and shoved him out of the apartment, slamming it closed again. "Well, we fucked up again, didn't we?" she grumbled to herself as she sat on the grey carpet in front of her glass coffee table.

This was the disoriented side of the good doctor he wanted to see. To learn what made her tick. Clearly, she was a terrible people person. But the fact she could instill fear in a man nearly twice her size intrigued Cyrus.

"Fuck…" he whispered to himself. He didn't *want* to be intrigued. He wanted intel. "You could've assigned someone to do this…" he muttered, shaking his head rapidly.

Movement beyond the door caught his attention. Cyrus watched as she pulled out her holoport. He couldn't fight the grin that crossed his lips as he heard her complain to herself.

"This one lasted the longest. Maybe let's not allow them in the bedroom, yeah?" She groaned as she leaned forward to plop her forehead on the surface. "Now I have to look for a new roommate. Again." She said each sentence with a bounce of her forehead against the glass.

It was odd seeing her as almost normal. Being alone, that typical arrogant sneer was gone, softening her features. It proved just how young she was, being only thirty, and it made her accomplishments that much more impressive. Too bad she was so fucking arrogant.

New roommate?

An idea brewed in an instant, but when he turned to leave, he noticed her sitting up straight and looking out at the yard. Her awareness was astounding, but tempted as he was to show himself just to see how she'd react, he remained in the shadows, watching as she stood and stretched. Her shirt rose to expose the bottom of her bare ass as she walked over to the double doors. Well, fuck.

Fangs slowly broke his gums as he watched her put a hand on the glass, staring right at him despite not being able to see him.

A slow grin tilted her lips, and he could barely catch her statement, "I wonder who is watching me. I know you're out there."

What she did next made his body react against his will, his

dick hardening to steel.

Doctor Broderick's tongue darted out as she licked the glass languidly and said, "Come out, come out, whoever you are..."

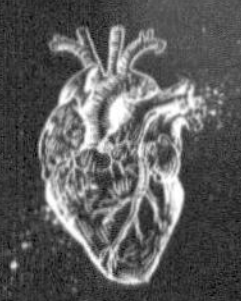

CHAPTER 6

ABSENCE MAKES THE DICK GROW HARDER

EARLY THE NEXT EVENING, Cyrus sat in his office, staring at the holoscreen and rubbing his temples. Shit was stirring in Asherai. He wondered if Aida knew her home country was close to falling to pieces, then shrugged to himself.

It wasn't his business. What was his business was her interesting behavior. He knew there was something more to her than she let on, and what he knew of her barely scratched the surface.

A knock on the door made him bark, "Come in!"

"Hey, boss," Bex said, fully entering.

The sight of them instantly lightened a bit of the weight on his shoulders, his body relaxing in his chair, and he didn't know what to do with that tidbit.

"Take a seat." He leaned forward, resting his elbows at his desk. "I have an assignment for you."

"In addition to this serial killer?" they asked as they plopped down, crossing their fishnet-covered legs.

They wore black leather shorts over them and a hot pink tank under a mesh shirt. A matching hot pink collar graced their neck, the black ring swinging as they moved. Their hazel eyes were clear, and Cyrus found himself relieved that they had honored his request. Why?

"Yes, actually. I've found that almost all the victims have ties to The Den and the Crow's Cauldron."

"Do you need me to go down there to question the twins?" they asked as they absentmindedly played with their lip ring.

"No, I've got that part handled. What I need from you is to

gain Aida Broderick's trust."

"The doctor?" Bex questioned with a quirked brow. "What do you need?"

"Word on the street is that she's looking for a new roommate. Her previous one pretty much leaped from her house." He chuckled. "I just know there's something up with her. Find out what it is."

He tapped a holoport and handed it over. Bex's hazel eyes widened as they looked over the details.

"When you said doctor and consultant, I wasn't expecting..." They snapped their mouth shut as they flicked their gaze up at him before returning to the image.

"Expecting an annoying, hot as fuck young woman?" he grumbled.

After what he had seen the previous night, he had jerked off at the idea of her mouth on his dick, choking and gagging.

Stop it.

He shifted in his seat, his nose flaring when he saw the lust crossing Bex's face.

"You are not to fuck her."

For some reason, the thought had him both irrationally irate and aroused. Cyrus was not a possessive man by any means but fuck if he couldn't help but feel it when it came to Bex. He barely knew them!

"What?" they snorted, looking back at him with confused expression. "Have you seen her? If I'm going to be her roomie and she gives me the time of night ... I am not promising anything. What I do outside of this office is none of your business."

His eyebrow lifted slowly at the wolf's defiance. They quickly lowered their gaze to the floor.

"You're right," he said, knowing it caught them off-guard by their soft gasp. "Look at me." Those hazel eyes snapped up, dilating almost to a deep green. "How about we *try* not to go out of our way to fuck her? I am not ... Exactly sure of her sanity."

"Gee, boss. Are you concerned for me?" A smirk tilted up their fuckable lips. He wouldn't admit the answer was 'yes' because he didn't understand why he cared. "Do you think she's the Carnicero Cerebral?"

"Fuck no," he said with a snort. "She's a bitch, yes. And she's not exactly all there." He tapped his temple. "But I highly doubt she's a serial killer."

"Do you know why I'm in line to be the next Spymaster?" Bex asked suddenly, uncrossing their legs to sit up and lean their elbows on their knees.

The o-ring at their collar clinked gently with the movement. Their tongue darted out to play with their lip ring. Their every movement had him hyper-aware of just how addictive they could be if he allowed himself to indulge. This wasn't good. Not at all.

"Why?" he inquired, wondering where they were going with this.

"I am good at pretending. I am good at transforming and being someone else. I know how to get information without putting a hand on a person. Torture techniques are nice and all. But I use other methods." Somehow, the words didn't put Cyrus at ease. Of course it was their job to be a flawless liar, but would they lie to him? Not knowing the answer sat uncomfortably. "I can also kill a person with just my hands. I am sure I can handle a mildly insane doctor." They bit their tongue with a grin.

"Cocky little wolf, aren't you?" Cyrus returned their grin, keeping his gaze on their mouth.

"Just a bit." Bex held their forefinger and thumb close together. Somehow, the act was utterly endearing.

Endearing? What?

"All right. Get into her home. Find out what secrets she's keeping."

"Can I ask a question?" Bex stood, stretching and exposing their smooth stomach under their mesh top.

How did he miss their navel piercing? He had the sudden urge to bite it, suck it into his mouth, and bring them a bit of pain.

"You just did. But sure, ask another." He bit back his snort when they scoffed.

"Are you sure she isn't the Carnicero Cerebral? You've just

discovered that she's got a few marbles loose, and you think she has secrets." They leaned their hip against the desk, their gaze roving over him, equally distracted. Desire unfurled in his stomach, heading south in an instant.

"If she is … Well then, I'll bring her in." And damn if that thought didn't do something to him. "Let me know as soon as you've become her roommate. And keep me updated."

Bex knocked their knuckles on his desk as they stood straight and headed for the door. They looked over their shoulder at him, eyes glowing gently.

"You've got it, boss."

"Hmm. That's good to know," Cyrus said as he leaned back in his chair, unbuttoning his cuffs and pushing up the sleeves of his shirt to his elbows. The wolf quirked an eyebrow, tracking his movement as they turned to face him.

"And what's that?"

"That you take orders without question," he said huskily. He bit his lip, pushing the thoughts of what he wanted to do to them to the back of his mind. "See you next week."

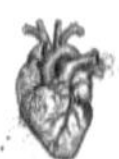

BLOOD POURED INTO CYRUS' mouth as he latched onto the human man currently riding his cock. He cupped the man's chin, tilting it up for better access to his throat. The human's back was to Cyrus' front as they fucked on a lounge couch in the middle of The Den's Exhibition Hall. Cyrus growled, lifting his hips to make the human bounce. The sensation of the man tightening around his erection, mixed with the blood filling his mouth, made his eyes roll.*

"Oh fuck!" the man cried out.

The sounds of gagging and a wet pop made Cyrus reluctantly pull away from the human's throat. Blood cascaded down his chin, staining his cream henley. Looking past the man's shoulder, he found a familiar head of navy hair bobbing on the

---

* "Descending" by Sleep Token

man's cock.

"Well, look who it is," he purred, gripping Bex's hair to pull them off the human. Cyrus cut off his protests when he bucked his hips, still fucking his tight hole as his gaze connected with Bex. Their mouth remained open, tongue licking the underside of the man's cock. "The filthy slut is just eager to have their throat fucked."

He pushed them back down onto the man, smirking when they gagged. He knew they didn't have to and purely did it for the show.

"My lord, please," the human panted, whimpering when Cyrus dragged his tongue up the man's throat to capture the blood that lightly streamed from the tiny puncture marks.

"You are not to come in their mouth," he growled, gripping the man's chin tighter. That damn possessiveness was getting the best of him. "Come in their mouth or on their face, and I will personally tear your throat apart." The human's fear wafted to him, making his cock thicken and stretch his hole wider. "Do you understand?"

"Ah! Fuck, okay."

The human rocked his hips, panting as pleasure took over. He cried out when Cyrus sank his fangs into his throat once more, pulling slowly. The desire to drain the human was strong and was only staved off by the fact that he desperately wanted to throat fuck Bex. It would be poor taste to kill a man while he was getting head. Gripping their hair tighter, he controlled their movements, sliding them up and down the man's dick just like a toy.

"That feels so good. Shit, I don't know how long I'll last."

Cyrus pulled away from his throat, licking the wounds closed. Using his hold on their hair, Cyrus removed Bex from the man's dick, moving them to the side. He grinned at their pout, their lips swollen from all the head they'd likely been giving all night. Cyrus flipped him and the man over, bending him over the couch.

"This tight, filthy hole loves being fucked raw, doesn't it?" he growled, pounding into the man.

"Yes, fuck yes," the human moaned, rocking back into

each rough snap of Cyrus' hips.

"Little wolf, jerk him off. Make him come all over the floor."

Bex didn't hesitate, kneeling next to the human. They spat into their hand, reaching in front to do precisely as Cyrus commanded.

"I'm coming!" the human cried out, body stiffening and his ass clenching tight around Cyrus as he came. Cyrus pulled out, ignoring the man's protests. The human panted, looking at Bex. "Can I return the favor?"

"No," Cyrus responded, smirking when Bex narrowed their hazel eyes at him. He grabbed a rag from the sterilizer and cleaned his still-hard cock. "No, their orgasm is mine tonight," he clarified.

"And if I said yes to him and no to you?" Bex raised an eyebrow, dilated eyes dropping to his erection.

They licked their puffy lips on instinct. Their question rang through him, and a growl vibrated in his chest. He gripped the man's hair, bringing him up to his knees.

"I mean, sure. Go ahead." Cyrus bluffed.

He wasn't sure what he would do if Bex denied him. He couldn't just let them leave. Not with thoughts of them choking on his cock and watching streams of dirty tears roll down their face plaguing his mind. How willing and obedient they were at his feet.

"I am totally okay with moving on," the man breathed, wincing due to Cyrus' grip on his hair. "I don't need to be caught between whatever you two have going on."

"There's nothing between us." Cyrus was suddenly defensive.

There was absolutely *nothing*. Cyrus was a fuck first, ask questions never sort of man. He didn't allow people into his mess of a life, and he didn't plan on starting now.

"Right. Can I go?" the human stared at Bex and then Cyrus.

He let him go, and the man left without any more chit-chat.

Cyrus rose and sat on the couch, his semi-hard cock going rigid once more at the sight of Bex. "Crawl to me."

Bex's throat bobbed, the scent of arousal wafting from

them as they slipped to the floor and prowled their way to him. As they settled in front of him, they sat back on their heels in expectation.

"Do you like being told what to do?"

"I do…"

Cyrus leaned forward, taking hold of their collar. "And do you like being a filthy slut?" He watched as Bex's pupils dilated, their chest heaving.

"I do…" they gasped when he jerked them toward him.

"What's your safeword?" he growled as he stroked his dick.

"Lotus, my Lord."

"Stops?"

"No penetration. Come on it, eat it, bite it, do anything but penetrate."

He nodded in acknowledgment.

"Open your mouth, little wolf."

Bex slowly licked their lush lips, and Cyrus groaned when they opened up. His grip on their collar tightened, taking away their ability to move. He spat in their mouth, making them moan.

"Hmm," he purred, spitting once more. "Keep it open," he commanded. Their lids fluttered in acknowledgment, and he rewarded them by plunging his fingers in. Pushing his digits deeper, he was reminded of their lack of gag reflex. "You must love having your throat fucked like a dirty whore." He slid his fingers out, pulling saliva and letting it drip over their chin.

"Please…" Bex whimpered as their gaze dropped to his cock.

"Does the little wolf want me to make them filthy again? Are you ready to be my cum slut?" He sank his hands into their short hair, pulling them closer and allowing his glistening tip to brush their lips.

"Yes, please, my lord."

"Please, what?" he growled.

"Please make me your cum slut."

It was all he needed to hear before gripping tightly and thrusting into their mouth. Bex's eyes closed as they moaned around his length.

"Eyes on me. I want to watch you cry for me." Their hazel eyes flared a neon green as they looked up at him, bobbing in time with each pump of his hips. "Shit," he groaned as he held Bex still so he could fuck their mouth. Saliva pooled around their mouth, soaking him in the process.

Despite their evident practice, they gagged, tears catching on their lashes and spilling down their cheeks. Streams of mascara coated their flushed face, and the sight had him nearly ready to come. But not yet. He had more playing to do first.

Bex gasped when he pulled out, gripping their chin tightly.

"How much pain do you like?" he asked as he stroked himself, pushing himself closer to the edge.

"Break me. I'll tell you if it's too much," they said confidently.

Fuck, that turned him on even more. He rubbed their cheek, smearing their mascara-blackened tears.

"I think I want to keep you," he whispered, slapping them hard enough to sting.

"Harder," Bex moaned.

He happily obliged, smoothing over the skin after he did so. He pinched their lip piercing, tugging at it to make them whine.

"Do you have somewhere you need to be after this?" he asked, letting go of their lip to stand up.

"Yes," they panted, keeping their glowing green eyes on his.

"Good, get up and bend over the table," he growled. Bex stood and did as he asked. Bex cried out when his hand cracked down on their ass. "I don't normally fuck people twice," he breathed in their ear as he cupped their sex. Their arousal coated him, and his replying growl was feral.

"Why me, then?" Bex asked as they dropped their forehead to the table. Moaning, they swayed their hips, arching their back as he slid his fingers to their clit. "Oh fuck," they whimpered, turning their head to the side so they could look at him over their shoulder.

"I don't know," he answered candidly.

Aside from Killian, he couldn't think of anything but Bex.

That thought alone should scare him. He'd never been beholden to someone or their needs before. But he wasn't using his big head at the moment.

Bex yelped when he grabbed their hips and lifted them to place them on their knees on the table. Remaining bent forward, their pussy was his to devour. He gripped their ass, spreading them open. He spat on them, dragging his tongue up their center.

"Oh fuck!" they whimpered when he tugged at the piercing at the hood of their clit with his teeth.

They tasted better than he imagined. Their juices coated his mouth and chin. Gripping their ass tighter, he felt their legs quake as he continued eating them out.

"Fuck, you're delicious," he growled in between licks.

They keened and cried, pleading breathlessly as he licked and sucked on their clit. Each moan slid further under his skin. It would be so easy to become addicted to their every sound. As they bucked and tried to push back on him, he reached with his free hand for their navel ring, tugging it between his fingers.

"Oh f-fuck!" Bex cried out at the pain he brought them.

"Come on my face, little wolf," he said as he continued his meal.

Flattening his tongue, he circled it around their clit. Bex's body shuddered as they came with a scream.

He backed away, pulling them from the table by their hips. Once their feet were solidly on the floor, they groaned in protest, and he slapped their ass.

"You're just begging for my dick, like the filthy little wolf that you are." He dragged his lips across their neck, pushing them to their knees in front of him.

Bex moaned as the head of his cock glided along their lips.

"You haven't known true ruination until me, little wolf," he growled as he thrust into their mouth. "You think you've broken before? Think again." Gripping Bex's hair, he held them still as he pumped. "I will break you more than you've ever thought possible. You will sob at my feet, take every inch of this dick down your throat." With each statement, he snapped his hips, thoroughly fucking them. "I don't care who you fuck. But when you're with me, I own you, slut. Do you hear me and agree?"

"Yes!" Bex gasped when he pulled them away. "I agree."

He snatched their collar and pulled them up to stand again, turning them so his front was flushed with their back. His free hand slipped it between their legs, swiping circles on their swollen clit.

"Now, break for your Lord," he growled, running his fangs along their neck.

He had never enjoyed wolf blood, but something about Bex tempted him regardless. Bex sobbed, throwing their head back against his chest as they shattered for him. Their body shook as he continued through their orgasm to give them another.

Groaning, he slid his dick through their slick to use as lube and stroke himself near the edge.

"Fuck!" he yelled.

Forcing them to bend over the table, he came with a roar. His cum covered them, coating their pussy. Cyrus smiled smugly as he watched his seed drip down their thighs, satisfaction filling him. His brain short-circuited when they reached behind themselves to scoop some of his spent arousal and lick it clean off their fingers.

"Thank you for your cum." Licking their lips of his arousal, Bex pushed themself onto their hands to look over their shoulder at him with a grin.

"Isn't it—" they started but cleared their throat, "Isn't it bad form to fuck your colleagues?"

"Let me make this clear," he said as they turned to face him. "When it's you and me alone, I am your Lord, you are my slut." He licked his thumbs, cleaning the mascara from their cheeks. "But in any other capacity, you are the Spymaster in training, and I am the Cortesano to the King. You are more than just a colleague. I'll never treat you less than that or indicate otherwise without consent. Understand?"

He wasn't prepared for the softness of his tone. What the fuck was up with him?

"Yeah. Sure." Bex looked up at him, their breaths mingling as he pulled a warm rag from the nearby cart and cleaned their face properly.

He pushed some of their dark navy waves from their forehead, the stubborn strands returning to where they were.

"I don't normally do this..." he whispered as he cupped their face, thumb gliding along their jaw. Cyrus leaned in, lips almost touching theirs.

"Do what?" they breathed.

Kissing was a form of intimacy that Cyrus didn't share with many. He could count on one hand how many people he had allowed to kiss him. For some reason, he wanted Bex on that list, and it freaked him the fuck out.

"Nothing," he said quickly, taking a step back.

"Okaay," they dragged the word out. "I've ... gotta go." Something passed Bex's gaze before they looked away.

"Go then," he said as he stepped back. He stopped them with a hold on their arm. "Just ... remember something."

"And what's that?" they huffed, looking exasperated.

It made him chuckle.

"Remember whose cum is dripping down your thighs. Wherever you go, remember that soreness in your throat, and know I'll give it to you whenever you want if you beg for it hard enough."

"O-okay," they said with a nod.

"Okay, what?" he growled.

"Okay, my Lord."

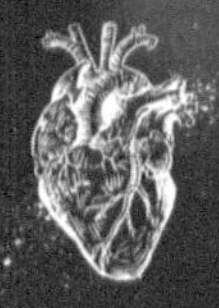

CHAPTER 7

SHOULD THEY OR SHOULDN'T THEY?

IT WAS DISORIENTING TO walk into The Den during off-hours. The lights were on, removing the allure of darkness and sex. Low jazz played in the distance, more as background noise than anything else. The smell of burgers made his mouth water.

Cyrus followed the music, noticing how pristine the club was. Clearly, the place was important to the twins. He couldn't wrap his head around the fact Killian was considered a suspect in their Carnicero Cerebral case.

His gut told him there was more to this case than what met the eye. But was he sure it was his gut or his hormones that refused Killian having a hand in this?

"I am *not* doing this right now," Killian said, speaking from an open door that likely led to the kitchen office.

"Why not? You think you can fuck someone else and I not find out about it?" came a gruff masculine voice.

Cyrus clenched his jaw as he listened, unwanted jealousy taking a lap in his body.

"It's not your business! We broke up because you're a fucking ass wipe," the human snapped.

The crash of a chair hitting the wall brought Cyrus into the office with inhuman speed. He found the asshole against the wall, a knife against his throat, and Killian holding the handle.

"Try to put your hands on me again, and you'll have to find new ways to jack off."

"I imagine that wouldn't be a fun experience."

Cyrus' vision burned as the man's throat bobbed against the blade, blood welling under the small slice. He was rugged and not in a handsome way. Blonde hair plastered to his forehead, blue eyes dilated, the man was high off potions. Killian flicked his gaze to Cyrus, knife pricking the man's throat once more.

"Can I help you?" he asked as if he didn't have a much larger man against the wall, who paled at Cyrus' appearance.

"Are you done? I need to talk with you," he said dryly, trying to hide the arousal he felt from Killian's boldness.

The man looked fucking hot. His black hair was disheveled as if he ran his hands through it one too many times. Kohl lined green eyes were piercing as always. His black leather vest hung open over a red tee, and his jeans fit over his thick thighs, accentuating his ass.

Cyrus raised an eyebrow impatiently, which made Killian sigh and let go of the asshole.

"Get the fuck out of here, and don't come back."

"But..."

"No, Ric. You don't get to come here high, try to claim rights ... Try to *hit* me! And think you can come back." Killian punched him in the nose before the man could say anything more.

"Fuck Killian!" he yelped.

The bartender grabbed Ric's dirty jean jacket and pulled him along. His biceps flexed, tattooed forearms tightening with apparent strength. Cyrus watched with amusement, following behind as Killian kicked open the back door and hauled Ric outside.

The other man dropped to his knees, wincing in pain. "I'm sorry!"

"Fuck you," Killian hissed, slamming the door closed. He looked up at Cyrus. "What did you need?" he asked casually. He wasn't even panting, in clear control of the entire situation.

"Deal with this often?"

"I co-own a bar..." he crossed his arms.

Right. That should've been obvious.

"I have a few questions to ask you. Might be best if we sit."

"Well, I was making some burgers before that jerk walked in. Hungry?" He motioned for Cyrus to follow, stopping abruptly. "I've never asked before ... But do vampires eat?"

"Yes, Killian. We have a bloodborne disease, and yes, we need blood, but we also still need food to live. Just not as much of it. Are the burgers medium, or do you think they're well done at this point?" Cyrus patted Killian's shoulder, and the man narrowed his eyes.

"Don't make fun of me," he said, shrugging off Cyrus' hand. "They weren't on the grill yet, jerk."

The kitchen they entered was more extensive than he thought it would be. Off to the side were raw burgers with two already cooked on the other. He noticed condiments and plates on the island.

"Servers and kitchen staff are coming in soon. I like to keep them fed." Killian shrugged as he held a hand over the hotplate to test temperature and threw on two hefty meat patties. "Bacon?" he asked, even though he was already putting some on.

"I'm impressed," Cyrus said as he draped his coat on the back of a stool, rolling up his sleeves and pulling on gloves. He went to work cutting the vegetables.

"Can you—" Killian's words cut off when he looked at Cyrus. "Oh."

"Speechless?" Cyrus snorted. "That's a first."

"Oh, shut up," the man said with a grin.

It was infectious, and Cyrus found himself returning it. What was it about this guy that had Cyrus feeling out of sorts and out of his own body? He felt lighter as if there wasn't a worry in the world. He could get lost in Killian's orbit; he knew that much. He briefly rubbed his chest, his heart pounding heavier than he'd like. He needed to get grounded and fast.

Killian bounced on his toes, dancing as the music in the kitchen changed to a faster pace. He popped buns out of the toaster oven, spinning on the balls of his feet, his sneakers barely making a sound. Was he a good dancer? Absolutely not. But it was still enjoyable to watch.

"I can feel you eye-fucking me, Cy." The man halted in his dance, turning slowly to look at him with a blush across his light tan face.

"Cy?" he mused, smirking. "We barely know each other, and you're giving me nicknames already." And damn, did it feel good. Better than Cyrus wanted to admit.

"I mean, it sounds better than Cyrus. Rolls off the tongue smoother." Killian returned his smirk, clicking his tongue ring against his teeth.

Cyrus rounded the island, walking toward him, making Killian tilt his head back to look up at him.

"You know what else rolls off the tongue?" he asked, voice dropping an octave.

"Burgers?"

"W-what?" Cyrus blinked a few times, taking a moment to process. That was *not* what he was preparing for, and his face instantly heated. Killian grinned, holding a plate out to him. The both of them burst out laughing as they gathered their food.

"Look, a sexy man like myself needs to be fed," Killian huffed, motioning to his husky form. *Sexy, indeed.*

After grabbing drinks to accompany their food, they sat on stools at the kitchen island.

"So, uh, what did you want to talk about?" Killian asked between bites, occasionally wiping his mouth clean with a napkin.

Cyrus nearly inhaled the burger, it was so good. He had no shame as he washed it down with beer.

"First ... That was great." He nodded to the food. "Unfortunately, the second thing isn't as fun. We found your bartender," he said plainly.

Cyrus' stomach clenched when the color drained from Killian's face. He didn't like the look on the man's face and instantly wanted to figure out a way to erase it. To make him feel better.

"She's dead, isn't she?"

"How many of your employees have stopped showing up to work?" Cyrus hedged, noticing how Killian's pulse raced against his throat.

"Just the one. The others quit. Or at least, they sent me resignation pings," he said uneasily. "Are you saying—"

"They're all dead. Are you aware that they all had a history of abuse or a record?"

"What? No. I looked into each of them," Killian said with sincerity.

"Personally?"

"Well … No. I hired a company." The man sighed, dipping his head low. He tapped his comms and held it out for Cyrus. "This is their contact information. I've never been able to get them on the comm, only via pings. I should've been smarter than that. It's been so busy, and I needed to hire new people for my brother."

"You mean to tell me you were not clued into it at all? That none of them seemed suspicious?" Cyrus cocked his head, hating what he was about to do. "You have a record yourself. You've been attacked. I would expect you to be more sensitive to these things."

He rubbed at his face, not happy with the idea of interrogating Killian.

"Fuck you!" he yelled as he stood up abruptly. "So, what? Once a victim, always a victim?" He rubbed his wrists as he shook his head. "No. Most abusers don't look or act like it at face value. I did not spend enough time with any of the new hires to truly learn who they were. Also, they only worked here for, at the max, a month. That's not enough time to understand who someone is."

"Are you sure about that?" Cyrus remained seated, drifting his gaze down to Killian's hands. "I've gathered a lot about you in just two interactions with you."

"I doubt you learned anything about me besides the size of my ass and how good I look in these jeans."

"Stop deflecting," Cyrus said with an eye roll.

"I am not. I did not spend one-on-one time with any of them. Did you forget that I also own the Crow's Cauldron? I can't be expected to be everywhere at once and speak to every new hire for The Den. And with limited interactions, there's little time to learn."

"Do you know if they spoke with anyone on the regular? Two of them were hauling guests from the bar, drunk and drugged, to be trafficked."

"What?" Killian barked. "No fucking way."

"Unfortunately, yes. This doesn't look good for you or your businesses." Cyrus wanted to wipe the look of dismay from Killian's face. "Whether it was you or your brother, or you were set up, word will spread."

"I swear, I didn't do it. But I will help you in any way possible. If this killer is pulling people from our bar, maybe we can—" Killian sighed, plugging a thumb into his full lips to chew on the nail.

"Leave that to me," Cyrus said, unable to stop himself from pulling the finger from Killian's mouth, letting his own linger on the lower lip.

The man's pulse raced, the sound making Cyrus almost groan. The scent of leather and espresso wafted from the human with an undercurrent of arousal. "Do you have any reason to believe someone is targeting you? Choosing victims that happen to be your employees?" he questioned.

"No, I don't." Killian's tongue darted out to lick the digit, taking a step back, but not so far to put distance between them. Cyrus let out a deep exhale, adjusting his seat. "We didn't—"

"I believe you. I don't think you did it either. Or your brother."

Cyrus asked himself if it was truly his gut or something else that led him to this belief. He was analytical. The evidence pointed to the twins, yet he refused to believe it.

"Good, you should," he murmured. "I have to get ready. The staff will be here any minute. Once they're settled, I have to head to the Cauldron. I was getting ready to bring on some new hires. Should I not?"

"Give me their names, and I'll personally research each of them, but proceed as usual. Don't make any sudden changes that might clue the killer in, or they might change their hunting ground." He winced at his choice of words, noticing Killian paling again.

"All right. We can't lose this place. It's the only thing we have and—"

"Killian..." Cyrus spoke softer than intended, cupping the man's face.

His gaze dropped to the man's lips. The one thing he didn't do was kiss people, yet here he was, his lips colliding with another. He wasn't sure what he planned to do when he pulled Killian in. All he knew was that he wanted to shut down his spiral.

It was an odd feeling. The instinct to help someone feel better, especially someone he barely knew. But he didn't hesitate. If Killian ended up being the Carnicero, he had to soak up this moment. There was no telling what would happen once the Governors found out and if he could do anything to prevent it from getting out of hand.

All remaining thoughts exited his head when Killian's mouth moved against his.

Cyrus teased with his tongue until the man opened for him, grabbing his shirt to pull himself closer. He growled, gripping Killian's hips as their kiss deepened. The man's tongue ring glided along his tongue, sending desire straight to his dick. A moan escaped into his mouth as Cyrus turned his hands to Killian's round ass.

"Seems you like me after all," Cyrus whispered against Killian's lips, sucking in the lower one. He returned the favor, teeth gliding along the flesh, and pulled away, breathless.

"I don't know about that yet," Killian said, cheeks flushed.

Cyrus dug his hands into the man's hair to pull him close and devour his mouth. Another moan escaped the bar owner while Cyrus sucked on his tongue. Fuck, he wanted to hear more of those sweet sounds. He moved his lips down Killian's chin, nipping at the skin and finding the sweet spot under his ear lobe. Killian's grip on Cyrus' shirt tightened as he sucked on the man's neck and left a lip-shaped hickey.

"Is that a challenge?" Cyrus growled, echoing the other night. He took immense satisfaction in the shiver that traveled the man's body.

"I don't know, is it?" Killian asked with an arched brow as he untangled himself from Cyrus, mussing up his own hair as if to fix it. All it did was make it stick up in a million places, as usual.

Cyrus stood as he looked down the line of Killian's body, finding the man just as hard as he was. His gaze landed on the hickey he left, and a smug smile pulled up at the sight. Leaning in, he planned on leaving another when his comm blared. He bit back a groan as he stepped back.

"If I had more time, I'd show you how much of a challenge I'm up for," he chuckled.

"Aw, what? One minute wonder?" Killian snorted as Cyrus narrowed his eyes. A gasp escaped him when Cyrus wrapped a gentle hand around his throat.

"I can't wait to prove to you just how wrong you are."

"Who says I want you to?" Killian breathed.

"Your dick." Cyrus stole another kiss, leaving the man unsteady on his feet as he let him go. "I love making a brat heel. Test me. Find out how quickly I do it."

Killian's emerald eyes darkened, almost black, as he let his gaze travel down Cyrus' body and up again.

"I guess we'll find out. I always love a good test."

The sounds of doors opening drew their attention, making them step further apart. They stared at each other for a minute, Killian's lips swollen from their kiss.

"Send me those names. I'll make sure to plug in some plain clothed Guards. Just…" Cyrus had to fight from bouncing on his feet. "Be careful."

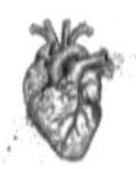

"YOU EVER TURNED SOMEONE before?" Tristan asked the next night in between bites of apple pie. "Like into a vampire … Duh." He snorted, shoveling more food into his mouth.

"Do you ever *not* eat?" Cyrus chuckled.

"What? I love pie. It's like I have a permanent sweet tooth," he responded, tapping the now-empty plate in his hand. "And *you're* the one who got it for me."

"That's wholly unsanitary, Tristan." Cyrus shook his head as the Ice Wielder plopped his dish on the counter.

"It's not like I didn't use a plate. None of his bits got on mine." Tristan shrugged as a pained groan rose from between them. He looked down at the man on the surgical table. "Well, hello there, buddy. About time you woke up."

"I—"

"If you tell us you don't know anything—*again*—I assure you that we will make this infinitely more painful for you, Tyson," Cyrus said casually. His vision tinted red at the smell of blood, fangs descending slowly.

"Stop!" the wolf screamed, trying to move his restrained wrists. Bound to armrests outstretched from the table, thin wiring cut into his skin, a brick weighing it down underneath.

"Y'know, the more you move, the quicker it cuts. The quicker it cuts, the closer you are to being amputated. Hands are important, aren't they?" Tristan wriggled his fingers. "Feet too, right?" He tapped Tyson's toes, making him arch his back. Like his arms, the man's legs were outstretched from the table.

"P-please…"

"Tell us why you were trying to sell military secrets to The Martyrs," Cyrus snapped. "Where did you get the information?"

"I-I never met them in person. Only through c-comms." Tyson sobbed, every wrack of his body slicing his ankles and wrists more.

"Now we're getting somewhere!" Tristan clapped. "Where are your comms?"

"A-apartment. If they're not destroyed by now." The man's body wracked again, skin paling. The blood loss was finally getting to him. "F-fuck it. The M-Martyrs are planning something. I-I don't know what."

"I'm assuming this mystery person told you this?" Cyrus asked as he looked through his tools to find his favorite knife.

"Y-yes." The man's pupils dilated as he faded, tears streaming down his temples. "S-shit is about to go down in Asherai. We were told to be prepared."

"We? Who's we?" Tristan asked too late, the man having passed out once more. Cyrus wasn't sure he would wake this time. "Boss … Maybe wiring at the wrists wasn't a good idea."

"Yeah..." Cyrus sighed, sucking his teeth. "Higher up? I didn't even get the chance to mark him as a traitor yet." Pulling a knife, he shrugged and worked on the wolf's chest anyway.

"Wait ... You're a vampire," Tristan said suddenly as they finished working on the wolf. Cyrus hummed in agreement, cutting with precision to spell out the word 'TRAITOR'. "And you fuck and drink blood."

"Where are you going with this, Tristan?" he asked, dropping the knife into a sterile container.

"Well, don't you do both at the same time? Isn't *that* unsanitary, too?"

"That's different," Cyrus said with a snort.

"Is it really, though?" Tristan shrugged, winking. "You never answered my question earlier."

"What is this, man? You're awfully nosey tonight."

"We spoke about this..." Tristan sat and spun on a stool, obviously determined to wait for Cyrus to answer. Cyrus grunted as he crossed his bloodied arms, smearing it across his white shirt.

"No. I have not."

He stood there as Tristan continued to spin before the Ice Wielder came to a stop. He looked to the left, then right, and slid his cobalt eyes back to Cyrus. Tristan pursed his lips, raising his eyebrows expectantly. When Cyrus remained silent, the man groaned.

"Okay, why not?" he rushed out, moving his hands in a circular motion to suggest, "Keep talking."

"Tristan, really?" Cyrus asked, exasperated.

"Yes, Cyrus. Really!" The Ice Wielder's eyes widened, voice pitching up as he popped out of his stool to follow behind him as he left the interrogation room.

Cyrus hit the sanitize button and lead the way to the changing room.

"Are you going to follow me into the shower as well?"

"Maybe..."

Knowing Tristan, he probably would. Cyrus let out a long-suffering sigh.

"I'm sure you're aware that without Jacinto's compulsion … I'm not all the way there," he murmured, tapping his temple as he started removing his clothes.

"Mhm, go on."

"The virus fucked with my brain chemistry. In the thousands of years of vampiric evolution, it's very rare that it creates berserkers." Cyrus hesitated, blinking back the red that threatened to encroach on his vision again.

He needed to feed, and soon. Fuck. The stress of impending political upheaval was getting to him. It was the most he had ever fed since his creation, and without Jacinto's compulsion, he would be tearing cities apart right now.

"Okay, tell me more…"

"If you keep cutting me off, I'm going to stop talking altogether," Cyrus growled. Tristan sucked in his lips between his teeth and nodded. "Since vampirism is a bloodborne disease, and often some traits are passed over… I am worried that I'll pass on my condition." He dropped his clothes into the incinerator and wrapped a towel around his waist.

"I know it's unheard of. For a vampire to not turn a human in their lifespan." He shrugged. "I just don't want to risk it."

"Have berserkers ever made other vampires before?" Tristan inquired, almost scratching his scruff with his bloodied, leather-gloved hands. He winced, turning to the sink to wash them off.

"Most haven't even lived as long as I have, so I am unsure. I don't know if I'm the exception or not." Cyrus shook his head, vision flashing red again. "But I do know I need to blood a lot more than regular vampires."

"Well, I'll leave you to it," Tristan said, approaching him to pat Cyrus' cheek a few times and then squeeze his cheeks. "Just so you know, you're amazing. Yes, you are!" he exclaimed as if talking to a baby.

Cyrus jerked his head back with a bark of laughter.

"Get the fuck out of here, Aries."

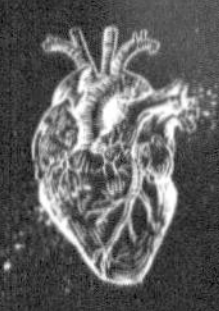

CHAPTER 8

I LIKE MY COFFEE BLACK

"**C**YRUS, WHY IS THIS** case so important to you?" Tristan asked, leaning against the table and crossing his ankles. "You rarely involve yourself in murder investigations."

"There is something about it that has been nagging me. I can't put my finger on it, but I need to figure it out."

"Oh, so you hyperfocus." Tristan nodded. "I once went down this rabbit hole learning about Euhaven history. I didn't let it drop for months."

"Exactly. So far, the common denominator has been the connection to the Den and the Crow's Cauldron. It feels too easy. There has to be something else. The Governors are still breathing down my neck about this, too. It's all a clusterfuck."

Whimpers rose from the table behind Tristan, making the man spin on the balls of his feet and clap his hands.

"Sorry, I got distracted and almost forgot about you, sweetheart," Tristan said gently, pushing the human's hair from her sweaty forehead.

The woman on the table had her arms out to the side, wrists bound tightly. Inserted in the tops of her feet were IVs, dripping a slow-acting narcotic into her bloodstream. Tristan squeezed the IV bag, pushing a rush of liquid into her veins and earning a scream.

"Stop! Fuck, stop!" she panted, sweat covering her body. The tee and shorts clung to her damp skin.

"How did you pass your background check?" Cyrus asked, playing with the knife in his hand. Shedding blood seemed like the perfect outlet for the madness brewing in his mind. Fuck! Would he ever get a reprieve?

"I didn't speak to anyone directly. I received a ping with

instructions, and I followed them," she said as she squeezed her eyes close. "Fuck," she whimpered as she fought her bindings. "I promise, I wasn't planning—"

"What did we say about lying?" Tristan snapped, gripping the IV itself and pushing it further into the woman's vein. She screamed again, the sound piercing through Cyrus' already sore head. "We know what you do with intoxicated women. You are good at covering your tracks but not good enough."

"I don't know who they are!" she yelled, body trembling.

Cyrus grunted as he strolled around the table, placing the tip of the knife at her shoulder and piercing her skin.

"Please! Don't do this!" Tears fell from her eyes.

Cyrus' vision tinted crimson at the sight, bloodlust rising to the surface. The high he got from torture flooded through his body.

"I don't think it's a coincidence that each person that has gone through—" Tristan paused to look at his comm "—DRB Consulting is a criminal." He pursed his lips, looking at Cyrus with questioning cobalt eyes. "Shell? Cover-up? I'll find out."

"Perhaps," he lifted one shoulder. "Why did you apply for The Den?" he asked, returning to the siren.

"Rumors," she wheezed, eyes circling the room, the narcotics doing their work through her system. "It's no secret that Royal and Killian hired criminals. But then again, I guess it wasn't *them,* per se," the woman grumbled.

"Rumors? How many people are taking advantage of this?" Cyrus growled, digging the knife till he hit bone.

He was right. Someone was setting up the twins, and the thought was driving him closer to madness. He planned to not only torture the person responsible but tear them limb from limb and feast on them as he did so.

"Stop!" she cried out. "I don't know! We got job alerts. I only heard about it from someone else who was recently hired. But they stopped responding to my pings."

"Probably because they're dead," Tristan snorted as he quirked an eyebrow. "Does this one get a 'traitor' or..."

"'Dumbass' is a good alternative. Though I'm not sure it'll

fit…"

"You get one arm, and I get the other. Which one do you want? 'Dumb' or 'ass'?" Tristan mused, picking up a knife.

"Hmm, 'dumb' works." Cyrus carved the D, the squelch of splitting skin helping to abate the bloodlust. "I don't think she has anything left to say."

"Rodon!" she screamed, body convulsing.

"The vampire kingpin?" Cyrus asked, pausing in his torture. "What about him?"

"Rodon!" she screamed again, crying. "Please!"

Her eyes shot open, pupils dilating as she seized. Tears streamed, and before Cyrus could do anything further, her body stilled, and her heart stopped beating.

"What is her connection to Rodon?" Tristan asked, dropping the knife into a nearby tin. "Shit…" He turned the woman's chin to the side and lifted her hair to find an elegant, scripted R behind her ear. "She was a familiar."

"A familiar? What was she doing working at the Den?" Cyrus wondered, walking out of the room with Tristan and hitting the cleansing button.

"None of his familiars would work uptown unless he didn't know. Fuck, none of them would be involved in the skin trade either. Rodon is a lot of things but a trafficker he is not." Tristan shook his head. "Aren't they compelled to stay out of the area?"

"That's right. Unless there's more going on." Cyrus sighed, rubbing his temples, not caring for the blood on his hands. "Rodon wouldn't be so blatant. For all we know, she went rogue. There are ways to get around a compulsion if done correctly."

"Should probably check the other victims and see if they have any connections with him too," Tristan suggested, and Cyrus was inclined to agree.

"I need to speak with Killian. I am certain he and his brother have nothing to do with this."

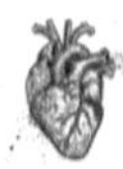

WITH HIS HANDS IN his pockets, Cyrus strolled down the street until he arrived at one of the busiest coffee shops in Malagado. The scent of espresso and brown sugar hit him first as he entered. The Crow's Cauldron was unlike any coffee shop he'd been in, with deep violet and teal gradient walls that mimicked a crow's wing in the light. Black marble with silver veins covered the floor and bar top. All the equipment was monochromatic teal, which shone bright against the darker counters. People milled about, waiting in line for their drinks to be called.

Rather than go to the counter, he chose an open seat by the window, sinking in and keeping his attention on the door. About a half hour later, things had slowed down, and in walked Doctor Broderick.

Predictable.

Her sneakers squeaked gently as she made her way to the front, her plum scrubs covered by a black leather jacket. Under her arm was a hovercycle helmet for her magenta and gold cycle.

"Hi, Doctor Broderick," the barista at the register said, clearly nervous. "The usual tonight?"

"Of course."

The doctor barely spared them a glance, making Cyrus clench his jaw. After paying, she waited at the counter, watching the barista as they made her drink.

"It's rude to stare. Makes them nervous," he said from his seat, nearly chuckling at how she stiffened.

Slowly, the good doctor turned, storm-grey eyes meeting his.

"Cyrus…" His name came out clipped, barely contained anger evident in her voice. "What are you doing here?"

"Thought I'd see if Killian was around. Decided to hang out for a bit first." He grinned at her frustration, flashing her his fangs. He was beginning to love getting a rise out of her.

"You don't seem like the 'hanging out' sort."

"Here's your drink, Doctor Broderick," the barista said.

Aida snatched the drink, again not sparing them a glance or so much as an acknowledgment.

"You'd be surprised," Cyrus said as he approached her slowly. Always impressing him, she remained where she stood, looking up at him as if he didn't tower over her.

"You might be a doctor. You might have a fine education and be highly resourceful…" he turned to the barista, smiling at them and tapping their comm watch to transfer credits to their tip fund. Their face lit up, golden eyes brightening in gratitude as they turned to finish their work. "But it doesn't excuse being a bitch to the people who make your life a little more comfortable."

"Maybe they—"

"Don't bother to finish that sentence," Cyrus snapped. "*You* choose to come here. *You* choose to order yourself a cold brew with a shot of espresso." He grinned as her eyes widened.

"You…"

"Enjoy your shift, good doctor."

"Stop calling me that!" she snarled, gripping her helmet tighter.

"No, I don't think so." Cyrus chuckled. "Run along, don't want to be late."

"Fuck you," she seethed as she pushed past him.

"Thanks," the barista said from the counter, pushing a coffee toward him. "A quad over ice, right?"

"Yes, thank you," he said, sipping the drink. "Is Killian around?"

"In his office," they nodded with their chin in the direction he should head.

Cyrus returned the nod and walked toward the 'employees only' area. A few of the bakers bowed their heads as he walked past.

"Coming around!" came Killian's booming voice as he rounded a corner.

Cyrus shifted to the side, barely moving out of the way as

Killian rushed past with a tray of pastries. He looked at Cyrus briefly, focusing on his destination. He leaned on the wall next to the door of Killian's office as he waited for the man to return.

Workers moved about, clearly prepping for an upcoming rush. He had never learned how to bake, and watching them work made him wish he had. The smells alone had his mouth-watering, and he wished he had a...

"Banana nut muffin?" Killian offered as he appeared in front of Cyrus.

"How'd you know?" he asked, flabbergasted, taking the treat.

The man shrugged, walking into his office for Cyrus to follow. The door clicked as it shut, and the thought of being in the enclosed space alone with Killian made his pulse race.

Fuck Cyrus. Stop acting like a teenager.

"Lucky guess? You seem like the type to like nuts, is all." Killian grinned, making Cyrus chuckle. "See? *That's* how you land a pun."

"Oh, shut up," Cyrus snorted, grabbing Killian's shirt to pull him closer. The human gasped at their proximity. His hand glided up the column of the man's throat to rest comfortably. "What about spanks? Want me to show you how to land those?" he whispered against Killian's lips.

"I..." His heart rate increased against his palm, matching the pace of his own.

"Speechless?" Cyrus grinned, pulling Killian into a fiery kiss. He refused to consider what it meant, knowing he yearned for the man's touch. Yearned to feel Killian's lips on his own. It was all he thought about since the last time they spoke.

The man opened for him, allowing Cyrus to push his tongue into his mouth. Killian's piercing rubbed against his tongue, sending desire straight to his dick. He wrapped his arms around Cyrus' waist, his soft body lining with his hard one.

"Well, damn," Killian chuckled breathlessly as they parted.

He gave Cyrus soft kisses, nipping gently and dragging his teeth along Cyrus' lower lip. The act was sensual in ways Cyrus had never experienced before, and he returned it in kind.

"Go on a date with me," Cyrus blurted, surprising himself. Based on the look on Killian's face, the man was equally perplexed.

A date? What was he thinking?

"What?" Killian asked, face turning red as he stepped back.

Cyrus' hand fell to his, holding it loosely. What was he doing? He cleared his throat, nearly rocking on his feet.

"A date. Ever been on one?" he huffed, nerves suddenly bunching in his stomach. *Didn't I say stop acting like a fucking teenager, Cyrus?*

What was he doing?

"Yes, but have you? You don't seem like the dating type, Cy." Killian was perceptive, that was for damn sure. He squeezed Cyrus' now clammy hand.

What the fuck? Clammy hands? Really?

"Yes! Of course," he mumbled. Killian raised an eyebrow, green eyes lit with mirth. "No…" he let go of his hand to rub the back of his neck. If he wasn't so dark-skinned, he imagined he'd have been scarlet by now. "It's cool if it's awkward. I honestly don't know what made me ask."

"Well, I would hope it was that fantastic kiss we just shared." Killian chuckled. "I'd love to."

"Okay. Cool," he said, nodding. "So, uh … What do you like?"

"Oh no, we're not doing that," Killian snorted, walking further into his office. He pulled off his deep purple apron, hanging it on a hook, and sat in his chair with a sigh. "Just surprise me. Send me the evening and time." He winked.

Cyrus blew out a nervous breath. Nervous! Cyrus barely recognized himself.

"But I'm sure you didn't come by to ask me on a date. What's up?"

"I came to talk with you about the investigation." Cyrus leaned against the desk, almost forgetting his muffin. He bit a piece, savoring it. "Wow, that's good…" he said more to himself.

"That's what he said," Killian grinned. Cyrus shook his head, polishing off the treat and following it with his espresso. "*And* you drink espresso over ice. You're a walking stereotype, my guy."

"Shut up," Cyrus snorted. He sighed and got back to business. "The consulting company is luring these criminals into the Den."

"Well, fuck," Killian groaned as he grimaced. "I guess I'll have to fire them."

"No, don't yet. We can't let them know we're on to them. I'm hoping with this knowledge, we can find out who they are sooner rather than later. I've got my best technicians on it." Cyrus' gaze locked with Killian's, whose lips parted slightly.

"Well, thank you…" Killian rubbed his wrists, eyes going mildly vacant. "I don't know how I feel about knowingly allowing these people to work for us … Even in the interim. What if it backfires? What if someone gets wind and the Carnicero Cerebral finds out? What if people start to assume it's us…"

"I wasn't lying when I said I know you and your brother had nothing to do with it," Cyrus said. "I know it is hard. But trust me when I say firing the consulting firm will give them a warning, and they'll shift gears. This is the best lead we have right now."

"All right. All right." Killian nodded, standing to pace. "I'll let Royal know. He and his partner should be back next week." He looked at the various plants and flowers he had lining his wall. "I'm trusting you, Cy."

"That's all I ask. I know what I'm doing," he reassured, coming up behind Killian to pull the shorter man against him.

Resting his chin on top of Killian's head, he wrapped his arms around him. He wanted to pull Killian tighter into his embrace and blanched at the thought. He needed to end this. He was becoming too invested. In a human, nonetheless. And yet…

"I am more than the Cortesano…" he said softly.

Being affectionate was never something Cyrus was known for. But being with Killian, in the man's very atmosphere, Cyrus found himself doing things he had never done before.

"What do you mean?" Killian asked, gliding his fingers along the petals of a bioluminescent lily, the flower glowing with the moon's power.

"Just that I can guarantee that I will figure out who is doing this and make them pay."

"Okay," he whispered, seeming to detach. "I have to get back to work." He stepped from Cyrus' arms, leaving him confused.

"Did I say something wrong?" he asked, watching Killian grab his holoport and what looked like a menu.

"No! No..." Killian shook his head, giving Cyrus a small smile. "Just a lot to think about." He approached Cyrus, raising on his toes, and kissed him softly. "If you're serious about that date, send me the details."

"I'm very serious," he said, returning the kiss. "I might have some ideas already."

"Oh really?" The warmth in Killian's smile returned, the haze in his eyes lifting slowly.

"Yeah, and they all end with me utterly ruining you."

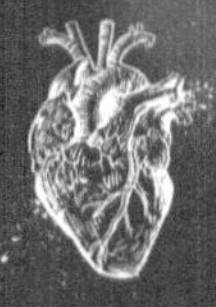

CHAPTER 9

SKY'S THE LIMIT OR SOME SHIT

BASS FLOWED THROUGH CYRUS' body. It vibrated his bones and had his head buzzing with energy. His chin dipped occasionally as he bopped to the beat, walking through the mass of sweaty bodies that smelled of sex and blood. The latter briefly reddened his vision, quickening his footsteps toward the club's second level. The increased smell was distracting, making his fangs ache and his dick twitch.

As he approached the double doors leading into the Exhibition Hall, a loud yell drew his attention, and his fangs descended.

"Yo, what the fuck!" came a gruff, masculine voice.

"I'm sorry, it was an accident!" The familiar alto voice of a particular little wolf had him changing direction.

"I wasn't ready," the man growled, coming into view as Cyrus narrowed his gaze on the pair.

Bex was on their knees and bound with a chain linking their collar to a set of hand and ankle cuffs. Other than the bindings, they were naked and covered in cum. The sight would've been erotic had it not been for the bruise on their face and their blown pupils. The large vampire had his hand in their hair, gripping it tightly, his softening dick still dripping.

"But you held me. How was I—"

"Shut up!" the man snarled, readying to smack them. Cyrus was there before he could lift his hand, removing the entire arm from the vampire's body. "Fuck!" the vampire screamed.

Cyrus swung the arm like a bat, landing a blow that knocked the man off his feet.

"You took it too far. You touched them beyond consent.

For that, you die."

"Please! Wait. She's just—"

"*They* are more than whatever the fuck you were about to say."

Cyrus punched through the vampire's throat, wrapping his hand around his spine to sever it. Red cleared from his vision as Cyrus shuddered from shedding blood. He licked his fingers as he stood, heedless of the crimson that stained his cream henley. Bouncers hauled ass, and once they saw who he was, bowed their heads, immediately taking care of cleaning up the mess.

Taking them by their biceps, Cyrus helped Bex stand.

"Cyrus," they said softly, looking down.

He put a finger under their chin, tilting their head to look at him.

"Clean yourself off. You're done for the night," he growled.

"What? You can't tell me what to do. You don't have a claim on me," they hissed, narrowing their eyes.

They had a point, but he didn't fucking care. The thought of someone hurting them made him irate, and he didn't know what to do with that.

"How many times did that asshole hit you?" A fury he never felt before raged through him.

"It doesn't matter. I wanted it. We were having a good time." Their eyes ping-ponged around the space, tongue darting out to play with their lip ring.

"Fine. How many times did he hit you *without* your consent? You can't tell me that bruise was consensual."

The way their gaze darted away told him everything he needed to know. He shook them by their collar, which made them look at him and let out a growl. Their wolf was close to the surface; he could smell it.

"It. Doesn't. Fucking. Matter. Now let me go," Bex snarled.

He took a better look at them; the way sweat clung to their skin, their body flushed from whatever the fuck they had been doing all night, their nose flared wide and red, and their eyes almost black from their enlarged pupils.

"I'm cutting you off. You're high as fuck, and you've had enough," he said as he knelt to wrap his arms around their thighs to hoist them over his shoulder. They were still bound and couldn't put up much of a fight.

"You're not my keeper, asshole! Put me down," they yelled, body shaking as he walked toward Killian's office. His grip around Bex's thighs tightened when they squirmed to get free. "Cyrus!"

"It's 'my Lord,' and you better get it the fuck right," he snarled as he burst through the office door.

As he expected, the room had its own bathroom and a pull-out bed in the corner. He figured Killian was the type to sleep at work if he had a busy night. Cyrus snapped the door closed with his foot and took them to the bathroom. He was impressed at the small but neat space. There was a shower stall with an overhead detachable shower head.

"It's only 'my Lord' when I'm on my knees begging for your cum," they grumbled.

Gently, he placed them in the shower stall, turning them so that he could work the chains free.

"Such sass," he remarked.

"Well, you're ruining my high, so naturally…"

"Can I remove your collar?" he asked, running a finger across it. It was magenta tonight.

"Yes…" they whispered.

"I'll make sure to wash it for you." He placed the collar and cuffs in a sanitary bin.

Damn, Killian really thought of everything. He was certain Royal's office was the same.

Bex groaned when he turned the shower on, the water frigid. "Fuck!" they hissed, jolting from the cold and turning to face him.

Cyrus raised a brow. "You're overheated; you need the cold."

"No shit, I know that. Doesn't mean I enjoy it. Don't wash my hair. No shampoo or anything," they said quickly when he reached for hair products. He nodded without question.

Grabbing a wash rag and unscented soap, he lathered it up, washing Bex's body. He knelt on one knee, ignoring the water soaking his black jeans. He delicately took their foot, resting it on his thigh as he glided the rag up their long leg.

"Why do you do it?" he inquired, tapping their foot for them to switch with the other. They let out a hum of contentment as he massaged their tattooed leg. He could feel every knot under the skin.

"Do what?" Bex asked with a groan.

"Potions..."

"Well, I mean, it feels good. So, there's that," they snorted.

He gripped their leg, looking up at them. Neon glowing eyes met his, mouth slightly parted.

"You know what the fuck I mean, Bex." He looked away to lather more soap and wash the cum off their torso. He stood up, their eyelids fluttering closed as he cleaned their face.

"Honestly, it's not really any of your business. And no, it doesn't affect my ability to do my job." Bex sniffed, keeping their eyes shut as he turned off the water. He grabbed a towel from a shelf and wrapped it around them. They shuddered, curling into the warm cloth.

They were right, and he decided not to push. Cyrus looked at all the oils Killian had stocked, shook his head, and grabbed the apple-spiced one.

"Do you shower in here?" he asked as he walked them toward an ottoman in front of the pull-out bed.

"Yeah, Killian has been good to me," they said with a small smile.

"Killian ... You know him?" Cyrus hedged as he knelt again to massage the oil into their skin. It didn't get past him how languid their body turned under his ministrations.

"Yeah. We're best friends." Something must have shown on his face because Bex laughed. "Oh, I already know about you two sucking face."

"And does he..."

"Know about us?"

"Yeah."

"Sure does. He *saw* us that first night. He's not an idiot." Bex's full lips turned down in a frown. "Is it a problem?"

"No!" He held their hips, directing them to turn so he could work on their heavily tattooed back. "Sit," he commanded, and they complied, plopping onto the ottoman. His fingers worked through the knots in their shoulders, and they moaned softly from his touch. "I was going to tell him anyway."

"Why?" they wondered, leaning forward to rest their elbows on their knees.

Cyrus wasn't sure how to answer. He bit his lip, focusing on what he was doing instead.

"How long have you known him?" he asked, hoping to change the subject.

Bex turned to face him, legs on either side of his body as he knelt between them.

"A few years."

They shrugged, focusing their attention on him. They were still high, albeit slightly less, and it bothered him. It bothered him when it shouldn't. Cyrus wasn't sure why when it was never his concern.*

"So..." they hummed, returning his focus to the present. "Why were you going to tell him?"

"You don't let up, do you?" he snorted, hands idly gliding up and down their thighs, raising goosebumps along their skin.

"Tell me," Bex said firmly, sitting closer to the edge of the ottoman. "And fuck me while you do."

"No," he said as he stood. He smirked at their protest as he pulled the mattress from the couch. "I'll tell you, little wolf. But I won't fuck you."

Bex yelped when he scooped them up and placed them on the bed. A frown turned their lips down once more, and they whimpered when he denied them access to his lap.

"Why not?" They rose to their knees, sliding their hands up his thighs to tug at his belt.

* "wRoNg (feat. Kehlani)" by ZAYN, Kehlani

As badly as he wanted them to continue, he decided against it, grabbing their hands to still them. Having sex while high and with other high people had never been an issue for Cyrus. But something about the state Bex was in made him hold off, to just let them rest, even if they didn't believe they needed it.

"I… I can't explain. Just that I won't." Cyrus let out a groan when Bex nudged his shirt up with their nose, exposing a sliver of his lower abdomen. Their lips touched the sensitive area, and he had to hold onto their shoulders. "Do you want to know the reason or not, little wolf?" He gently pushed them back onto their ass.

"Fine. Yes." Bex pouted at him, crossing their arms.

Cyrus scratched his forehead as he crossed the office to grab a bottle of water from the mini-fridge. He sat on the ottoman across from Bex and thrust the bottle at them. They rolled their eyes, snatching and cracking it open to guzzle down.

"Don't be a brat. That's not in your nature." Cyrus grinned when they chucked the empty bottle at him. "I wanted Killian to know that I have a cum slut," he said plainly, watching as their eyes widened.

Before they could react, he snatched their foot, pulling it into his lap. Their soft moans let him know that the impromptu massage was worth it.

"I wanted him to know I have a toy that I like to fuck and play with." His voice was raw and husky, a soft growl vibrating through his body.

"Oh!" they cried out when he worked through a knot and moved to their other foot. "And? I doubt he cares." They shrugged. "I'm not important, so—" His teeth latched onto their big toe. It wasn't hard enough to break skin but enough to shut them up.

"*And* I wanted to tell him that I don't plan on giving you up," he breathed, soothing the bite with his tongue.

"Cyrus," Bex groaned.

Their pupils had returned to normal, and he almost sighed in relief. Why did it matter to him so much? He never cared what others did on their own time.

"Don't ever tell me you're not important." He blurted as he

dropped their foot.

Fuck, he hadn't meant to say that out loud. *Important?* Did he genuinely feel that way?

"O-okay." Bex quickly sat up to wrap their legs around his waist. Hooking one foot over the other, he grunted in surprise when Bex used their werewolf strength to pull him on top of them on the bed.

"Bex…" he breathed, leaning on one hand to hover above their lithe body. His free one cupped their face as his eyes drifted to their lips.

"Cyrus," they whispered. "Kiss me."

A battle roared inside.

Trust didn't come easily to Cyrus, and as much as he'd grown to enjoy Bex's light, could he trust a spy? They were a master at manipulation, proving they could become anyone they needed to be. How did he know if they were being authentic? Why did it even fucking matter?

Giving his body, fucking, and fighting that was no problem. Intimacy? Softness? Those were concepts beyond his understanding. He had no use or desire for them. Or hadn't. First, it was Killian, and even that rocked his world. Now? Now, he was looking at an earthquake that would shatter everything.

They stared at each other for a long time, but when Bex tried to push him away, he refused to let them go.

Fuck it.

Sinking his hand in their hair, he pulled them into a hungry kiss. Their lips on his own was like coming home. It sent sparks up his spine and caused a strange tightening in his chest.

Fuck, was he dying? If so, then this was the perfect way to go.

Cyrus moaned as Bex thoroughly tasted all of his mouth, tongue fighting against his. As they parted, he pulled their lip ring with his teeth, making them whine in pleasure.

"Fuck my throat, please," they whispered against his lips. He kissed them once more, using all his willpower to push off the bed. "Cy…"

"You need to sleep. I think you've been come on enough tonight." He grabbed a blanket and plopped it over their face to shut up their protests.

Bex grunted as they pushed it out of the way, a genuine smile gracing their lips. It was a stunning smile, the kind that showed off their small but sharp canines, made their eyes light up, and tugged at that tightness in his chest he refused to acknowledge. All he knew was he couldn't get enough of them and would always want more.

"Fine," they said with a yawn, snuggling into the blankets. "Where..." They shook their head, cutting themself off.

"What? What were you going to say?" he asked as he stripped out his still-wet henley. Thankfully, his undershirt wasn't as wet.

"Nothing. It's none of my business," they mumbled, turning away from him to burrow further into the blanket.

He sat at the edge of the couch, sinking his hand into their hair to pull it back and make them look at him. They whimpered, their eyes briefly flaring neon green.

"Little wolf..." he warned.

"I was just going to ask where you were off to. But seriously, it's not my business," they breathed out quickly.

His grip loosened immediately, fingers lightly massaging Bex's scalp.

"I have business to get to," he said as he continued his ministrations when he noticed their eyes had fluttered closed.

"Oh, okay. Pleasure or work?" they mumbled, voice growing softer with sleep.

"This time? Work."

"Hmm ... Sexy..." they chuckled, sleep taking them over.

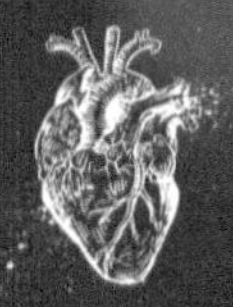

CHAPTER 10

IT'S USUALLY THE ONES WHO SMILE THE MOST

CYRUS' HOVERCAR HUMMED AS he stopped in front of Killian's sleek house. A wall of black glass faced a cliff drop, the Temisraine splashing softly below. Everything was angular: the magenta roof was flat, and the floors were stacked in a zig-zag formation.

Exiting the car, he made his way up the walkway. Green fluorescent lights glowed under his feet, quickly disappearing with every step. Bioluminescent flora and vines covered Killian's front porch in an organized, chaotic way.

Cyrus rang the door comm, shifting from foot to foot as he waited. They were supposed to have met up, but the human never showed. With the Carnicero Cerebral on the loose, thousands of potentialities flooded his mind.

Time ticked on, and he hit the comm again, wondering if he was being pushy. Maybe Killian was occupied with someone else? A growl made its way out his mouth at the thought.

Hypocrite.

After no response, Cyrus' heart crawled into his throat, his pulse pounding. Putting his hand on the door, he planned to burst through, but it opened with ease as if it had already been slightly ajar.

He walked through the still house, not paying attention to anything except for the sound of Killian's erratic heartbeat coming from a floor above. With only one heartbeat, Cyrus knew no one else was present.

Fuck, was it even Killian?

He moved quickly, finding the stairs and taking them two at

a time. The sharp, coppery scent of blood had his fangs dropping in an instant. His vision reddened, bloodlust fighting to rise in his system. He followed the smell, trying to calm himself as he got closer.

"Killian?" he hissed, stopping in the doorway of the man's room.*

Killian looked up from where he sat on the floor with a shocked expression. Blood covered one of his forearms, and he held a razor blade in the opposite hand. Dark, wine-colored stains covered his grey sweats where his arm rested on a propped-up knee, clear that the blood had dried.

"What are you doing here, Cy?" he asked roughly, dropping his head back against the edge of the bed.

Killian swallowed, his throat bobbing as he did. It drew attention to his racing pulse, and Cyrus had to grit his teeth against the temptation to drive his fangs in deep.

"Can I come in?" His voice was guttural, his bloodlust burning in his chest.

"Not if you keep looking at me like I'm a snack," Killian sighed but nodded. "I'm a three-course meal at minimum."

"The fact that you're even laughing right now baffles me," Cyrus said as he slowly entered the room, taking in the high platform bed covered in emerald and amethyst sheets. He sat beside Killian, careful not to slip on the black marble flooring.

"You get used to it." He shrugged.

Now that he was close, Cyrus could see the slice marks on Killian's skin. Several thin cuts traveled from his wrist to his inner elbow. They were fine enough to make them bleed but not deep enough to cause injury. In the middle of them were scars from previous sessions.

"What happened?"

Cyrus took a few deep breaths, the blood cloying and tempting. He shifted away a bit, putting space between them. Killian frowned but remained where he sat.

"Why are you here?" he asked as he rubbed his fingers on

---

* "Jaws" by Sleep Token

the blunt edge of the razor blade.

"Answer my question first," Cyrus said with narrowed eyes.

With concentration, he slowly reined in his bloodlust. His need to be close to Killian outweighing the alternative. All he wanted was to make sure he was okay. To find out why he was harming himself and how he could get him to stop.

"No, you came into my house uninvited. You answer me first."

"Brat."

"And?" Killian retorted, looking away to focus on the gun resting on his open lap.

How Cyrus missed it, he wasn't sure, and it pissed him off that he'd been so distracted.

"We were supposed to meet up, Killian." Cyrus itched to snatch the weapons away from the human. What was going on with him?

"Well fuck," Killian sighed. "I… forgot."

Cyrus didn't want to acknowledge how much those words hurt.

"You forgot?" His gaze locked with Killian's, whose lips parted slightly.

"I'm sorry…" he whispered.

The sadness in Killian's voice made Cyrus want to wrap his arms around him. Something about Killian drew Cyrus into his orbit, and it was unclear whether he wanted to remain there.

"Tell me what's wrong." Cyrus inched closer.

"Why do you think anything is wrong?" Killian arched an eyebrow.

He lifted the blade to his tongue, licking his blood off it and somehow managing not to slice his flesh. He snorted at Cyrus' expression as he tossed it into a nearby trash can.

"When you're experienced with these things, you learn some stuff."

"I mean, *these things* are why I'm asking. Why are you harming yourself, and why is there a gun in your lap?" he practically growled.

He didn't like the idea of Killian hurting himself. He didn't want to see him hurt in any way, whether it was by the hands of someone else or his own.

"I'm not sure how to answer that question," Killian said candidly.

He picked up the gun, scratching his forehead with the muzzle. The action had Cyrus on edge. In his many centuries on Euhaven, he'd never been in this situation and had no clue how to treat it.

"Start with one sentence," Cyrus whispered.

"Simple answer? I don't know." He shrugged, biting his lower lip in thought.

Cyrus gave him time to process, all the while spiraling internally. Could he try to wrest the gun from him? What if that put Killian over the deep end? How did he navigate this? He didn't enjoy the feeling of not knowing what to do.

"Complicated answer? It feels like it's right. It's a form of release. The pain helps me clear my mind, watching the blood seep and drip … It's almost meditative." His eyes closed as he lay his head back once more. "The gun? Well, I think things would be better if I weren't here."

"What? Why?" Cyrus blurted, reaching for Killian in panic.

The man smiled, taking his hand into his free one.

"There is no reason. It just is. No amount of positive thinking or mantras makes the thoughts go away. Maybe for a little. Shit, maybe even for years. But they always come back. *Always.*" Killian scrunched his nose as if trying to keep himself from crying while tapping the gun on his forehead.

"But you have a pretty decent life," Cyrus said, sounding utterly naïve, he realized.

"You can have a decent life and still be suicidal, Cy."

Killian scratched his forehead again, placed the muzzle on his chin, and turned his gaze on Cyrus. His depthless emerald eyes were dark and full of deep sorrow, made more haunting by the smudged kohl around them.

"I don't get it. Logically, I know I have things in order. My life could be worse. It's decent. I survived more than once. And yet, these thoughts don't go away. The anxiety that I'm failing at life doesn't go away. Wondering if everyone would be happier…" he took a long shuddering breath, "…if I just wasn't around anymore. Maybe they'd feel less stressed out. You know?"

"Give me the gun, Killian," Cyrus said sharply, making the man snap his eyes open to stare at him while he placed the gun to his temple. "*Now*."

"Relax … Tonight isn't the night," he huffed, pulling the trigger.

"No!" Cyrus recoiled, his body tensing as he expected to hear the sound of a gunshot and feel the hot splatter of Killian's blood and brain matter on his face.

That was when he realized the gun was empty.

After the initial panic subsided, he glared at Killian. Cyrus' reaction told him everything he needed to know about how he was beginning to feel for the human. The realization scared the shit out of him.

"That wasn't fucking funny," Cyrus snapped.

"Nice to know you care," he said with a smirk, letting the weapon clatter to the ground and dropping his knee. "I'll be fine. I'm still here, aren't I?"

He scratched his ear, and Cyrus noticed the semi-colon tattooed just below his ear lobe.

"How many times?" he murmured, letting his finger trail over the tattoo. Killian shuddered, letting out a slow breath.

"Clarify what you're asking for me," Killian said tiredly.

"You have a semi-colon. How many times?"

"Oh…" Killian breathed, turning to fiddle with something on the bed. He grabbed a pack of medi-pills and wound care items. "Four…"

"Four?" Cyrus blanched, eyeing the tools he used to clean up his arm and wrap it in gauze.

Killian downed one medi-pill dry with a wince. It was just enough to heal but not enough to prevent scarring.

"Each occasion has a story, none of which I want to talk

about right now," Killian said, scooting close enough that his knees touched Cyrus. "But I do need something from you." Killian smiled, tongue darting out to lick his own lower lip. His piercing flashed in the low light, drawing Cyrus' attention to his mouth.

"And what's that, pet?"

"Ohhh. Hmm, I think I like that," the man purred.

The shift in Killian's demeanor should've concerned Cyrus, but all thoughts left his brain when he tilted his chin to bare his throat to Cyrus. The action awakened his dick, his fangs descending.

"See, I have a throat begging for a fist around it." Cyrus slid his hand around the tender flesh, gripping it slightly. "Tighter, Daddy," Killian breathed.

Cyrus' brain short-circuited for a moment, the moniker making him hard as fuck. He pulled Killian closer, kissing the man's chin to bring it back down so they could lock gazes.

"What are you doing?" he growled against Killian's lips.

"I need to feel something..." he whispered, straddling Cyrus. "Something other than this." Killian motioned to his head and chest. "I need you."

The man's erection pressed into Cyrus' lower stomach. He groaned, his own grinding against Killian's plump ass.

"Are you sure?" he asked. "I can be whatever you need me to be right now, but I need to know you're sure."

Cyrus was yet again surprising himself with his need to protect and care. How he got himself wrapped up so quickly, he didn't know. And that was what concerned him the most.

"Look at you asking for consent," he chuckled as best he could with Cyrus' hand still around his throat.

"Consent is sexy, didn't you know that?" Cyrus smirked, stilling Killian's hips with his free hand. "Tell me what you want, Killian..."

"You. I want you. I am so fucking sure, it nearly hurts, Cy. Please." Killian begging was his final confirmation. "Kiss me."

Using his free hand, Cyrus dug it into Killian's thick, straight hair, pulling tightly, and kissed him deeply. Killian moaned, tugging at Cyrus' shirt. They broke their kiss long enough to pull off his top and Killian's. Their lips clashed again, tongues running wild. Cyrus' fingers trailed down Killian's tattooed chest as they kissed. He stopped at the man's nipple, rolling it and making Killian break away with a gasp.

"Oh shit!" he moaned, continuing to rock his hips against Cyrus.

Cyrus let his fingers continue their trek south until they got to the waistband of his sweats. He slipped his hand into the man's pants, cupping his erection. "Oh fuck," Killian whimpered as Cyrus pulled out his dick.

Cyrus held his hand up to the man's mouth. "Spit," he commanded.

Killian's emerald eyes never left Cyrus while he obeyed. Saliva pooled in Killian's mouth, and he slowly let it drip into his hand. The sight had Cyrus' cock aching. It was perfect lubrication as he stroked Killian and made the human shudder in pleasure. Cyrus bit and sucked Killian's lips, bringing out sounds he could listen to all night.

"You're so hard for me, Pet," he rumbled as he pumped Killian's dick with one hand and tightened his grip around his throat with the other. The man's hips bucked, fucking Cyrus' fist. Pre-cum leaked between his fingers as he increased his pace. "Do you want to come?" he asked, loosening his hold enough to allow Killian to take a deep breath.

"Yes," he whimpered against his lips, tongue darting out to lick them while keeping their gazes locked.

"'Yes' what?" Cyrus growled as he gripped Killian's length tighter, but not so much it hurt.

"Yes, Daddy," he moaned as Cyrus captured his mouth in a bruising kiss.

Their tongues thrust against each other in a war of wills. Lips sucked on lips, teeth clinked together. The kiss was rough and fierce and brought moans out of them both. Cyrus broke the kiss first, taking in Killian's flushed appearance. His lips were pouting and red, pupils dilated with desire. The creasing between his brows deepened as he panted and rocked faster.

"Mmm, fuck my hand just like that," Cyrus groaned. "Make yourself come on us both."

He tightened his grip around Killian's throat, and the man's eyes rolled back as he shattered. Cum shot out in jets as he cried out, coating both their stomachs. Letting go of his throat, Cyrus dug his hand into Killian's messy locks and pulled him in for another electric kiss.

"Fucking Orcus, Cy," Killian panted as they parted.

Cyrus smirked smugly as he ran his hand over his cum covered abs, collecting it on his fingertips.

"Open up, Pet," he commanded. Killian obliged without question, allowing Cyrus to push his fingers into the man's mouth. "See how good you taste?" he murmured.

Killian whimpered with a nod as he sucked on the digits. After he slid his fingers out, Cyrus licked up any lingering arousal from Killian's lips.

"How are you feeling?"

"Better," he said softly. Cyrus caught his wrist when he attempted to reach between them. "Wha—"

"Not tonight. This was for you." Cyrus caught the tears that glided down Killian's cheeks. "As much as I love your cum on me, it's gonna get sticky soon. Have an extra washcloth I can use?" Cyrus smirked victoriously when Killian laughed breathily.

"Yeah, of course," he said as he stood on shaky legs, pulling up his sweats.

Cyrus grinned as he got up and followed Killian to the bathroom.

"If you're having a hard time walking with just my hand..." he joked, pulling Killian toward him, the man's back to his chest. "I can only imagine how you'll walk after I finally fuck you."

"You don't have to wait, Daddy." Killian turned in his arms, rising to his tiptoes to plant a kiss on his lips.

"But I do. Anticipation is the best form of torture, and I'm a sadist."

"Tease." Killian stuck his tongue out, turning back around.

"You'll learn to enjoy it."

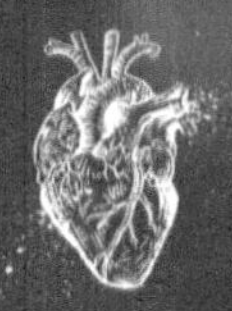

CHAPTER 11

UNHINGED IS AN UNDERSTATEMENT

"I HAVE TO BE HONEST. I don't know why people say she's difficult to be around," Bex said, pacing his living room excitedly.

Cyrus sighed, leaning back on his couch and letting his head hang off the top. The wolf had been going on for at least thirty minutes, sharing all the ways the good doctor was great. It not only exhausted him, it made him unreasonably jealous. He hated the feeling with his entire being.

"Are we even talking about the same person? How did you even get in with her so fast? You've been living with her for two weeks already?" he asked, closing his eyes to fight the bloodlust threatening to break through.

He hadn't fed, and he was perfectly aware just how fucking stupid that was, but he couldn't focus. Again. Lately, all of his focus had been thrown into the trash. This wasn't good, but he didn't know how to stop or refocus how he needed to. There was simply too much going on, and managing it all took a toll.

"Um, hello? Spy?" Bex pointed at themself. "Anyway, she's hot as fuck. She's confident and feminine but with a masculine side too. She clearly knows what she wants, and she's intelligent." They listed each statement as if talking about their favorite dessert.

"Bex…"

"And she trains. Did you know that? She has Guard training from Junior Academy. Her whole family is military. Explains her physique. That's what bonded us. She wanted a roomie she could train with."

"Bex…" he tried again with a long sigh.

They chuckled. "Said she was tired of weak people in her atmosphere."

"Fuck, what?" Cyrus picked up his head to furrow his brow at them. "She *said* that? Why am I not surprised?"

"Like I said, she's confident. And she takes no shit. Maybe people find her difficult because she's so self-assured."

"No, it's because she's cocky and arrogant," Cyrus snapped.

"The same can be said about you..." They put up their hand to keep him from responding. "But people still like you—"

"Like is a strong statement ... More like they fear me. Maybe they tolerate me because of my proximity to the King. Or—"

"And you know why?" Bex continued loudly, barreling through his commentary. "Because you're a fucking guy. They'd be less inclined to like you if you were a woman or femme."

"Oh, come on, we haven't held those views in centuries!" He shook his head. He was way too fucking tired for this right now.

"Doesn't mean the bias isn't still there. It just presents differently," Bex said with narrowed hazel eyes. "Now, she isn't perfect. There are some ... social cues she misses a lot. She's blunt and doesn't filter her thoughts."

Cyrus snorted. "Yes, I'm aware."

"She *does* have those creepy specimens. While she was at work, I took the liberty of getting small DNA samples of each as a precaution. None of them were linked to our victims. All of them were cadavers approved for scientific purposes." Bex shrugged. "But otherwise, I haven't found anything amiss. I think she's misunderstood. She's the youngest double board-certified—"

"Yes, yes, I know her credentials, Bex," he groaned.

"I'm just saying ... Maybe she doesn't need to be targeted."

"Touchy, touchy. Does the wolf feel protective?" And damn, did the thought make Cyrus feel some type of way.

"No," they said much too quickly.

"Have you fucked her yet?" he asked coolly.

Bex's gaze dropped to the floor, not in shame, but to hide their sly smile.

"Share with the class."

They looked up slowly, a glint in their eyes.

"Come watch." Bex arched an eyebrow.

"Excuse me?" He stared at them incredulously. Were they seriously suggesting…

"She is an exhibitionist … She likes to fuck in front of her glass doors. Come. Watch." Bex sank to the floor, nestling themself in between his spread knees.

The sight hardened his dick. Heat flushed through his body as their hazel eyes drank him in.

"Little wolf, I don't even like the woman. Why would I want to watch her have sex?" He bit his lip as they waited for him. "You have permission to touch me."

Bex's hands glided up his thighs, moving to the center to rub his thick erection through his slacks.

"I think your opinion of her would change once you saw how wet she gets when she's eaten out from behind. Or how she rides a strap." They undid his belt, removing it and unbuttoning his fly. "She almost has you beat as a domme."

Cyrus dug his hand in their hair, yanking their head back with a growl.

"What the fuck did you just say?" That unreasonable and unwanted jealousy rushed through him once more.

"Just come watch, and you'll see what I mean," Bex breathed, chest rising and falling as they panted.

He gritted his teeth, trying to ignore the fact that the thought of watching them had his balls aching.

"Please, my Lord."

Fingers still locked in their hair, he gripped their chin with his free hand to pop their mouth open.

"I love it when you beg," he purred, spitting.

Bex moaned, sticking out their eager tongue for more.

"So fucking greedy." He gave them what they wanted. Plunging two fingers in their mouth, he thrust them deep enough to make their eyes water. He removed them to smear the saliva across their face. "So fucking filthy."

Cyrus leaned in for an ardent kiss. He bit and sucked at their lips, making Bex moan, their hand finding its way into his pants to pull him out. He growled as he continued to tongue fuck them while they stroked his cock.

"Will you come?" they breathed against his lips, tongue flicking along them.

"If you keep doing that, I will," he joked. Holding their hair, he guided them down to wrap their mouth around the head of his erection. The cool metal of their lip ring sent a jolt of pleasure through his body. "Choke on my dick, little wolf, and maybe I'll consider it."

Moaning, they relaxed their tongue, allowing him to thrust up and deep. Their hot and wet throat sucked him in. "Look at me while I fuck your mouth," he commanded, making them snap their gaze up to him, eyes glowing neon green. "Such a dirty slut, aren't you? Eager for my dick." He held their head as he surged his hips up, groaning as their saliva poured over his length. "Eager for my cum." He thrust again, getting closer to his orgasm.

The sounds they made were sloppy, wet pops and gagging. "Fuck, Bex!" He gripped their hair and pulled them away so that he could fist himself and come on their face. They left their mouth open to catch some and licked their lips with a sigh of contentment.

"Thank you for your cum, my Lord."

"Fuck," he moaned as they swiped the cum from their face to suck off their fingers. He kissed them again, this time licking his pleasure from their lips. He rubbed their scalp, making them hum softly. "This evening, after Ithea sets. I will be there."

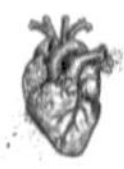

CYRUS WONDERED IF HE was making a mistake. It wasn't the voyeurism or the fact that he was basically stalking the doctor at this point. It was the idea of watching her fuck turning him on that bothered him.

He didn't *want* to find her fascinating. He didn't *want* to imagine her mouth around his dick or the feeling of her wet pussy. With no new bodies to be found, he hadn't seen her since their last altercation. Oddly, as much as he couldn't stand the woman, he wanted to see her, if only to argue. He enjoyed it more than he should.

Now, here he was, propped in the shadows of the large tree, staking out Aida's apartment again. He watched as the pair walked in, lights flickering on. Doctor Broderick roughly grabbed Bex by their lavender collar to pull them into a kiss. The sight brought on a wave of that unwanted jealousy, and he had to fight a growl from crawling up his throat.*

This was a bad idea, but he couldn't look away if he wanted to.

Tuning into his hearing, he listened as if he were in the living room with them.

"I have to tell you something," the doctor whispered as she led Bex to the living room. "Sit."

She pointed to the floor, the wolf complying instantly. Cyrus arched a brow, watching the exchange.

"What is it?" they asked as they sat back on their heels and placed their hands in their lap. Their tight, electric blue shorts rose to expose the bottom of their ass.

"I have a stalker." Doctor Broderick slowly stripped out of her lilac ripped jeans and black graphic tee, exposing her white lace bra and thong.

"Holy fucking shit…" Cyrus murmured to himself, taking in every muscular curve of the doctor's body. Tight abs flexed as she removed her clothing, and the muscles in her thighs were evident as she walked.

Bex's hazel eyes flared neon green briefly. Lust filled their gaze along with a rapid pulse that Cyrus could see in their throat. "What … uh, what makes you say that?" they stammered as Broderick removed her lingerie.

She nodded toward the large glass doors. He smirked,

* "Slumber Party (feat. Princess Nokia)" by Ashnikko, Princess Nokia

wondering if she knew he was in the shadows.

"I know these things. I'm always aware of my surroundings. I didn't go to the Academy because I couldn't. I didn't go because I didn't want to." She shrugged, her small breasts shifting with the movement—her small, round, and very much pierced breasts.

"My, my. What a surprise, good doctor," he said gruffly, palming his dick to keep it from getting hard. Naturally, he failed.

"How about we put on a show?" she asked as she raised her hands to her breasts, pulling at her nipple rings.

Fuck, what did Cyrus get himself into? He wasn't sure what he was expecting when Bex asked him to come tonight, but it sure as fuck wasn't how alluring the doctor was. How she seemed to suck in his attention despite his will to look away.

"A show?" Bex asked, eyes flicking to him and back.

"What? I thought sluts enjoyed exhibitionism. Are you not my little slut?" the Storm Wielder asked, hardness in her tone.

The wolf's eyes widened as they dropped their gaze.

"I do, Mistress."

Mistress. Fuck that. The growl he'd been fighting against escaped his lips. He was both angry and aroused, the mixed emotions a heady cocktail.

"I was just wondering if it was a good idea to provoke them."

"I'm sure they'll enjoy it. If not, they can tell me themself. Whoever they are." Aida sat on the couch, spreading her legs to show her dripping pussy to the wolf. "Look at me and crawl."

Cyrus clenched his jaw so tight that his ears popped as he watched Bex, *his* Bex, crawl to another person.

Wait. *His?* He internally shook his head. No, that was unacceptable. Claiming meant sentimentality. He wasn't in the position for sentimentality.

"Yes, Mistress," Bex breathed as their gaze connected with Aida's core. Licking their lips, they crawled to her, stopping at her feet.

Doctor Broderick tugged the wolf's collar to bring them into a hot kiss. She sucked in their lower lip, teeth catching on the ring. Bex's whine traveled straight to his dick. That ridiculous protectiveness clawed at his insides, and he was tempted to rush in and tear into Aida's throat for touching what was his.

Fuck, again?

"Are you hungry, whore?" she asked along Bex's mouth.

"Yes," they whimpered.

She sat back, gripping their hair tightly. Bex moaned as Aida's fists pulled at the strands.

"Then feast," she growled. Bex dove in, tongue lashing out to lick a line from her center to clit. "Oh fuck!" the doctor cried out, rubbing herself along Bex's face. "Make a mess. Be the dirty slut I know you are."

Cyrus was not at all sure what to make of what he was watching. He was pissed that Bex was getting filthy for someone else, even though he had no right to be, but was also aroused because he wanted to be in there with them. Eating Bex while their face was buried in Doctor Broderick's pussy.

There was a muffled groan as the wolf pushed themself against her, making circles with their head to spread her juices all over their face.

Aida looked out her large door right at him, and for a moment, he thought she could see him. The way her unfocused gaze occasionally looked away told him she hadn't.

"Fuck, keep doing that," the Storm Wielder moaned when Bex sucked on her clit.

Keeping her attention on him, she licked a circle around her lips. She mouthed, 'Fuck you,' grinning maniacally. Cyrus started as his vision darkened to red briefly, taking a few involuntary steps forward. He almost gave up his position with the urge to teach her a lesson. He wondered what she'd do with that fuckable mouth if he got ahold of it.

No. Stop that.

"Up, get on your back," the doctor commanded. She took in their glistening face as Bex did what they were told. "You're coated with my juices." She wasted no time straddling Bex's shoulders and rode the fuck out of their face.

Doctor Broderick turned her gaze back to him, and it unnerved him that she was so perceptive. She grinned again, lips parting as she moaned and played with her pierced nipples. Fuck, she had amazing tits.

No! What did we say? Stop it.

"Oh fuck, you're going to make me come!" she yelled, silver eyes rolling briefly as Bex gripped her ass.

Watching his little wolf get ridden had him aching to stroke his dick.

Again, with this nonsense? *His?* How many times would he tell himself to stop those invasive thoughts?

Cyrus aimed to fuck up Aida's high, so he threw a rock. It wasn't hard enough to shatter the glass, but enough to make her jolt her eyes open and look at the backyard. A smirk pulled up on her kissed-swollen lips.

'*You should join us,*' she mouthed, letting out a breathy moan. She rode Bex's face faster. He shouldn't have thrown the damn rock. What was wrong with him? Now she knew for sure he was out there.

Get your shit together.

"I'm coming. Drink my juices like a good little slut," the doctor hissed, falling apart as her orgasm crashed through her.

"My turn," she said as she got up. "You deserve a reward."

Cyrus finally pulled his gaze from the apartment, not needing to watch their marathon. He had to fight the urge to barge in there and take Bex with him. Another part fought against the idea of throat fucking them while the doctor rode their strap.

Why did he let Bex convince him to watch?

Did it show him a new side of the doctor? Yes.

Did it show him how damn sexy she was? Yep.

Did it make him hate her any less? Absolutely. Fucking. Not.

CHAPTER 12

WHAT IS HAPPENING HERE?

THE WORLD WAS ENDING.

Again.

This was what? The third time in the last two hundred years? Granted, the first two times were not nearly as severe. But really, why did life have to be so fucking complicated?

An Angel? An actual fucking Angel. The damn thing crashed into Trezora, nearly demolishing the capital of Asherai. Just another thing on his plate. It was only a matter of time until that bullshit made it onto Potroya's doorstep.

Oh, and the cherry on top was a serial killer he had yet to find. Yeah. That was fun.

Cyrus was growing tired of it all. But being the Cortesano meant he had to live with the responsibilities his Sire placed on him, which he would honor regardless. He owed Jacinto his life. The King gave him the power to get revenge on the men who killed his family. Without him, Cyrus would be on a bloodlust rampage.

So tired as he was of his responsibilities at times, he'd never shirk them or take his King—and best friend—for granted. Jacinto meant too much to him to be so foolish.

Cyrus stared at the holoscreen, rubbing his temples. A knock on his office door pulled him out of his spiral, and he leaned back with a grunt.

"Yeah, come in," he said, exhausted.

Bex poked their head in, hazel eyes glinting neon briefly.

"Have a moment?" they asked with an arched eyebrow.

For you? Always... He shook the thought from his mind, though he had been having difficulty doing that lately.

"Sure." He motioned to the comfortable couch he liked

having in his space. He stood, stretching briefly and undoing his cuffs to push his sleeves up. The top buttons of his shirt were undone, and his vest was discarded somewhere.

"Rough evening?" Bex asked as they sat with Cyrus, pulling their fishnet-covered knees to their chest.

He couldn't help but trace their collar. It was black with crimson splattered across it.

"What gave it away?" he murmured, hooking his finger in the o-ring and tugging them toward him.

Would he ever get enough of Bex? The answer was likely no. How the fuck was he meant to deal with these feelings when emotional attachments were dangerous for a man like him?

"No vest, shirt unbuttoned, cuffs up ... and your eyes," they whispered, lips close to his own. "They burn golden when you're tired or upset. With the tiniest of red at the pupil."

Cyrus considered their words. Did they pay that much attention out of interest or because it was their job to be hyper-aware? Why did it matter?

"Observant," he whispered back, eyes dropping to their plump, pierced lips.

"It's my job."

Cyrus stiffened, stopping just shy of kissing Bex. It hurt. It hurt hearing those words, and he didn't know why. It shouldn't bother him. So why did it? Did he really wish it had been more than just a job? What did he do with that?

He sat back, ignoring their pout, and grabbed the decanter filled with tequila. He poured himself a glass, offering some to Bex, who shook their head.

"You get high off potions, but you don't drink," he said with a bite in his tone.

He winced internally at himself, noticing how the wolf's eyes shuddered. Their jaw clenched, and they shifted away from him, dropping their heavy booted feet to the ground.

"Compulsion," Bex said, making Cyrus go still.

"Compulsion?"

"Yes. All the victims are either familiars or have a Sire bond."

Bex sighed.

"The serial killer has been abducting people under compulsion," he mused out loud to himself. "For what? Experimentation? What kind…"

"Might want to ask the doc about that," Bex snarked, scratching the back of their neck. As they stood, Cyrus rose with them, snatching their wrist.

"How long?" he snapped.

"What gave it away?" they echoed, trying and failing to tug their arm free.

"A glossing of sweat, erratic heartbeat … and *your* eyes. The hazel leans toward green, your wolf anxious." His grip tightened, not caring for their hiss of pain or what it did to his dick.

"Well, now look who's observant," they snarled, eyes flaring neon, canines descending.

"I have to. It's my *job*." Cyrus' jaw clenched, watching as the realization dawned upon them.

They shook their head, their lips pulling back.

"Let me go," they growled, the echo of their wolf underneath.

"Answer the fucking question." He needed to know. He yearned for it in a way that made him hesitate.

"Two nights!" Bex barked. "I considered … Fuck! It doesn't matter. Let me go!" They tugged once more, and this time Cyrus let them, only to snatch their collar.

"You considered what, Bex?" he asked. Their lips parted as they panted, looking down. "No, look at me and tell me."

Those neon eyes snapped up.

"I don't know … I thought maybe I'd quit…" The fight in them drained as they dug into their pocket and pulled out a bag filled with silver potion. "I'm not strong enough."

When Cyrus reached for it, they clenched their fist tight around it.

"I wish I could say you are … But only *you* can convince yourself."

He didn't attempt to take the bag again. If they wanted

it—needed it—then he wouldn't stop them. It wasn't up to him how they handled life, no matter how it made him feel.

"Yeah, well, that hasn't gone anywhere," they said, pushing the drugs back into their pocket. They sniffed, eyes returning to hazel. "Can you let me go?" they asked calmly.

Cyrus did so reluctantly, allowing his hand to linger and his thumb to glide along their jaw. Bex leaned into the touch.

"You're not a job." Their voice was soft as they looked at him intensely.

"I know…" he said, unsure if he believed himself. Fuck, he *wanted* to believe them. Against his better judgment, he pushed down the doubts. He would deal with them later.

Bex's eyes widened, their head shaking as they stepped away from him. They lightly scratched the back of their neck as they began pacing.

"Undercover…" Bex started. When they noticed his raised brow, they added, "I was undercover when I started potions."

"You don't have to tell me if you don't want to," he said softly, stuffing his hands into his pockets to avoid reaching out to stop them in their tracks.

"Nah, it's okay. I haven't spoken about it in a while. Stopped going to NA months ago." They shrugged. "Anyway, about ten years ago, I was drafted into the Guard to be trained as a spy. They put me through rigorous testing, and when they felt I was ready, they gave me assignments. It was my fifth one … a typical drug ring that needed infiltration and shit. Boring, I know."

"Not true. But continue," he said with a nod.

"To keep up appearances, I needed to become an addict. It wasn't my intention to use. I was given a placebo, but then I was cornered and stuck in an office with these major players. They wanted proof of product, and if I tried to cheat, I would've died right there on the spot. So, I did it. Took the silver, snorted it down, and floated like a kite." They sniffed, scratching the back of their neck again.

"I buzzed, Cyrus. It felt electric, like everything around me was tangible, even the air. It eased my anxiety, it increased my focus … It made me feel like I could do anything. But then they placed the green in front of me to take next." They paused their pacing, rocking back and forth, heel to toe. "High off the silver, I didn't question it. I just snatched and straight injected it." Bex ran a shaky hand through their messy navy hair, pursing their lips as they processed.

"Do you know anything about the green? Silver is the most common; red is the most fucked up. They tried to get me to do the red, and I had enough sense to say no. I didn't want that synthetic Wielding anywhere near me."

"The green … Lust, arousal…" he answered, rubbing his jaw slowly.

Fuck. A lot more made sense.

"Yes. Straight ecstasy. If silver is like adrenaline, then green is like dopamine. Once it hit, I wanted to fuck all of them." Bex smirked. "It wasn't as if I wasn't already hypersexual. I love sex, as you may know." He snorted but let them continue. "But this was different because they *weren't* the kind of people I'd have sex with, far from it. Green doesn't care, though. It gets the engine going, and you plow through until you're wiped."

"Is that why…"

"Yeah," Bex sighed. "I wasn't much of a penetration fan to begin with. After that night, I never wanted to again."

Cyrus made a mental note to find these fuckers and place them in an Interrogation room. Would Bex like to watch?

They turned their hazel eyes to him, a glint in them, pulling him out of his thoughts when they said, "The silver is what caught me, though. I never did the green again. But after the comedown, I crashed so hard that the silver was the only thing that helped me bounce back. I started needing it more and more. So much so that going without it was painful. Agonizing. I tried rehab. Almost overdosed about five years ago, so I figured I should give it a try. That's where I met Killian. He was … well, that's his story. But I remember thinking about how young he was. Twenty-three…"

"Why—"

"Don't ask me why I still do it. I don't know. I … need it," they said, gazing at the floor.

"I am not one to judge, Bex. I'm literally addicted to blood and turn feral if I go too long without it," he said candidly.

"What do you mean?" they asked, snapping their gaze up, confusion coloring their expression.

"Ever heard of a berserker?" It was his turn to pace, rubbing his jaw as he thought about his past. "The rare vampire that cannot abstain from blood for longer than a week, maybe less. And usually has no control over how much they consume."

"You? No way ... I have never met one, but I've heard plenty. You're too calm and collected. Too old, no offense," they said with a shake of their head.

"I'll pretend you didn't say that," he said with a smirk, pleased when they returned it. His eyes widened when he was struck with realization. "Compulsion."

"What?"

"Jacinto ... My Sire. He uses compulsion to keep me regulated. Sometimes, he needs more push, especially if I go too long between feeds. It's the only reason I'm still alive." He stopped in his pacing abruptly, thoughts shifting course. "The fact that the killer is specifically choosing compelled victims ... Makes me wonder if they're trying to synthesize the ability or morph it. They'd have to understand the brain..."

"Where'd you go? Do you know who did it?" Bex asked, stepping closer to him with one hand in their back pocket and the other scratching the back of their neck again.

"I need confirmation first..." He appreciated it when they didn't push.

Bex's anxiousness was taking a toll on them, he could tell. He had no say or control over what they did in their life. Did he wish they would slow down? Take a moment? Of course. But it wasn't his place to say or make mention.

"You do your thing. I am going to head out," they said with a nod.

He stepped in front of them to stop them from leaving.

"This is new..." he remarked as he glided his finger across

the soft black and red leather. Hooking it into the o-ring, he tugged them close.

"It's yours," Bex whispered.

His eyes widened, taking in their flushed cheeks.

"When I wear this one, I'm yours to own. To use. To fuck. To destroy. However you see fit. No one else but you."

That damn tightening pulled painfully at his chest. His heart rose to his throat, and the sensation was something he couldn't put into words. Cyrus could admit that it scared the fucking shit out of him.

"Open your mouth," he growled, yanking them even closer.

Bex complied instantly, greedy tongue sticking out and beckoning. He let his saliva drip from his tongue to theirs, the rumble in his chest deepening when they let it slide down their chin. Without warning, he latched onto their lip ring. His teeth pulled at the jewelry, making the wolf yip. He sucked on the entire lower lip. A groan escaped him as it turned into a kiss, their tongue clashing with his. Too soon, he pulled away, needing to get a handle on himself.

"Come with me..." Bex said suddenly.

"Go with you? Where?" Cyrus quirked a brow, waiting as they played with their lip ring in thought.

"No, meet me." Their cheeks went red as they fumbled their words. They took his hand and tapped their comm with his. "Meet me at my place. Later tonight. Before you go hunting for the serial killer."

He looked down at his wrist, brows lifted.

"No one knows where you live," Cyrus said softly, more to himself than anything.

Surprise would be an understatement of what he felt. If Bex trusted him enough to tell him where they lived... maybe he could trust that they were authentic and not pretending to be what they thought he wanted.

Bex smirked, tapping his chest a few times. His eyes met theirs, and he couldn't help but return their smile.

"So you better not tell anyone, Cy." Bex wriggled their

eyebrows, stepping away from him slowly on their way out. Hooking a finger in their o-ring, they winked. "I'll see you in a few, boss."

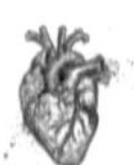

CYRUS' HOVERCAR WHIRRED AS he followed the GPS to the coordinates Bex gave him. They lived on the outskirts of Malagado, further than he assumed they would. Considering how much time they spent in the city, he wondered how often they went home.

He pulled up in front of a small ebony cabin surrounded by trees covered in teal leaves. A garden with a bench in front of the bay window was a surprise. Deep purple, black, and magenta flora took over the space, and the nearly full moon above gave them much-needed nutrition. The home was quaint, soft even. It was the last place he expected someone like Bex to live.

"You're staring," came the wolf's alto from the front door. He hadn't noticed them at first, and looking at them now, he couldn't understand why. They were fucking stunning, wearing low cut, black sweats, and a dark magenta sports bra. But what made them even sexier was the splatter of paint on their arms and face. Although there was a glaze in their eyes, their energy shined bright.

"I wasn't expecting you to be into goth cottage-core," Cyrus smirked, closing the distance between them. He cupped their face, thumb gliding across their lower lip.

"Eh, wait till you see the inside," they breathed, sucking the digit into their mouth.

"Naughty wolf. Already so needy, and you haven't even told me why you brought me here," he purred, removing his thumb to replace with his lips.

Bex's tongue clashed with his as he dug his hands into their hair to consume them in a kiss. They whimpered when he broke it just as quickly as it started.

"Show me inside then, little wolf."

"Welcome to my humble abode," Bex snorted, leading him into their mysterious home. "Shoes off," they prompted, nodding to his feet.

After slipping out of his boots, he stood at the entrance and took in the small but comfortable living room. Three small black plushie wolves were strewn about their couch, all having a collar of various colors. *Cute.*

An easel with a fresh canvas sat in the corner. A table littered with acrylic paint and other supplies stood next to it. That explained the paint on their body. A finished piece rested on the floor, upright and leaning against a paint-splattered wall.

"You're an artist," he said in awe. As he walked over to the painting, he let his hand glide over their black leather couch, the emerald carpet soft even through his socks. Cyrus' eyes widened when he got a closer look. "You're the Florist?"

His hand hovered over the completed piece. The artwork was a messy, graphic arrangement of red, black, and white plants and wildlife. Blood dripped from the leaves, making the large piece even more stunning.

"I've seen these all over Malagado. Jacinto has one in his office, too."

"Yeah. Being a spy pays very well, but these … are fulfilling." Bex stood next to him, crossing their arms. "Painting has been my passion since before I could even write. I could've been a serious artist if life had taken me in that direction." They shrugged.

"As a spy, you must pretend to be someone you're not. It's easy to forget yourself and confuse your fake identities with your own." Bex bumped their shoulder against his arm. "My real name isn't even Bex. Did you know that?"

He turned to face them, surprised.

"No, I didn't." How could he have missed this? With all of his resources and power, he never knew Bex wasn't … well, Bex. "How—"

"By being very good at covering my tracks," they finished. Bex smirked, nudging him to look back at the painting. "My name was Lizbeth. I grew up in Milagros and found myself in a very shitty fucking situation. Such a situation led me to be recruited by the Guard." They let out a long sigh. "Apparently, being very good at hiding who you are, even from the government, makes you a high-demand asset."

"You're more than an asset, Bex..." He paused.

"I am not Lizbeth anymore. Don't call me anything other than Bex."

"You're awfully intuitive," he snorted.

"The line of questioning was predictable." Bex's voice held a playful tone. "But this..." They nodded their chin toward the artwork. One of their bare feet bounced, and he looked at them with a furrowed brow.

"Are you all right?" he asked, sensing their nervousness.

"Y-yes," they replied, glancing at him briefly. Their paint-splattered hand gently touched the large piece. "I wanted to show you this..."

"It's beautiful," he said, though he was looking at them.

"Art has a hold on my heart," Bex whispered. "When the silver works its way through, I don't always show up at The Den. I channel through this work. I take a break from the rest of the world. Away from the requirements of work and life." Slowly, they turned their glassy gaze up to him. "I've never invited anyone here because it's my safe space. It's *my* space."

"So why am I here?" he asked, unsure why it was important to know.

"Because I trust you." Bex looked away again, their attention returning to the art.

"What's the significance of this piece?"

The artwork felt familiar, and he couldn't figure out why. It compelled a part of him, and he suddenly wanted to know everything about Bex. What was their childhood like? What else did they do in their free time? What were some of their favorite foods? Their nearly inaudible reply cut off his inquisition.

"You," they whispered so softly he thought he misheard them.

Sliding to the floor, Bex sat crossed-legged in front of the large canvas. Realizing he still had his jacket on, he shrugged it off, placing it on the couch before joining them on the floor. His heart was in his throat, pounding roughly, as he drew close and put a leg on either side of them. Bex leaned back, allowing him to wrap his arms around them. The intimacy of the moment had his stomach in knots.

"What do you mean?" he asked, resting his chin on their shoulder. Bex tilted their head to the side, drawing his attention to the red and black collar.

"When I painted this, I thought of you and only you."

The admission tilted his world on its axis. The fact they created *art* with him in mind had him speechless. Fuck. Again. If it wasn't Killian, it was Bex rendering him without words.

Bex's chuckle vibrated through him.

"Relax, it's not like I'm asking for a hand-fasting ceremony or something."

A soft gasp left them when he cupped their face and turned their attention to him. He didn't have words, so he kissed Bex instead. It was slow and lazy, their tongues gliding across each other like a dance. He gently bit along their lower lip, sucking on it until it was plump and swollen. His thumb stroked along their jawline, his mouth eating their moans. The wolf turned in his arms, straddling his lap. Their arms wrapped around his shoulders as they leaned in to kiss him once more.

"I am more of a sports guy," Cyrus said, interrupting the moment.

"What?" Bex chuckled in surprise.

"I enjoy sports." He bit his lower lip. Fuck he sucked at small talk. "I played Wielderball. All the way through upper school. Thought I'd go pro eventually. I was one Orcus of a catcher and even better at bat. Being at home plate was *my* happy place. The game hasn't changed much in the last two hundred years. At the time, being a human ballplayer from Mutuba and making it pro would've been historic. But life had other plans for me, too." It was his turn to shrug. "Turns out I was better as a soldier. I haven't been to bat since." He dropped his forehead to their shoulder, and they let out another startled snort. "I know it's not as eloquent as art…"

"No, don't say that, Cy." Bex leaned back, forcing him to lift his head and look at them. "Sports are just as important as art. If it made you happy, it made you happy. If it made you passionate about life, that matters most."

What was going on here? When had he ever spoken about his past? About anything outside of his job? Something was brewing that he wasn't even sure he wanted. Cyrus knew he had to take control of the situation before it got out of hand and ended up with him hitting rock bottom. So, he did what he always did best.*

Cyrus gripped Bex's small ass, grinding them on his growing erection. He drank down their whimpers as his mouth crashed with theirs. He groaned when they rocked against him. His kiss turned brutal, hungry … needy. Their tongues lashed at each other, teeth clinking together. He let Bex push him onto his back, their hand reaching between them to rub his cock.

"Hmm, shit," he groaned, breaking the kiss.

Bex's lips found his neck, their tiny fangs gliding along the flesh and making his body shudder. As if consumed by need, they tugged at his henley, nearly ripping the material. He sat up briefly to take it off, Bex doing the same and chucking their bra across the room.

"I need you, my Lord," Bex panted, sliding down his body. Their hazel eyes glowed as they undid his belt and jeans. "Please."

"Such a needy little slut. Hungry for my dick," he growled, lifting his hips to permit them to remove the rest of his clothes. As soon as his erection sprung free, they sucked him in to the back of their throat. "Fuck!" he groaned, sinking his hands in their thick hair.

With every bob they made, he bucked up into their mouth, fucking it deeply.

"That's it. Cry for me." Bex's teary eyes looked up at him, mascara and eyeliner running down their face. "Such a beautiful

---

* "Who Do You Want" by Ex Habit

fucking mess." He pulled them off his dick, smirking at their pout. "Get rid of the pants."

"Yes, my Lord," Bex responded, shucking them quickly.

He gripped their ass, stopping them from moving back down, shifting them to straddle him once more.

"Rub that filthy pussy on my dick like a good little slut."

Without penetrating them, he glided the head of his erection along their swollen clit. Their wetness coated him, making it easier for him to slide back and forth.

"Mmm, fuck," they moaned, rolling their hips.

The sensation had his eyes nearly seeing the back of his head as their pussy ground against the length of his cock. His grip on their ass tightened, allowing him to push Bex onto him harder.

"Cy, please," they whimpered.

"You're making a fucking mess all over my dick, Bex," he groaned. The wolf strategically moved their swollen clit to the head of his erection, rubbing along the sensitive tip. The sounds of their wet pussy made him lift his hips faster. "Does the little wolf want to come?"

He staved off the approach of his orgasm. "Yes, yes, please! My Lord, let me come."

"Such a needy little beggar," he growled. He jerked them by the collar to bring them into a fiery kiss. He tugged their lip ring sharply, sucking on the already swollen flesh. Bex's rocking turned erratic, their breathing coming out in harsh pants. "Come for me, little wolf," he breathed as their kiss broke.

Bex cried out, body shuddering as they came. Their cum gushed over his dick, covering him in its sweet essence.

Bex's sweat-slick body slumped onto his as he allowed them a moment to breathe. Cyrus was perfectly aware this was their first time having sex together completely naked. He decided he wouldn't look further into what it meant. He kept failing at keeping these thoughts and concerns out of his fucking mind.

Bex rose onto their hands, tongue gliding along his lips. They wriggled their ass, spreading their wetness even more.

"On your back. I know what the cum slut wants," he

commanded.

As they flipped over, he couldn't stop himself from admiring Bex. Their flushed skin glowed in the moonlight that filtered through the bay window. Hazel eyes pierced through his, occasionally flaring neon green as they watched him hungrily. He pushed their knees up and out.

"Hold on and keep yourself spread for me. I want to see this filthy pussy covered in my cum."

"Yes, my Lord." Bex complied, biting their lower lip as they watched him.

He cupped their pussy, covering his hand in their gushing arousal. He used it as lubricant, stroking himself and occasionally bouncing the head of his cock on their clit.

"Oh fuck!"

"Oh, I remember. The filthy slut likes being slapped."

He gave them a firm slap on their inner thigh, doing the same to the other in rapid succession. Their pussy gushed more, drenching the rug underneath. He massaged the reddened skin while continuing to rub himself against them.

"Please. I need your cum!" Bex moaned, spreading their knees even further apart.

With his free hand, he gripped their thigh. He slapped their clit with his cock once more, stroking himself faster as he got closer to the edge.

"Do you want your pussy covered like a cum slut? Greedy, greedy," he growled. He grew thicker in his hand, his strokes erratic. "Answer me!"

"Yes! I'm your greedy cum slut. I need your cum on my pussy. Please!"

"Fuck, that's what I like to hear. You begging me like a needy little whore."

A loud groan escaped him as he came, covering their pussy and lower stomach in his seed. Satisfaction flooded him at the sight of it dripping down their ass. He noticed their fingers wriggling and smirked, taking hold of their knees to keep them spread. They snaked their hand between their legs, scooping up his spent arousal.

"Thank you for your cum, my Lord," they said as they licked it off their fingers.

He dropped their legs and leaned in to kiss them silly. Their legs wrapped around his waist as they moaned into his mouth.

"If I didn't have a murderer to find … I'd stay and give you the most delicious skull fucking you've ever had."

"Promise me you will?" Bex smirked, lips swollen, wet mascara drying on their face.

Such a beautiful fucking mess.

"Always," he said, giving them more kisses.

"Then, hurry up. Chop, chop. I'd love to have you make good on your promise sooner rather than later."

They chuckled when he buried his face in their throat, the collar not stopping him from getting close and inhaling their spiced apple scent. His dick twitched, making Bex's back arch. He didn't stop himself when he rolled his hips, especially when they whimpered.

Cyrus knew he had a job to do. He had the Deities damned Governors breathing down his neck, demanding answers. Never had he allowed personal shit to get in the way of his responsibilities, and yet...

"You know what?" he started, rising to his hands. He ground against them with a smirk. "Maybe I *do* have the time..."

CHAPTER 13

OH ... WELL FUCK.

CYRUS KNEW WHAT HE was doing when he stood outside Doctor Broderick's apartment. Leaning against the large tree, the teal leaves swaying in the breeze, he knew stalking was a habit he didn't have the time for, but he couldn't help it. The good doctor had secrets, and what better way to hunt prey than in the shadows?

Cyrus waited for Broderick to exit her home for her nightly run. Wearing a black hoodie and jeans, he blended into the night. His leisurely pace easily kept up with her quick steps. A bright magenta running jacket clung to her muscular body, and leggings tightly hugged each dip and curve.

For a woman as arrogant as she was, she sure loved bright colors. Running seemed to be the only time she didn't have a scowl.

He followed her to a park, where she jumped onto monkey bars to hang and start her pull-ups. He would be a fool if he didn't admire how she moved. She jumped down, panting as she stilled. Turning in his direction, Cyrus could've sworn she looked straight at him, which would've been impossible, considering he was in full cover of darkness.

"Aida, get your shit together," she muttered to herself as she resumed her jog, clearly more focused on her destination than her surroundings. It surprised him, but he didn't question her motivation. "That fucking vampire," she grumbled.

He smirked, knowing she was talking about him and his annoying tendency to show up randomly. He almost wanted to jump in front of her to prove a point.

Cyrus followed for what felt like an hour, impressed with

her stamina. He stayed behind as she stopped in front of what looked like an abandoned building. Tilting his head to the side, he watched as she used a keycard to gain access. Before the door closed, he shifted, moving quicker than sight to place his foot between it and the frame. He waited until it was quiet and slipped inside. Following her scent, he found Doctor Broderick two floors down in what looked like an … operating room.

Cyrus took in the sight before him. With her back to him, she removed her running jacket and placed it on a nearby chair. The doctor sighed, stretching her body, barely a drop of sweat on her.

"You're an interesting one," she said softly, almost a purr, as she looked over the man on the operating table.

Aida stepped to the side to grab gloves, and Cyrus' eyes widened. The man was strapped down, an IV in his hands and feet. His eyes were wide, shifting around the room in fear. But that wasn't the most interesting part. What impressed Cyrus was the brain pulsing in full view under a protective curtain. On a rolling cart was the top half of the man's skull.

"Your compulsion is strong. Stronger than the others. Let's see if I can break it. Maybe you'll be the first one to live," she said with a shrug as if the man wasn't leaking fear through his pores.

So, the good doctor is the Carnicero Cerebral.

Cyrus knew Doctor Broderick had secrets. He knew she was unhinged. When the common denominator for the victims was compulsion, he knew instantly that a doctor had to be behind their deaths. A very specific type of doctor: a neurosurgeon, to be exact.

The news surprised him only in that he missed it. He should've known and wondered if Bex knew about the good doctor's hobby. Did the little wolf know this entire time? Cyrus fought the growl that tried to crawl up his throat. If the spy knew and hadn't told him … He wasn't sure what he'd do.

Cyrus had two options. One would be to barge in there and take her in. The Governors would be pleased with him finally bringing the killer to their table. But … Fuck them. Right now, the other option was far more interesting.

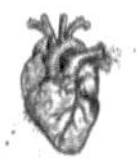

IDEAS SWARMED AROUND CYRUS' mind as he walked toward the Exhibition Hall of The Den. It'd been a week since he discovered who the Carnicero was, but he had yet to act. He wasn't sure when he would confront her, only that when he did, it was going to be fun.

It was interesting to watch Doctor Broderick act as if she wasn't the one putting those victims in the morgue. He wouldn't have thought it was her if he hadn't seen it himself. He hadn't confronted Bex. Not yet. He knew they weren't at risk, considering Broderick only went after compelled individuals. But he also wondered if they'd tell him first. That was if they knew.

"Doing the usual?" came a familiar voice, drawing his attention.

His gaze shifted to Killian leaning against the upstairs bar. The sounds of fucking fell into the background as he took in the man. His emerald eyes seemed almost black in the dim light, his black hair sticking up as usual.

"Actually, no. I'm here to talk with you," Cyrus said, his gaze dropping briefly to Killian's full lips. The man licked them, tongue ring flicking out.

"Okay, follow me," he said, motioning toward an office door.

Cyrus did, ignoring the hungry looks of the humans and the paranormals around him. He blinked rapidly, knowing the red haze wasn't due to the strobe lights. They entered the office, and the overwhelming sounds died once the door closed.

"Hey, boss." Bex's smooth voice made Cyrus' gaze snap to the couch, finding the wolf lazing about, long legs propped on the ottoman. They sat on the very couch he allowed himself to be vulnerable on and kissed them.

"Bex," he said as he looked at Killian, who wore a bemused expression. "What is this?"

"Nothing," he said with a shrug as he leaned against his

oak desk. "Maybe I should ask what you've been up to in here?"

A sculpted eyebrow arched. Cyrus' eyes shot throughout the room, landing on a corner of the ceiling. The almost completely invisible camera was in a prime spot to record the entire office.

"Oh," was all Cyrus could say. He'd never felt so ... shy? No, not that. Embarrassed? No, not that either.

"Oh, look. He's speechless!" Bex cackled.

That ... That was what he was.

"Did you know the camera was there, little wolf?" Cyrus growled as he stalked over to them. "Up," he said with a snap of his fingers.

They stood without question, their yellow mesh-covered chest rising and falling.

"Oh, well damn," Killian whistled as he watched.

"Shut up, I'll deal with you next," Cyrus said while focusing on Bex. He sank his hand into their hair, gripping it tightly. Their pierced lips parted as their eyes fluttered, and that was when he noticed how dilated they were. "Did you know the camera was there?"

"Yes," they breathed, tongue flicking out briefly.

"And why didn't you say something?" he asked, hooking a finger in their orange collar ring to jerk them close. Their eyes rolled briefly, their body rocking on unsteady feet.

"I was a bit preoccupied," they snorted, looking back at him again. Their face was flushed, lips plumper than usual. "Can't exactly tell someone about a camera when you're so high, you're hearing colors."

Cyrus clenched his jaw, wanting to toss them over his shoulder and take them home ... Bex's home, not his. Right? *Fuck*.

"What did you need to talk about?" Killian cut through his thoughts, and he let go of the wolf.

"I know who the Carnicero Cerebral is," Cyrus said roughly, watching as Bex's eyes widened.

"Oh really..."

"Yes," he snapped. "*You* said getting high didn't fuck with your ability to get your job done."

"It doesn't!" they snarled, canines elongating in their anger.

"Then how did this get past you? I found out a week ago. A *week*." Cyrus arched a brow. "Or were you too invested in her pussy to see anything else?"

"Fuck you." Bex attempted to step away from him when he snatched their arm.

"I'm starting to wonder why Kayne recommended you as his successor," he growled.

"Because I'm good at what I do," they said as they tugged their arm. "Let me go, and I'll show you."

Reluctantly, he did as they asked, and Bex grabbed their backpack from the couch. Hanging out the side was one of those wolf plushies he saw back at their cabin. This one was navy with purple eyes. Pulling out their holoport, Bex tapped a few things and handed it to Cyrus. On the screen was Aida's operating room with a different victim on the bed and the good doctor hovering over them.

"You *knew!*" he yelled, stepping back before he did something stupid—like choke them or worse.

He didn't know what was worse: the fact that they knew and hid it from him or that he wasn't sure if it would stop him from wanting them.

The berserker in him wanted to lash out. Bloodlust hovered on the surface of his consciousness. He ignored that it was ridiculously foolish for Aida to have been captured on a recording.

"Yes, I knew," Bex said, canines retracting. "But I had wanted to confirm it before sharing it with you. You beat me to the punch, it seems." Their voice was oddly clear, despite how obviously high they still were. "I told you, I am still effective. How did you figure it out?"

"I already knew she had been hiding something. When you told me the victims had all been compelled, I put two and two together. Only someone with medical experience would alter brains in such a manner." He shook his head, fists clenching. "You should've told me the minute you found out! How long have you known?"

He worked to control his anger, his nose flaring as he took deep breaths. He was vaguely aware of Killian standing to the side, watching their altercation.

"I had suspicions the minute you assigned me to look into her. *You* underestimated her."

"How long ago was that? You've been at her place for weeks, Bex." Cyrus pointed at them, Bex's lip curling up in response as they growled. "You should've told me of your suspicions. It is your fucking job!"

"I didn't tell you because I wanted to get it on a recording first!" Bex snatched the holoport from him and returned it to their bag.

"Really? Or were you too distracted by her pussy?" Cyrus snatched Bex's collar, dragging them close. They raised their hands to grip his wrist, grunting when they tried to get him to let go. "You have allowed her to cloud your judgment."

Cyrus was one to talk despite his rising anger at Bex. The distress in their gaze cut through his chest. He did not easily give trust, and the wolf was giving him reasons to withhold such a precious commodity.

"I had it handled," they bit out. "I promise, I only just found out two nights ago! With the full moon coming up, I didn't have the chance to tell you."

"Why don't I believe you?" Cyrus growled. His grip on their collar tightened, restricting their air.

"Cyrus, let them go!"

Killian's words cut through the rising crimson that flooded Cyrus' vision. He clenched his jaw, reluctantly letting the wolf go. Bex gasped, stepping backward a few paces, rubbing their raw neck. Cyrus took deep breaths, working on reining in his temper.

"You don't fit the doctor's motive. I have a plan for picking her up. I am going to let you walk out of here in the hopes you don't royally *fuck* this up and tell her," Cyrus said as he smoothed down his vest, collecting his calm bit by bit.

"Why would I tell her?" Bex rasped.

"Stop. It's clear you're infatuated with her."

"I don't know what you are talking about..." they started.

"Cut the bullshit, little wolf," Cyrus snarled. "I should *really* put you in a cell."

He wondered why he hadn't already dragged them there in the first place. No. He knew why, but he wouldn't give it any of his attention at the moment.

Cyrus opened his mouth to speak when Killian cleared his throat. They both turned their attention to the man staring down Bex. Anger lit in his emerald eyes. He pushed forward to stand in front of Bex.

"Wait, wait. Your roommate ... The doctor you kept talking about... is the Carnicero?!"

Bex blanched. "Killian—"

"No! You've been fucking the serial murderer hunting in my place of business this whole time?! And you knew?!" Killian turned that fiery anger on Cyrus. "And you ... you didn't think it pertinent to tell me?" The human's emerald eyes bore into Cyrus. "You're making all this fuss about Bexie not telling you, but what about me?"

"I have plans on how I'm handling this," Cyrus said, feeling like a broken record. "I don't have to explain my process."

"This is my business, Cy! This is my livelihood, my brother's. We deserved to know."

"That is not how investigations work, Killian," Bex said. "The fewer people who know, the better when preparing for an arrest." They cupped Killian's cheek, the man looking at his best friend with furrowed brows. "I know you're frustrated. But Cyrus has this handled."

"It doesn't mean I can't be upset." Killian stepped back, shaking his head, walking to the desk to sit on. The wolf frowned, looking at Cyrus now.

"I promise, I only just found out about her being the Carnicero." Bex stepped toward him, gently placing a hand on his chest. "I wasn't planning on keeping it a secret."

Their voice turned soft, and Cyrus clasped his hand over theirs, gripping tighter than he wanted. And just like that, his anger drained.

"Killian," Cyrus said softly, stepping back from Bex. Both of them looked at him, and his stomach flipped. "It's hard, but trust that we know what we're doing."

Was Cyrus the pot calling the kettle black?

"All right," Killian sighed. "I'm trusting you both. Please don't fuck it up."

"We won't. But I have to go," the wolf said, rubbing their nose gently. "It's the full moon, and I need to get this out of my system before I run." Cyrus opened his mouth to say something when Bex shook their head. "I won't do anything, I promise. I'll let you handle it."

"Good," he murmured, hooking his finger in their collar to pull them close. "Be alert, little wolf." He licked their lower lip, making them hum in pleasure.

"Yes, my Lord," they whispered, kissing him.

It was gentler than he expected and judging by their wide eyes as they pulled away, Bex hadn't expected it either. Reluctantly, he let them go, watching as they slung their backpack on and left the office.

"So…" Killian started, drawing Cyrus' attention.

The tension in the room was still high, and Cyrus didn't know how to drain it.

"I'm sorry…" Cyrus said as he let out a long sigh. He took off his jacket, tossed it on the couch, and pushed the sleeves of his black shirt up to his elbows.

"Don't be." Killian shrugged. With his chin, he nodded to the wet bar, allowing Cyrus to help himself to a double pour of tequila. He lifted the glass to sip when Killian said, "You care about Bex."

"What?" Cyrus coughed, the tequila burning his throat.

Killian chuckled at Cyrus' expense, the sound helping to reduce the thick energy surrounding them. "You care about them. It's very clear," he said, bemused.

Killian watched as Cyrus walked over, casually settling between the man's legs. Killian leaned back on his hands to look up at him.

"Is that a problem?" Cyrus asked, realizing he was acknowledging the truth of Killian's words.

"Nah. I mean, if I were into pussy, I'd be down to bang in an instant. They're hot. But they don't have all the parts I like," he said with a snort. "But other than that, Bex is fun and a riot. We've been friends for a while. I just worry…" He shook his head, biting his lower lip in thought.

"How did you two meet?" Cyrus inquired, idly gliding his palms up and down Killian's thick thighs.

"Rehab," he said bluntly. "It was after my third suicide attempt and their fifth—or sixth—stint. Some things just don't stick." Killian's response was dry as he held up his scarred forearm. They were easy to miss with all his tattoos. "We made quick friends. And honestly, I don't think I'd have been able to get out of that place without them." He sat up, wrapping his arms around Cyrus' waist, his forehead just at his sternum. "Bex has always had issues with potions. But that is their story to tell, not mine."

"I respect that," Cyrus said as his fingers tangled into Killian's hair, and he tugged to tilt the man's chin up. "Will you tell me yours?" he breathed, leaning down to hover his mouth above Killian's.

"My story?" Killian breathed when Cyrus kept him still by his hair, not allowing their lips to connect.

"Yes. Your story. Your past. Your present. Who you are. Everything. I want to know everything, Killian."

He captured Killian's mouth with his own. Moving his hands to Killian's hips, he pulled him closer. The man gripped his shirt tightly, moaning when Cyrus sucked in his lower lip, fangs gliding along the sensitive flesh gently.

"It's messy. I'm messy," he breathed as they parted. "Who cares about my mess…"

"I do," Cyrus said without hesitation, cupping the back of Killian's head as he kissed him once more. "We're all messy. I have had over two hundred years to accumulate mess. I can handle more. Especially if it's yours." The look the man gave him had his heart fluttering in his chest. Was he... Was he having a heart attack?

"I don't know where to start..." he whispered.

"Start with one sentence," Cyrus whispered back.

There was something fragile about the intimacy they shared. He didn't want it to shatter. He was scared it might anyway. Burying his face in the man's neck, he inhaled his delicious scent. A scent he never wanted to forget. Espresso, brown sugar, and leather.

"Um ... Hi, I'm Killian. Twenty-eight. Human. Gay."

Cyrus stepped back to narrow his eyes at the man.

"Yeah, no shit." They both laughed, more of the tension releasing. An idea occurred to him. "How do you feel about moving at high speeds?"

"What?" Killian snorted in surprise. "I mean, I ride a hovercycle. Like that?"

"Hmm," Cyrus smirked. "Think faster..."

CYRUS' FINGERS LOCKED WITH Killian's as they walked through the sliding glass doors of the raceway. They passed a large sports bar with multiple games and races playing on several holoscreens. When the idea came to him to bring Killian here, he told the man to meet up with him in an hour and to wear protective gear.

"I don't think I've ever seen you outside of your fancy suits, Cy," Killian said with a grin.

"Is it bad?" Cyrus asked with a raised brow, returning the grin.

"No, definitely not. I am digging the leather and jeans look," the human said, slowly biting his lower lip. "It's sexy."

Cyrus paused, making Killian look up at him with a question in his eyes.

"Sexy?" he purred as he stepped into Killian's space, leading the man into a darkened hallway.

"Yeah," Killian breathed. "Is there a problem?"

"Absolutely not," Cyrus said as he snatched Killian's hands to push above his head, his body pushing into his against the wall. Killian gasped when Cyrus leaned in to kiss his throat, right above the jugular. "I just like how dark your eyes get when you look at me." He nipped the flesh, making him moan.

"Fuck," Killian whimpered, gripping Cyrus. "You're so fucking sexy. You're delicious to look at."

Desire shot straight to his dick, hardening against the shorter man's stomach.

"Keep saying those pretty words, and I might just do something about it." Cyrus shifted to take both of Killian's wrists in one hand so he could use his free hand to cup Killian's erection.

"Cy, someone could walk around that corner and see us," he moaned, grinding against him regardless.

"Pet, I fuck in a sex club. You think it bothers me?" Cyrus sucked on Killian's neck, removing his hand to rest on the wall beside the man's face instead. "But if it bothers you, I'll stop."

Killian leaned forward to catch Cyrus' lower lip between his teeth, slowly dragging him into a kiss. A growl vibrated up his chest as their tongues rubbed together languidly. Letting go of Killian's hands, he gave him a few more soft kisses and stepped back.

"Thank you," he said, breathless. His cheeks were flushed, pupils nearly blown. He ran a hand through his spikey hair, fanning himself with a chuckle.

"Come," he held his hand out for Killian to take.

"Maybe later, sexy," he replied, snickering.

Cyrus tugged him closer, briefly letting go of his hand to wrap his arm around the man's shoulders instead.

"What did we just learn happens when you use those pretty words?" Cyrus asked as they walked toward the sounds of engines pumping and whirring.

"Are we seeing a race?" Killian asked, his arm sliding around Cyrus' waist.

"Sort of."

"What do you mean?" Killian insisted as Cyrus led them into

a garage.

Massive in size, there were at least twenty race hovercars in varying colors and sponsors. Each vehicle had its own assigned parking space, and some of its drivers or mechanics worked on it. The smell of grease and gas clogged the air in the best way. Several of the cars were on, their humming engines filling the space. There was nothing like the energy of a garage full of high-speed vehicles and their teams.

"Ever been in a race hovercar?" he asked, smiling at the intrigue in Killian's eyes.

"No. Fucking. Way."

The man practically thrummed in Cyrus' arms, and it felt so damn good. He bit his lip to keep the big ass smile from overtaking his face. Killian's excitement bubbled over as he pointed out the different hovercars and racers.

As they approached a deep emerald machine, Cyrus stepped away from Killian to run his hand over the smooth, matte surface. Faintly on the hood was a symbol of his home country before it was renamed. The elegant curves took up the entirety of the space, lined in a very thin black—the face of a lion.

"Wow, this is beautiful," Killian said in awe. "You know the racer?" His hand hovered over the hood, seeming torn between wanting to touch it or not.

"You can touch her..." Cyrus purred, moving to the passenger side.

With a press of his palm, Cyrus pushed the door open, and it hissed as it rose skyward. Killian let his fingers glide over the metal as he rounded the car to look at Cyrus.

"This is yours?" he asked, eyes wide.

"Get in," he prompted.*

He didn't have to ask twice. Cyrus laughed as Killian happily jumped into the hovercar. After securing the door, he slid in through the driver's side and leaned back. The interior lit up as he turned the vehicle on, different dials and screens telling him everything he needed to know about the car. He reached into

* "CHIHIRO" by Billie Eilish

the backseat and pulled out two helmets, passing one to Killian.

"You race…" the man said in disbelief, strapping it over his head.

If the helmet wasn't the answer, Cyrus assumed the five-point harness seatbelt they had locked themselves in was.

"You. Fucking. Race!"

Killian's excitement was infectious, and he couldn't fight the smile any longer.

"I don't do it often. Not as much as I'd like. I wish I could." Tapping a few buttons put the vehicle in drive, with important diagnostic details hovering above the dash.

"How'd you even know I'd like it?" Killian asked.

He could feel those emerald eyes on him as he pulled out of the parking garage and headed toward the raceway.

"I saw the flags in your office," Cyrus said, somewhat embarrassed. For what? He didn't know. "Escobar is your favorite if the signed ticket you have framed is any indication."

"Cy…" Killian gasped as they rapidly sped toward the on-ramp.

He didn't dare risk a glance at the man, knowing that looking off the road could cause disaster. But the awe and emotion in his voice tugged at Cyrus' heart.

"It's just a free track tonight. There is no serious racing. It's only for experienced drivers, though. Novices can't do free track nights. Too dangerous." With another few taps, the hovercar accelerated to breakneck speeds as they merged onto the raceway.

"Oh. My. Deities!" Killian squealed as the lights blurred from their speed. "This is fucking awesome."

The pure elation in his man's voice had his mind spinning…

Wait. *His?*

Not again…

"Hold on," Cyrus said, using his chin to indicate the handle by the top of the door.

Using his periphery to ensure the man did what he asked, he tapped the screens, flipping his hand palm-side up to grip the steering wheel's underside. With one smooth turn, the hovercar tilted sideways, riding the raceway walls, following a few others doing the same.

"Fuuuuck!" Killian squealed.

For the next hour, as he continued laps, Cyrus explained the mechanics of handling a race hovercar and how it was drastically different than a regular hovercar. Killian asked questions, and their mutual interest blossomed.

"Before our father died, Royal and I went to races all the time. Though, he didn't enjoy it nearly as much as I did. It's one of the fonder memories I have of him," Killian said, breathless from the adrenaline. "It always stuck with me."

As they finally pulled off the raceway, he glanced over at Killian for the first time since they started. Through the helmets' clear visors, Killian's green eyes were lit with excitement, an emotion in them that Cyrus couldn't decipher. The man let out a contended sigh as they parked.

"Would you like to learn?" Cyrus asked as they removed their helmets to leave in the vehicle's backseat. Exiting the hovercar, they headed toward the exit.

"What? How to drive one of the most dangerous machines in the world?" Killian deadpanned. "Of course! I'd be mad if you didn't teach me."

He popped to his tiptoes to wrap his arms around Cyrus' neck, bringing their lips together. He held onto Killian's hips, kissing him hungrily in turn, matching his fervor.

"Killian?" Cyrus breathed, pulling from the kiss to lock his gaze with the human's.

"Y-yeah?"

"Can I ruin you tonight?"

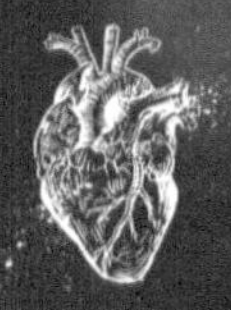

CHAPTER 14

DADDY? I MEAN, DADDY?

KILLIAN GRUNTED AS CYRUS pressed him against his living room wall, mouth on his. Once they arrived at Killian's place, they couldn't keep their hands off each other. Cyrus lifted the shorter man, Killian's legs wrapping around his waist. Their tongues danced as Cyrus ground his erection against Killian's.

"Fuck," Killian whimpered when Cyrus' licked and sucked on his neck.

"Soon," Cyrus chuckled, holding the man and stepping away from the wall.

With his vampiric speed, he rushed them to the bedroom. Killian gasped when Cyrus dropped him on the bed and nestled himself between the man's legs.

Killian wrapped his legs around Cyrus' waist once more, tightening to raise his hips so their erections could grind against each other. Growling, he grabbed Killian's hands to push above his head, breaking from the kiss to move his lips along his jaw.

"Do you want me to fuck you, Pet?" He swiveled his hips, making the man moan.

"Yes," he whimpered.

"Yes, what?"

"Yes, Daddy. Fuck me right now."

Cyrus stood up to pull off his shirt and smirked when Killian took him in as he followed suit. Cyrus ran his hands up the curves of Killian's stomach and chest, his lips following the path. They trailed along a thick scar on Killian's ribcage. The man gasped when Cyrus sucked on his nipple, tongue flicking it in circles. As he

---

continued to tease Killian, he slid a hand between them, cupping Killian's erection.

"Oh shit," Killian moaned, hips lifting to add more friction.

"Tell me your safeword, Pet," Cyrus whispered as he hovered his mouth over Killian's, stroking him over his jeans.

"Juniper," he breathed, letting his tongue play along Cyrus' lower lip.

"Mine is moonlight." When Killian nodded, Cyrus pulled him up to stand. "Something tells me you aren't into degradation, am I right?" he asked as he knelt to remove Killian's remaining clothes.

As he peeled down the man's briefs, his erection bobbed out, glistening on the tip. Cyrus couldn't help himself and gave it a lick, making Killian grip his shoulders tightly.

"F-fuck," he groaned, clearing his throat. "No, I'm not. I'm more of a 'tell me to shut the fuck up and take this dick like a good boy' kind of man. I like a fight."

Killian wriggled his eyebrows, but it quickly morphed into an expression of passion when Cyrus sucked on the head of his dick. The man's pre-cum lit up his tastebuds. Cyrus groaned and palmed his cock. Taking Killian further, he bobbed his head, enjoying the feel of Killian's velvety hard shaft along his tongue. Killian's hold on his shoulders tightened as he cried out, thrusting his hips. Cyrus continued sucking until he could feel Killian's dick swelling. He let go of Killian with a pop as he stood.

"Hmmm... I don't have an issue with that," he growled, hand going around the man's throat.

With his free hand, he undid his jeans and pulled out his aching erection. Killian's kohl-lined eyes widened as his gaze trailed a hot path from Cyrus' dick to his face.

"I'll be honest. I'm sort of scared," he said with a grin. Killian's eyes fluttered as Cyrus rubbed their cocks along each other.

"Don't worry, Pet. It'll fit." He pulled Killian close to give him a rough kiss. "Now, you are going to get on your knees and get throat fucked by my dick."

"Not unless you ask nicely," the brat smirked. A gasp escaped him when Cyrus tightened his grip around Killian's throat.

"Get on your fucking knees and suck my dick, Killian."

Killian did not miss the command in his voice, and he enjoyed watching the man's pupils dilate. Letting him go, Killian dropped to the floor and removed Cyrus' shoes and pants. Cyrus tangled his fingers in Killian's thick hair, gripping tightly.

"You look good on your knees." He groaned when the man took his length in hand and licked up the shaft, tongue ring sending shivers up his spine.

"Do you like that, Daddy?" Killian asked huskily.

Cyrus responded by tightening his grip in his hair, making the man moan and suck him in.

"Fuck," he breathed as he rocked his hips in time with Killian's bobs. "That fucking tongue ring, shit."

Killian hummed, one hand working the base of Cyrus' shaft where he couldn't reach with his mouth and the other stroking himself. Cyrus pulled out, smirking at Killian's pout.

"Ready to get your throat fucked, pet?"

"Fuck yes, I am," he breathed.

"Good, open wide," he growled, thrusting into the man's mouth.

He gagged briefly before relaxing, allowing Cyrus to slide in deeper. As his dick ran over the piercing, his body jolted with pleasure. Tears fell from Killian's eyes as Cyrus watched himself thrusting in and out.

Their eyes connected, emerald meeting yellow. Killian's waterproof kohl made his gaze even sexier. His brows pinched together as he panted through his nose, his strokes picking up.

"You are not to come, you hear me? I want to be in you when you come."

He pulled out and brought Killian up to stand to crash his lips against the other man's. Killian whimpered when Cyrus took over and jerked him off.

"Top drawer of the nightstand," Killian breathed as their kiss broke, Cyrus kissing down his jaw to suck on his neck, leaving a matching hickey on the opposite side.

A surge of bloodlust coursed through him as he licked over

Killian's pulse, his fangs threatening to crest. He had to take a reluctant step away, focusing inward to calm the raging hunger. Rounding the bed, he pulled open the top drawer with more force than necessary. Finding the lube, he stalked back over to a panting Killian.

"Bend over, ass up," he rumbled, uncapping the bottle.

The man rested his elbows on the high bed, craning his neck to watch Cyrus. The lube was cool as he poured some on his fingers. Reaching around, he stroked Killian's dick to spread it.

"Touch yourself. *Slowly*, Pet. Don't make yourself come."

Killian nodded, taking over.

"You listen so well."

"Oh, well fuck, Cy," he moaned.

Cyrus grinned as he rubbed Killian's ass cheek, warming the skin.

"Oh, do you like praise? Hmm?" he whispered, giving his ass a firm slap.

"Yes!" Killian panted, wriggling for more.

Cyrus gave him what he wanted on the other side, massaging the hot skin.

"You're doing such a good job, Killian." He gave the man's ass two more slaps, watching as he shuddered. "My handprints look good on you."

He grinned as he put lube on his fingers and inserted one into Killian's ass. The man's back arched, hips tilting for more. "Look at you, so eager and willing," he whispered as he leaned over, his dick grazing Killian's balls. He continued working him, adding more lube to insert a second finger.

"Fucking Orcus," he gasped.

Cyrus stretched him slowly, pumping his fingers in time with Killian's strokes. Killian bucked his hips, sliding himself between his fist. Prepping Killian some more, he added a third finger and continued his ministrations.

"Are you ready for me?" he asked as he gripped his own erection, needing to keep himself from coming from the sounds this sexy man was making. He removed his digits, replacing them with the head of his dick, just barely edging him, and added more lube to slicken him further.

"I've been ready," Killian said, gasping when Cyrus slapped his round ass.

"Tsk, so impatient." He continued to edge Killian, entering inch by inch. Muscle stretched around him tightly, each shallow thrust pushing himself in deeper.

"You're such a tease. You—" Killian's words were cut off when Cyrus wrapped his free hand around his throat and tightened.

"Shut the fuck up…" he growled as he slid in and pulled back. "And take this dick like a good boy." He drove in with a slap, loosening his hold to let Killian cry out.

"Ah! You're so damn big," Killian panted. "Fuck, you feel so good," Killian whimpered as he rocked back as Cyrus thrust deep.

He fucked him hard; the sensation nearly had his toes curling.

"I told you it'd fit," Cyrus moaned, grabbing hold of Killian's ass to spread and watch his dick pumping in and out. "Your tight hole is taking me so well. Stretched wide as I fuck it."

"Cyrus!" he cried out, throwing his hips back to meet each thrust.

"Hmm?" he growled, fucking him deep with harsh slaps.

"Daddy, please. I'm getting close," Killian groaned, grunting in frustration when Cyrus pulled out. "What?"

"I want to see your face when you come," he panted. "Turn around."

As soon as the man did, Cyrus hooked his elbow behind Killian's knee and drove into him hard. They both moaned, Cyrus rolling his hips to work deeper. He leaned in and captured the man's mouth in a kiss. Their tongues clashed, Killian's piercing rubbing along his seductively. Each matching rock of Killian's hips had his cock rubbing between them, the wet tip leaving pre-cum on Cyrus' lower stomach.

A whimper escaped Killian as Cyrus sucked on his lower lip until it was plump and swollen.

"Fuck, fuck," Killian cried out when their kiss broke.

Resting on one hand, Cyrus reached between them to grip the man's soft, round stomach. His fingers glided along the scar on Killian's rib cage, Killian inhaling sharply at the touch. His curiosity would have to wait.

"I fucking love how soft you are. How you feel in my hands," he breathed against Killian's mouth. "How you're taking my dick like a good boy." He moved his grip to Killian's cock, stroking in time with his thrusts in Killian's ass. "You feel so fucking good too."

"Please," Killian moaned as their fucking turned into a frenzy.

"Please, what?" Cyrus purred.

"Please, Daddy, make me come."

"Fuck!" Cyrus yelled as he thrust hard, making Killian's body tremble under him. "Look at me while I make you come."

As their gazes connected, Cyrus could feel that fluttering in his chest again. He took in Killian's parted, kissed swollen lips and how hot and flushed his body was under him. The emotion in Killian's eyes matched what Cyrus realized he felt in return. Sweat glistened on their bodies, making them slick as they approached the edge.

"I'm going to fill your ass with my cum, Killian."

"Fill it. Fill it up, please!" he cried out as his body shuddered and his cum shot out in jets, covering their stomachs.

Cyrus soon followed, roaring as he came, his release flowing out to cover the bedsheet. Their bodies jolted, pleasure coursing through them as Cyrus kissed Killian. It was slow, languid, and passionate. The feel of Killian's mouth on his was something he hoped he'd never forget. He needed more, yearned for more. Soft kisses peppered his chin and jaw as Killian moved from his lips to his neck.

"I don't think I ever came that hard in my life."

Cyrus chuckled, removing his arm from under Killian's knee and gently putting it down. "That's what good dick will do to you," he huffed a laugh when Killian playfully smacked his chest, then shook his hand with a pout.

"Ow ... Your chest is so damn hard."

"Is it now?" Cyrus grinned, flexing his pecs for added measure, making Killian roll his eyes.

"You're so full of yourself," he snorted.

"And you're full of me, so..." He grunted when Killian smacked his chest again.

He pulled him in for another quick kiss. Smoothly, he turned, pulling Killian on top, keeping his still-hard dick in the man's ass. Killian's erection stood proudly, the younger man's stamina rivaling his own. His face was flush, swollen lips parted as he rested a hand on Cyrus' stomach and began rocking his hips.

"Yes, so full," he moaned. Cyrus gripped the man's waist as he rolled languidly. A grin crossed his lips. "So full of this thick dick of yours."

Killian threw his head back, leaning on his hands as he continued his slow grind. Cyrus groaned, matching Killian's pace. It allowed him to work himself deeper, feeling every little thing. The tightening of Killian's muscles, how it felt to slide in and out. His hands glided up Killian's thighs, running circles as he warmed the skin.

"Can I?" Cyrus asked, garnering Killian's full attention.

"Yes," he breathed.

Cyrus gave his thick thigh a firm slap, making the man jolt and tighten around his cock.

"Fuck," Cyrus groaned, slapping the opposite thigh. He massaged them both, flexing his abs to sit up. Grabbing Killian's knees, he jerked the man even closer. "This ass is so greedy, isn't it?"

"Yes," Killian panted.

"Hungry for my thick dick," he thrust up, making Killian bounce.

"Starving," he moaned, riding Cyrus faster.

He quickly found the lube, pouring some in his hand.

"Fuuuck," Killian whimpered when Cyrus took his cock in hand, the lube allowing him to glide over it easily. With his free hand, Cyrus gripped Killian's ass, encouraging him to ride him faster.

"Shit, you smell so good," Cyrus groaned, running his nose up Killian's throat, following with his tongue.

He nipped and sucked over the sensitive pulse, the man's erection thickening in his hand. For once, the bloodlust didn't tempt him. For once, he could be in the moment without the need to spill blood. The relief that came with it flushed through him. It felt fucking amazing.

"Cyrus, please," Killian cried out, each rock of his hips rougher than the last.

Cyrus pumped Killian quicker, running a thumb over the wet tip.

"Be a good boy and come for Daddy," Cyrus growled, capturing Killian in a passionate kiss.

Killian's whimpers were swallowed by Cyrus' tongue as cum shot out and covered more of Cyrus' stomach. With a few more bucks of his hips, Cyrus followed, breaking from the kiss to let out a loud groan.

"Ah, fuuuck!"

"You did it," Killian panted, body trembling as he wrapped his arms around Cyrus' neck and rested his forehead against his.

"Did what?" he asked, equally breathless.

"You ruined me," he giggled.

"Did you just—"

"Shush. We don't talk about that." Killian grinned.

"Secret's safe with me," Cyrus joked, returning the grin.

"I ... You don't know what you do to me, man," Killian let out a breathy chuckle, giving Cyrus soft kisses. "Can I tell you something without you freaking out?"

"What's that, Pet?" he asked, returning those sweet kisses he didn't realize he adored until that moment. "Honestly, things don't freak me out."

"Yeah, but..." Killian looked down, bumping his forehead against Cyrus' chin. "I think I'm falling for you."

"What?" Cyrus whispered, cupping Killian's face, tilting his face up.

Emerald eyes shone as they pierced his anima. How did he find the words to explain he was falling, too? It felt all too soon. First Bex, now Killian. It was too much and overwhelming.

"I…"

"Look who's speechless again," Killian smirked.

"It's just…" Cyrus' throat felt thick as if the words were too big.

"You don't feel the same," Killian said softly, looking down again.

"No, it's not that," Cyrus said quickly. "Look at me." The man's gaze drifted up once more. He swallowed, pulse pounding. "I just don't know what to say."

Was it truly that hard? What was he afraid of?

"How do I…"

"Start with one sentence," Killian echoed with a small smile.

Cyrus bit his lip as he pondered for a few moments. He cupped both sides of Killian's face.

"Killian…" He took a deep breath, finding it difficult to speak through the pulse pounding in his chest. "I think I fell for you the moment you drank my tequila."

"Really?" A surprised chuckle left him as he sat straighter, bringing his lips close to Cyrus.

"Yes, really, you brat." Cyrus grinned, consuming him in a kiss. He thrust his tongue into Killian's mouth, the man's piercing gliding and playing, sending surges of pleasure straight to his dick once more.

"Whoa now," Killian breathed as they parted. "I need a bath and probably at least one business night to recover."

"Aw, did my thick dick spear you in half?"

Cyrus laughed when Killian sank his teeth into his shoulder playfully. Aggressively cute, the man tried to bite down but quickly groaned in frustration.

"Yes…" He bit his lower lip, a flush creeping up his neck to cover his face.

"Half a night." Cyrus raised an eyebrow.

"Half a night?" Killian squeaked, and despite what they

had just discussed, the man's half-hard dick twitched.

"Don't worry, Pet, you can handle it." He chuckled as he helped Killian slide off his lap, pushing him face down. He lifted the man's hips, making him yelp in surprise.

"Cy—"

"Don't worry," he said as he spread Killian's ass to watch his arousal flow out. He let his thumb glide over the sensitive muscle, collecting his seed and making the man whimper. "Whose cum is this, Killian?"

"Yours," he breathed.

"Whose tight hole is this?" he growled, pushing his thumb inside.

"Ah, fuck! Yours!" Killian shuddered as Cyrus pumped his digit shallowly.

"I'll ask again. Whose tight hole is this, pet?"

"My tight hole is yours, Daddy!"

He slumped forward into the bed when Cyrus pulled his thumb out. He scooped Killian into a cradle hold, Killian resting his head on his shoulder. His body was soft and plump. Pliable in his hands, and he fucking loved it.

"How do you feel about paddles?" Cyrus smirked when Killian wriggled in his arms.

"Love them," he said as he turned his head to kiss Cyrus' jaw. "Planning on spanking me some more?"

Cyrus hummed in thought as he placed Killian down on the bathtub ledge.

"That and then some," he said as he filled the tub, grabbed some of Killian's bath oils, and put a few drops into the water.

"I take it tonight was only the beginning of my ruination?"

"Tonight pales in comparison to what I want to do you," he said, giving Killian a feral grin.

The man's lips parted, eyes widening in surprise while Cyrus picked him up again to place in the tub. He slid in behind Killian, pulling the shorter man into an embrace. The water was warm, soothing the worries that tried to plague his mind.

Falling for Killian was not part of his plans. A man like himself didn't fall for anyone, and yet … He found himself falling for more than one person, and he didn't know what the fuck to do with that. A soft sound of pleasure escaped Killian as Cyrus washed him, taking gentle care of the man's reddened thighs.

"Thirteen," Killian sighed as Cyrus lathered his hair.

"Thirteen?" he asked with a quirked brow.

"I was thirteen when I first attempted suicide. It was silly, really," he murmured. Cyrus continued washing the man's hair, moving to conditioner as he let him process. "Believe it or not, I was the smarter twin when we were younger—the one who was an overachiever. I did everything I could to be the best. Royal was a bit of a troublemaker." Killian paused to allow Cyrus to finish before he turned to face him, emerald eyes bright but haunted. "I was jealous."

"Jealous?" Cyrus asked while Killian let his fingers glide along his jawline.

"Yeah. Despite how hard I worked, he got all the attention. No one ever paid me any mind. No one told me 'good job'. It sounds so stupid when I think back on it, but at the time, it was big enough for me to feel like I was a burden. So, I thought, hey, let's just relieve them of it and die. Apparently, my family didn't like that idea. Almost put me on watch after that stunt."

Cyrus grasped his hands, fingers linking together.

"I started cutting when I was fifteen." Killian shrugged as if it wasn't a big deal. "It started with me wanting attention from an ex. I blamed him for the reason I needed pain to make me forget him. I sent him pictures telling him that it was his fault I bled." Killian sighed with an eye roll. "It became a habit I couldn't kick. Still can't. I just *need* it."

"I can understand that bit," Cyrus said candidly.

"The second time I tried to commit suicide, I nearly wrapped my hovercycle around a poll. I was nineteen at the time." Killian lifted his arm to indicate the thick scar down his ribcage. "Guess it wasn't my time, despite how badly I wanted it to be. I was in an abusive relationship. Being told you're a piece of shit for two years does a lot to an already suicidal person. It didn't matter that I took self-defense courses and learned how to fight."

"What's his name?" Cyrus growled instantly.

Killian just gave him a sad smile.

"He was on the bike..." the man looked down, ashamed. "It … It wasn't my intent. He'd been berating me during the ride, and I just gave up."

Cyrus learned about the accident during his background check on the twins, but he never knew it had been intentional. Thus, it made sense that Killian didn't like degradation.

"You don't have to explain to me," Cyrus said softly, thumbs catching tears that cascaded down Killian's cheeks.

"I tried to do it again shortly after that, though. I felt so guilty. I *killed* someone. Whether it was intentional or not, I knew the risks when I aimed the cycle at the poll." He shook his head, letting go of one of Cyrus' hands to run his own through his wet hair. He pulled the man onto his lap, allowing Killian to straddle him. "I … The self-harm got worse. I was doing it near nightly. Royal found out..." His chuckle was weak. "He came to me with a business idea. He felt getting my mind on something productive would help. He wasn't wrong. Who would've known the roles would reverse? Him levelheaded and me downright awful."

"You're not awful, Killian," Cyrus blurted, cupping the man's face. "You've had awful things happen to you. You made some awful decisions that felt necessary at the time. But that does not make you an awful person."

"I'm not so sure about that." Killian shook his head before Cyrus could rebut. "I can admit starting The Den was a good idea. And then venturing off to open The Crow's Cauldron. It kept the thoughts away for a bit. But then I turned twenty-three..." His jaw clenched as he looked away.

"I'm cold," he whispered as he stood abruptly.

Cyrus quickly joined him, grabbing a towel to wrap around Killian.

He muttered a weak "Thanks" as he left the bathroom, water dripping behind him.

Cyrus wondered if he should say anything as he watched

Killian moisturize his body. The man threw a bottle of oil over his shoulder for Cyrus to catch, and he went through the motions. His gaze never left Killian as the man's fingers bounced on his vanity. Random makeup was strewn about, rattling with each rough tap.

"What do you need?" Cyrus asked gently. Clearly, the last suicide attempt was especially triggering, and he wouldn't push for the story.

"I need to be alone," Killian sighed as he continued his incessant tapping.

Pain shot through Cyrus' chest. A pain that he didn't like. A pain that felt as if he was being torn in two.

"Are you sure?" He took slow steps toward the human, hoping not to spook him.

Killian turned to look up at him. He wondered if Killian could see the pleading in his eyes. The plea to help. The need to make sure he was okay. Cyrus had never been transparent, but at that moment, he wished he was. They stood there, staring at each other, naked as the night they were born.

"Killian…"

"This is not a you thing. Please understand that," Killian said quickly. "Nothing about this night is what bothers me. It was magnificent, beautiful, and overwhelming in the best ways." He rose to his tiptoes to cup Cyrus' face. He leaned into the touch, bending to meet Killian's lips in a kiss. "Memory Lane is not my favorite tourist destination…"

"I'm sorry," Cyrus said as he wrapped his arms around Killian. "You don't have to tell me anything more. Not if it hurts."

"Thank you," he whispered, giving Cyrus gentle kisses. "I'll see you later."

"All right," Cyrus breathed, putting up a mask to hide his worry. "But, Killian?"

"Yeah, Cy?"

He pulled the man close, nuzzling his nose against Killian's.

"I'm really glad you're still here."

Killian pulled back, his emerald eyes connecting with Cyrus'. Melancholy crossed the man's expression as he cupped Cyrus' face. Whatever Killian saw in Cyrus' gaze made him shudder, and a tear cascaded down his cheek.

"Thank you," he whispered, voice almost imperceptible. "Thank you for seeing me."

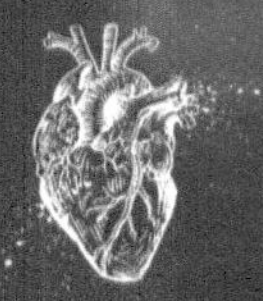

CHAPTER 15

COME OUT, COME OUT, WHEREVER YOU ARE

CYRUS HATED MORGUES, NOT because of the dead bodies or bodily fluids. He dealt with both daily. It was the smell, the stench of bleach and fresheners.

He sniffed a few times as he looked at the body on the autopsy table. The victim was a few nights old, meaning the doctor took her time with her victims. It was a level of sophistication and intimacy that he didn't see often with murderers.

"Is Doctor Broderick on her way?" he asked Lyn as she worked on the autopsy, lips turned down in a frown. "What is it?"

"His brain doesn't have the black striations." She scratched her head with the back of a pen before writing more notes.

"What?" Cyrus quirked an eyebrow as he joined her to inspect the now-open skull. "Interesting," he murmured, wanting to touch it to examine it further.

"The sample we pulled showed an unidentified drug likely caused those anomalies. Or kept them sedated?" She chewed on her lower lip for a moment. "I was hoping Doctor Broderick could—"

The door bursting open cut the coroner off as the woman in question barged through. Her eyes narrowed as she took Cyrus in.

"Surgery ran late," she said as she pulled on gloves and looked over the body on the table.

It was fascinating to watch her feign interest as if she wasn't the one who put him there.

"His brain is intact?" She looked up at Lyn, whose brow was furrowed as if trying to figure out the world's most complicated puzzle.

"Lyn, can I have a moment with the good doctor?" he asked smoothly, nearly smirking when the Storm Wielder's nose flared.

"I told you to stop calling me that," she hissed.

"You said you were good at your job. Thought it apt to remind myself." Now he smirked, Lyn's cough making it hard not to.

"All right. I'll be back in a few. I want to review more labs anyway." The coroner dipped her head and left.

"What do you want?" Aida asked as she removed her gloves and discarded them in a bin. Cyrus pursed his lips as if in thought, finding much joy in making her squirm. "Well, are you going to speak or stand there looking stupid?"

"I know what you did," he said in a sing-song voice.

Slowly, his bloodlust rose, and the need to hunt guided him. She quirked an eyebrow, not giving anything away in her expression. He undid his cuffs, pushing his sleeves up to his elbows as he stalked around the table toward her.

"And what is that?" she asked, stepping back.

"I'll have to bring you in," he said as he walked, not answering her question. Doctor Broderick took a few more steps back, a grin playing on her sumptuous lips. "Have you show me your technique, and then I can practice on you. Mind you, you won't want to lie to me. Don't want to accidentally kill you too soon or put you through too much pain."

His grin was feral as he continued advancing.

"There's a problem with that," she snarked.

Her racing pulse echoed in his ears and tempted his already impending bloodlust. As she continued backing up, the scent of her arousal wafted toward him, taking him by surprise. It only pushed his need further.

"You have to catch me first, and I know this hospital like the back of my hand."

He realized she had backed into the exit and let her bolt through the door. He loved a head start.

"Tsk, good doctor. You can try and hide, but I *will* find you," Cyrus snarled as he went after her.

He immediately slowed his pace when he turned a corner and found it busy with medical staff. Fuck. She blended in while he stood out. He inhaled, singling her scent out from all the others. Her blood called to him, his bloodlust practically driving him now.

"Excuse me, would you happen to have seen where Doctor Broderick went?" he asked a passing nurse, barely keeping enough control to avoid ripping out her throat.

"Yeah, I saw her get on the elevator. Um, I think to the fifth floor?" She smiled at him, pointing the way.

"Thank you," he muttered, making his way to the lift. Slipping inside, he clicked the doors shut so no one else could enter. Her petrichor and lilac scent enveloped him, and he found his body responding against his will.

"Get it together, you dick," he swore to himself.*

As it came to a stop, he exited cautiously. He looked around; the floor being under construction made for some barriers, but it wouldn't stop him from finding the doctor. No one was around, walls of tarp cutting off grids for new rooms. The thought of finding her and utterly destroying her had his vision shading the room in red and his heart racing.

"Come out, come out, wherever you are." Cyrus prowled as he inhaled and caught the doctor's scent again. His lip curled up when he found her lab coat hanging on a vacuum cleaner. "I *will* find you, and when I do, you're going to wish you had let me take you in before the bloodlust hits. Now? I am not sure what I'll do to that pretty little neck of yours."

A racing heartbeat drew his attention to the far side of the floor, away from the elevator and any stairs. His next step placed him in a cloud of petrichor, the scent filming on his tongue as it filled his lungs. It tasted of metal and the ozone of a coming storm. He knew he was getting closer when he caught whiff of her arousal.

"Smells like your pussy is wet for me," he growled. He pushed tarps to the side, hoping to find her behind one. "Aaai-

* "RUNRUNRUN" by Dutch Melrose

daaa. Come out to plaaay," he sang, "and I promise not to *fuck* you too hard." He chuckled darkly. "That is … unless you want me to."

He saw a flash out the corner of his eye just in time to duck the knife aimed at his head.

"Your dick isn't getting anywhere near my pussy," she hissed, throwing a jab at his chin.

His head snapped to the side as her punch landed. He spat out blood from his busted lip.

"Are you sure about that? Whether you admit it or not, you're fucking drenched," he said as he dodged another knife swipe.

He crouched, popping up to elbow her wrists and disarm her quickly. She grinned, a flash of wildness in her gaze, as she pivoted and jump-elbowed him across the jaw. He hissed as his hand came to his bleeding skin. Shit, she really packed a punch.

"Fuck off," Aida snarled.

A laugh bubbled out of him, and it only got worse at her questioning look. "And if I don't?"

He shook his head, regaining his bearings. She snapped the heel of her palm up, hitting him straight in the nose. Blood poured, and he grinned, letting it cover his mouth, and flashed his now red teeth.

Aida bolted, slipping under his arm and running for the stairs. He stalked after her, smirking at her attempt to escape. Oh, how he loved to play with his prey. She rolled, dodging in between tarps, and he lost sight of her.

"If you weren't so fucking aroused, I wouldn't be able to find you," he chuckled.

He heard a shuffling of feet and turned to see her running again. He smirked, chasing her, his rising bloodlust giving him a boost in speed. With all her athletic training, it made sense that she'd have as much stamina as she did.

"It's funny how you think it's because of you!" she yelled over her shoulder.

The moment of distraction cost her. She fumbled slightly,

allowing him to catch up and wrap his arms around her waist to yank her off her feet.

"Let me go, you motherfucker!" She threw her head back, but he dodged. The movement allowed her to slip out of his hold, and she turned quickly to face him.

He caught her by the throat when she tried to hit him again. She gasped as his grip tightened, and he slammed her against a wall. Her head thunked, making her bare her teeth at him.

"Let me go," she said, voice dripping venom.

"No." He gave her a dry look that made her scream and throw on an innocent voice with a menacing smile that didn't match.

"Help me!"

Cyrus jolted her from the wall and slammed her against it once more. She grunted softly, electricity skittering from her hands to his shoulders.

"No one to hear you, good doctor," he growled as he pushed his hips into her stomach, letting her feel his erection.

She twisted, bringing her elbow down to buckle his arm and let her go. He laughed, slapping a hand over her wrists to pin them above her head. Aida's silver eyes darkened as she glared at him, struggling to escape his hold. He chuckled as he ran a thumb along her lower lip. He nearly groaned when her tongue darted out to lick it.

"If you want me to fuck off, why does it smell like you're wet? Hmm?"

"I'm wet because vampire or not, Cortesano to the King or not, there are ways to kill you, and fantasizing about them has me wetter than a waterfall," Aida snarled.

"And what are some ways you'd kill me, murderess?" he asked, leaning in to inhale her addictive scent.

Fuck, she smelled so good. Why had he never noticed how good she smelled? He hissed when she suddenly latched onto his lip, catching it between her teeth. His free hand slid down her body, coasting over her breasts and hardened nipples through her scrubs. The taste of his blood made him grin as he pulled his head back far enough for her to let him go eventually.

"Stabbing you in the dick works," she said, his blood coating her teeth.

Cyrus snorted, using his finger to run circles over her pierced nipples. He didn't miss how her body arched into him or the way she licked her lips. Pushing in closer, he worked his knee between her legs, feeling her heat on his thigh.

"You'd have to get close enough for that to happen."

"I have my ways," she snapped.

The venom dripped from her words while her hips rocked against his leg. Her pulse roared in his ears, an indication that she wanted him as badly as he wanted her.

"Really? Are you sure you won't be more focused on the feel of your pussy around it instead?" He slid his hand down to play with the waistband of her pants.

"Let me go and find out," she growled, lifting her hips for more. A breathy moan escaped her when he slipped inside, and his fingers found her wet clit.

"I don't know. I rather love my dick."

"Let me go!" she snapped, pussy drenching his hand.

He loosened his grip enough for one of her hands to get free. She immediately grabbed his wrist. She pushed it closer instead of pulling his hand away like he expected.

"If you're going to finger me, the least you could do is fuck me with them." She guided him in making them groan at the same time.*

"Fucking you is the plan."

"Good," she growled as he thrust his fingers in her pussy.

He let go of her wrist from the wall to push his hand up her shirt, pulling the cup of her bra down to grasp her breast. Aida whimpered as she rocked her hips, and he pulled at her nipple piercing.

"So fucking wet for me. Hmm?" he whispered. "I will destroy you, Doctor Aida Broderick," he rumbled as their combined fingers in her pussy pumped faster.

---

* "Desire" by MEG MYERS

"Not if I destroy you first, Cyrus," she breathed, tilting her head back and rolling her eyes. "Make me come."

"No," he said with a grin when he stopped his thrusting, pulling out and gripping her hand to keep her from continuing. It didn't matter; she found a way to continue grinding against the heel of his palm and orgasmed anyway. She bit her lip as her body shuddered, coming on his hand.

"I see how it is. You take without permission."

"I'll never ask for permission," she snapped as she opened those glowing silver eyes to glower at him.

The feral look in her gaze had him collaring her throat and latching on to it with his lips. His fangs glided over the flesh, making her jerk against his palm.

Suddenly, she pushed him away, panting.

"Aida," he threatened with a low voice.

Somehow, she managed to free herself from his body, his knee no longer between her legs. Before he could grab her, she turned to face the wall. She arched, presenting her ass for him.

"Fucking me was the plan, right?" she asked, voice hoarse with need. She held his gaze over her shoulder, silver eyes glowing like electricity. "So, fuck me."

He grabbed a nearby construction table, pulling it toward them. He pushed her scrub bottoms and panties down to her knees, taking a good look at her exposed center. He slapped her round ass, smirking when she moaned.

"You're dripping for me, murderess," he rumbled as he freed his cock. He picked up her petite body, dropping her on her knees on the table.

"And you're so fucking hard for me," she gasped. She kept her gaze on him from over her shoulder, and her eyes widened when she took a look at his erection.

"I'm going to stretch this tight little pussy over my dick and fuck you raw."

Gripping her waist with one hand and wrapping the other around her throat, he rammed into her needy cunt. An indistinguishable sound left her as she rocked back against him.

Aida's wetness made it easier for him to slide in and out.

"Fuck!" he groaned as he fucked her with abandon.

"Harder!" she cried out, scratching the table for something to hold on to. He pushed her face to the hard surface, lifting her ass higher. Cyrus growled, fangs descended as he pounded into her.

"Admit it, my dick feels good in your pussy," he hissed against the shell of her ear as he bent over. He continued driving into her, making her legs tremble.

"Yes!" Her tiny body shook as he slapped against her, abusing her cunt with the force of his thrusts. "Fucking Deities!"

"Nuh huh," he chided, pulling out to flip her around and against the wall. She pouted at him, grabbing his hand to suck on his fingers. Fuck. "If you're going to call out anyone's name while I'm fucking you, it's going to be mine."

She slipped out of her sneakers while he pushed her pants off completely.

"Get your dick inside me again, and maybe I will," Aida panted, gripping his button-up and ripping it open. Buttons went flying, the shirt hanging at his elbows, as she pushed his undershirt up to run her hands over his abs. "Deities damn you for being so hot," she groaned.

"Ditto." Cyrus pulled off his shirt, and he pressed against her again. Her lips found his nipple and he gripped her coily black hair. "Shit!"

Cyrus snatched her small but fit body up, thrusting into her as soon as she wrapped her legs around him. Her back slammed against the wall as she clawed at his biceps.

"Fuck, Aida!" he growled, pumping inside her, her juices drenching him.

She cried out, laughing as she locked her manic gaze with his.

"You said my name first," she panted as he thrust roughly.

She licked the top of her teeth as she bounced. Her pussy clenched tightly around him, and he slowed to a torturous pace, using his grip on her ass to control just how much he gave her. He pulled out just enough that she couldn't come even if she wanted to.

"Say my name, and you get to come," he growled, hunching over to place his lips on her tender neck. "Say my name before I completely lose myself to the bloodlust."

"Do it," she moaned when he dragged his tongue along her skin.

Her blood sang to him, and he knew he wouldn't be gentle about it.

"Cyrus, bite me and fuck me."

"Demanding, aren't we, murderess?" he hissed, sinking his fangs in time with a deep thrust.

Cyrus couldn't explain the rush of power he got as her blood filled his mouth. He'd never experienced the euphoria that overcame him as he pulled from her throat while fucking her into oblivion.

"Cyrus!" she cried out as her core clamped tight.

Growling, he continued drawing from her, the coppery liquid leaking from his mouth.

"Oh, o-oh fuck."

Her moans were breathless, her whimpers driving him into her with hard slaps. He wasn't sure how, but he managed to unlatch himself from her to watch as she was overcome with raw pleasure.

"Come for me, Aida," he panted as he lapped up the blood that dripped from the puncture wounds. "Come for me now," he demanded, her small body bouncing with each rough snap of his hips.

"Cyrus!" she sobbed, shuddering as she came. He was about to pull out when she tightened her muscular thighs around his waist. "You will not come on my pussy. You will come inside me or not at all."

He stilled, blinking a few times at her demand.

A smirk pulled up his lips as he dropped her suddenly, catching her so off guard she couldn't help but let go of his waist.

"You don't get to make demands," he growled as his

orgasm rushed in, and he came on her stomach.

"You asshole!" she cried out, though her eyes dilated further as his cum splashed against her body.

She could deny it all she wanted; it was clear she loved having his seed all over her. For a moment, everything was silent, with the exception of their heavy breathing. His eyesight cleared, no longer tinted red, as Aida's powerful blood coursed through his veins.

The realization of what they did crashed down on him. He just fucked the serial killer that he was investigating. This crazy, wild, and utterly unhinged woman just pulled out one of the most blinding orgasms he'd ever had. He fucked the woman who had been using the twins' club and cafe as a hunting ground. Fuck!

"I'm sorry," she whispered, returning his attention to the present.

He quirked an eyebrow in question, wondering what she was apologizing for. Before he could ask, the sting of a needle bit into his neck, heat flowing through his veins. As he fell backward, she stepped over him when he hit the floor.

"Or maybe I'm not..."

It was the last thing he heard when the world went black.

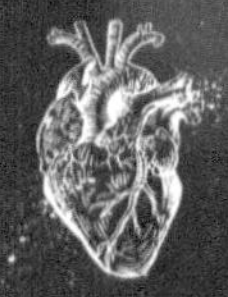

CHAPTER 16

WHAT IN THE EVER-LOVING FUCK?

"**B**ERSERKER..." THE VAMPIRE SAID as Cyrus finished tearing into the human who had raped his mimi. A strong hand grabbed his shoulder, yanking Cyrus to his feet. Blood poured down his chest, bits of flesh in his mouth. He spat it out and looked at the large man.

"What the fuck is a berserker?" he snarled, voice guttural.

A second Asherite was tossed into the room, and red completely glossed Cyrus' vision. He stepped forward when the grip on his shoulder tightened. Cyrus gnashed his teeth, needing to sink his teeth—no, fangs—into the Asherite and tear him limb from limb.

"You see red, verdad?"

"Yes," he bit out, fighting against the firm hold. "Let me go. I need ... I must!" He reached out for the sobbing human on the floor.

"You don't just want to feed. You want to destroy."

"Yes! Fuck! Let me do it. Let me tear him apart. Let him feel what I feel!" Cyrus bellowed, almost falling over when he was abruptly let go. He grabbed the Asherite's shirt without hesitation and pulled him up to stand.

"Do you want to know what it feels like to have your stomach turned inside out?"

He punched his fist into the man's abdomen, cackling at his gurgled screams. He wrapped his fingers around the intestine, brutally pulling it from his gut. With a roar, Cyrus tore into the man's throat and moaned at the rush of blood that filled his mouth.

"Calmáte. We have more to go. You will have your revenge," the vampire said, the compulsion making Cyrus l against his will. *"Let him go and look at me."*

He dropped the Asherite and turned his gaze to his maker. He couldn't ignore the command, his body doing what was asked without consent.

"What ... What is a berserker?" Cyrus panted, throat raw.

The tall vampire knelt in front of him, taking hold of his bloodied chin to examine him. He turned his face from side to side. Stunning golden eyes met his, long brown hair flowing over his shoulders. The man was beautiful.

"An abnormal vampire. One that will tear through anything and everyone unless controlled. A step in vampiric evolution that no one understands yet." His maker ran his hand over Cyrus' head. He couldn't help but lean into the touch.

"Why me?" Cyrus rubbed the back of his hand across his chin. He chuckled when he realized it was pointless, considering he was covered in the red, sticky fluid.

"I have been where you are. I see something in you. And you are now mine."

"Who are you?" Cyrus asked, red vision bleeding back to normal.

"Yo soy Jacinto. King of Potroya."

"WAKEY, WAKEY," CAME A sing-song soprano, waking Cyrus from his dream.

Groaning, pain seared his head as he slowly blinked his eyes open. The bright ceiling lights made him want to shut them again, but he had to take in his surroundings. Everything was white. He couldn't move his head left or right, and the lack of sensation shot a pulse of panic through him.

Where the fuck was he? Why couldn't he move? What the fuck...

"Oh, there he is!"

The feminine voice sounded from somewhere above him,

and he realized he was lying on a bed of some sort. The scent of lilacs and petrichor was followed by an assault of memories from the previous night.

"Good doctor…" Cyrus growled as she came into view, surprised he could speak, considering the rest of his body was paralyzed. "Or should I say, Carnicero Cerebral?'"

The smile that graced her face was sinister, full of dark promise, and manic. But the worst part? She looked fucking hot.

"Well, Cyrus, we've got ourselves a pickle, don't we?" Aida mused as she hit a button that lifted the bed head first so he was virtually standing. "See, you weren't supposed to figure me out." Lightning flashed through her dark grey eyes. "And you weren't on my list. I honestly couldn't have cared less about your mind."

"Let me go, Broderick," he snapped, trying to move his frozen limbs.

"However…" she started, slapping on surgical gloves, "… Then you informed me you were the Interrogator."

She turned to a medical cart, wriggling her fingers as she looked over the tools.

"Is it true you need the King's compulsion to stay sane?" she whispered as she turned to him with wide eyes.

A tingling sensation raced up his arms, and he had to fight the instinct to move or smirk at Aida's mistake.

"How do you know about that?" Cyrus asked.

"I think that is fascinating. I've not studied a specimen such as yourself before," she rambled as if he hadn't spoken. Grabbing a comm, she hit a button and held it to her mouth. "Tonight, I am studying another vampire under compulsion. This specimen is older than previous vampire specimens. The goal is to determine if it can be broken without the Sire present or if the attempt would kill them first."

"How do you know about the King's compulsion?" Cyrus asked louder.

The buzzing under his skin grew as feeling returned to his limbs. His vision briefly tinted red, making Aida gasp in delight.

"Oh! You'll be surprised at what you find out when no one

thinks you're listening," she chuckled as she carted over an ECT machine.

She took the electrodes and stuck them onto his temples. He could feel everything she was doing to him despite being unable to move. She yelped with a snort laugh when he tried to bite her as she attempted to put in a mouth guard.

"I mean, unless you want to chip those pearly whites, I suggest you bite down on this."

"Fuck you! Let me go, and I won't make you suffer," he bit out.

"No mouth guard it is," she said with a nod, plopping it onto the cart.

As she focused on the machine, he wriggled his fingers. Sensation was returning to him more rapidly now.

"Why are you doing this?" he asked calmly.

"I want to understand," she said as she turned back to him to place more electrodes on his chest.

"Understand what?"

"How compulsion works. How to break it." Aida said it as if it should've been obvious. "Do you know what vampires have made people do with their compulsions? What they force upon them?"

She tapped a button on the machine, which caused a surge of electricity to course through him. He bit back a yell, his jaw clamping tight. It ended as soon as it started, and he slumped in relief.

"So…" he panted, "You were a victim."

"No," she said simply. "My best friend was. And now she's permanently under their control."

She shrugged as she tapped the machine again. This time, he couldn't stop the scream from escaping his mouth. Pain seared through his entire nervous system, and his vision turned deep red. He could feel the rising bloodlust, and his gaze snapped to the steady pulse in her throat.

"Hmm." She turned it off, and he shuddered.

"Why The Den? Why the Crow? Malagado is full of the

unsavory. Why lead them there?" he asked, trying to calm the rage pushing at his skin. Aida ran the back of her hand down the side of his face.

"You are an interesting specimen. I underestimated you," she said with awe. The crazed look in her eyes did nothing to abate the beast wanting to break through. "To answer your question ... herding the wicked to one location didn't take much work. The Crow was a happy coincidence."

"So you did it because it was easy?" He almost grinned as more sensation returned, and her eyes widened ever so slightly.

"Actually, yes. I'm surprised you figured it out," she snorted and shrugged. "Now... How do we get you to unleash?" she whispered, rising to her tip toes to bring her mouth close to his. "I have a feeling last night was only the surface. I bet you can lose so much more control," she purred, letting her tongue glide along his lips.

He had to fight the urge to turn his head, not wanting her to know he could move. Not yet.

"You're just as insane as I am, bitch," he hissed, his tongue tracing hers.

Her gasp had him grinning. Fuck. She was unraveling him, and by the look on her face, she knew it too.

"Oh, you're right about that!" Aida laughed as she backed up. She tapped a few settings on the ECT machine, biting her full lower lip as she concentrated. "Compulsion can't be explained scientifically. Only that it works between a Sire and their progeny or a vampire and a human." She flicked her silver gaze to him. "I might be able to mimic the compulsion to fry the connection completely. Magic is susceptible to electricity. Maybe compulsion works the same?"

"You're playing a dangerous game," Cyrus snarled, patiently waiting as he almost regained complete control of his body. His fangs descended as he inhaled her scent, her blood calling to him in a way that no other blood, save Bex's, had before. "You unleash me, and I'll be every bit the monster you claim me to be."

Aida looked up at him without fear and rose to her toes again.

"Good," she said against his mouth. She sucked on his lower lip, and his body fucking betrayed him as he grew hard and thick in his pants. "I want to see the monster."

She backed up quickly, hitting the machine and sending wave after wave of pain through him. He could feel every compulsion given to him fray at the edges.

"I will tear you apart, Aida!" he roared as his body convulsed. "I will destroy every bit of your fuckable little body and drink you dry."

"Fascinating," she said, awed and not at all afraid at his outbursts.

She clicked off the machine, and his body slumped once more. He bared his teeth at her as she scrutinized him like the specimen he was. Picking up her holoport, she jotted down some notes.

"Tell me, I wonder what Bex would say about your actions?" Cyrus snapped. Her movements halted for the briefest of moments.

"I don't know who you're talking about," Aida said, keeping her eyes on the device.

"Are you sure? The sexy little wolf who loves my cum on them?" His lips twitched in a smirk when she gripped the holoport. "My playful slut?"

"They are *my slut*!" she yelled at him, snapping her angry gaze to him as she slammed the holoport onto the table.

He scoffed, rolling his eyes.

"They are *mine*. Who do you think sent them to be your roommate, good doctor?" His smirk grew into a wide grin as emotions flittered through her expression.

Her mask slammed back down again.

"You're lying," she said as she turned to the ECT and turned it on, lighting up his nerve endings with sharp pain.

"Killing me won't change it!"

"Change what?" Aida asked through gritted teeth when she shut the blasted thing off again.

"That Bex was mine first and will always be *mine.*"

Cyrus wasn't sure when he realized Bex was his and that he'd never let them go, but what was done was done. He wasn't going back now.

"No, fuck you!" Aida grabbed his face, eyes darting between his own.

"Don't believe me? What about the sounds they make when they're being made a mess of? Or how they happily drown in cum? The light in their eyes when they crawl with obedience."

Or their wide, toothy smile. Their sarcastic and dry humor. How achingly sexy they were when they were being snarky. Fuck. He wouldn't say that out loud.

"Deities damn it," she hissed, stabbing him in the neck with a syringe. "Good night, vampire."

And all he saw was black.

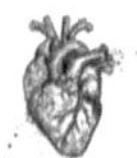

AN ACHE IN HIS head startled him awake. If that bitch cut into him, he was going to lose his shit. He opened his eyes slowly, finding her staring at him intently. He was back to lying flat. She looked down at her wrist comm calmly as if she hadn't had an outburst over Bex.

"Two hours. That was fast. You burned right through that sedative. Something is different. What changed?" she mused more to herself.

He found he could move his head, but the heaviness in his limbs had returned. Fuck.

"Let me go, good doctor," he said with vitriol.

"I don't think so. There's something different about you, and I want to know what it is." Aida sauntered her way over to him, palpating his face, down his neck to his bare chest. "Isn't this an amazing paralytic? You can feel this, can't you?" she whispered as she flicked his nipple, making him inhale sharply.

The desire flooding him at the way she treated him should've pissed him off. Instead, he wanted her to touch him more, but he refused to admit it.

"Don't fucking touch me," he snapped, even as his eyes almost rolled when her fingers glided down his stomach to play with the soft dusting of hair that trailed into his pants.

A smile tilted those sumptuous lips upward at the way his erection hardened under her gaze.

"Hmm, I think you want me to. While you can't move, your dick is perfectly capable." Her tongue darted out, and she licked his sweat-glistened abs. "You taste amazing."

Her mouth found his nipple and sucked on it tightly. Cyrus tried and failed to bite back his groan. If he could roll his hips, he would've.

"Fuck you," he growled.

"No, no. None of that. I won't fuck a paralyzed man," she said simply while popping the button of his slacks. "But touch … Yes, I can do that."

"Shit," he breathed when she cupped him on the outside of his pants. Buzzing skittered up his arms as feeling started to return. He fought against the urge to grin. "Do you always touch your victims like this before you kill them?" he asked with an arched brow.

"Most certainly not," Aida said seriously. "But none of them were like you." She pulled the zipper of his fly down, kissing up his body and stopping at his mouth. "None of them fucked me so hard I almost forgot my name," she whispered.

Her hand slipped into his pants and boxers, gripping his hard length and pulling him out. More feeling returned to his limbs as his beast pushed at his skin. He was stuck in between wanting to fuck her again and tearing out her throat.

"What makes me so different?" He bared his fangs at her, growling when she spat in her hand and stroked his length.*

"It wasn't until you told me you were the Interrogator that I realized you were like me. And because of that, I could understand compulsion more if I got a look at the true you." She

* "Go Fuck Yourself" by Two Feet

licked his lips as she continued pumping his dick. "I was already making plans until you cornered me. Well, then I just *had* to see how unhinged you could get."

She gave an utterly sexy chuckle.

"You barely scratched the surface, murderess. Hmm … fuck." He didn't fight the moan that crawled out of him, pre-cum leaking onto her hand.

"Oh, I know, sweet man," she said, the nickname completely juxtaposed to who he was. Her pace increased, and his breath came out in pants.

He knew the moment he regained full function of his limbs, and he had to fight the need to roll his hips and fuck her fist.

"I wonder what you'd do to me if you could move?" she asked rhetorically.

"Would you like to find out?" he snarled, snapping one of his wrist bindings to grab her by her hair. Her widened eyes were the only giveaway that he caught her off guard. "You should really do your research, good doctor."

Yanking her toward him, he sank his fangs into her throat. The moan that left her had him finally raising his hips against her tightening hold around his cock. He ripped through the other binding and gripped the front of her scrubs.

"How the fuck—" she breathed as he drank deeply.

The blood rushed into his mouth, fueling him with needed power. The scent of her arousal had him in overdrive as he fucked her fist, so close to coming. Pulling away from her neck, he glared at her, keeping her gaze with his own. She slowed her movements, and his grip on her hair tightened.

"If you stop, so help the Deities, I *will* tear out your throat," he growled, voice guttural.

She pumped him with renewed vigor, grinning like a mad woman as she watched him succumb to the pleasure.

"Come, sweet man."

He hated the command in her voice. He would've pushed her away if he hadn't been so close. Close as he was, he gripped her tighter as he came, coating her hand and the front of his pants. He snatched her wrist when she tried to let him go.

"Lick it," Cyrus said, abs flexing as he sat up slowly. Her eyes widened slightly as he snapped the bindings at his ankles. Gripping her hair to keep her head still, he forced her hand to her face. "Lick my fucking cum off your hand, murderess."

"Fuck you," she snapped.

It didn't matter, though, because she did exactly what he told her to do, and the sight had him wanting to fuck that pretty mouth of hers.

"Now..."

He stood abruptly, stuffing himself back into his slacks and not caring that they hung low on his hips. He wrapped his fingers around her throat and slammed her against the wall. She gasped when the back of her head smacked against it.

"Have you ever heard of berserkers?" he growled, his grip so tight his nails pierced her skin. Aida whimpered, but instead of fear, the smell of arousal floated up to him, making his bloodlust claw at the surface.

"M-monsters," she barely bit out.

Pulling her away from the wall, he brought her to the surgical table, throwing her against it hard enough that it snapped backward more. Her Wielding lit, not at full capacity indoors, but enough to make him let her go. She took a long gasp of air, scrambling away from him.

"Call me a monster one more time." Cyrus stretched his neck, muscles flexing as the berserker consumed him. He moved faster than she could track, in front of her instantly. He grabbed her chin, loving how her teeth ground under his fingers. "You played with fire, little murderess. And now you'll suffer the consequences."

"What if I want to suffer?" she laughed despite his hold on her chin. "There's nothing you can do that I wouldn't want. I told you I never ask for permission."

She reached between them to cup his renewed erection. It shouldn't, but the unhinged glint in her eyes had him rolling his hips into hand.

"I want to see the beast."

"Hmmm," he purred, turning her face to the side to bare her neck.

Blood coated his tongue once more as he licked the puncture wounds he left. There was something about Aida that his inner berserker wanted to know more about. The fact that he hadn't torn out her throat yet was an indicator he couldn't ignore.

"You want to see the beast?" Her body shuddered as he dragged his fangs along the flesh.

"Yes. Show me."

"Fine." He pulled her away from the wall only to slam her back against it, thoroughly knocking her out. "I will show you the beast."

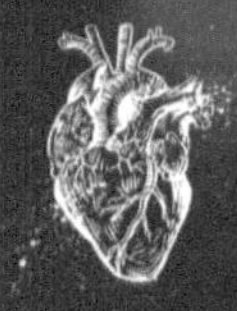

CHAPTER 17

BEASTS & MONSTERS LIVE HERE

CYRUS WHISTLED AS HE adjusted his white suit. A good shower would put anyone in a better mood. With slow steps, he walked around a very passed-out Aida in one of his interrogation chairs. Her head hung down, her hands zip-tied behind her, and her ankles secured to the legs of the chair. He knelt in front of her, taking in her seemingly peaceful sleep.

After knocking her unconscious, he gave her a sedative to keep her that way. Payback of sorts. He smirked as he took her chin and tilted her head back. Running his fingers along her lips, he wondered how much she touched him while he had been unconscious.

"Tsk... All you had to do was ask," he murmured as his fingers trailed down her neck, lingering on the puncture wounds where he'd bitten her—twice.

Other than Tristan, Cyrus hadn't met anyone else who shared his brand of insanity. The doctor confused him in ways he couldn't fathom. He pushed her mouth open, dragging his fingers along her lips.

"Responsive, aren't you..." He noticed how her nipples hardened under her top, her body responding to his touch. He slid his digits into her mouth, and surprisingly, her lips closed over them despite her being asleep still.

"Does the good doctor like a good mouth fucking?" he pondered as he pumped his fingers and enjoyed the soft sounds that escaped her. He pulled out, turned on his heel to grab smelling salts from the counter, and settled in front of her again. "I'll enjoy playing with you. Time to wake up."

He placed the salts under her nose, and she jerked awake,

her eyes unfocused.

"Ugh, fuck..." Aida groaned as Cyrus watched her come to.

He stood, crossing his arms, and waited for her to register where she was. The doctor looked up at him and focused on him as she took him in.

"You..."

"Me..." he mocked.

"You fucking drugged me," she breathed, voice groggy. She attempted to move but almost fell over when she realized her wrists were bound.

"Sucks, doesn't it?" He moved forward, using his knees to spread her legs. "Sucks feeling vulnerable. Not knowing if I took advantage of you."

He leaned in, placing one hand on the back of her chair and the other on the seat between her thighs. He planted the heel of his palm on the smooth surface, dangerously close to her heat. Aida sucked in a breath, her arousal traveling up his nose.

"You love this shit, don't you?"

"Love what?" she snarked, though her gaze told him just how hungry she was for him.

"Don't fuck with me," he growled, pushing the chair until it nearly hit the wall. He stopped shy of it, ensuring not to crush her hands.

She flinched briefly before schooling her features.

"I imagine that, as a surgeon, your hands are important." He dragged his fingers along her lips. "Did you know I practically fucked your mouth with these while you were out?"

At that, she opened up and caught his digits between her teeth. He laughed, pulling them away. He shifted his hand on the seat forward, firmly pressing against her core.

"Let me go," she breathed as she tried to grind herself on him.

"You get off by being a sadist," he pressed harder, making her gasp. "You like to take without permission."

"Take off the zip ties." Her back arched as he allowed his

thumb to glide across her pussy over her scrubs.

"You're right, you know. We are a lot alike."

He pushed in, feeling her wetness through the fabric. Aida turned her steel eyes to him; full lips parted as she panted. Fuck, she was sexy, and he hated it.

"I bet you want me to fuck that little pussy of yours again." The pulse under his thumb told him the answer.

"Let me go, now!" she snarled, struggling against her bindings while also rubbing herself on his hand.

Having his legs between hers, she couldn't close them even if she wanted to, though he had a feeling she didn't. With his free hand, he dug it into her hair at the scalp and gripped it tight enough to make her wince.

"No." He continued, rubbing on her clit. "Thought I'd return the favor."

"Fuck you," she moaned as her hips rocked faster.

"Maybe if you behave."

"I'll never behave," she snorted.

Cyrus smirked, moving to slip his hand in her pants.

"You're so wet. You sure you want me to let you go?" he asked huskily as he plunged his fingers into her cunt.

"Fuck!" she cried out, still struggling to get free.

She tightened around his digits, and he hooked them, hitting a spot that had whimpers dropping from her lips like a song. Groaning from the other side of the room snagged their attention. He continued finger fucking her as he looked over his shoulder to find the man in another interrogation chair regaining consciousness.

"Looks like our guest is waking up," he said as he shifted to the side so Aida could get a good look at the bloodied man.

"Jay?" she whispered, grunting when he thrust his fingers roughly. "Fuck, don't stop." She was completely unbothered by the sight of her ex-roommate.

"Hmm, that's it for now."

He stopped his thrusts as soon as her body told him she was close. She growled at him, attempting and failing to move her hips to finish herself off. He moved his grip to her chin, holding tightly to force her mouth open.

"I plan to destroy you tonight." He grinned, knowing it was manic by the slight widening of her eyes. He removed his fingers from her cunt to push them in between those fuckable lips of hers.

She glared at him, and he almost laughed. She could look at him however she wanted; her body told him a different story as she sucked on his digits.

"Let's meet our guest," he said as he pulled his fingers out and patted her cheek.

"Let me go!" she yelled.

He ignored her as he grabbed Jay by the lapels of his jacket, loving how he groaned in pain.

"You wanted to see the beast. You wanted to see how I work. I can show you that without you having to fucking cut into my head."

Cyrus grabbed one of the meat hooks that hung from the ceiling and dug it into the man's left shoulder. The sound of flesh tearing and blood spurting had a shiver running up Cyrus' spine. Adrenaline filled his veins, making the berserker under his skin roar in pleasure.

"Do you know why you're here, Jay?" he hummed as he grabbed the second hook and gave Jay's right shoulder the same treatment.

"N-no! Please. S-stop," the man sobbed.

Cyrus sucked his teeth as he walked over to a chain and pulled, jerking the man upright. He screamed as his body weighed down on the hooks in his shoulders.

"Genius," Aida said, awed. "He won't die that way, but the pain must be immense."

She leaned back, swaying her knees back and forth as if she didn't have her hands and feet bound. Licking her lips, she said, "Why Jay? He was my roommate, but I have no other ties to him. Watching him tortured won't affect me."

"Oh, I know. But I think you might be interested in what he has to say. He'd already been here before you *kidnapped* me."

Cyrus spun Jay around to face Aida.

"Aida?" the human whimpered.

Cyrus scrunched his nose at the smell of the piss that wet the man's pants.

"Pissing yourself already? You're weaker than I thought," Aida scoffed.

"Perhaps he's just terrified of your face?" Cyrus chuckled, not missing the hint of a smirk on her face.

"W-why are you doing this?" Jay panted, sweat coating his forehead.

Cyrus brushed past him, making the man yelp.

"Because you've made stupid fucking choices," Cyrus said as he looked at the tools laid out on the counter. His gaze slid to Aida. "Bone saw or barbed wire?"

"Barbed wire," she responded without hesitation.

He smirked, as that was his choice regardless of what she said.

"Perfect choice. Good girl," he said huskily.

Her widened stare and accelerated breathing told him more than she realized.

"I don't know why I'm here! Please, don't…" The man's cries were cut off when Cyrus wrapped barbed wire around his throat.

"When I originally brought you in, it was because you were shouting to the world that you knew who the Carnicero Cerebral was."

"I-it was just a t-theory," he whispered, trying to keep the wire from cutting into his flesh.

Cyrus looked at Aida and jabbed a thumb at Jay.

"It was just a theory…" he mimicked with an eye roll.

Aida snorted, pulling in her lips in an apparent attempt to not grin. Returning his focus to the man, he grabbed some more barbed wire. He shifted the man's pant legs up and wrapped the wire around Jay's ankles. Reflexively, the man tried to kick out, only serving to dig the barbs deep into his skin.

"F-Fuck!" Jay yelled and then sobbed as the wire around

his neck tightened and blood spurted.

They wouldn't cut deep enough to hit his jugular vein, so Cyrus wasn't concerned. The sight, however, had him wanting to tear into the human's throat. To feast and get his fill. But he knew he couldn't do that. Not yet, at least. He was surprised at the control he managed to have over his beast.

"See, if it had been just a theory, you wouldn't have been trying to tell the hospital CEO, the Guard, or anyone else with a desperate ear." Cyrus grabbed Jay's wrists, pulling them forward. The movement had the man screaming in agony, his shoulders popping as the hooks tore flesh above his scapula. "So. Share the theory with the class," Cyrus said casually, as if the man in front of him wasn't trembling.

He whistled as he wrapped the wire around Jay's wrists. He felt Aida's stare on his back, watching him work and storing the information for later.

"I-I can't. I was wrong," he cried. "P-please. I thought you were t-trying to find the C-Carnicero Cerebral to bring them in…" he hiccupped, snot running down his chin.

Cyrus took a few steps back to take in the view. Delicious. Blood ran in rivulets from Jay's throat and shoulders.

"Oh, I was. I truly was. But not for the reasons you think."

"Then why…" the man's eyes fluttered, rolling briefly.

Cyrus smacked him, jolting him awake from the total body torture it surely gave.

"Who do you think the Carnicero Cerebral is?" Cyrus wanted to hear him say it.

"I think it's obvious…" Aida quipped.

He stalked over to her, gripping her chin and making her hiss.

"It doesn't matter if it's fucking obvious. It's about *him* saying the words. It's about taking their control away and watching what happens when people have no choice but to speak. Who do they become under pain and torture?" He let her go abruptly, making her head snap back.

"All right. All right." She stretched her jaw, eyes flaring bright with lightning.

She truly loved being manhandled, didn't she? Cyrus spun on his heels to clap his hands and stalk back to the sniffling man.

"As I was asking before, I was so rudely interrupted … Who do you think the Carnicero Cerebral is?"

"Her! Doctor Broderick … A-aida." He sniffed, a sneer covering his features despite the apparent fear that encapsulated his being.

"Uh-oh. And why is that? Because she's stronger than you?" Cyrus asked with raised eyebrows. "Or because you're afraid of her?"

"B-because she's a freak! She has all those weird b-brains in her apartment. And we all know the Carnicero Cerebral fucks with brains." Jay was breathing heavily, his body seemingly having gone numb due to his lack of reaction to the pain.

Cyrus heard her chair shuffling behind him while Aida grunted.

"If I weren't tied up right now, I'd murder you myself, Jay," she growled.

His dick twitched at the menace in her voice. He had half a mind of pushing Jay to the wall and fuck Aida in front of him while the man writhed in pain. *Fuck.* Cyrus adjusted himself and unraveled more barbed wire.

"Did anyone believe you? Give you any merit for this *theory*?" he asked as he circled behind the sobbing man.

"N-no. Despite her arrogance, everyone thinks she's an amazing doctor," he grunted. "N-no one believed she'd be c-capable of doing it."

Cyrus tilted to the side to look at Aida from behind Jay.

"See what I mean? Get to a certain limit, and they won't shut up." He winked at her eye roll. Yeah, she knew he was right. He patted Jay's shoulder, making him cry out. "She was your roommate. You both fucked. Is this what you do? Become a traitor because you are afraid?"

"Us fucking had nothing to do with it. She's a fucking psycho and a monster!"

"Hey!" Cyrus barked, reaching in front and hooking the wire in Jay's open mouth. "We don't say that around here."

Red clouded his vision, his bloodlust rushing to the front. The man screamed as best he could as Cyrus wrapped the wire several times around his head, across his open mouth. Blood and saliva poured down Jay's chin.

"Aw, defending my honor?" Aida asked. He looked around Jay again to glance at her. She had an eyebrow arched, a slight grin tipping up one side of her mouth.

"Do you know what we do to people down here? We mark them with a word. Sometimes it's 'traitor'. Or a recent favorite of mine: 'dumb ass.' In your case, I think 'coward' works best."

Cyrus grabbed a scalpel from the counter and returned to the back of Jay's body. He ripped the man's shirt down the middle, baring a smooth canvas for his artwork. As he began to work, he bit his lower lip in concentration. Blood sprayed when he occasionally dug deep, and he enjoyed the feel of the hot, sticky fluid.

"Do you always wear white when you ... Interrogate?" Aida asked as if the man between them wasn't screaming bloody murder.

Cyrus snorted as he kept up with his carving, up to the A already.

"Always. I like the color of blood. Scares the prisoners, too. Added bonus," he said, flicking his gaze up to hers. "Starting to understand me a bit more?"

Something clicked, both of them staring at each other in total understanding. He returned his focus to the man in front of him. Jay abruptly stopped screaming right as Cyrus finished the last letter. He was surprised the man even lasted that long. He was still alive, but barely. Grabbing Jay's wrist, he dragged the man to the wall, courtesy of the tracks the hooks were attached to. He pushed him face-first against it, his back a raw mess.

"See, I'm always looking for new ways to interrogate, and knowing what I know now, I think you can help me with that. So, I've taken care of this leaky motherfucker so that any suspicion can be quieted down. After all, he decided to take an extended vacation due to his embarrassment."

"Can you let me go now?" Aida asked as Cyrus turned to face her.*

He marked the noticeable heat in her eyes, and he stalked toward her, dick straining in his pants. He ripped the zip ties at her ankles and collared her throat to pull her up to stand. She sucked in a sharp intake of breath, pupils dilating.

"Have you ever been fucked against a body before?" he growled.

"No," she whimpered when he pulled her close, hand on her ass.

"Well, tonight's your lucky night."

He snapped her wrist binds only to scoop her up. Her muscular legs tightened around his waist as he pushed her back against Jay's. Blood coated her, and she didn't seem to care.

"Grab the chain," he breathed, looking to where the hooks were hanging. She did as he asked, biceps flexing as she held her weight.

"I told you I'd destroy you. Watch me do exactly that," he snarled, his berserker roaring inside to fuck her until she couldn't walk. To fuck her until all she felt was him, with no idea where he started, and she ended.

He stepped away briefly, Aida holding herself up with ease. He slipped off her pants and panties, leaving her bottom half bare. He stood, pulling his aching length out.

"I'm going to fuck this pretty pussy until it is swollen and sore." He ran the tip of his dick along the seam of her core, making her whimper and wrap her legs around his waist. "And then I'm going to fuck it again so that when I'm done with you, you'll beg me for more."

"I'll never beg," she breathed as he edged her, her juices coating him. He slid inside her inch by inch, groaning at the feel of her wet heat as he stretched her wide. "I take without permission, remember?" She tightened her thighs around him, hooking her

* "MAKE ME CUM" by Witchz, a calmer place., Erika Sirola

ankles, and jerked him forward so that he thrust deep inside her.

"So demanding," he growled. His fangs descended as he ran his tongue up the column of her throat. He lingered on the puncture marks he left, sucking and dragging his teeth along them. "Well, so do I."

He sank his fangs into her throat at the same time he gripped her ass and thrust hard.

"Oh fuck!" she cried out, pussy gushing.

The barely alive Jay groaned softly as they fucked against him. Cyrus grinned, ramming into Aida roughly as her blood poured down his throat. He parted from her, his berserker having him seeing red. He licked her chin, spreading her blood along it.

"Fuck," he groaned as she tightened around him. Gripping her ass, he bounced her on his cock. The wet slaps of him fucking her drenched pussy echoed throughout the room. "Come on my dick like I know you want to."

He bit into her top, sucking on her pierced nipple through the fabric.

"Holy Deities!" she screamed as her body convulsed and she came.

Pulling out of her, he carried her to the counter, placing her on her feet and spinning her around.

"You like the way I fuck you," he growled as he bent her over and thrust two fingers in her.

"No," she denied even while moaning.

"You're so fucking wet, good doctor. Are you sure about that?" He added a third finger. "The way your pussy is taking my fingers, say differently."

He took one of her wrists to hold behind her back, kicking his feet between hers to spread her wider. She cried out when he added a fourth, stretching her cunt.

"The way you're about to take my whole fucking hand says differently, murderess."

"Ah! Oh shit. Fucking Deities!" she cried, arching her back to give him more access. She gushed over him as he worked himself deeper until his hand was fully inside.

"Want to tell me again that you don't like the way I fuck you?" he growled as he worked her canal, pumping slowly.

"Fuck, all right! You're right." Her legs shook as she clamped down around him.

"I'm right about what?" he asked, bringing her toward another orgasm.

"I like the way you fuck me!"

"That's a good girl," he purred, and she shattered, sobbing as she came once more.

He slowly slid his hand out and turned her to face him, picking her up to place her on the countertop. He smeared her arousal along her face and stuck his fingers into her mouth.

"Suck."

She didn't hesitate, keeping her eyes on him as he pumped in and out. He groaned as he removed his digits. The copper taste of her blood lingered on his tongue as he rolled his hips and rubbed his cock on her stomach.

"Show me how much you like fucking me, too," she panted as he removed his fingers. "Your dick was made for me, sweet man, no matter how much I hate you for it." Lightning flashed in her eyes, her plump lips parted as she breathed heavily.

"I hate you too," Cyrus snapped as he tore her top down the middle.

He pushed it off her, ripping through her bra. He gripped one of her breasts and bit her pierced nipple. She gripped his bloody shirt, moaning as his tongue flicked her tightened peak. Removing his button-up and undershirt, he tossed it aside and hissed when she dragged her nails down his chest and abs.

"I hate you so fucking much," she growled as she gripped his dick and stroked.

His lips found her neck, tongue dragging along the puncture wounds. Sinking his fangs into her flesh, his dick pulsed in her grip. He drank but not as deeply as he had earlier. No, this was just for pleasure.

Fuck, he hated this reaction Aida brought out of him. He hated how he knew, after tonight, he wouldn't be able to get enough of her insanity. He hated this gorgeously dangerous woman whose pussy was made for him too.

Pulling away from her neck was a task shy of impossible. Cyrus spun her around again, bending her over the counter roughly, her knees at the edge. He slapped her ass, the sound echoing. Moving with vampiric speed, he grabbed a zip tie and bound her hands behind her back. She fell forward, cheek flush with the countertop.

"What—"

"Shut the fuck up," was all he said as he lined up and railed into her soaking pussy. "The only sounds I want are your screams and cries."

Aida did precisely that when he grabbed her binding like a harness and fucked her as if there was no tomorrow. Aida pulled at the zip ties around her wrists while Cyrus gripped her ass hard enough to bruise. She tightened around his cock, and he let her come without permission.

"Fuck! I'm coming," she cried out, her body shuddering.

He pulled out suddenly, gripping his erection. She peered over her shoulder at him with an eyebrow arched in question.

"On your knees," he growled. Taking a fist full of her hair, he pulled her off the counter and onto the hard tile floor. He stroked himself quickly, keeping her head still as he did so.

"Don't you fucking dare," she hissed as she fought against her bindings.

"Fuck you," he groaned as he got closer to his peak. "This is for drugging and kidnapping me."

Hot cum shot out and covered her face. The sound that escaped her was either from pleasure or anger, he wasn't sure, and he didn't fucking care.

"Argh! I fucking hate you! You will pay for that," she snarled.

"Doubt that, good doctor." He smeared the cum on her face, gripping her chin tight enough to pop her mouth open. "Fuck. You."

He pushed his cum coated fingers in between her lips, grinning when she involuntarily moaned.

A soft chuckle sounded, the sound familiar and sultry, as he pulled up his slacks.

"Well, what do we have here?"

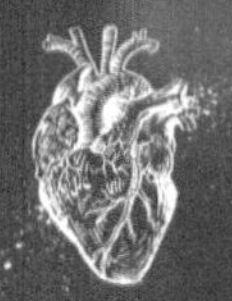

CHAPTER 18

LITTLE WOLVES DESERVE TO PLAY

CYRUS CAST HIS GAZE upon the sexy as fuck werewolf leaning on the doorframe of the interrogation room. Their long, leather-clad legs and bare arms were crossed. The chains on their leather vest clinked softly as they breathed, hazel eyes dark with desire. Their sumptuous lips were pulled up in a grin, their tongue playing with the piercing through it.

"This is a sight I'd never thought I'd see," Bex said, gaze taking in the room.

He knew how it looked—blood, sex, and violence.

"Let me go, Cyrus," Aida snarled, drawing his attention.

He raised a brow, tempted to gag her with his cock. He looked at Bex, who stared at Aida. Desire clouded their eyes, along with something else. Something he didn't like.

"Bex, clean the good doctor up and put her in a cell," Cyrus ordered.

"What?" the wolf breathed, looking at him now.

That same look was aimed at him, which did something to his gut. Fuck.

"Clean her up and put her in a cell. Is that hard to understand?"

"But…" Bex looked back at Aida. "I…" Their brows furrowed, clearly struggling with obeying his command.

Cyrus knew he wouldn't punish them if they didn't follow his order.

It was then that he realized just how deep he had gotten.

Clenching his jaw, he bit out, "On your knees." Bex followed his command without question. "Crawl to me."

Their breathing turned heavy as they slowly made their

way to him, crawling through blood as if it weren't there.

"Bex..." Aida started but gasped when Cyrus tightened his grip on her hair.

"No, shut the fuck up," he growled.

Bex knelt next to Aida, and something about seeing them both on their knees did something to him. Double fuck. Using his free hand, he ran his fingers along Bex's jaw, tilting their face up to him. He plunged his fingers into their mouth, and they sucked.

He kept his gaze locked with them as he said, "Be a good cum slut and clean her face with your tongue."

A sound left Aida, and Cyrus didn't hold back his manic grin when the scent of arousal wafted to him. Bex complied, turning to the doctor.

"Hey," the wolf said huskily.

The way Aida's gazed softened ever so slightly as she looked at Bex had him grinding his teeth. Starting with her mouth, Bex licked Aida's lips, sucking the cum off as they did so. A moan escaped the doctor as Bex kissed them deeply.

"None of that," Cyrus snapped, pulling Aida away with a rough pull of her coils. "I said clean her, not kiss her."

"Aw, jealous?" Aida snarked.

He held up a finger to signal Bex to pause. He noted the distress in their eyes, even if it wasn't particularly evident in their face. Reluctantly, he ignored them. He had a point to make. Slowly, he made Aida stand with his grip in her hair. She winced when he tightened his fist.

"Let's go," he growled, dragging Aida with him, not caring that she was half-naked and covered in blood and cum.

"Where are you taking me?" she shouted, trying her hardest to plant her feet. Her much smaller body was no fight for his larger one.

"To a cell. Where all prisoners are kept."

"Do you fuck all your prisoners?" Aida snarled.

Cyrus had to give her credit for continuing her struggle. However, it didn't go unnoticed that she was highly aroused. He ignored her, dragging her out of the interrogation room. He felt

Bex behind him, following in silence. He eyed the cells, each of them bleak save for one. One that he used to lull his prisoners into a sense of security. He pulled Aida in, pushing her onto a cot.

"If you want to leave here with your body intact, you will listen to me and shut the fuck up," he growled, motioning for Bex to stay at the door.

Aida's nose flared as she bit out, "Fine. Go ahead, then."

"Your interest in compulsions and your process has intrigued me. It's the only reason you're still alive." *That, plus the little wolf who has you wrapped around their finger.* Cyrus cursed internally at himself. "So, we're going to lay some ground rules."

Aida shifted on the cot, wincing as she tried to stretch her shoulders.

"Cut her free," he sighed, speaking to Bex.

The wolf wasted no time in unbinding the Wielder.

"Thank you," she grumbled, stretching her arms and wrists. "What rules?" she asked, glaring at him.

"No more hunting at the twins' businesses. The Crow's Cauldron and The Den are off limits." He refused to put Killian and Royal in that position.

"And…" Aida urged.

"Get approval from me first."

"What? No," she snapped.

"Do you want to live?" he asked calmly, waiting until she nodded with an eye roll. "I have no problems letting you continue, so long as you share your process. Fail to do so, and I will lock you up and kill you slowly." The menace in his voice worsened the tension in the cell.

"So … You want me to continue my experiments?" the doctor asked slowly, eyebrow raising in surprise.

"Yes." Cyrus crossed his arms, not caring that his still bloody hands smeared along them.

"And you, what? Want to observe?"

"Absolutely. I will even give you prisoners to work on. I want to learn how you do it. It'll help us break the compulsions of anyone who can give us answers. And it'll be a new way for me to

Interrogate. That shit is painful as fuck," he said candidly.

He allowed Aida the space to think on his offer. As she did, he looked her over, arousal flooding him at the thought of fucking her blind again.

"All right," she said, drawing him from his thoughts.

He saw the way her eyes raked over his body, the blood on his hands caked and dry, the sweat that still glistened. Cyrus' lips turned up in a feral grin.

"Good girl," he purred, nearly laughing at how she glared at him. He snatched Aida from the cot, ignoring her protests.

"Bex…" he said, nodding with his chin for them to move in front.

"Yes?" They followed his order, staring at him with those stunning hazel eyes. He clenched his jaw as he shoved Aida their way. "Cyrus—"

"Take her to my penthouse … Clean her up." He wouldn't admit how much the light in their eyes made his chest ache. *"Don't* fuck her, or I swear to the Deities I will punish you and not in the fun kind of way," he warned.

When Bex nodded enthusiastically, he almost groaned. If they asked him to let the doctor go, Cyrus had to admit he would do it in a heartbeat. Especially if it meant they'd keep that look in their eyes.

Fuck. He was royally screwed.

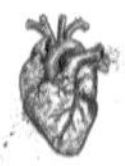

AFTER MAKING SURE THE interrogation room was sanitized and Jay's body had been reduced to ashes, Cyrus took a quick shower in his private locker room. He sighed as he slipped on a fresh suit. The shower wasn't nearly enough to remove the blood still crusted around his hands and random spots over his body.

He needed to get to the penthouse as soon as possible but needed to look clean enough to keep eyes off him. No one knew he was the Interrogator, and he planned to keep it that way.

Cyrus stuffed his hands into his pocket, casually going to the penthouse. What the fuck happened over these last two nights? He didn't like that his life was in disarray. Things had been getting increasingly convoluted, driving him up the wall. Why did he fuck the doctor?

Because she's just as unhinged as you are, he scowled at himself. *Shut the fuck up.*

But he had to admit his inner voice was right. The woman was a menace. A straight-up wildcat on her best nights, a terror on her worst. He'd never met anyone like her. Not anyone he wanted to fuck, at least. And the wild part was that he wasn't even interested in her until he saw how unhinged she was. What kind of fucked up shit was that?

The first thing he noticed when he entered his home was the smell of his body wash. The whiskey and oak scent traveled to him, and he sighed unhappily at the thought that Aida would smell like him. The sounds of water sloshing grabbed his attention, and he silently walked toward the bathroom.

Soft moans could be heard, and his dick instantly hardened. Fuck!

"Please…" Bex whimpered.

The door had been left slightly ajar, and he could clearly see his sizeable russet tub, which could easily fit six people. A ledge separated the tub from a waterfall shower built into the far wall. On a bench, halfway submerged, he found the wolf and Wielder.

Bex straddled Aida, hands on both shoulders. The woman held Bex's tiny ass, biting her lip as she looked up at Bex with … adoration?

"We can't," she breathed. "As much as I want this pretty pussy on my tongue…" What she said next surprised him. "I don't want you punished because of me."

Moving her grip from Bex's ass to their hair, she pulled the wolf in for a kiss. It was passionate in a way that made him both angry and horny. They never spoke about exclusivity. It wasn't in the cards for Cyrus, anyway. But he would be lying if he said it didn't bother him. Maybe it was because he hated the Storm

Wielder.

"Besides, the only time you get punished will be because *I* punish you."

"Now, now, do continue," Cyrus said, making himself known.

Bex snapped their gaze to him, Aida rolling her eyes.

"I mean, the little wolf will still be punished for even trying."

"Fuck you, Cyrus," Aida growled, moving Bex off her lap and standing.

Water traveled down her muscled, toned body, pierced nipples tightening in the cool air. Bex rose with her, their tattoos glistening with moisture.

"Did that, done that. I'll admit it was pretty fucking good," he snorted, removing his jacket and vest. Unbuttoning his shirt, he looked at Bex and motioned with his chin. "Come here." Aida attempted to keep the wolf from moving. "Let them go, *now*."

The snarl that came out of him was nothing short of animalistic. Panic rose in Bex's eyes before they slammed their mask down.

"It's okay, mamita," Bex said, leaning down to kiss Aida's shoulder. She looked back at the wolf, her scowl quickly turning into concern. "I need him as much as I need you. You understand?"

Cyrus fought a growl as the two kissed once more. He didn't know if he wanted to rip the two apart or join them. His head was all fucked up, and he needed to do something about it.

"Little wolf," Cyrus breathed, barely keeping himself composed.

Their eyes lit with a flash of neon green as they parted from the kiss. Bex's lithe form exited the bathtub to walk up to him, placing a hand on his chest.

"I'm sorry," they whispered, pupils dilated.

His heart pounded against their palm. He wondered if they had any idea of their power over him.

"You will be," Cyrus growled, sinking his still blood-encrusted hand in their messy hair to pull them into a passionate kiss.*

* "Gorilla" by Bruno Mars

Desperate. That was what it felt like. Pure desperation consumed him as he held them close, thrusting his tongue into their mouth. He ate their moans as they pushed his button-up off and tugged at his undershirt. He removed it quickly, returning his hold on their hair.

"Cy…" Bex whimpered against his lips, sliding their hand inside his pants to grasp his hard cock. "I need you, please." The last word came out as a whine.

It seemed the desperation went both ways.

Fuck. Fuck! He wanted to give them everything they wanted, but he made a promise. Reluctantly, he grasped their wrist to keep them from stroking him. He wanted to bite their pouting lower lip.

"And I need a shower." He pulled their hand out. "But the doctor can keep you warm for me."

He looked over at the Storm Wielder to find lust clear in her eyes. Her sweet-smelling arousal reached his nose, and he wondered how he hadn't noticed it before. Then again, he'd been wrapped up in Bex. It was hard to notice anything with the wolf around.

Bex looked at Aida and looked back at Cyrus. "I think she wanted your pretty pussy on her tongue, right?"

"Yes," Bex said with a nod.

"Then go to her. Let me watch while I shower," he commanded.

When Bex turned, he caught Aida's silver gaze. Her brow arched, suspicion clear. He only smirked, removing the rest of his clothes to follow behind the wolf.

"Go ahead, good doctor. Sit down and let them smother you with their juices."

Surprisingly, Aida did as she was told. Bex stood over them, feet on either side of her thighs. Cyrus closed in on them, sliding his hand down the wolf's heavily tattooed thigh to grip and lift.

"Give me your pussy, slut," Aida said huskily, catching on to Cyrus' direction. She took Bex's knee and draped it over her shoulder. She gripped the wolf's ass and pulled them closer. "So dripping wet. So filthy, wanting to be fucked by the both of us."

Bex was not kidding when they said Aida could give him a run for his money as a dom. He was hard as a rock as he stepped backward onto the shower ledge, turning it on. The hot water rained down on him while he grabbed his soap and washed up. Water flowed from the shower opposite the tub, keeping the grime from invading the pool. From his angle, he could see Aida's mouth on Bex's pussy. He watched as the Storm Wielder's tongue licked and lapped. With her free hand, she spread the wolf's lips to expose their swollen clit.

"Oh fuck!" they cried out when Aida latched onto it.

Their gaze connected with Cyrus', slowly moving down his body to find him stroking himself. Slowly, he pumped, the feel of his hand nothing compared to their lush lips and hot mouth. He kept his gaze on theirs as the water rained down his body, his abs flexing with each breath.

He swiped a thumb over the tip of his cock, biting his lip at the sensation. Their hazel eyes nearly rolled as they gripped Aida's tight coils. Bex's hips rocked into Aida's mouth, and with each one, Cyrus stroked himself.

"Hmm, looks like the slut is ready to come," he said as he walked into the tub to stand behind them again. His erection pressed against their lower back. He wrapped his arms around their waist. "Come, Bex."

Aida's eyes widened as she caught the smirk on his lips. Just as Bex hit their orgasm, he pulled them off the Storm Wielder, effectively ruining their high.

"Cy!" the wolf whined, tilting their head to look up at him.

Their face was flush, lips swollen from all the rough kissing they'd done. He quickly turned them, chest to chest, bringing them with him as he stepped back into the shower.

"Excuse me, what?" he asked with a raised brow, his erection jumping at their whimpers.

"My Lord ... Please, I'm sorry."

The shower plastered Bex's hair to their forehead, framing their hazel eyes. Their black eyeliner and mascara ran in rivulets down their cheeks.

"Prove it," he snapped, pointing to the floor. "I had a worse punishment in mind when I first came in here. You're lucky a ruined orgasm and cuckolding is all you're getting."

"That's kind of you," Aida said sarcastically.

She had moved to the tub's ledge, sitting on the bench, her small, muscular body half submerged. A sexy smirk played on her full lips, and fuck, he hated how much harder it made him. He kept his eyes on the Wielder while placing a hand on Bex's shoulder to push them to their knees. They let out a gasp that he took advantage of, thrusting his dick into their mouth. Their moan vibrated up his body, causing him to thicken and slide deeper into their throat.

"Come here, good doctor," he purred, smirking when her lips parted and her pulse sped up. Despite how her body responded, a glare was found in her eyes.

"Stop calling me that," she snapped while still doing what he asked.

"Hmm, what should I call you then? Whore?" He groaned when Bex's teeth glided along his length, hand between his legs to massage his balls. "Slut?" They tightened their grip, and he almost laughed despite the sharp pain. "Oh, I don't think our little wolf likes that idea." He snapped his mouth shut, gripping Bex's hair to make them stop.

"Our?" Aida cooed, dragging a finger from his lips to his neck and collarbone.

Fuck. He looked down at the wolf, their eyes glimmering with neon green. He pulled out of their mouth and made them stand. That damn fucking tug pulled at his chest. He was losing his mind. He was sure of it.

"Ours..." he whispered, shutting the shower off. He hated how vulnerable he felt—how he sounded. He cleared his throat and glared at Aida. "Only because they obviously care for you. Otherwise, you'd have been dead already."

The Wielder snorted with an eye roll.

"Sure. Okay." Her expression softened as she wrapped her

arms around Bex's waist from behind. "Now, I believe the sweet man over here was saying something about cuckolding?"

He bristled at the nickname, vowing he'd make her pay for it eventually.

"Actions have consequences, and I still have a point to prove," he growled, wrapping his fingers around Bex's throat. They whimpered when he pulled them from Aida's arms. He led them to the bathtub's edge and forced them to sit on the bench. "You don't get to play anymore."

"Cyrus! No..." they whined, pierced lip popping out in a pout.

"Are you being a brat?" he asked with a raised brow.

Aida angled her body toward Cyrus' side, gliding her nails along his abdomen. As she worked her hand lower, Bex's eyes zeroed in on the movement.

"I..." They crossed their arms and blew out a breath. "No."

"Don't worry. You're not being punished because of Aida. You're getting punished for disobeying me. *She* is getting punished for you and doesn't get to come."

"What?" Aida snapped.*

"You said you didn't want them punished for you. So, I'm punishing you instead. Have a problem?" His glare met hers, and he could sense how Bex practically buzzed.

The woman nodded and looked at Bex.

"Spread your legs. I want to see how wet your pretty pussy gets when you watch us fuck, knowing you can't participate," Aida ordered, taking hold of his erection. Her tiny hands barely wrapped around its girth, but she worked him with both.

Cyrus groaned as Bex did what was ordered and spread open.

"Put your hands on the ledge. You're not to touch yourself," Cyrus said, fisting Aida's coils. "Open," he snapped.

"Make me," she snapped back.

Using his free hand, he grabbed her chin until she couldn't help but pop her mouth open.

* "Please" by Omido, Ex Habit

"Tongue out. Don't make me rip it from you." As soon as she did, he thrust his fingers into her mouth, making her gag.

Her back arched, eyes fluttering as he did it once more. Despite the glare in her eyes, it was clear she loved it. Dragging her with him, he sat on a ledge across from Bex. Though he was seated, Aida was still too short to reach eye level. But it didn't matter; she still managed to look down her nose at him.

"Have I mentioned how much I hate you?" she growled, sliding to her knees on the bench in front of him when she felt him putting pressure on her head.

Her mouth stretched wide over the head of his cock. He heard her jaw pop softly as she worked her way down.

"You still plan to choke on my dick, so it doesn't matter," he said, thrusting deep and making her gag again.

"My Lord, please," Bex whimpered, fingers opening and closing.

Cyrus kept his gaze locked with theirs as Aida swallowed him down. He cupped the Wielder's throat, feeling his cock buried deep in it. He hissed, pulling Aida away sharply.

"Use your teeth again, and I'll personally rip those piercings out of your fucking nipples. Keep playing with me."

"But you're so fucking big. You can't expect me not to use them at least a little," she rasped with a maniacal grin. "What's wrong? Can't handle a bit of pain?"

"Bitch," he snorted, not being able to help himself. "Get back to work. Our slut is getting jealous."

She laughed, wrapping her lips around him once more.

"I knew you had a fuckable mouth, shit," he groaned, rolling his hips to thrust into her throat.

"I'm sorry," Bex breathed, chest rising and falling as their arousal increased.

"You should've listened to the good doctor," he said, gripping the woman's hair to keep her on his cock. "You should've waited."

When her body jerked, he let her go so she could pop off and take a large gulp of air. He didn't wait much longer, pulling her back down immediately.

"This could've been your mouth I was fucking."

Aida's sweet-smelling arousal blended with Bex's, making him swell. The Wielder moaned as she bobbed with each lift of his hips.

"I'll listen next time! I won't disobey again," they sniffed, hips rocking.

"Look at how wet the cum slut is," Cyrus said, letting Aida come up for air once more.

She licked her swollen lips, heat glossing her eyes. She turned around and stood in front of Cyrus.

"You're soaking. I bet you want a tongue on you, don't you?" she taunted as she brushed her back against his length.

Cyrus' large hands snatched her waist and picked her up like the doll she was. Aida planted her feet on the tops of his thighs, spreading her knees wide.

"Ohh, fuck," Bex whimpered, licking their lips. "Please, can I taste Mistress?"

With Cyrus' support, Aida slowly edged herself on the head of his cock. Her arousal dripped down his length, her core tight as he worked his way inside.

"No, watch only," Cyrus growled.

"Shit!" Aida moaned, her pussy stretching around him.

He knew she was sore from the fucking he gave her for the last two nights, and the thought made him surge his hips up, impaling her in one thrust.

"Ah!" she cried out, reaching behind to grab the back of his head.

He slipped his hands under her thighs and began lifting her up and down.

"So small. A doll for me to fuck," he rumbled, fucking into her hard. She bounced with harsh wet slaps, her pussy gushing.

"This dick of yours is the perfect fuck toy," she panted, tightening her core around him. "For me to use." Using her powerful abs, she leaned back and rotated her hips with each bounce.

"Fuck!" He grunted, swelling thicker.

If he didn't pace himself, he was going to come before he was ready. He *hated* how much of a good fuck Aida was.

"I hate how good your dick feels fucking my pussy," she eerily echoed his thoughts.

He held her thighs tight, slowing their frenzy to a torturously languid pace.

"Little wolf, you've been patient enough. Are you ready to please your Lord and Mistress?" he asked, looking at Bex from over Aida's head.

They nodded eagerly, rocking their hips in anticipation.

"What do you think, good doctor?" He almost laughed at her slight growl at the nickname.

"Crawl to us and feast, baby."

Bex dropped to their knees and made their way over. Aida's back arched, and Cyrus hissed in pleasure when he felt Bex's tongue lap at where Cyrus and Aida met. They sucked on his balls, licked up where he fucked Aida, and from what he could feel, ate Aida like they were dying of starvation.

"Keep going, slut. You're doing such a good job with that filthy mouth," Cyrus moaned, bending to place his lips against Aida's pulse.

"Cyrus," Aida panted, pussy squeezing around him. "Bite me right now."

There was no question. She simply demanded it of him, and if he weren't already lost to the arousal and increasing bloodlust, he'd have pulled her off him. Instead, he sank his fangs in, her blood hitting his tongue like rich spiced wine.

"Holy shit!"

Cyrus bucked into her, Bex's tongue and lips on both him and Aida, driving him closer to the edge. Rivulets of red flowed down Aida's body as he drank greedily. She gushed, legs quivering.

"Fuck!" Cyrus yelled as he pulled away from her near-addictive blood. He kept her knees apart as he buried himself deep and came.

"Deities damn it, vampire!" Aida growled as he lifted her, sliding out of her pussy. He could feel his cum leaking onto his dick.

"I told you. You don't get to come. Clean us up, cum slut."

"Yes, my Lord," Bex replied huskily.

Aida moaned as the wolf cleaned her first.

"Don't you dare make her come," he warned, earning another growl from the Wielder.

"How do we taste? You just love drinking his cum, don't you?" Aida asked, breathless.

"Yes, Mistress, I do." Bex let out a happy sound, sucking Cyrus down. They thoroughly cleaned his still-hard erection, bringing him closer to another orgasm.

"Our slut deserves a reward," he said, stopping Bex from continuing. He moved Aida off his lap, motioning to the floor. "On your back, bitch. Let them ride your face." He grinned at her glare.

"You're lucky this is for Bex," she snapped, lying flat nonetheless.

The wolf straddled her face, giving Cyrus a good view of their pussy rubbing along the doctor's lips. Aida sucked and prodded, causing Bex to twitch and moan.

"I need your dick down my throat, Cyrus. Please. I need your cum on my body."

"Because you asked so nicely," he started, sliding to the edge of the bench. He gripped their chin, their mouth opening on their own volition. "Eager, eager."

He spat, saliva dripping from his tongue to theirs.

"Choke on it." He fisted their hair and brought them onto his cock. They moaned, relaxing their mouth to slide him further down their throat. "Fuck, I love the way you suck my dick. Letting me face fuck you as long as I want."

Bex gave a garbled whimper, breathing heavily through their nose. He could hear their wet pussy on Aida's mouth. He pulled them back, allowing them to gasp and splutter. Tears and saliva poured from their face.

"Please, I'm going to come," Bex panted hoarsely.

"You have my permission to come." He brought them back to his cock and slid down their abused throat. He groaned, fucking their mouth thoroughly. "I'm going to come! Wear it like a filthy whore."

He pulled out and covered their face and chest in his hot cum. At the same time, their body shuddered, and they cried out, coming hard. Dragging their fingers through his seed, they sucked it clean off their digits.

"Thank you for your cum, my Lord."

Cyrus snatched them up, making them straddle his lap. He made sure not to penetrate them, moving into a position that avoided it. Growling, he kissed them greedily, hands sinking into their short hair to tug. They moaned into his mouth, tongue lashing against his.

"I'm sorry," Bex panted as their kiss broke.

"You're forgiven," he breathed, nipping at their lower lip, catching their piercing between his teeth. They sucked in a breath, whimpering when he pulled and let it go with a pop.

"And me?" Aida's voice drew his attention. He looked around Bex to find her sitting on the bathtub floor. The water had drained at some point.

"Not any time soon, that's for damn sure," he said as he possessively gripped Bex's ass to keep them close. Aida's silver eyes narrowed as she caught on to his movement. "If you seriously think I'll forgive you—"

"No, not that asshole," Aida scoffed. "I mean, what are we doing here? Am I safe to go home? Is Bex going with me? Or does it not matter anymore since I'm no longer an assignment for them?"

The last question ended bitterly, and if he didn't know better, he'd say she was hurt. Bex stiffened, gently tapping his shoulder so he could let them go. He didn't want to. He wanted to keep them in his lap and give them as much of his cum as he could all night. With a sigh, he let Bex slide off him to sit on the floor at his feet.

"You stopped being an assignment weeks ago, mamita," Bex murmured.

"Loathe as I am to admit, the little wolf was fascinated by you from night one," he said candidly, albeit unhappy in doing so.

Aida's silver eyes sparked with lightning as she scooted closer to Bex. Their lips met in a passionate kiss, and Cyrus had to fight back the impulse to separate them. If only to put one of their mouths to better use. Fuck, watching them make out was doing things.

When the two parted, he observed how they gazed at each other. It was the softest he'd ever seen the doctor. As Bex turned their attention to him, his heart stuttered. He stood abruptly, staring down at both of them.

"You're safe to go home. Bex can choose to go with you or not. That is their call." He turned to leave when the wolf's hand grabbed his.

"Thank you," they said as they stood, Aida doing the same. "I…" They bit their pouty lower lip as they seemed to think about something. They took Aida's hand and stood between him and her. "I understand that you hate each other," Bex said, startling a chuckle from him and the doctor. "Just thank you. I've never had anyone besides Killian go to bat for me."

"Always," Aida said gently.

"Forever," Cyrus said at the same time.

Bex beamed between them. Regardless of his feelings about the doctor, if tolerating her meant that Bex was happy, he'd do it. No questions asked.

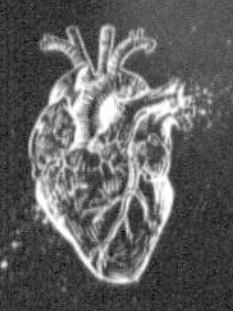

CHAPTER 19

DARKNESS IS OUR ALLY

CYRUS WAS LOST IN thought when he heard a grunt from the interrogation room next to his. One week. It had been one week since he and the doctor came to an accord. And it had been one week of dealing with her anger and frustrations.

"You said you could have a room turned into a surgical suite by now!" Aida yelled, her grunting continuing as she punched into something meaty. He groaned and went to see what she was up to.

"My, you sure are bitchy when you haven't murdered someone," Cyrus snarked, taking in the bloodied and bruised prisoner she'd been using as a punching bag. They hung from the ceiling, barely recognizable at this point.

"Shut up," she snarled, barely breathless from her exertion.

The light bounced off the divots of her muscular arms, her dark skin accentuating their shape as she threw a few more jabs. Sweat glistened on her abs, staining her grey sports bra with it. Low-hanging sweats exposed the band of her briefs. He had to give it to her; her rough and unhinged side was just as sexy as when she worked with a scalpel.

"We came to an agreement, and so far, you're not holding up your end."

Well, that wasn't exactly true. The surgical suite had been completed three nights ago, but he wanted to see what she would do. How long would she be able to hold off before caving? He shouldn't have been surprised that she was more patient than he thought.

"Come with me, good doctor."

"*Stop* calling me that!" she snapped, following him out of

the room.

He just shrugged, white suit whispering as he walked. Cyrus could almost feel her steaming as he guided her toward the last room in the corridor.

"What are we doing? Why—" Her complaint stuttered short when she looked at the suite he presented.

"Took longer than planned. Is this up to your standards?" he asked, watching as she entered and took everything in. It was fully equipped with everything a surgeon would need.

"This tech is experimental! How did you…" She shook her head. "Never mind." He could tell she was trying to hide her excitement. "This is good enough," she said calmly, though the brightness in her eyes gave her away.

Cyrus crossed his arms and leaned on the doorframe as she walked around the suite, occasionally touching the equipment.

"Perfect. Get cleaned up. I have someone for you." He fought a smirk at the way her eyes lit up further. "I keep my promises, good doctor."

"Stop—"

"You're wasting your breath," he chuckled.

"Whatever, *sweet man*." It was her turn to chuckle as he straightened and narrowed his eyes at her. "I must return to my apartment to get my kit and gear."

"Nope," Cyrus said, nodding toward a door at the back of the suite. "Everything you need is in there."

"No … Seriously?" she asked.

He wondered if she realized she had let the awe in her voice slip through. A gasp escaped her as she opened the door to a massive utility closet stocked full of scrubs, surgical tools, and everything else she needed to perform her work not already in the suite.

"I…" Aida sucked her bottom lip in, craning her neck to look up at him.

Cyrus didn't fight the urge to place his thumb on the pouting lip and pop it free.

"You're welcome." He glided his digit along the soft flesh

and nearly groaned when she sucked it in, letting her tongue glide around it. "You can show me how grateful you are later." He snorted when she nipped at his finger, letting it go. "Right now, I need to Interrogate a familiar who's been compelled to silence."

While Aida readied herself, Cyrus entered the interrogation room across the hall. He pulled a gurney with a passed-out Earth Wielder on it, the woman's dirty blonde hair a matted mess on her sweaty forehead. Rolling her to the entrance of the surgical suite, he placed his hand on the wall next to the door frame. The wall shifted into glass, allowing him to watch Aida work and communicate with her without interfering with her actual process.

"So, what do you need to know?" Aida asked as she pulled the gurney into the suite and snapped the door closed.

"She is a familiar of Rodon, the Kingpin—or at least one of his vampires' familiars. I want to know why they're inserting themselves into The Den when it's supposed to be neutral ground. The Guard has been investigating him and the limits he keeps pushing. We tolerate him because his hold on the lower district is strong. But it's escalated now that he is trying to petition for the position of Governor."

"You think he's trying to expand? Gain more favors?" she asked from behind her mask as she prepped the familiar, injecting a paralytic that Cyrus didn't know the name of. He only remembered how it felt, sending an unwelcome shiver down his spine.

"Yes and no. I think he's recruiting. And he's seeing how far his influence can reach—making himself more valuable. The Den is supposed to be neutral territory. I wouldn't have known he was making attempts if it hadn't been for … you and your methods."

"Ahhh, so that's why you spared me," she said, amused. Working in her element seemed to have brought her a sense of calm, her voice light and airy. It was a drastic contrast to her night-to-night. "Let's see if we can duplicate the process I took with you. The electroshock was a new trial. It seemed to work."

He could tell by the way her eyes glittered that she was smiling.

"Don't remind me," he mumbled, which made her snort. "Will it work differently because she's a Wielder?"

"Most likely," she responded. "Before I cut into her skull, I'm going to see if I can ask her a few questions. If she's unresponsive, then I'll dig in. She might not survive the questioning after that point. Humans and Wielders … are fragile."

"Understood. Proceed."

Over the next hour, through many screams and sobs, their interrogation proved useful.

"The twins!" she screamed, monitors blaring in response. Her body slumped as Aida stopped feeding electricity directly to her brain. It pulsed in front of the doctor, mild black striations starting to form.

"The twins? What about them?" Cyrus snarled, slamming a hand on the glass so hard a crack traveled up the center. Anger lit him up, bloodlust rising to the surface. His chest ached; the thought of anyone approaching the twins—near *Killian*—for anything made his world unravel.

The Earth Wielder's eyes were glassy, breathing erratic. "I … I can't s-say."

"No one likes lies," Aida said with a scoff, lighting up the woman's brain once more.

His vision deepened, his breathing erratic. Tremors wracked his hands as his beast pushed him to do something, *anything*, to keep Rodon away from fucking with what was his … His? Yeah, that felt right. Killian was *his*.

"Stop!" she wailed. "I'll tell you!" The familiar shuddered as Aida laid off. "He wants to recruit them. Bring their businesses under his control. And—"

Cyrus didn't stop his berserker from taking over as he barged into the suite, fury making his muscles swell and add to his already hulking form.

Mine. Mine. Mine.

The words played loudly on repeat in his mind, near deafening.

"Cyrus, don't!"

Aida's shout came a moment too late as he tore into the woman's throat, all common sense lost to the rage. Animalistic sounds escaped him as he fed, chewing and swallowing down chunks of flesh in the process.

No one would fuck with what was his.

NO. ONE.

Cyrus' body shook as his vision slowly returned to him. Sound shortly followed, and all he heard was his heaving pants.

No, Killian was not to be fucked with. Cyrus would make sure of that. If he had to tear into more familiars, he would without question. Hopefully, Rodon knew what was good for him and backed off when he found out who Killian belonged to.

Cyrus staggered to the edge of the room, nearly slipping on the blood-covered floor. Leaning against the wall, he dropped his head against the cool surface. Blood and gore covered the front of his white suit, and he grunted as he spat out a piece of meat. Wiping his mouth with the back of his hand, he grimaced. It'd been a while since he fed on flesh.

"That … That was insane," Aida said with wide eyes. Her scrubs were just as blood-soaked as his clothes. "I have never seen anything like that."

Cyrus shouldn't be surprised that she wasn't afraid. Like everything else, he was a fascinating specimen. He stepped up to the gurney, eyes locked with Aida's.

"I'm surprised you're still standing," he said, using his forefinger to push the familiar's head back and forth. "Or maybe the sickest part of me wanted to see you covered in my insanity."

He grinned, knowing how he must look. White suit, face a bloodied mess, teeth stained. Her pupils dilated, arousal wafting to him, and he had to fight the urge to palm his dick.

"Probably the second," she said, clearing her throat. "Clearly, the twins are a sore topic?"

"What makes you think that?" he asked dryly, pushing the familiar's head, watching it as it separated from the neck and plopped onto the floor with a wet thud.

"You chewed and ate a woman's throat and neck," Aida

said with a smirk. "You're a glorious type of monster." She gasped when Cyrus snatched her by the throat, pulling her close enough for his breath to be hot against her lips.

"You better think twice about calling me a monster. You have yet to glimpse its magnitude. Don't fucking test me." His voice was a low growl.

"Okay. Okay!" she squeaked, barely able to get a word out.

He let her go, not caring that she landed on her knees. She rubbed her throat as she narrowed her eyes at him.

"You didn't have to threaten me…" she said, looking upset.

He couldn't find it in him to care.

"Clean up. Do whatever you need here. I have to go."

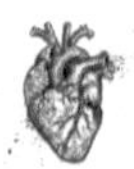

THE SMELL OF ESPRESSO and syrup accosted Cyrus as he entered The Crow's Cauldron. He had to speak to Killian. He hadn't seen him since his kidnapping. He knew how fucked up it was. But Cyrus found himself feeling … Nervous, was it? Worried? Regretful…

Guilty. That's what it was. He didn't know how Killian would react to what happened with Aida. Was he going to be pissed? Was Killian going to tell Cyrus to fuck off?

Avoidance was his best option … Until it wasn't. The familiar had rattled him. It made him realize just how fucking foolish he was being.

He thanked the barista for his espresso and for getting permission to head to the man's office.

"Hey, what're you doing here?" came Killian's smooth voice as he greeted him at the door.

Cyrus' lips turned into a frown as he looked around the office. What was usually a very neat space seemed tossed. The couch made it clear that he'd been sleeping there for some time. The human's tired eyes had bags under them, and Cyrus had a sinking feeling he might have something to do with it.

"Are you all right?" Cyrus asked as he stepped in and nudged the door closed with his foot.

Killian shrugged, mussing up his already messy hair even more.

"I don't know. Haven't seen you in a bit," he murmured. "You know … After I told you I was falling for you."

Oh, fuck.

"I didn't ghost you, I promise," Cyrus said, cautiously placing his hands on the man's hips. When Killian stepped away, his stomach sank to his feet. "Sit … I have a lot to tell you."

"No, it's okay. Things have been … A bit crazy around here. I have paperwork to catch up on," he said, scratching his forehead.

That was when Cyrus noticed fresh cut marks precariously close to his wrist.

"Killian, I was kidnapped," he blurted out when the man went to open the door.

He turned immediately, grabbing Cyrus' hands.

"What? Holy shit. You should've led with that! Are you okay?!" he exclaimed. Killian's grip tightened, the man's pulse racing under his fingertips. The fear that dripped from him triggered Cyrus' bloodlust, and he had to shake his head to clear it. He was not expecting Killian to react this way.

"I'm okay. I'm okay," Cyrus reassured him. He wanted to bring the human into a hug but decided it would be best to wait until he told him the rest of the story. "But we really do need to talk."

He motioned to the couch, and Killian nodded, sitting with him. "When I confronted Aida … Well, she injected me with a sedative that knocked me clean out…"

Killian's expression paled as Cyrus told him the rest of the story, not in detail, but enough for Killian to get the gist of what happened between him, Aida, and Bex.

"So … You just decided to … what? Fuck her? Like she wasn't a serial killer? Like she wasn't using both the coffee shop and the club as a hunting ground?" Killian's angry snarl was everything Cyrus expected. The man stood, walking to his desk to lean on, crossing his arms.

"Bloodlust," Cyrus admitted. "I've never told you about it. It makes me lose myself." He sighed. "But that's not an excuse. What I did was wrong…"

"I think 'wrong' is the understatement of the century, Cy." Killian's green eyes darkened. "You're telling me I wasn't enough to make you think twice?"

"That's not—" Cyrus barked as he stood abruptly. Killian flinched, dropping his arms to fiddle with his wrists. "No … You are more than enough. The problem was that I *wasn't* thinking. No thoughts came to mind until it was too late." He clenched his jaw. "It doesn't excuse what happened after I was kidnapped."

"No, it fucking doesn't. Are you going to stop?" Killian asked, a threat in his tone.

"I don't know," he said candidly. If Aida hadn't called him a monster earlier, he was sure he would've fucked her on the floor in a pool of blood and gore. "It is so much more complicated than that…"

"Of course…" Killian sucked his teeth. "I know that we aren't exclusive. But Aida? Of all the fucking people in Malagado, Aida? Why? She killed my workers, and despite how vile they were, that shit put my businesses at risk. She turned them into some sort of sick playing ground! Do you know how much danger she put me and my brother in? Fuck, Cyrus!" He gripped his hair tightly.

"She won't be doing that any longer. I have stipulations in place…" Cyrus knew any assurance he tried to give would be in vain, but he had to try anyway.

"Oh, and that just makes everything better," Killian scoffed. "Why am I surprised? Tell me … why her?" The decibel his voice had dropped to caused an ache in Cyrus' chest. "Why Cyrus?!"

"I'm fucked up!" he yelled when Killian opened his mouth to say more.

The man snapped his mouth shut, jaw clenching in anger. Cyrus ran a hand over his head, vision red as he paced.

"I. Am. Fucked. Up. I am not sane. I am not safe. I am

dangerous. I am violence personified." He shook his head, bloodlust threatening to crest as his emotions grew. "I saw myself in her. She saw the worst parts of me and didn't flinch. She saw herself in me, too. And I couldn't help myself. I hate myself for it, Killian. I hate it so fucking much." He took deep breaths, trying to gather his wits. "The deepest, most fucked up parts of me rose to the occasion, and I didn't deny it. I rarely do."

"Why do I find that hard to believe?" Killian scoffed. "You've never been like that around me. If this were true, why haven't you done it? Been dangerous and fucked up?" He shook his head, eyes red-rimmed and brimming with tears. "How can I believe you? So … make it make sense. Why—"

Cyrus was in front of Killian before he could finish his question. He cupped the man's face, gazing over it, taking in his parted lips and emerald eyes. He could hear Killian's heart racing, and one thing Cyrus never wanted wafted off him: fear. And not just any kind of fear. It was fear of *him*.

"Because, despite everything I just said, I never wanted you to feel unsafe around me," Cyrus responded. "When I told you..." he cleared his throat. "When I told you I fell for you the moment you gave me the time of night, I meant it. I … never want you to see that fucked up side of me."

The tears welled in Killian's eyes spilled over.

"Why? Why me?" he whispered, holding Cyrus' wrists gently as if to keep himself steady. "What makes me so special?"

A lump formed in Cyrus' throat.

"I … I don't know how to explain it," he said candidly. "I just know you are..."

"Cyrus, what am I supposed to do with that?" Killian whimpered, letting go of Cyrus to pace to the other side of the room. "I can't just guess at what you feel. I can't make assumptions. Assumptions are dangerous. I'm not just falling, Cy. I've fallen. I've hit the bottom. Knowing what you did … It feels like I'm being stabbed three times over." Killian rubbed his chest, tears still falling. He swiped them away angrily.

"Killian, I don't want to hurt you. That wasn't my intention."

Cyrus ached to hold him in his arms. A whole wave of guilt threatened to drown him. "I wish I could promise you I won't repeat my actions with her. But one thing I am not is a liar. I will not do that to you."

"Cyrus … if this isn't working, I need to know—"

"No! Killian, I want this to work so damn bad," Cyrus said, pleading with the man, finally taking strides to stand in front of him.

Killian looked up at him, eyes red. He hoped the man could see just how badly he wanted this—wanted *them*.

"I am no good with words. I don't know how to explain my feelings when I don't even know *what* I feel. When the only thing I can say with surety is that I want you. That I *feel* something for you. I just can't explain it. Maybe that's what it is. There are no words. None that can speak to the whirlwind in my heart."

"Cy," Killian breathed, gripping Cyrus' henley. Something shone in the man's eyes. Something that Cyrus wasn't sure he was ready to acknowledge further than what he already admitted.

"I wish I were a better man, Killian … But I'm selfish. I'm a selfish fucking person, and I don't know what I'd do without you."

"This isn't fair … You can't come here, throw me this bomb, and then clean it up with words you said you were no good with." His grip tightened, an apparent war in his eyes. "But I'm selfish too. Because despite it all, I want you. I want you through it all. And I'll take you however I can, so long as I have you."

"Can I kiss you?" he whispered, wrapping his arms around Killian.

"I don't know … Can you?" A small smirk lifted the man's mouth.

"Brat," Cyrus growled, slamming his lips against Killian's.*

Their teeth clinked as they hungrily kissed each other. Cyrus groaned as he thrust his tongue against Killian's, the man's piercing sending jolts of electric pleasure throughout his body. He let Killian push him toward the couch, their lips never parting as he sat and pulled the man to straddle his lap. Killian ground his round ass against Cyrus' growing erection, whimpering as he did so. The

* "Change (In the House of Flies)" by Deftones

man's erection pressed against his stomach.

"I missed you," Killian panted as their kiss broke. "I missed the feel of your lips on my body and the way your tongue feels against mine." He sucked on Cyrus' lower lip, then thrust his tongue back into his mouth. Cyrus groaned, gripping the man's ass. "Fuck, I missed your hands on my body," he whimpered, breathless. He reached in between them, rubbing Cyrus' erection. "I missed how hard you get for me."

Killian's eyes lit with emerald fire as he slid off Cyrus' lap to rest on his knees.

"I missed you too," Cyrus admitted. "I missed your thick body and the way it fills my hands," he groaned as Killian pulled him out, stroking him slowly. "I missed the sounds you make for me."

His hands sank into Killian's thick hair as the man took the head of his dick between his lips. "Oh fuck, I missed your hot mouth." he moaned, rolling his hips.

As the man's mouth slackened and he relaxed his throat, Cyrus slid in deeper. He raised his hips to pump into Killian's mouth. He could already feel himself getting to the edge, so he gripped Killian's hair to pull him off.

"If you keep up, I'm going to come down that throat of yours."

"Face fuck me, Daddy," he panted, tears of pleasure cascading down his cheeks. "And then you can take me back to my place to wash and fuck me in return."

"Since you asked so prettily," Cyrus growled, pushing the man back on his cock. Killian whimpered, throat stretching over his girth. "You're doing such a good job, Pet."

Cyrus lifted his hips, thoroughly fucking his man's mouth. He gently ran a hand through Killian's hair, the human's gaze meeting his own.

"You're mine, Killian." That look returned to his eyes, and his chest tightened, knowing he was on the cusp of feeling the same. "You're mine, and I don't plan on letting you go."

Killian's pace increased, matching each pump of Cyrus'

hips. He breathed heavily through his nose, using his hand to stroke where his mouth couldn't reach.

"Oh no, take it all, pet. I know you can do it." Cyrus held Killian's head down, the man expertly taking a deep breath through his nose, sucking him down, and sliding Cyrus as far as he could down his throat.

"Fuck yes," Cyrus groaned. "That's it. Make Daddy come."

Cyrus let Killian come up for air before the man sucked him back in without pause. The peak reached him quickly, and he roared as he came, pouring his arousal down the man's throat. He kept sucking until he pulled every drop out of Cyrus.

"Am I really yours?" Killian asked, a broad smile on his face, eyes glazed over.

Cyrus stuffed himself back into his pants, standing and bringing Killian up with him. He kissed him silly, tasting his lingering cum.

"Yes, and I intend to prove it to you all night."

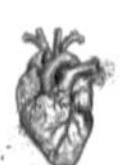

CYRUS AND KILLIAN BARELY made it through the door before he picked up his man to rush him to the shower. Within minutes, they were undressed, but as Cyrus guided Killian under the spray of the hot water, he slowed down. He leaned in and gave him sweet kisses, nipping and sucking, trailing down his chin to his throat. Cyrus ran his tongue over the man's pulse but pulled back abruptly when the bloodlust threatened to take control.

"Let me wash you," Cyrus said, groaning when Killian stroked his hard cock.*

The man pouted but nodded. Cyrus took his time, washing the shorter man's hair and moving down his body. As he stood, he met Killian's hazy gaze. He gave him more soft kisses on his chin, cheeks, lips, and forehead. He took Killian's hand into his own, pulling it up to kiss each scar on his wrist and forearm before

---

* "Yen" by Slipknot

moving to the other. A gasp escaped the man as Cyrus pulled him close.

"I am so glad you're here," he reminded him.

"Cy, I—" a kiss cut off Killian's words.

He wasn't ready for the rest of the sentence hanging in the air between them.

"Turn around," Cyrus commanded. Without hesitation, his man turned. "Hands on the wall."

Cyrus smirked when Killian followed his orders. His fingers found the man's ass, circling the ring of muscle.

"Oh damn," Killian whimpered, arching his back.

"Is this tight hole greedy for Daddy's dick?" Cyrus found a bottle of water-resistant lube on the shower rack and smirked. He poured some on his fingers, pushing one in and then two.

"Yes, so greedy," Killian moaned.

Cyrus scissored his fingers, making room for a third, slowly stretching his man. He pumped in and out.

"That's it, Pet," Cyrus cooed as Killian backed into him, fucking himself on his fingers. "I think you can take more."

"What?" His exclamation turned into a cry when Cyrus added a fourth digit. He splashed more lube on his fingers before slowly working in the last, his hand fully seated in the man's ass. He continued slowly pumping. "Oh … Oh shit. Please … Please!"

"What do you need, Killian?" Cyrus whispered as he leaned in and kissed the man's shoulder, gradually fucking him with his fist. His hard erection rested on the mound of Killian's ass as a tease. He slicked it with lube, stroking it with his free hand.

"I need your dick in me," he panted, body slumping when Cyrus gently removed his hand.

He quickly replaced it with the head of his thick erection. Cyrus moaned, pushing himself into Killian's well-stretched hole.

"You need me, Killian?" he growled, thrusting deep and holding Killian's hips. "I want you to warm this dick for me first." He sat on the nearby shower bench, firmly planted inside Killian.

"No, please," he whimpered, trying to rock his hips.

"You're mine, Killian. Do you know what that means?" Cyrus

asked, reaching around to stroke the man's cock.

"N-no," he panted, erection jumping in Cyrus' hand.

"It means this hole is mine," he said as he slowly moved his hips. "It means this dick is mine." He stroked Killian faster. With his free hand, he cupped Killian's throat, tightening just enough to make his man whimper. "It means your orgasm is mine," he growled as he thrust up hard.

Killian moaned, rocking against Cyrus as he made the man bounce in his lap.

"F-fuck," he cried out when Cyrus loosened his grip on his throat. He began fucking his man in earnest, stroking him with each thrust.

"Are you mine, Killian?" he whispered seductively against the man's temple.

"Y-yes, Cyrus. I'm yours," he moaned, ass clenching tight. "Are you mine?"

Cyrus' heart stuttered at the question. Using his hand around his throat, Cyrus tilted Killian's chin to look at him.

"Always," he said, passionately kissing him. He bounced Killian on his cock; each thrust making Killian fuck his fist. "Come for Daddy, Killian."

His man tensed, body locking as he came with a shout.

"That's it. Such a good boy." Cyrus lifted him to push against the wall. He snapped his hips, fucking Killian deeper. "Take my cum in your greedy hole." A few more thrusts had him coming so hard he saw spots.

"A-ah damn," Killian panted, legs shaking.

Cyrus pulled out with a soft moan, smirking as his seed dripped out of the man's ass. He turned him around and cupped the back of his head.

"You get one hour," Cyrus smirked, noticing how Killian's still-hard cock jumped.

"One hour?" Killian asked with a raised brow.

"One hour to get properly prepared to have your back blown out. Don't plan on walking tomorrow."

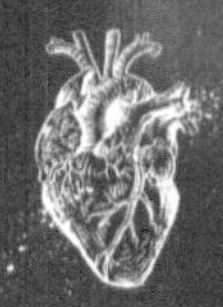

CHAPTER 20

SHARING IS CARING

TRISTAN NUDGED CYRUS AS they walked through the upper level of The Den. Cyrus needed blood, and he needed to get his shit under control.

Backlash from the Angel crashing in Asherai was causing havoc on the Dark Continent. Every time he settled one issue, another cropped up. He had hoped worrying about Rodon would be the most of his worries, that the shit in Asherai would've stayed there. Naturally, that wasn't the case.

Cyrus rolled his eyes as he looked at the Ice Wielder, who was wearing a navy and black flannel button-up shirt and comfortable black jeans.

"What is it, Aries?" Cyrus asked as they found a couch to sit on.

Tristan sank into the cushion, spreading his knees wide as he pushed his sleeves to his elbows. The Ice Wielder plucked at Cyrus' henley.

"Y'know, we've been to the bar downstairs a few times … But seeing you dress casually is still weird. Crimson is for sure your color," Tristan said with a chuckle. "But I don't think I've ever seen you in jeans."

"First time for everything," Cyrus chuckled, shrugging. "Have you been up here in the Exhibition Hall before?"

"A few times, yeah." Tristan licked his lower lip as his eyes traveled to the many people dancing or fucking. "So, tell me about the doctor," he said while focusing on a femme vampire tied up and suspended from the ceiling.

"Fuck, I need to find someone to do that with," he muttered

more to himself, though Cyrus heard him regardless.

"Aries, are you a rope bunny?" Cyrus chuckled at Tristan's snort.

He turned cobalt eyes to him.

"No, boss. Trust me, if ropes are involved, *they* are the ones being tied up. And they'll be happy for it, like a good little bunny." The Ice Wielder winked as he turned his gaze back on the vampire. He adjusted himself in his seat as he asked, "Well?"

"She's insane. Like clinical. She might just be up there with you and me." Cyrus took the wrist of a server, pulling her into his lap. He pushed her hair over her shoulder, and she shuddered at his touch. "She's a great hate fuck, I'll give you that. Try as she might to deny it, she loves being called a 'good girl' while being manhandled."

He leaned in to run his tongue over the pulse throbbing in her neck. "Can I feed from you?"

"Yes, sir," she whimpered, craning her head more.

He groaned as he sank his fangs deep, his dick hardening under the server's round ass.

"I'm not even into blood, and that shit looks hot as fuck," Tristan said with a smirk, his blue eyes now meeting Cyrus once more.

A familiar doctor in a lavender dress caught his attention, and he pulled away from the server. He licked the puncture marks, thanked the woman, and sent her on her way.

"Well, speak of the murderess, and she appears." He laughed at Aida's scowl as she looked around to ensure no one heard him.

"What are you doing here?" she hissed, crossing her arms, which pushed her small breasts up.

Cyrus would be lying if he said he didn't find her tight, athletic, little body fine as fuck. The minidress hugged her, the halter top showcasing her muscular arms and back. He let his gaze burn a fire down her body as he lifted his wrist, the neon purple symbol of an exclusive member lighting on his wrist. It also indicated he was down for anything.

"While exclusive, it's still a public place."

Cyrus leaned back, widening his knees, not hiding his obvious reaction to her. Why fight it? She took notice, her breath quickening ever so slightly as she dragged her eyes down his body to land on his erection.

"You might not remember, but the first time I ran into you was in this very place. But you were a bit drunk and with *Jay*."

She snapped her silver eyes back up to his face with another scowl.

"Whatever. Just don't fuck up my night."

"You're not supposed to be here, Aida. We spoke about this," he said, watching her body tighten at his words. "I told you what would happen if you came in here."

"Oh please, you can't kill me, and you know it." She gave him another perusal that ended with a roll of her eyes.

"Killing you and hurting you are two different things. I might not be able to do the first, but I can do the second. And you'd love every moment of it," he growled. He saw the way his words affected her. Aida's pupils dilated, the scent of arousal wafting toward him. It made him want to fuck her senseless.

When she started to walk away, Cyrus asked, "Afraid, good doctor?"

"Afraid of what?" she snarled.

"Of how wet that pretty pussy gets when I'm around," he grinned.

"Oh, so *this* is the insane doctor you've told me about." Tristan whistled, getting Aida's attention.

Her pupils dilated as she took in the Ice Wielder, like a predator who found some prey. Tristan's eyes flared a neon blue in a show of dominance that had Aida narrowing hers.

"Try me, sweetheart."

"Fuck you, Cyrus," Aida growled as she stepped in front of him, her small body nearly between his knees. "How many times have you fucked your fist since that Interrogation room? Or the shower with Bex?"

"Oh whaaat?" Tristan gasped, bringing his hand up to his

mouth. "This stunner right here is the one you fucked…"

It didn't go unnoticed that Aida puffed a little at the praise.

"I told you about this…" Cyrus groaned.

"That's beside the point. I'm saying that you ain't say she was stunning." Tristan let his lust-filled perusal of Aida drag from her stilettos to her short coils. "I'm Tristan, by the way."

"Aida," she said, voice clipped.

"Oh, I know your name already, sweets." Tristan grinned when Cyrus groaned.

"My, have I left such a lasting impression that you talk about me?" Aida's gasp feigned shock. "Didn't take you for the pussy whipped type. But then again, Bex…"

"Shut that shit down right now," Cyrus growled, snatching her wrist before she could turn and try to walk away again. He sat up, drawing Aida in close. "Say what you want, good doctor, but don't act like Bex doesn't have you wrapped around their finger, too."

"I'm trying to figure out if I should leave or…" Tristan hummed.

"Stay."

Both Cyrus and Aida said in unison, glaring at each other.

"I wonder what you would do if I fucked you right here, right now, like a dirty whore?" Cyrus rumbled as he glided his hands up her muscular thighs, pushing her dress up as he did.

"Normally, I'd probably drug you again," she said with a dark smile. "But I'm too horny to care. You're just as much a whore as I am."

"You are *definitely* as insane as we are," Tristan said huskily.

"Oh yeah? What's the worst you've ever done?" she asked as she moved to sit between him and Cyrus.

She was engulfed by the both of them. Putting one ankle on Cyrus' lap, Aida leaned into Tristan, who draped his arm over her shoulder. His fingers glided along her décolletage.

"Hmm, it's a toss-up between scooping someone's eyes out and forcing them to eat them…" His voice dropped an octave, hand cupping her throat, "And blowing up a Monarch."

Cyrus watched as his grip tightened, and Aida moaned.

"You've killed a Monarch?" she gasped as Cyrus slid his hand up the leg she placed over his lap, spreading her wide.

"Not just one," Cyrus murmured.

Aida's eyes widened, turning them to Cyrus.

"Do you like to share?" she asked, her question turning into a moan when his fingers found her soaking thong.

"What's there to share? You?" Cyrus chuckled at her narrowed expression. "Sharing implies that I care. I don't."

"Cyrus, you're an asshole," Tristan chuckled.

"Fine. Forget it," she groused, getting ready to sit up.

Tristan pulled his hand away immediately while Cyrus gripped her leg to keep her still.

"Do you *want* to be shared is the question," he said intelligently.

Her lids lowered, catching on to what he was implying. It wasn't his decision to share her.

"Yes. I want to be shared. With you in my pussy," she pointed to Cyrus. "And you down my throat," she said, looking up at Tristan.

"First, let's get something straight," the Ice Wielder said as he gently wrapped his hand around her throat again. "I don't do the degradation. What you do with him ain't gonna be what you do with me. He can say it all he wants, but you won't get it from me." His grip tightened. "Now, I heard you like being a good girl, so that's what you're gonna be. Are we clear, sweets?"

Aida arched a brow, and Cyrus watched her battle her desire to dominate. She turned slowly to kneel between them on the couch, her back to Cyrus.

"We're clear," she said with a nod, respecting the Ice Wielder's boundaries.

"Limits?" Tristan asked, his fingers gliding along her bare shoulders.

"Bondage is okay so long as it doesn't cut circulation. Hard pain is fine and desired, but in absolutely no way are my hands to be harmed. I'm partial to degradation but don't mind praise from the right person."

Tristan's face lit up, a devious smirk pulling up his lips.

"*I'm* the right person," he said as he kissed her shoulder and neck. "Just behave for me, and you'll get all the praise."

"Oh, I can tell," she moaned, peeling the front of her dress down.

"Oh shit, you didn't tell me she was pierced," Tristan groaned as he cupped her breasts. Aida's back arched as the Ice Wielder played with her nipples. "Safeword, sweetheart," Tristan breathed against her skin.

Cyrus licked his lips, watching their exchange.

"Bananas," she said with a snort.

"Bananas?" Cyrus chuckled, dragging his teeth along the opposite shoulder.

"The words 'no' and 'stop' mean something different in my kink vocabulary," she said candidly, moaning when he bit her gently enough to smart but not enough to break the skin. *

"I knew you liked to be manhandled," Cyrus whispered in her ear as his hand found her center and snapped the thong clean off. "You like to fight." He pushed a finger in her soaking pussy. "You want it taken from you. To be forced and tamed. Treated like a filthy ragdoll to be used and tossed away." He tasted the salt of her skin as he ran his tongue along her pulse. "I can give you that if you ask."

"Fuck!" she moaned, rocking her hips as her pussy gushed on his hand.

"Already so wet. Ready to have your holes fucked," Cyrus growled, adding a second finger.

"Ever come so hard you went blind?" Tristan rumbled, sliding his hand down her front to meet Cyrus' at her pussy. While Cyrus pumped inside her, Tristan rubbed her clit.

"O-once," she whimpered.

"Tell the truth, shame the Deities," Cyrus said sharply as he drove a third finger in her, thoroughly fucking her cunt. He could feel Tristan increasing his pace on Aida's clit, matching Cyrus'.

* "on your knees" by Ex Habit

"C'mon now, sweets. Don't make me take this prize away from you. You've been doing such a good job." The Ice Wielder's words made Aida clench tight around his fingers.

"Three times!" she cried out.

"We'll beat that record tonight." Tristan grinned over her shoulder at Cyrus. The man couldn't help himself. He got off on getting others off. "Think you can do that for us? Come so hard you'll be bow-legged for nights?" The men continued to work her pussy.

"You won't even have to ask permission to come," Cyrus chuckled. "We'll use you until you're a mess, filled with cum."

"Sound good?" Tristan reiterated.

"Yes!" she cried out, her body shuddering as she came.

As if they shared a mind, they continued working Aida until she came again.

"That's two," Tristan chuckled, sliding his fingers from her to push into her mouth. He groaned when she sucked them clean. "Look at you, already off to a good start. But I wouldn't say those were the blind ones yet."

"What?" she panted when he pulled his fingers out. "That wasn't?"

She caught her breath, placing her hands on Tristan's shoulders. Tristan's body went rigid, and he took her wrists to slide them down to his lap instead.

"Put your hands behind your back, murderess," Cyrus commanded as he pulled his belt off. She looked at him from over her shoulder.

"Fuck you," she snapped with a grin.

She gasped when he grabbed her hands from Tristan's body and pulled them to the small of her back. While she struggled, he wrapped the belt around her wrists in a figure eight, making sure not to make them too tight to mess with the blood flow to her highly valuable hands.

"I think that filthy mouth needs to be filled," Cyrus growled. Aida arched her back as he reached in front of her to pinch her pierced nipples. "Mind giving me your belt, Aries?"

Tristan's lips tilted into a grin as he followed Cyrus' train of thought. He complied, removing it from his jeans and handing it over.

"Come here, sweets," Tristan said as Cyrus pushed her toward him to raise her ass in the air. He caught her to keep her from falling completely over. "You look so pretty. Bet you'll look even prettier sucking my dick."

"Yes, I would," Aida purred.

While Cyrus took hold of her ankles, he heard a zipper and shuffling. He wrapped Aida's ankles so she was bound. In this position, she was under his complete control.

"Show me your hand signal," Cyrus asked, knowing he surprised her by how her body stiffened briefly. She wriggled her fingers, and he slapped her ass in acknowledgment.

"Oh fuck, you're pierced too?" Aida gasped until her sounds were muffled by Tristan's dick now gagging her.

Cyrus kneeled behind her, admiring how she looked all bound.

"Might be the closest you get to having your own rope bunny, Aries," he chuckled as he undid his jeans to pull his aching cock out.

"Fuck, you work that sexy mouth so good," Tristan groaned, gripping Aida's coils as he encouraged her to continue bobbing. He leaned to look at how Cyrus had bound Aida and grinned. "Damn, boss. Making my dreams come true."

The Wielder's cobalt eyes were heavy-lidded as he licked his lower lip. "Nah, I'll find one. Just you wait."

"I've got one more idea."

Cyrus reached for the rolling cart containing sanitized compartments for various toys and accessories. He perused the contents, pulling out what he was looking for. He showed it to Tristan, who smirked and temporarily lifted Aida from him. She gasped, panting as her body trembled, still leaning forward.

"If you behave, you'll be filled. Are you going to behave for us?" Tristan purred, one hand firmly in her hair and the other on her small breast. When she nodded, Tristan sucked his teeth. "Use your words, sweetheart. Need to hear you say it."

"Yes," she breathed, gasping when Cyrus covered her asshole in lube.

"Yes, what?"

"Yes, I'll behave for you," she chuckled. "For him, I'll be a bitch."

"I wouldn't expect anything less," Cyrus snorted, slapping her ass aggressively. She yelped, wriggling for more. "You're so needy. Desperate to be filled up and used."

He played with her hole, pushing his finger in slowly. Her hips rocked as he added a second. "I'm going to plug this ass while I fuck your greedy pussy," he growled, a third finger joining the others.

"Why not the both of you?" she asked, her hands turning into fists as he continued to fuck her tight hole.

Tristan lifted the hand on her breast to show a teal, glowing symbol on his wrist.

"Only head for the night. Giving and getting. Free use." Tristan leaned his head onto the back of the couch to get Cyrus' attention. "Maybe after she's full of your cum, I'll clean it with my tongue."

"Yes, please?" Aida whimpered, and Cyrus watched as her arousal dripped down her thighs.

Sliding his fingers out from her, he replaced it with the tip of the lube-covered anal plug.

"So filthy, wanting a man to clean you of another man's cum."

"You made Bex do it," she snapped, Tristan's hand loosening enough in her hair for her to look over her shoulder at Cyrus.

His jaw clenched, and he pushed the plug in with the flared base settling in place. He placed his knees on either side of hers, bringing them close to tighten her center. The belt around her ankles prevented her from spreading her legs.

"I know Aries made you a promise, but I'm tempted to keep you from coming after that. Just turn you into a cum filled whore who gets nothing in return." If she wasn't as good of a fuck as she was … or important to Bex … He would've just left her there, wanting and waiting to be used.

His gaze connected with Tristan, who pursed his lips in thought. He sat up, turning Aida to look at him again.

"Didn't we agree that you'd behave for me?" Tristan asked. "If he doesn't let you come, then I don't either. That wouldn't be very nice, would it?"

Looking over her shoulder, Tristan stroked his still very hard cock, keeping Aida's gaze on it.

"No," she whimpered.

Cyrus coated his erection with her arousal, edging her opening. Wriggling her ass, she attempted to rock back into him, but he held her hips firm.

"Then say it again. Tell me you'll behave and ask Cyrus to let you come."

"I'll behave," she moaned when Cyrus pushed another inch inside her, allowing her pussy to accommodate his size. She looked over her shoulder once more. A look of anger in her gaze made him grin as she said, "Please, Cyrus. Let me come."

"Go do something better with that dirty mouth, bitch." Cyrus pushed her head back toward Tristan, who leaned his onto the back of the couch once more.

"That's it, sweets. Let's gag you." Hand in her dark coils, he pulled her back to his dick, groaning as she took him deep. As Tristan bucked up into her mouth, Cyrus thrust into her willing and ready pussy.

"If Bex didn't care about you so much, you'd already be dead," Cyrus growled as he fucked into her, making her tiny body jerk and rock between him and Tristan.

More of her arousal gushed down her legs at his words; her moans lost to the garbling around Tristan. The man gripped her hair, controlling every way she used her mouth.

Aida slowly raised her middle fingers, flipping Cyrus off.

"Fuck you," he couldn't help the laugh that escaped him. Tristan turned heavy-lidded blue eyes to Cyrus.

"She flipped you off, didn't she?" Using both of his hands,

he held her head still. "Fuck, right there. Use that tongue just like that, sweets."

"It's all right. Needy bitches get fucked, so that's what she's going to get," Cyrus said, using his grip on her waist to pull her into him with each snap of his hips. The plug in her ass hit his pelvis with each thrust. She breathed heavily through her nose, body tensing, pussy clenching.

"Ready to be blinded?" Tristan panted, rocking his hips. "Damn, sweets. Your throat takes my dick so well. Eyes on me. Let me see you blow apart."

Her trembling body told Cyrus she was close.

"Come for us, murderess, and take every ounce of our cum."

Aida's garbled moans vibrated down her body as he pounded into her clenching pussy. She shuddered, coming hard enough to bow her back while still keeping her mouth on Tristan.

"Fuck, I'm coming." Tristan thrust up a few more times and came with a loud moan. Cyrus grabbed a fist full of Aida's hair, pulling her from Tristan. "You look so pretty with my cum dripping down your chin," Tristan said with a grin.

"Come again, Aida."

With each rise of his hips, he made her bounce on his cock. His fangs glided along her neck as he hunched slightly, still fucking her while able to drag his tongue over the sensitive spot he'd bitten previously.

"Bite me," she moaned.

He didn't need to be told twice. He sank his fangs in, the rush of her spiced blood filling his mouth. It made him swell thicker, stretching Aida wider.

"I forgot how big you are," she whimpered, trying to rock her hips in time with his. "I'm going to come!"

Once more, she tightened around his cock, and this time when she came, he went with her.

"Well, that was hot," Tristan said, now sitting on the floor with his head back on the couch seat.

"Yes, it was," Aida panted.

Cyrus drew his fangs from her, licking the wounds. She shuddered as Cyrus pulled out of her slowly.

"Bring her here," Tristan said with a slow lick of his lips.

"You weren't kidding?" Aida squeaked as Cyrus lifted her to place her knees on either side of Tristan's head, her bound ankles resting in front of his throat.

"Fuck no, sweets," the Ice Wielder chuckled, grabbing her hips and pulling her to his mouth.

The woman's abs flexed as she balanced and rocked her pussy along Tristan's mouth. Cyrus stood, hard cock in front of her.

"Clean me," he growled. When she took him in her mouth without a fight, he nearly came again. She looked up at him with watery eyes, tears streaming down her cheeks as he fucked her mouth deep. "Look at you. You're a cum slut, too, and you know it. You look better bound and gagged."

Her gaze narrowed, and she grunted when his grip tightened on her hair. Those silver eyes flared as her body tensed, Tristan obviously eating that pussy like a man starved.

"Drink it. I know you're thirsty, and once wasn't enough," he moaned as he came. He watched her throat work as she drank his cum. He pulled out right as she was finishing, causing some of it to pour out and dribble down her chin and onto her chest. "Tell me you don't like the feeling of my cum on your body."

He knelt, eyeing the way her thighs tried to tighten around Tristan's face, but the man's firm hold kept her from doing so.

"I—"

Before she could finish the sentence, he ran his hand up her cum covered chest to snatch her throat.

"Don't lie. Or I'll tell Aries to stop."

The man groaned against her pussy, clearly not liking the idea.

"Fine!" she panted, trying again to rock against Tristan's mouth. "I do."

"You do, what?" Cyrus grinned.

A growl emanated from Tristan, drawing Cyrus' attention to find a Shadow Wielder settled between Tristan's knees, his dick buried in her mouth.

"I like wearing your cum," Aida admitted.

While there was a look of hatred and anger in her eyes, something else was there. An understanding. They might not like each other very much, but they had one hell of a sexual connection, that was for sure.

"Was that so hard?" Cyrus purred, petting her gently, clearly surprising her.

"No, but I am," Tristan huffed as he picked up Aida for a moment. "Are you done talking? Because I'd really like for her to come in my mouth." He winked at Cyrus, "Yours is pretty good, by the way."

"Is everyone a cum slut here?" Cyrus laughed, bringing out a chuckle from Aida as well.

"No! Whoa. Wait. *I* am a cum connoisseur. Yes, it's different. No, don't ask me why. Just consider me well experienced." With that, Tristan pulled Aida back to his mouth, being the *connoisseur* he said he was.

"Oh, fuck!" Aida moaned, almost losing her balance.

Cyrus caught her, keeping her upright while she came. She panted as Cyrus helped her off Tristan.

"Be careful, lean forward, and rest your head on the top of the couch."

"I'm a doctor. I know what to do," she chuckled, doing what he said anyway.

He didn't fight his smirk as he helped undo the binds at her wrists and ankles. Slowly, he pulled out the butt plug, making Aida sag. She groaned and turned to sit on the couch, a look of contentment on her face. He'd never seen the expression on her before. Clearly, she needed a good fucking to get out of her head.

It sounded a lot like himself.

"How do you feel?" Cyrus found himself asking as he fixed himself and pulled his jeans up.

Usually, Tristan would be the type to ask, but he was currently on the floor with another woman riding his face. The man had moved on and was no longer focused on Cyrus and Aida.

"Do you mean that, or are you just trying to be nice?" she asked, shutting down her face.

He knelt before her and gently took her hand, slowly massaging her wrist. As he rubbed the sore skin, she let out a soft gasp.

"I mean it, Aida," he said as he moved to massage her other wrist.

She winced but sighed.

"Yeah, I'm fine. Not so bad, I've done worse." He quirked a brow at her smirk.

"I'll ask you another time. Don't think I'll forget." Cyrus smirked back, undoing her strappy stilettos and placing them to the side.

She gasped, biting her lip as he massaged her ankle, slowly moving up her calf.

"Will there be another time? You've threatened to kill me quite a few times now." She squeaked out a laugh when he pressed on her inner knee to massage a knot.

Was she … Was she ticklish? He kept that in mind as he massaged her other ankle, taking his time up her calf.

"I hate you. That much is true. But unless you give me a true reason, I won't. As we already agreed … For Bex's sake." Cyrus again applied pressure on her inner knee, snorting when she laughed again.

"Stop!" she squealed, kicking him with her tiny feet.

He caught them, placing them on either side of his waist and pulling her toward him.

"Truce?" he asked, kneading her hips now. "Officially. Between us two, without putting a show on for Bex."

She let out a slow exhale, melting into his touch, pierced nipples pebbling further. Sitting up, she scooted closer, wrapping her legs around him and her arms around his neck.

"Fine. For Bex. Yes." She bit her lip when his thumb found her pussy, casually gliding along her slit but not pushing further. From what he could feel, it was swollen from his attention. "Can I ask you a question?"

"A fresh truce and already asking?" Cyrus snorted, grinning when she moaned as his thumb parted her to rub circles on her clit.

"Did you mean what you said?" she whimpered, his thumb pushing inside her swollen pussy.

"About what?" he asked as he slid the digit from her to suck on.

"Deities damn it," she breathed, eyelids dropping halfway. "Earlier, you said you could give me what I want. I haven't met anyone who could give it to me the way I desire…"

"Are you asking me if I wouldn't mind forcing you to your knees so I can fuck your ass while you cry for me to stop?" he growled, hand covering her throat.

She moaned, nodding.

"Yes."

"You want me to take you in an alley? Hmm? Or drug you? Fuck you while you're unconscious, so you wake up with my cum dripping from your pussy?"

"Yes." Her eyes fluttered closed but snapped open when he let go of her neck.

"Wear a symbol. Let me know when you want to play … and we'll play. Send me a voice comm of your preferences and your signal…"

"All right." Her grin was the most authentic smile he'd ever seen from her.

He stood suddenly, keeping her legs wrapped around his waist.

"What are you doing?" she gasped as he walked away from the booth, leaving Tristan to his antics.

"Taking you to the baths."

"The baths?" she asked, wariness in her tone.

Despite that, she plopped her temple on his chest. She was so light, like a doll. Yes, she was fit and muscular but fierce and small compared to him. Her personality and drive more than made up for it.

"I hate you a little less tonight, good doctor. That means I will bathe and make sure you get home safely. Is that all right?"

Aida gripped his shirt as she seemed to want to bury herself in him.

"That'll be nice ... Thank you."

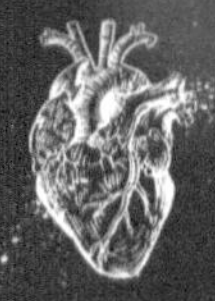

CHAPTER 21

IS IT WARM IN HERE?

CYRUS STARED AT THE holographic atlas that hovered above his comm watch, a long sigh leaving his lips. A Demon had revealed himself in Silvermoon, and he'd yet to tell the King. An ache formed in Cyrus' temple.

He'd been buried in … Everything. The chaos of Asherai and the risk it brought to Malagado, and now a Demon? Oh, he couldn't forget the Asherite foreign contingency making their way to Potroya.

The need to feed had gotten worse. It was almost daily, though he held off. He had to. Too much was happening, and his lack of feeding affected his temperament. His berserker was near the surface.

Lost in thought, Cyrus almost breezed past Tristan's apartment. He clicked off the atlas, using the hand sensor to alert Tristan that he was there.

"Uh. One second!" came the Ice Wielder's voice.

The man sounded strained, and Cyrus' eyebrow quirked. There was a bang and the sound of stumbling before the door wrenched open. Tristan's face was flushed, his heavily tattooed torso on display while a pair of sweats hung lazily on his hips. His hair and body were soaking wet, and it seemed the Wielder had just jumped out of a bath. Cyrus grinned at the man's disheveled appearance and the purple hickeys littering his neck.

"Am I interrupting something?" he asked, not holding back the teasing in his voice.

Tristan leaned against the doorframe, pushing his door open further. In the middle of the living room was a large aquatic tank, three mermaids giggling inside. Triplets? Fish nets hung around the tank. Cyrus noticed one of them was bound.

"Found yourself a rope bunny, eh?"

"Uh, more like a rope fish?" Tristan shrugged with a grin. "What's up, boss?"

"I'm here for the dossier you assembled for the Asherite team making their way here."

"Right, two seconds," Tristan said, disappearing into his apartment.

Cyrus raised a brow at the triplets, who giggled once more, two waving at him. He winked in response, and they giggled louder.

"All right, boss," the Ice Wielder said, popping back in front of him. "Here's what we got." He passed Cyrus a comm.

He pulled up the team members, looking through each of them.

"Thank you. This is great. I'll bring this to Jacinto." Cyrus continued swiping until Tristan snapped his fingers.

"Oh! Wait, this guy," Tristan pointed to the team's Captain. "He looks familiar."

"Really?" Cyrus asked sarcastically. Tristan narrowed his eyes, not pleased. "You did all this research and didn't bother to check the family history?"

"I only pulled what was relevant, Cyrus. That's how it is. Family history isn't relevant." Tristan pursed his lips, pushing his wet hair from his forehead when realization dawned on his face.

"Oh, there it is…" Cyrus smirked. "He looks familiar because we fucked his little sister."

"Wellll, fuck." Tristan blew out a breath. "You didn't tell me Sweets was related to the Captain of Alpha Phoenix…"

"Didn't think it mattered," Cyrus said, shrugging. "Would it have stopped you?"

"Eh, not really," Tristan said, mimicking Cyrus' shrug.

"Daddy, are you going to keep us waiting?" one of the mermaids whined from inside.

"Daddy? You too?" Cyrus smirked.

Tristan put a forefinger to his lips. "A man never tells."

"Tristan … you are an over-sharer."

The two of them barked out a laugh.

"I'm wrapping up things here," Tristan said with a smirk, amused with his pun as the bound mermaid behind him whimpered. "But I will be heading to Faysos. The King has given me an assignment which may pull me away for at least a month."

Cyrus admitted to himself that he was bummed about it. Over the last few months, his friendship with Tristan had grown. Even if the man could be insufferable, Cyrus enjoyed his companionship.

"Well … All right. I don't need to tell you to be safe. Just be diligent. The shit from Asherai is leaking all over Potroya."

"I know. I'll do regular check-ins when I can. But I'll likely be off-grid." Just as Cyrus readied to turn away, Tristan asked, "You ever consider settling down?"

"What?" Cyrus snorted, completely caught off guard by the question.

"You know … Finding a partner, or partners, and taking it easy?"

"Do I look like the type to settle down?" Cyrus asked blandly.

"Well, no … I guess not," Tristan laughed. "I guess the better question is … Do you ever see yourself falling in love?"

"Where is this line of questioning coming from?" Cyrus asked, feeling defensive.

"Eh, I don't know. I don't see it for myself. With my lifestyle, I doubt I'll ever settle down or find someone I can love." The man had a far-off look, his aura unlike his usual chipper self. "I had it once, but it didn't end well. He hated me for who I was."

"You're being awfully sentimental," Cyrus said, stating the obvious.

Sighing, Tristan shook his head and ran a hand through his dark blonde hair.

"Maybe all this chaos going on in Asherai is getting to me. Getting out of town will do me some good, I think." He held out his hand to Cyrus, who gripped it in a shake. Tristan grinned, and the man pulled him into a bear hug without warning. "I'll see you, boss. Be back before you know it!"

"All right. All right!" Cyrus laughed, peeling the Ice Wielder off him. "Maybe by the time you get back, I'll have an answer to your question."

"That's my boy," Tristan said with a knowing smile.

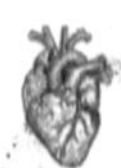

THE FOLLOWING WEEK, CYRUS found himself in his home office. He'd been posted up in there more often than not, finding it easier to handle all his needs in one location. Sure, he'd go to his office if it was official business. Lately, he'd been more secluded than ever. If the King hadn't forced him to feed the last time he saw him, he wasn't sure where his head would've been or how much blood he would've shed.

Cyrus sighed as he looked over the satellite feed of the Temisraine, specifically the red yacht that housed the Demon from Silvermoon. He was arriving sooner than they planned. He didn't know how he got across the Temisraine so quickly.

Jacinto had been communicating with King Rizor, the Ice King, to build up their trade. The King of Gailux sent a shipment of their latest high-tech handguns and mission visors, while Jacinto sent vaccines and other medical instruments. Cyrus had seen war enough to know what they were gearing up for.

The sound of his penthouse lift dinging made him groan.

"He's early," he grumbled.

As he stepped out of his office, the scent of spiced apples wafted to him, instantly making his heart pound in his throat. Standing in front of the lift doors was Bex. He wasn't sure how to handle how quickly his mood lifted.

"Expecting someone else?" they mused with a grin.

Bex looked him up and down, raising an eyebrow. "I don't think I've ever seen you in sweats." They wet their lower lip, hooking a finger in their red and black collar, drawing his attention to it. "Especially grey ones."

"Spin for me," he said, voice mildly hoarse.

Bex held their hands out as they did what he commanded. Chunky ankle boots lengthened their fishnet-covered legs, adding to their already tall frame. The fishnet crawled up their torso and down their arms, with a crimson crop top underneath. Fuck, a body suit. "Bend. Let me see that ass in those tight little shorts."

"Yes, my Lord," they said breathless, their submissiveness quickly kicking in.

As they bent over to grab their ankles, he walked up to them and grabbed their hips. He ground his aching erection against their backside.

"Hmm, perfect," he growled.

"Like what you see?" they breathed, looking over their shoulder to stare at him.

"Get on your knees, slut," he demanded.

Bex complied instantly, sitting back on their heels with their hands in their lap. Cyrus leaned down to cup their cheek.

"Look at you. So sexy at my feet, little wolf." His thumb glided along their lower lip, and they sucked it in, tongue rolling around the flesh. "Eager, aren't we?"

"Yes," they said when he removed the digit from their mouth.

His brow furrowed when he noticed their dilated pupils and the light gleam of sweat covering their forehead.

"You're high," he stated plainly, dropping his hand.

Bex's throat bobbed as they nodded.

"Yes..." They sniffed on impulse.

"Is that why you're here?" Cyrus shook his head, taking a step away. He had to resist the urge to rub his chest.

"No! No, I promise," they said with wide eyes. The panic was evident as they shook their head. "I had already planned on coming here before..."

"Your hit."

Cyrus wished he could say he didn't understand why he was upset, but he knew why. It was plain as Ithea, and he'd been avoiding it like he tried to avoid feeding, thinking he'd be all right.

"Are you upset?" they asked, remaining on their knees.

"No," he lied smoothly. "You can stand. I have a meeting in a few." Bex frowned as they stood, and he hated it. Did they notice his lie? "Isn't tonight the full moon?" he asked, trying to distract himself from his thoughts.

"Yes … But I wanted to see you before my run," they said softly, eyes still pleading with him.

He didn't like seeing them distraught, so he reached for them and pulled them close. "Does the little wolf want to stick around?" he asked, sliding his hand up the column of their throat to wrap his fingers around.

Bex's eyes fluttered, hazel eyes flaring neon green briefly.

"Please?" they begged, resting their hands on his waist.

How could he say no?

Using his grip around their throat, he brought them into a brutal kiss, his frustration channeling into it. He dominated their mouth, pushing it open with his tongue and thrusting it in. Bex whimpered, grabbing his shirt as he latched his teeth on their lip ring and tugged. He did it harder than usual, and their arousal wafted up to him. A growl escaped him when Bex bit his lower lip, sucking on it. How badly did he want to fuck their mouth right now?

"I have an idea," he panted when their kiss broke. The wolf smirked as they rubbed his hard-on. "Damnit," he groaned, rolling his hips into the movement. "Come with me."

"I'd love to," they said with a wink.

"Killian is rubbing off on you," Cyrus chuckled, leading them to his office. He grabbed a pillow from the nearby couch, rounding his oak desk.

"Nah, he got all his jokes from me," Bex said as they looked around his space. "Why am I surprised you have a whole ass office in your home?"

Cyrus snorted, sitting in his massive chair. He glanced at one of his open holoports, the screen showing a shipment confirmation for art supplies. He quickly shut it off, returning his attention to his wolf.

"I'm the Cortesano. Gotta be available whenever I'm needed." He clicked his tongue when they attempted to sit in the chair across from his desk. "No, you're not sitting there." Bex's eyebrow rose slowly as they looked at him curiously. "Here, at my feet, under the desk." The space was more than large enough for their lithe body. He placed the pillow on the floor for them.

"Oh," they whispered, falling to their knees and crawling to him. They settled in, sighing a grateful breath for the pillow. They looked up at him, eyes glinting with a neon glow. Bex licked their lips when he pulled out his aching erection.

"You're going to keep my dick warm with that filthy mouth while I have my meeting. I think it'll be a challenge considering who I'm meeting." He petted their thick, wavy hair, gripping it tightly. "You are not to suck, lick, or bob your head. You are not to clean your saliva or wipe your teary eyes. I want your mascara running, your face covered. I want you messy. Because that's what you are. My messy little cum slut."

"Yes, my Lord," they whimpered.

"Open up," he growled, spitting in their mouth as soon as they did. They moaned, leaving their tongue out. "No sounds. You are a toy. Something for me to use." He bounced the head of his cock on their tongue. "Go ahead. I will tell you when to stop."

The smile on their face lured a matching one to his lips, blunting some of his dominant edge. He pulled them forward, thrusting into their mouth. They sucked him in instantly, relaxing their throat so he could slide down it. He allowed them to bob several times, gripping their hair tighter when they moaned in pleasure.

"Okay, stop," he bit out. He smirked at their sounds of disappointment. "You tap my knee if you need me to pull out," he said, looking down at them. Their mascara had already started to run, and if he didn't have as much control as he did, he would've come from the sight alone.

His penthouse lift dinged as if right on cue, and Jacinto was at his door within seconds. The smirk on his face told Cyrus the King knew exactly what was going on under his desk. The thing was huge, going entirely to the floor in front. There was no way to see under it. But scents didn't lie, and Cyrus didn't fight the urge to smirk back.

"Well, sorry I'm late," Jacinto said as he sat across from Cyrus. Cyrus shifted slightly, his cock pushing into Bex's mouth further. Like a good little slut, they didn't break the rules.

"Eh, it's all right. I had some other things to focus on," he said with a shrug. "So, the plans for the masquerade ball are coming together." He grunted in annoyance. "I passed the job off to Ericka because what the fuck do I look like planning events?"

"I figured you would. What did you need from me?"

"Two things. First, Rodon is testing his limits further. He has familiars at The Den, and his runners are trying to expand. Are we going to do anything about him?" Cyrus asked, choosing to withhold the information about Killian.

"I understand the issues with his attempted expansion. But you have to admit the man is also very strategic and smart. You can't do all jobs. Being Cortesano and interim vampire Governor has been running you ragged. I have considered a proposition for him … Pull the runners back, become Governor."

"What!" Cyrus snapped. "No. Absolutely not. He should not be rewarded for trying to overstep his boundaries."

"Oye, he isn't being rewarded. By becoming Governor, we get a hold on his business and can cut his allowances in half if he steps out of line. He'd been on my choice list for months. I will not entertain any further conversation about this. What else do you have to speak with me about?"

"I think I have a new method for Interrogations." Cyrus pulled up records on his holoscreen to show Jacinto. "With everything that's been going on, I haven't reported about the Carnicero Cerebral." An image of a brain popped up, with black striations throughout.

"Sí, I remember. I assumed you caught them because I haven't heard of any new victims. Pero, was I wrong?" Jacinto leaned back, relaxing in his chair. "Mira, I always loved these," he said as he patted the arms and closed his eyes with a sigh.

Cyrus took a good look at the vampire. He was obviously tired, though he'd never admit to it. As Jacinto stretched, his white tee pulled tight on his muscular body. Cyrus' dick twitched in Bex's mouth. If the wolf hadn't been in the office, Cyrus would have had half a mind of giving his King a good fucking. It was clear he needed it.

"I caught her, but I didn't arrest her," Cyrus said, smirking when Jacinto's eyes popped open.

"Her?" he asked as he ran his hand through his hair. "Dime. Tell me more."

"Well, first, I can say she's a complete menace and on her way here." Cyrus huffed, reaching down to grip the wolf's hair when they involuntarily swallowed at the mention of the doctor. He licked his lips slowly, placing his hand back on the desk. Jacinto's eyebrow rose as his near-crimson stare raked over him.

Damn, did he want to bend his Sire over this very desk…

Maybe having the wolf keep your dick warm was a bad idea, Cyrus. He internally cursed at himself. It was as much a torture for himself as it was for them.

"She's a neurosurgeon and psychiatrist," Cyrus began, hoping the facts could put his focus where it needed to be. He explained everything he knew of Aida and his experiences with her, including the kidnapping and subsequent hate sex.

"She fucking kidnapped you, and you didn't say anything?" Jacinto snarled.

"Relax, I'm okay. Clearly. I had it handled." Cyrus shook his head, shifting once more and spreading his knees wider. Bex settled further, hot saliva dripping down his cock. A soft groan escaped him before he could stop it.

"You all right over there?" Jacinto asked with a heated stare.

"Yep," Cyrus said after clearing his throat.

"You're a terrible liar, hermano," his Sire snorted. "Do you share?"

Cyrus contemplated whether he wanted to but was interrupted when the penthouse lift dinged.

"All right, what the fuck did you need me for?" came the doctor's voice.

After a few moments, Aida walked in, wearing tight, navy, washed-out jeans and a soft, pink, off-the-shoulder sweater. Fuck, it made her rich dark brown skin look warm and lickable. Her eyes widened slightly when she took in his appearance. She opened her mouth to speak when she turned to look up at the King who stood when she entered. He towered over her, making her look like a child in comparison.

"Oh…"

"So, this is the Carnicero?" Jacinto purred, holding his hand and palm up so Aida could place her delicate small one in it.

He brought it to his lips, lightly brushing it across her skin. The Wielder's breath hitched, and Cyrus had to bite back a chuckle. Jacinto had that effect on people.

"Maybe?" she asked as she turned her eyes onto Cyrus, a glare now piercing through them. "Am I being arrested?"

"No. I've just been informing the King what we've been up to. The experiments. It was time you both met." Cyrus fought the cocky smirk that wanted to tilt his mouth up at Aida's exasperation. He watched her reel it in as she looked up to Jacinto.

"I'm Doctor Aida Broderick," she said, voice firm despite the slightly wide-eyed look. "It's a pleasure to meet you, your Eminence."

Jacinto's grip on her hand tightened.

"No, por favor, call me Jacinto," he said, voice rumbling.

Aida might be a brat and a Domme in her own right, but Cyrus was enjoying watching her squirm underneath the King's gaze. A pulse of arousal traveled through him as he watched Jacinto nuzzle his nose along Aida's wrist to inhale her scent. The man's tongue darted out, licking the veins slowly.

"O-okay," the doctor breathed. Cyrus was sure the King could turn this woman into a pure puddle if she let him.

"You attend The Den, sí?" He kissed the delicate skin, and Cyrus could see that goosebumps had risen along her flesh.

Her arousal was potent, driving his own. His cock was aching at this point. Subtly, Cyrus brought one of his hands down to run over Bex's hair, petting them gently. He was more than ready for this meeting to be over with so that he could finally fuck Bex's mouth properly.

"I do," Aida said, chest rising and falling as she kept her silver eyes on Jacinto's near-red ones.

His Sire smirked, letting her hand go slowly.

"Perhaps I'll see you there." That smirk never left his lips as he sat down, motioning for Aida to do the same in the free chair. "First, let's talk about how you murdered in my streets and kidnapped my Cortesano."

Aida's expression paled, much to Cyrus' satisfaction.

"Well…"

"I already explained everything. Don't have an aneurysm, good doctor." Cyrus chuckled.

"STOP—" Aida cut off her sharp tone and cleared her throat. "Stop calling me that."

"Oye, mira. What you can do is very dangerous. Not every time is successful, but the fact that you can even do it puts a target on your back if anyone finds out," Jacinto said, sobering the mood.

Cyrus continued to pet Bex, realizing it was as soothing for him as it probably was for them.

"I'm aware. It wasn't my plan to get caught," she said, glaring at Cyrus.

"Sí, pero, you did. No going back. Cyrus has already explained that you both came to an agreement."

"More like blackmail," she snarked, straightening in her seat and looking at the King. "I'm sorry." Cyrus was surprised at the apology. Well damn.

"No, you're fine," Jacinto chuckled. "He told me you had a temper. You can speak freely."

"Are you sure?" she asked. Clearly, there was something she had to say.

Aida caught her lower lip between her teeth, a movement his Sire noticed. If he didn't get these two out of his damn office, they were going end up fucking on his couch or some shit.

"Speak. Freely." Jacinto practically purred. "What does that pretty mouth have to say?"

"Ah..." she nearly squeaked.

Fuck, this was fun.

"Your progeny is an asshole," she snapped, pointing at Cyrus.

A startled laugh escaped him, making his hips buck once. The action pushed him further into Bex's mouth.

"That is not news," Jacinto said with mirth.

"I'm not surprised," Aida grumbled.

"She's neglecting to tell you how much she enjoys being manhandled by me." Cyrus grinned at Aida's surprised expression. "She's a good girl when she wants to be."

The doctor shot to her feet, slamming her hands on his desk.

"I am *not* a good girl, sweet man." She smirked when she noticed how he bristled at the nickname. "You enjoy the mindfuck just the same. Or was your dick hard while you were strapped down for nothing?"

"Fuck you," Cyrus bit out.

"Oh, I don't know. Maybe later," she said smugly.

If he didn't have Bex at his feet, he would've snatched this woman up and fucked her right then.

What in the Orcus?

There was too much pent-up sexual energy in the room, and he needed them out.

"Anyway, now that you've met, you can remain at your position at Malagado University Medical Center or come on board as the Palacio surgeon." Cyrus had mused this over, wondering if it was a good idea.

"I will need time to think about this. It's a big step," Aida said, though she couldn't keep the awe and respect out of her tone.

"Another thing you should know," Cyrus started, looking at Jacinto for confirmation. With a nod, Cyrus continued, "Your brother is arriving in Malagado within the next week or two."

"What!" Aida yelped.

"*But* you cannot reach out to him," Jacinto stated, stopping her when she went for her comms. "He is here on a diplomatic mission. We are being courteous in letting you know."

"Understood," she sighed but nodded.

"Great, good, perfect," Cyrus said with a wave. "Now that that's all settled, we can go about the rest of our evenings."

Jacinto smirked, stood, and extended his hand to Aida. She slipped hers in his, and he kissed her knuckles again before releasing her.

"Walk with me? I have questions about your experiments."

"Sure," she said, eyes lit with excitement. That excitement quickly drained when she looked at Cyrus. Of course. "Tomorrow. I need another by tomorrow."

"You'll get one when I say you can," Cyrus snapped, his hand now gripping Bex's hair as he made them slowly move up and down his cock. They didn't suck like he asked.

"Cyrus—"

"Another time, children," Jacinto chuckled. "Now, doctor, show me what you've worked on."

Cyrus shot Jacinto a grateful look as his Sire met his gaze over Aida's head. She had turned away from Cyrus. *'You owe me,'* Jacinto mouthed, turning his attention to Aida and walking her out of the office. Once the penthouse lift dinged and the telltale sign of its descent sounded, Cyrus pushed away from his desk.*

"Fucking finally," he said with a groan, looking down at his little wolf with his cock still stuffed in their mouth. He sank his other hand into their hair, pushing them down further. "Suck. Put your slutty mouth to use."

Without hesitation, Bex swallowed and allowed him to slide down their throat. Soft whimpers escaped them, their face a mess of saliva and wet mascara streaming down their cheeks.

"Fuck," he growled, standing up suddenly.

Bex took hold of the waistband of his sweats and tugged

---

* "EAT SPIT! (feat Royal & the Serpent) – By Slush Puppy, Royal & the Serpent

them down to his ankles. Kicking them off, he groaned as he gripped them tighter. Their nails dug into his ass as he fucked their mouth thoroughly.

"You did a good job keeping my dick warm." He thrust hard, rushing toward the edge of his orgasm. "Such a good fuck toy."

Holding their hair tight, he held their head still so he could rock his hips a few more times, pulling out to let them gasp for air. He didn't have to ask; they kept their mouth open, tongue out. Saliva poured down their chin, wetting their chest.

"Eager, eager," he growled as he came on their face. His vision temporarily went black from the force of his orgasm.

"Thank you for your cum," Bex croaked, swiping some off their chin to suck on. They licked a slow circle around their swollen lips, licking more of his cum from their mouth.

Watching them at his feet, he was sure there were no lengths that he would not go to keep them in his life. He didn't care how messy Bex was because he was just as filthy. He held his hands out for them to clasp and helped the wolf stand. Their legs shook from being bent for the entirety of his meeting.

"You're a beautiful mess, did you know that?" he asked softly, smearing his cum and their mascara when he cupped their face with his hands. "My beautiful mess."

Their still-blown eyes widened, and their lips parted as their breathing increased. He slammed his mouth on theirs, devouring them in a hungry kiss. Bex moaned, gripping his shirt as their tongues met in a clash. He bit their lip ring, tugging it like he knew Bex liked. Their tiny whine confirmed it. As they parted, their sloppy kiss left a bridge of saliva from his tongue to theirs. Bex left their mouth open, and he happily obliged by spitting in it.

"Can I call you mine?" they asked, seemingly unsure of his reaction.

For someone as sexy, wild, and carefree, Bex looked almost shy and innocent. It was a juxtaposition to the cum and saliva coating their face. Cyrus smiled, walking them backward to his desk while taking off his shirt. They gasped when he pulled at their fishnet body suit and tore it down the middle.

"I've been yours for longer than you think, little wolf," he said as he peeled off their tight shorts, allowing him to continue ripping the bodysuit. Freeing Bex of the damn fishnet, he pushed their crop top off.

"I was yours the moment we met." He palmed the back of their thighs and lifted them to place on the desk. They were bare except for their collar and chunky boots. "I was yours when you looked up at me with those hazel eyes and thanked me for my cum." He latched onto their throat, sucking and nipping his way down. "You've always been more than just a toy."

"Cyrus," Bex panted, back arching when he bit their tight nipple.

His tongue lashed at it, and he drew it further into his mouth. They rocked their hips, soft calves running up and down the outsides of his bare thighs.

"You have me on my knees, Bex," Cyrus breathed as he hit the floor before them. He gripped their hips and brought them to the edge of the desk. Their eyes glowed as they looked down at him, their lower lip caught between their teeth. "And I want to see all of you."*

"All of me?" they whimpered.

"Yes. I want you to show me your wolf, Bex. When I make you come, blow apart for me," he growled, pushing one of their legs up to rest their foot on the desk. The action bared their glistening core to him, and he groaned. "Such a perfect pussy," he said, giving it a long, languid lick. "*Mine.*"

He gripped their free thigh with one hand, placing their knee over his shoulder. With the other, he parted their slick center, exposing their swollen clit.

"Yours," Bex moaned as he ran his tongue over the sensitive bundle of nerves.

He worked in circles, occasionally tugging at their hood piercing. They leaned back onto their hands, back arching as he ate them like they were his favorite dessert. Cyrus licked, sucked,

* "I'm The Sinner" by Jared Benjamin

and prodded, pulling out sounds he never wanted to forget.

"Fuck … Please!" they cried out.

"Is the filthy little wolf ready to come?" he asked in between each swipe of his tongue. Without pushing in, he ran his thumb along their opening, collecting their arousal.

"Yes, yes, please," Bex panted, hips rocking faster as they ground their pussy along his lips.

"Come for me, Bex. Shatter for me."

As soon as the words left him, his wolf cried out in orgasm. Their scream turned into a howl as their wolf erupted through their body. Skin sloughed off to reveal wet fur. Hot, clear fluid covered Cyrus as they emerged in their tall werewolf form. Fur the color of steel was streaked with navy, covering most of their body. Their torso was the same warm, dark tan as their complexion. As they stood before him, their brown nipples perked in the cool air. They were just as lithe in their werewolf form.

Bex shuddered, ridding the rest of the fluid and drying their fur as they focused on Cyrus. Their neon green eyes glowed as they tackled him down to the floor, growling in his face. His fangs descended on instinct as he returned their growl. Bex straddled his waist, their hot pussy just above his pelvis, their soft furred thighs rubbing along his naked body.

"Hey, Cyrus," Bex said through a mouth full of fangs, four on top and four on the bottom.

His eyes nearly rolled at the tenor of their voice and how it had a growl behind it. Clawed hands rested on either side of his head as they dragged their short snout up Cyrus' face.

"You smell so good." They nipped his chin, warm breath sending goosebumps down his body.

"Fuck, you're stunning," he breathed, slowly running his hand through their hair and down the side of their face. The fur was so soft under his palm, softer than he expected.

Bex's eyes closed as they leaned into the movement, a soft growl vibrating their chest. His fingers cascaded over their furrowed brow, down the length of their short snout, and landed on their lips. Gripping their chin, he pulled them into an aggressive kiss. He trusted Bex not to bite him. Their teeth clinked together briefly, their rough tongue rubbing along his. He drew in their lower lip, dragging his fangs along it gently. When they returned the favor, he groaned.

"Shit," Bex panted as they broke the kiss. They licked his cheek without prompting, and the sensation wasn't unpleasant.

"Look at you, cleaning me up like a good little wolf," he breathed as they continued, moving to his neck. He ran his hands down their body, landing on their ass.

"Cyrus," they whimpered when he slapped it. They pulled back to look at him, and he raised an eyebrow.

"I didn't say stop. Clean the mess you made, slut."

"Yes, my Lord."

Their neon eyes glowed as they dipped their head, lapping at the fluid on his chest. He hissed when they dragged their tongue across one nipple and then the other. His cock stood at attention, throbbing as they continued their ministrations.

"Fuck," he groaned.

Bex's claws made soft clacking sounds as they moved down his body, their wet pussy gliding over his erection. Their tongue dragged along his abs, licking up the fluid with a moan. He gripped their hair, pushing them down further.

"You know where to put that tongue."

A whimper vibrated from Bex as they licked his cock from root to tip. Cyrus' hips bucked when they wrapped their tongue around the head. Slowly, they brought him inside their mouth, tongue working up and down. He was dizzy with pleasure as it wracked his body.

"You keep those teeth away from my dick, or we're going to have a problem," Cyrus growled, both playing but not.

Bex dipped their head in acknowledgment as they carefully worked his cock. He'd never received head from a shifted werewolf before. But damn, he knew this was not going to be the last. Moans escaped him as their tongue tightened just enough to give him the perfect amount of pressure. Their saliva coated him, making it easier for him to lift his hips and fuck into their mouth.

"Fuck. I did *not* know your tongue could do that." He threw his head back, the sensations making his world spin. "Do you want me to come on your fur or your skin?"

Bex chuckled, unwrapping their tongue from around his dick. He met their gaze to find their eyes twinkling as they moved away. They rested on their hands and knees and wriggled their ass.

"However you want to, my Lord," they said, voice husky with need.

Cyrus smirked, getting to his knees and positioning himself behind them. Their tail brushed against his chest, playing across his nipples. He groaned, sliding his hand between their legs, and found their soaking pussy. They let out a whimper when he ran circles on their swollen clit.

"Filthy little wolf. Pussy dripping all over the place."

Removing his hand, he replaced it with the head of his cock. He rubbed it against their bundle of nerves, bringing more whimpers from Bex. Placing his knees on either side of Bex's furred legs, he brought them close together, clamping their soaking pussy around his dick without him penetrating them.

"Head down," he commanded.

Instantly, Bex complied, resting on the side of their face to look at him from over their shoulders.

"Cyrus, please," they begged, attempting to move.

"Tsk, patience, cum slut. You'll get it when I say you can," he growled, gripping their hips tight. Slowly, he slid his cock through their wet slit, the head rubbing against their swollen clit. "So eager for my cum, aren't you?"

"Yes," they moaned, pussy gushing.

"Yes, what?" he said as he squeezed their legs tighter with his knees.

"Yes, my Lord. I'm eager for your cum. I need it!" Bex cried out when he leaned over and cupped their breasts.

He tightly pinched their nipples, loving the whines that left their lips. He felt himself getting close to the edge, equally eager to see them covered in his seed.

"I'm going to come on this greedy pussy," he growled, pushing away from their slick to stroke his cock. "How badly do you want it, little wolf?"

"My Lord, please. I'm your dirty cum slut. I want it so badly," they whimpered.

"Spread your knees, grip your ass, and bare that wet pussy to me," he said as he increased his pace.

As soon as they did what he demanded, he came so hard he partially blacked out. His cum shot out, covering their pussy and furred ass. Body shuddering, he took satisfaction at watching his cum drip down their thighs. Bex reached behind them to scoop up some and popped their fingers into their mouth to suck clean.

"Thank you for your cum."

"On your back," he said, suddenly urgent.

Their eyes widened as they did what he demanded, a questioning look on their lupine face. He kissed them roughly but not long enough for it to deepen. He slid his hands down their soft body, admiring their fur as he nestled between their legs, throwing one of them over his shoulder. Without preamble, he dove into their pussy, loving the growl that vibrated through Bex.

"Oh! Oh fuck!" they cried out as he worked them to orgasm in no time.

Using the flat of his tongue, he lapped and swallowed their cum as it to gushed over his chin. He sat back, looking at them. Their hazy but now sober eyes stared back at him. Cyrus grinned as he swiped their cum from his chin with his thumb. Slowly, he dragged his tongue up the digit, popping it into his mouth. Their neon eyes flared, a soft moan escaping them.

"Thank you for your cum."

"Cy…" Bex gasped. That was when he sank his fangs deep into their thigh. "Ah!" they yelped.

He thumbed their clit while he drank their rich blood, bringing them to orgasm once more. He pulled away, licking the soft puncture wounds to staunch it. Blood dribbled down his chin, but he didn't wipe it away.

"Yours," he said softly, releasing their knee from his shoulder.

He lifted them from the floor, and they instantly wrapped their long legs around his waist. He kissed them deeply and passionately, not caring how sticky they both were. As they parted, his and Bex's lips continued to graze along each other. Bex found his shoulder. Their sharp teeth brushed against the flesh of his deltoid, rough tongue licking his skin.

"I'm yours. Do it."

A growl vibrated from their chest to his, and he shuddered when he felt their teeth sharpen further. Quickly, they struck, embedding their fangs into his flesh. His eyes rolled, his grip on their ass tightening. The heat of their body felt like being next to a furnace, burning him in the best ways. He knew their bite would leave a permanent mark on his shoulder, and he didn't care.

Let everyone know who he belonged to. Who his heart belonged to.

With a gasp, they pulled back to look at him with perfect clarity in their gaze. Seeing his blood on their mouth and chin had him near feral with need.

Bex licked their lips, whispering, "Mine."

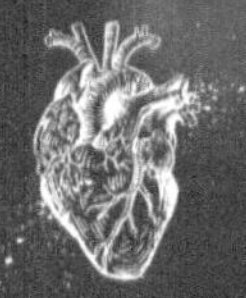

CHAPTER 22

TAKEN

"**T**HIS BRAIN IS DIFFERENT,** Cyrus," Lynn said as she shared with him the findings of the new victim.

After Cyrus learned who the Carnicero Cerebral was, he let loose to the media that the serial killer had been found and killed while evading capture. Looking at the body on the table before them, Cyrus wondered if they had a copycat. He and Aida had an agreement, and if she killed another one of her experiments without his permission, he was going to rip her throat out.

"There's a new body?" came the doctor's voice as she entered the exam room.

Her brows were furrowed, barely sparing him or Lynn a glance. She quickly washed her hands and forearms, putting on gloves. She inspected the victim's head, palpating where the skull was cut.

"Lynn, what exactly makes these different?" Cyrus asked as he rounded the table to hover over Aida. "Good doctor, did you do something?" he whispered, noticing the goosebumps lifting the hair on her arms.

"No! This wasn't me," she responded softly. "Look at the lacerations. I'd never be this sloppy."

As she pointed to the markings, her charm bracelet caught his attention. A broken heart dangled daintily in the center. It was her symbol, the signal they'd agreed she would wear when she wanted to play. He stepped closer, gently pressing his hips into hers.

"Stop it." She snapped, though her back arched slightly.

"Where's the fun in that, doctor?" he cooed, keeping his eyes on a distracted Lynn, who was fumbling through her notes.

"Fuck you." She moved away, glaring briefly at him, and focused on the brain again. "This brain has more than the black striations. The grey matter is completely destroyed, and the victim's pallor suggests they'd been bled out slowly."

"Ah! Here it is," Lynn said brightly, oblivious to the tension in the room. "Open one of his eyes," she said, nodding with her chin to the body.

Cyrus did as requested and nearly fell over as he jumped back. Black covered the entirety of it, including the sclera.

"None of the previous victims had eyes like that."

"I've never seen anything like this," Aida said, awed as she inspected the anomaly further. "I'll start working on theories." She turned, bumping into Cyrus and rolling her eyes. "Space. Ever heard of it?"

"I think so. Maybe?" he quirked a brow, loving how irritated she was and how it made her irises deepen to storm grey.

"Find something better to do. Like your hand, perhaps." With that, she left the room, leaving Cyrus chuckling internally.

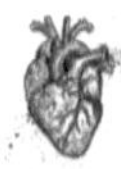

CYRUS LEANED AGAINST THE tree outside Aida's apartment, where he found himself more often than he'd like to admit. It had been an evening since he last saw Aida; her charm was a sign that she wanted to play. They agreed on a three-night window to keep it from being predictable. He smelled her before he saw her, the lilac and petrichor scent wafting in the wind.

Aida rounded the corner of her favorite jogging trail, sweat dripping down her muscular body. Just as she ran past the tree, he wrapped an arm around her waist and hauled her off her feet.

"What the fuck?!" she barked, twisting and landing an elbow to his masked face.

He grinned as blood pooled in his mouth. Aida backed

up quickly, hands in a guard position, body tense for a fight. Her gaze dropped to the chain around his neck. The other half of the charm she wore on her wrist dangled from it, letting her know who he was. She visibly relaxed though she kept her hands up.

"Aw, are you going to hit me again? I always love it when someone puts up a good fight. Especially when it means I get to fuck them afterward." Cyrus huffed a laugh at the slight widening of her eyes. "Just a case of wrong time, wrong place, beautiful. You happened to be the first person I ran into."*

Cyrus switched on his feet and slapped her across the face. It wasn't hard enough to bruise, but enough to give her the sharp sting and the split lip she craved.

"Fuck you and your limp dick dreams," she snarled, using the back of her hand to wipe blood from her mouth. She snapped her foot out, and for someone as short as she was, he was surprised by the force it hit him, briefly knocking the air out of his lungs.

"You won't be calling it limp when I fuck you with it," he growled as he side-stepped another jab and slid behind her. Grabbing a fist full of her coils, he pulled her head back, smirking at her flailing arms.

"Let go!" Aida yelled, trying to claw at his arm, but avoiding the use of her Wielding, as they had agreed.

Cyrus cupped his hand over her mouth, dragging her backward into the woods. He stood over a foot taller than her and lifted her from the ground, holding her like a toy doll.

"It's not smart to go running late after Ithea sets. You never know what sick fuck is out there waiting for a hole to fill." Cyrus pressed his aching erection against the small of her back.

Despite her protests, she arched, pushing into his touch. She screamed into his hand, unable to fight against his vampiric strength. He tossed her to the ground, and Aida let out a choked gasp as she landed on her stomach.

"Get away! Please. I'm sorry for what I said," she stuttered, scrambling in a military crawl to escape him.

He snatched her ankle, dragging her back toward him.

* "RAGDOLL" by Vana

Seeing her in this form of submission felt right, perfect. From the arousal dripping off her, he knew she felt the same. She needed it as much as he did. He was grateful for her trust in him.

"Oh, *now* you're sorry? Sorry for what? For calling me a limp dick fucker?" He straddled her thighs, immobilizing her further. "Or was it for trying to run? For pretending you don't want to get fucked in the grass like a filthy bitch?"

"No, no. That's not it. I wasn't thinking. Please let me go," she cried.

He chuckled darkly, digging into his pocket to pull out a zip tie. She struggled, fighting as best she could to keep him from grabbing her wrists and pulling them to the small of her back.

"Sit still!" he barked, taking both her wrists in one hand and using his free one to wrap the zip tie around them. "If you want to live, you'll stop fighting me," he snarled, tightening the ties, but not so much to cut circulation or fuck up her delicate hands.

"You're an idiot if you think I'd just stop fighting. Just let me go. Why waste your time with me? Find someone easier!" she grunted when he grabbed her hair again.

"You're an arrogant bitch. Did you know that?" he snapped her head down, pushing her cheek against the dirt. "And arrogant bitches need to be humbled."

"No, no," she cried as he slid down her body to grab her tight shorts.

Her struggle renewed when he dragged them down roughly, exposing her ass and cunt to the air. With a frustrated sigh, he pulled his empty gun from the band of his jeans, holding it to the back of her head. He'd never risk either of them with a fully loaded weapon.

"Keep it up. I'll put a bullet through your brain and fuck you afterward."

"Okay ... Okay, I'm sorry," she whispered, sniffling gently.

"Good girl," he praised, placing the gun on the ground where she could see it, but far enough that she couldn't reach it even if she managed to break the binds.

He finished dragging her shorts to her ankles, the tight

material keeping them bound. He firmly gripped her ass, spreading her cheeks so he could spit on her hole.

"Please don't do this," she whimpered, squeezing her eyes shut. "Please..."

"Shut the fuck up," he growled, pushing his thumb into her asshole without preamble.

He could tell she'd prepped for this and likely had each evening, unsure of when he'd 'attack'. She screamed, body tensing as it fought his intrusion.

"Stop!" She trembled, breathing harsh and shallow.

Cyrus knew she wanted him to fuck her with minimal prep, but he couldn't help but give her some anyway. He continued thrusting, spitting to lubricate her hole more. She slumped to the ground when he removed his thumb. As he unbuckled his pants, he showed how loud it was, letting her know what he planned to do next.

"No, no, no."

"Oh yes," he whispered, leaning over her to wrap the belt around her throat. "I am going to fuck this filthy hole raw, and you can't do anything but take it."

"Why are you doing this?" she cried, her voice hoarse as he slightly tightened the belt. It didn't get past him when she arched into him again.

"Because I want to. Because I *can*." Cyrus groaned, sitting up as he palmed his dick, pulling it out of his jeans. The head leaked pre-cum as he dragged it along her ass cheeks. He spat once more, covering his erection.

"Please don't do this," she whimpered, gasping when he pushed the head of his cock into her. "Stop!"

It was his cue, and he obeyed, thrusting in with a snap of his hips.

"This tight hole will be filled with my cum whether you want it to or not," he grunted, gripping her hips to bring her toward him as he began fucking her hard. She screamed, hands turning into fists and her back arching. She squirmed, trying to get away from the intrusion in her ass.

"No, why..." she cried. "Please, just stop. You're hurting me."

He listened to her second cue, getting rougher with each thrust.

"Exactly." He leaned into her, pounding into her ass, his cock filling her with each deep pump. "I don't want it to feel good for you. I am only here to fuck this hole for *my* pleasure." He felt himself thicken as he continued to invade her asshole.

"Please, nooo," she dragged out.

A few more thrusts and he came, filling her like he said he would. He slid out of her quickly, digging into his back pocket to grab the sanitary wipes they agreed on him carrying. He cleaned himself, tossed the wipe, and grabbed her hair to bring her to her knees before him.

"Open your mouth and clean this dick of my cum and your shit," he growled, his still-hard cock in front of her.

She stared up at him, tears spilling from her eyes. They were glazed in submission, and her mouth parted slightly as she panted. He loosened his grip, his expression softening as he checked in with her nonverbally. He hoped she could see it in his eyes, through the sockets of his skull mask. His thumb rubbed soft circles on her scalp. She gave him a slight nod, letting him know she was okay, before fighting against him once more.

"You're disgusting!" she screamed, trying to keep her face away from him.

Cyrus smirked darkly, bending to pick the gun up from the ground.

With one grip in her hair and the other pointing the nozzle at her head, he growled, "Open your fucking mouth, whore."

Her eyes were nearly black as she did what he demanded. He thrust in hard enough to make her gag. She sucked and gagged, saliva pouring from her mouth.

"Fuck yes, cry for me bitch." He held her head to his pelvis, feeling her swallow him down her throat.

He dropped the gun once more to place his hand on her throat and feel his cock buried in it. Her body convulsed, and he pulled out to let her take a large inhale of air.

Aida stared up at him, tears cascading down her pretty face. She licked her swollen lips, lapping at the head of his dick.

"Please," she whimpered. "Please don't hurt me anymore."

With a brief nod, Cyrus complied.

"Face down, ass up, bitch."

He pushed her, planting the side of her face onto the ground while keeping her hips raised on her knees. Dragging his hand up her soaking center, he collected her arousal, lubricating himself thoroughly. He pressed the head of his erection into her tight hole once more.

"Ow!" she screamed, trying to move away from him. He gripped her hips and aggressively pulled her to him, thrusting deep into her once more. "It hurts. Please stop, it hurts."

"Beg for it. Beg me to stop," he growled as he rutted into her ass, abusing it further.

"Please stop!" she cried, making him fuck her faster. "It hurts!" she yelled, making him thrust harder.

"Does it hurt? The way I use you for my pleasure?" he grunted as she began rocking her hips into him instead of away. "Fucking your hole so hard that if I let you live, you'll remember me for nights." With each violent snap of his hips, he could feel himself getting closer to the edge.

"Yes, it hurts! So much, so, so much," her cries morphed into moans, and he could feel her arousal dripping down her thighs.

"Tell me you want me to stop."

"Please stop!" she whimpered, her body shaking.

He leaned forward, reaching around her to find her clit. He pulled out slowly to slam back into her tight hole.

"Tell me how bad it hurts," he growled, torturing her with slow but punishing thrusts. Her tiny body rocked with each slap of his hips.

"It hurts so bad! Stop hurting me! Please!" she cried out, pussy gushing on his hand. "Fuck!" she moaned, her body shuddering as she came.

Thunder clapped, lightning streaking through the sky, as

she screamed her pleasure into the night. He followed right after, gripping her tightly as he filled her with his cum again.

They nearly collapsed, and he managed to keep a hand on her while using the other to hold himself up from the ground. He leaned into her, slowly dragging his nose from her shoulder to her ear lobe.

"I am going to lay you on your side for a moment so I can remove the bindings," he said softly, waiting for her to acknowledge him with a nod.

"O-okay," she whispered.

Slowly, he eased her onto her side and cut the zip ties at her wrists first. He massaged them, making sure her hands were all right. He removed the belt and helped scoot her shorts and underwear back up where they belonged.

"How are you feeling?" he asked, sitting on the ground and pulling her into his lap, her knees draped over one of his thighs. He removed his skull mask and tossed it aside, sweat pouring down his face.

"I..." she sighed, burrowing into his body.

He wrapped his arms around her instinctively. She was so small compared to him. Delicate, even though she was a fighter. A fucking firecracker.

"I am feeling perfect." Her small smile lit up her face.

It reminded him that she was a lot younger than how she presented. Tears filled her eyes as she looked up at him, and it did something to him that he didn't want to acknowledge.

"Can I take you to your apartment? Help you get into a bath?" he asked softly, running a hand over her tight coils. "You're dropping, and I want to make sure you're safe."

As soon as the words left his mouth, Aida started sobbing. He scooped her up into his arms, allowing her the grace to hold onto him and cry into his chest.

"Thank you," she whispered as he hurried to the apartment. "That was everything ... Everything I wanted," she let out a shuddering sigh, "Everything I *needed*. But couldn't find. Felt so guilty for wanting this..." she sniffed, the words seeming to tumble out her mouth. "The handful of times … it just wasn't it. It wasn't THIS." She fumbled to get her key from her bra and snorted a laugh when he dug right in to get it.

"Sorry," he murmured as they walked through the door. He headed straight for her ensuite bathroom.

"Should I be concerned that you know which room is mine?" she asked, voice slurring as exhaustion overtook her.

"Probably," he chuckled gently. "Don't sleep yet. Stay with me a little while longer. I know it's a lot. You've never done it to this extreme."

"Yeah, no. Never," she chuckled. "Thank you … again."

"Thank you for trusting me. For letting us see this out." He gingerly sat her on the edge of the large bathtub, catching her wince. "Was I too aggressive?" he asked, concerned.

She shook her head vigorously.

"No! No. My ass will be sore for nights, though." She smirked.

"Well, you asked for it." He winked, helping her undress.

"Technically, I didn't." Aida laughed at whatever expression had surfaced on his face. The doctor hissed softly as she slid into the hot water. "Ohhh, this is nice."

Cyrus whistled softly as he looked for a silk scarf. He tapped her shoulders so she could lean forward and gently wrapped her short coils in the scarf.

"You … know hair care."

"I had a few sisters and cousins. My hair was once longer. Even after hundreds of years, the care is still the same." He grabbed a fluffy sponge and lilac bar soap and lathered it to bathe her. She caught his hand, gripping it tightly.

"Would you mind joining me?" she asked, voice suddenly soft.

There was a vulnerability in her that he'd never seen before. Considering that, he nodded and pulled her palm to his lips, kissing it gently.

"Sure."

Cyrus undressed and slowly slid into the tub behind her. The water sloshed, splashing over the edge.

"I'm surprised this thing can fit the both of us," he chuckled, groaning when he felt a twinge in his rib cage.

"Are you hurt?" she asked, leaning back against him, and tilted her head to look up at him curiously.

He smirked, taking care to wash her slowly.

"Well, you fucking donkey kicked me in the ribs, Aida."

"Oh, shit, I did," she laughed.

"Lean forward," he said softly, massaging her back when she did.

Soft sighs left her as he worked through her tight muscles. She relaxed against him again, and they sat there, listening to the soft sounds of the water. She must've had a heater keeping the tub warm.

Cyrus wasn't sure how long they remained there, breathing in each other's scent. It was the longest he stayed in her presence without the need to strangle her. The thought made him smirk, and he decided to tell her his thoughts.

Aida turned to face him, something passing in her eyes again. The haze had lifted, and she seemed more alert.

"We're toxic, aren't we?" she asked as she stood, water dripping down her abs and firm, muscular legs. She bit her lower lip as he pulled her close.*

"We are," he responded, his mouth coasting along her diaphragm.

Even standing while he sat, she was only just a head over him. Her hands found the back of his head while his glided up her thighs. She gripped him tight enough to make him tilt his chin, looking at her through lowered lids.

"We're no good for each other," he whispered.

"Might be a good idea if we stop…" she breathed as she slowly slid down to straddle his thighs, his now growing erection bobbing between them.

"No more hate fucking," he said. "It's unfair to Bex and Killian."

"All right. Then, for our last time, tonight … Can we pretend?"

---

* "Aphrodite" by Sam Short

"Thought we did earlier?" he asked with a raised brow. He groaned when she sat up and angled his dick to her center.

"No … That was roleplay." They both moaned as she impaled herself on him, slowly allowing him to stretch her tight pussy. "I … just want to pretend for one night…"

He gripped her ass, moving her tiny body up and down on his dick.

"That we're just two regular people and not murderers with a few screws loose in the head?" He chuckled when she slapped his shoulder. His lips found her pierced nipple, earning a whimper. He pulled away with a pop, giving her a smile.

"Yeah. Because then I can tell you that you should smile more." She ran a hand over his head, her hips rocking against his.

"Those dimples of yours will make anyone weak at the knees," he responded. "Shit," he breathed when her pussy tightened around his dick.

"You're actually pretty smart," she snorted.

Her laughter turned into a moan when he latched onto her neck, tongue working a hickey that would show even on her dark skin. His fangs slowly descended, and he pulled back from the temptation to sink them into her throat.

"High praise coming from the good doctor," he chuckled. "It's not every night that I find someone who can keep up with me."

"I'd say I outpace you, but I'll let you have it for tonight," she huffed, rocking harder and faster. "You've got an amazing dick, that's for sure."

"Your pussy was made for it," he rumbled, bucking up with each grind of her hips. It made her bounce, her small breasts jostling with the movement. "Tight, wet, eager."

"Fuck!" she cried, gripping his shoulders tightly.

"This small, tiny body of yours is so fuckable." Moans fell from his lips as he latched onto her neck again.

"Cyrus, bite me, please," she begged. He didn't need to be told twice, sinking his fangs deep. "Ah!"

Her pussy tightened around his dick, and he growled

against her flesh, fucking up into her harder. Blood pooled in his mouth as he took gulps, some spilling to cascade down her body.

"I'm going to come. Oh fuck, I'm going to come!"

"Come all over my dick, Aida," he groaned as he pulled away from her throat.

He licked her wounds closed, burying his face in the crook of her neck as he held her while she came. Her body shook, back bowing, as she peaked. He soon followed, pumping his cum into her with a roar.

"Holy shit…" Aida breathed, panting softly.

Aida's fingers brushed against the still-sensitive scar on his shoulder, and she pulled back to look at him.

"What's this?" she asked. He caught her wrist, stilling her movement. "Bex?" She raised an eyebrow.

He kept his mouth shut, knowing his silence was answer enough. A look passed in her eyes, and he could've sworn it was pain. Or was it envy?

"It's okay. You don't have to tell me." Her voice was soft, almost vulnerable.

Aida's thumb glided along his lower lip, cleaning it of her blood. She leaned in to kiss him before he realized what she was doing, but he recoiled quickly, rearing his head back. Storm grey eyes widened in shock before shuttering.

"I can't…"

Kissing was too intimate. Things suddenly turned too intimate in ways he shouldn't have allowed. Fuck. Why did he let it get this far?

"I understand," she said with a nod, quickly standing. She snatched the chain off his neck, the metal biting into his skin sharply.

"Aida…" he rose, following her out of the bathtub. "Wait."

She passed a towel to him as she wrapped herself in her own.

"I'm tired. It's okay. Game's over," she sighed, swiping under her eye as she turned away.

Soft clinking echoed in the space as she dropped the

charm bracelet and his chain in a jewelry bowl.

"Aida…" he tried again but didn't take another step.

She whipped around, lightning crackling in her eyes.

"Go. Now," she snapped, jaw clenching.

He nodded, keeping the towel around his waist. He didn't bother to grab his soiled clothes. She could burn it for all he cared.

Without another word, he left. There was nothing more to say or do.

Gone was their moment, and he was sure they'd never have another.

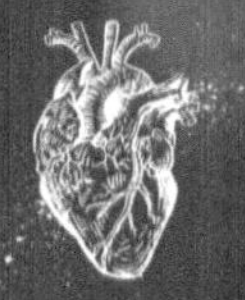

CHAPTER 23

WHO ARE YOU, & WHAT HAVE YOU DONE WITH CYRUS?

CYRUS PACED HIS LIVING room nervously, waiting for Killian, Bex, and Aida to arrive. His fucking life was blowing up. The Asherites had been held up and were a week behind schedule. The Demon from Silvermoon was as much an asshole as he figured he would be. The ridiculous fucking masquerade was closing in.

What was he doing?

His emotions were everywhere. He tried to process the depth of those feelings but could not bring himself to voice them out loud. Admitting such a thing made him vulnerable in a way he wasn't prepared to be.

Was it love?

That was the big question Cyrus had been asking himself ever since Tristan asked him if he'd ever fallen deep. To be honest, Cyrus had no fucking clue. He fell hard for two of the most unlikely people in just a few short months. Throw in the deranged doctor, and he didn't recognize himself anymore.

Who was he becoming?

Cyrus rubbed his hands on his pants and froze when his penthouse bell dinged. A smile grew on his face when Killian entered, the emerald of his shirt bringing out his kohl-lined eyes. His man returned his smile, meeting Cyrus halfway. He rose to his toes, wrapping his arms around Cyrus' shoulders.

"Hey, Daddy," Killian said playfully, kissing him.

"Hey, Pet," Cyrus replied, running his tongue along Killian's lower lip, nipping it.

Killian groaned, returning the favor, dropping to his heels. He looked up at Cyrus, making him squirm.

his hands to hold Cyrus'. "You seem … off?"

"Me?" Cyrus shook his head. "Why do you think that?" Damn the man for being so perceptive.

"I'm pretty sure your voice just cracked," Killian teased.

"What?" Cyrus coughed, clearing his throat. He led Killian to the couch, motioning him to sit. "I wanted to talk with you, Bex, and Aida…"

His man didn't sit, opting to cross his arms and scowl at Cyrus.

"Aida? Really?" Killian sneered.

"Don't be a brat. We need to talk about … all of this." He gestured to the room, indicating his fucking life.

"Brat? I am not being a brat. I am not pleased that I have to talk to that bitch who nearly cost me and my brother our businesses!" He shook his head, rubbing his wrists. "And you're *blindsiding* me. You should've told me before I came over."

"Would you have come if I had?" Cyrus asked. Killian clenched his jaw as he breathed a long sigh through his nose. "Exactly. Look, I know you don't like her—"

"Oh no. Let's get it right," Killian snarked. "I *hate* her. I am only putting up with this because she means something to you."

"Wait, no." Cyrus scoffed bitterly. "She means nothing to me. *I* only put up with her because of Bex." He groaned, aware of how it all sounded.

"Cy, this is all messy," Killian sighed, plopping onto the couch. "Can I at least get a double pour of whiskey?"

"Yeah," he sighed as he left the room. Cyrus returned with a decanter of the amber liquid and a few glasses, putting them on the low coffee table. He gave a glass to Killian, who snatched it, leaning back and resting his foot on the opposite knee.

The penthouse bell rang, and Aida and Bex arrived together, hand in hand. Noticing the teal collar around Bex's throat, Cyrus suppressed a growl.

Killian clicked his tongue. "Messy, messy."

"Fuck you for being so intuitive," Cyrus bit out, but there

was no real anger in his tone.

"Oh joy," Aida said sarcastically, looking from Cyrus to Killian.

There was no remorse on her face for what she did, and it pissed him off. Killian flipped her off, downing the rest of his whiskey.

"Joy indeed," the human snapped.

"What are we doing here?" Bex asked with an arched brow. They looked from Cyrus to Killian and back.

"What? No, hello first? Strike one, little wolf," Cyrus rumbled, ambling toward them.

Bex's lips parted as they stared up at him. "I'm sorry, my Lord."

Bex gasped when he hooked his finger in the o-ring and jerked them close. They melted into him when their mouths met in a kiss. Cyrus tugged at their piercing, enjoying the squeak of pleasure that came from them.

"You will be," Cyrus breathed against their lips when they parted.

"All right, all right," Aida said loudly, clapping her hands with each word.

Cyrus gritted his teeth, looking at the shorter woman behind Bex.

"*You* invited us here, me included. I don't need to sit here and watch you swap spit all night."

"Don't act like you don't like my spit, good doctor," he remarked, smirking at her glare. She took a step forward, eyes sparking. Cyrus moved Bex to the side, baring his fangs. "Try it, murderess."

Killian made a show of yawning, garnering everyone's attention.

"Are we done here?" His foot bounced where it lay on his knee.

Bex snorted, quickly moving to the couch to throw themself on him.

"Oomph!" he yelped.

"How we doing, Kill-man?" Bex smiled, sliding onto the seat

beside him and worming their way under his arm.

Cyrus leaned on the arm of the couch, looking down at his man with an eyebrow raised. "Kill-man?" he asked, amused.

Killian shrugged. "I don't know. Ask them."

"He's got kill…er looks." Bex huffed, making Killian snort. "Thank you for coming to my set. Please leave tips on your way out."

On the far end of the couch, across from Killian and Bex, Aida sat slowly, assessing the room and the human in front of her. After a beat, she poured herself a hefty amount of whiskey and leaned back.

"I know you're all wondering why I brought you here," Cyrus started.

"Yeah, no shit," Aida quipped.

"Shut the fuck up," Killian snapped, surprising Cyrus with the harshness of his tone.

"Killian…" Bex said softly, running a comforting hand on his forearm.

"Oh, the human has bite," Aida smirked, taking a large gulp of her whiskey.

"This. This is exactly why," Cyrus said as he motioned to all of them, sinking into a recliner. "Look. I know I am the epicenter of my life blowing up. I am aware that this is all messy. I don't know what the fuck I'm doing or what this is with you both," he said, speaking directly to Bex and Killian. "What I *do* know is that things would get a lot messier—and bloodier—if I don't have you in my life." He held up a hand before Aida could speak. "I am *aware* of how fucking selfish I sound."

"Where is this all coming from?" Bex asked, dilated eyes looking from him to Aida and back.

Cyrus couldn't remember the last time he saw them arrive at his place or office sober. He kept telling himself it wasn't his business outside of work, but it gnawed at his resolve. He knew he would have to ask and stop putting it off.

"I…" Cyrus scratched the back of his head. "I just want to try and clean some of this up." He motioned to Aida. "I only put up with you, for Bex's sake."

"But you have no problem fucking her because, hey, let's ignore Killian's feelings," his man said bitterly.

Fuck. FUCK. That was not his intent.

"No, Killian—" Cyrus started when he was cut off.

"Not that I have to explain anything to you," Aida started, nose flaring. "But we decided we weren't going to fuck anymore."

"What?" Bex whipped their head to stare at the doctor.

Cyrus was surprised she spoke first about it. Killian's expression shuttered, leaving Cyrus wondering what was going through his head.

"After … our last time together, things were heated." Cyrus sighed, suddenly feeling bone tired. "We realized our toxicity isn't worth it. It's not worth you or Bex," Cyrus said to Killian.

"I wonder how many times you both fucked before coming to this revelation," Killian said as he turned his eyes to the ceiling.

Cyrus found himself on his knees in front of him. The man gasped, clearly caught off guard as he snapped his eyes to him. He dropped his foot from his knee, spreading them apart for Cyrus to settle between.

"I am sorry," Cyrus whispered.

His man's eyes widened in disbelief. Aida chuckled, making Cyrus grind his teeth. Killian's gaze flickered to the woman.

"Don't look at her; look at me," he growled, garnering the man's attention again. Bex removed themselves from Killian's side but remained on the couch. "Baby, I'm so sorry." He cupped Killian's face. "I was an asshole. I said this before. And yet I continued doing it."

Cyrus rushed to place his thumbs under Killian's eyes to capture the tears threatening to fall. When he opened his mouth to continue, Killian shook his head.

"No…" he whispered, gaze flicking back to Aida. "Later … Just tell me later." He leaned in and gave Cyrus a chaste kiss, sitting back and out of reach.

"All right," he said softly as he stood and held out his hand for Bex to take. They stood, a look of confusion on their face as he rounded the table to sit with Aida on the couch. "I don't like that you've been caught between the good doctor and I."

"Cyrus..." Aida grumbled.

He succeeded in making Bex smirk.

"I can tell when you're distressed, especially when the three of us are in the same room," he said softly.

"You feel like you need to choose," Aida murmured, sliding her hand to lock with Bex's. "We both care about you enough to let you know you don't have to."

"We may not get along," Cyrus snorted, nodding his chin toward Aida, who shrugged. "We pretty much hate each other."

"You got that right," the doctor sneered.

Cyrus narrowed his eyes at her, making her smirk.

"I can't promise we won't fight, but it'll never be about you. You're ours, and we're yours, no matter what." Cyrus took Bex's other hand.

The wolf looked from him to Aida and then to their knees. One bounced as they contemplated what Cyrus and Aida were telling them.

"I ... We don't want you to feel obligated." Aida's voice was so full of compassion that it threw Cyrus off. "But if I'm being honest, I'm just as greedy as he is. I don't think I could let you go if I tried. It's selfish of me. I didn't plan to fall for you..."

Cyrus' breath became shallow as he waited for Bex to respond. He echoed Aida's sentiment, but for once, he wasn't going to overshadow her moment. Suddenly, Bex shot to their feet, bringing Cyrus and Aida up with them.

"I ... I need time," Bex said, scratching the back of their neck. "This is a lot. Too much. I'm overwhelmed." They let go of Cyrus' and Aida's hands. Their breathing was erratic, eyes flashing neon and back.

"I need to go." They bolted for the lift, Aida running after them.

"Bex!" she yelled, but the wolf ignored her, looking around as they watched the lift crawl floor by floor.

"Please don't follow me," Bex said as they turned to face

Aida. They cupped the woman's face and kissed her tenderly. "Don't follow me." Their words were barely a whisper as they looked up at him.

"Bexie," Killian breathed, standing up and approaching them. The lift continued to crawl up. Up. Up.

"Kill-man." They smirked sadly.

As the lift doors open, Bex backed into it. They tugged at their collar, scratching the back of their neck with their free hand. He knew precisely where Bex was headed, and he fucking hated that they felt the need to get high.

As the doors closed, Killian cried out, "Ping me later! Please!"

The last thing he saw was Bex's hazel eyes as the doors closed.

"Fuck!" Aida snarled, storming away from the door to head into his kitchen.

"What the fuck are you doing?" Cyrus barked, Killian hot on his heels.

"I need a fucking drink that's not whiskey; that's what I'm doing," she snapped, looking around his home bar.

Cyrus snatched her wrist away from his liquor.

"No. You can leave. That's what you can do." Cyrus bared his fangs at her, to which she responded with shocks of electricity going up from her wrist to his forearm.

"Just go, Aida. Bex doesn't want you to follow them, but that doesn't mean you need to stay here, either," Killian snapped angrily.

Aida turned her gaze to him, wrenching her wrist from Cyrus' grip.

"I get that what I did was fucked up," Aida said, a look of disdain on her face. "I don't regret it. It's not my fault you allowed stupid people to work for you."

"Get the fuck out!" Cyrus snarled, snatching her by her arm and ignoring her shout of protest. "You keep putting me in these fucking situations where I have to choose whether to kill you for disrespecting me and my man or let you live for the sake of Bex. I fucking hate you for it."

He kept a firm grip on her as he stabbed at the down button on the lift. It was the one time he regretted living on the top floor.

"So far, I'm alive, so it's clear who you favor," she bit out as she gripped his wrist to alleviate the pain in her arm.

"That's where you're wrong," Killian said, getting up in her face. "Bex and I are best friends. If they were hurt because of Cyrus, it would hurt me too. He's thinking about the both of us. In this situation, you're nothing but a nuisance. A necessary evil." He reached out to snatch Aida's throat.

"One night, your life is going to shatter, and you're going to be left alone to pick up the pieces because you don't know how to form bonds with anyone but your fucking self. You will be bitter, sad, and alone." He pulled Aida toward him, seething. "And I swear to the fucking Deities, if you hurt Bex by making Cyrus do something he doesn't want, I will end you myself."

"I was right. The human has bite," Aida panted, as if she didn't have two men threatening her. A manic smirk tilted her lips up. "Fine."

"Fine, what?" Cyrus snarled.

"Fine! I'll behave," she bit out.

Right on cue, the lift dinged. Cyrus shoved her inside with a growl.

"I'd hold your word to it, but I know your word is worth shit."

Aida gave him the finger as the doors closed.

Cyrus exhaled long, tension still keeping his shoulders up and rigid. His vision was nearly red, bloodlust so high that he feared looking at Killian. This entire night drained his emotional capacity to remain focused.

"Cy..." his man said, touching his forearm to draw his attention. He gasped and took a step back. "You need blood, don't you?"

"How can you tell?" he asked through his extended fangs. He clenched his hands into fists, just barely maintaining control.

"Your eyes are practically black ... With just a rim of red around the pupil."

"Killian, go lock yourself into my bedroom," he panted,

eyeing the way his man's throat bobbed. The vein that ran down his neck called to Cyrus, and he licked his lips as he thought about the bloodshed he so desperately wanted.

"No," he said, to Cyrus' shock.

"You've been full of surprises tonight, Pet." He took a slow, menacing step forward. He grinned when Killian's resolve faltered. "I don't trust myself."

"But *I* trust you," he said softly. "Cyrus, feed." He tilted his chin up, baring his throat.

"You don't know what you're asking," Cyrus growled, taking another step forward. He cupped the back of Killian's neck. "I am not a normal vampire."

"I know that, Cy," he whispered, this time being the one to close the distance.

Killian moaned when Cyrus licked his sweet pulse. His body shook with restraint, torn between instinct and protectiveness.

"Last chance to back out," he whispered along the man's flesh.

Killian gripped the front of Cyrus' shirt, tugging him closer.

"Stop wasting time and do it," the human panted, pulse pounding against his mouth.

"Brat," Cyrus breathed, sinking his fangs deep.

"Ah!" Killian cried out, but not from pain.

It was clear to Cyrus it was in pleasure. He growled, pushing his man against a nearby wall, pulling deeply. He shook his head, opening the wound just slightly, his tongue lapping at the blood that rushed out.

"Fuck," Killian whimpered, pushing his hips into Cyrus'. He growled as their erections ground against each other. "Cy," Killian whispered, voice breathless. The man's pulse slowed, his blood too sweet, too addictive to give up.

With a gasp, Cyrus put all his will into pulling away from Killian just in time. He quickly licked the man's wounds closed, his blood staining both his shirt and Killian's. While the puncture wounds were small scars, the bruises remained.

His bloodlust abated, but not completely. He would need

to feed on at least two more people, but he couldn't focus on that now. His man's eyes were closed, a small blissful smile on his lips.

"Killian?" Cyrus hedged.

The man was pale, so fucking pale. If Cyrus couldn't hear his thready but constant heartbeat, he would've thought he killed him.

"Killian!"

"Hmmm?" the man mumbled, hazy eyes opening to meet his. "Fuck that was … Interesting." Killian's knees buckled, causing Cyrus to catch him and scoop him up in a cradle hold. "Is it normal to be so horny?" he chuckled as if drunk.

"Yeah. Vampire venom will do that," Cyrus said with a smirk, pushing his bedroom door open with his foot.

He brought him to the bathroom, sitting him on the counter. Grabbing a rag, he cleaned Killian's throat, undoing his bloodied button-up and pushing it off.

"Are you all right?" he asked as he helped Killian out of his undershirt.

"Yeah. Tired," he mumbled some more.

Cyrus removed his shirt, tossing the bloodied mess into a hamper. He helped Killian attend to his needs, to which he grumbled, "I'm not a baby," under his breath, making Cyrus chuckle.

He helped Killian into his bed to lie down, whose eyes fluttered closed. He realized his mistake and pulled Killian up to sit, ignoring the man's whines of complaint. "Wait, don't fall asleep yet."

He opened his mini-fridge, rummaging around until he found a protein shake. He sat on the bed, opening it for him and gently smacking Killian's cheek to make his eyes snap open.

"Ow…"

"Shut up, it didn't hurt," Cyrus snorted, passing him the shake. "Drink."

"You just so happened to have protein shakes in your fridge?" Killian grumbled, nose scrunching as he took a sip. "Ew…"

"What? It's chocolate..." Cyrus quirked a brow.

Killian gulped some more down. "I like coffee flavor. Did you get these for me?" he asked, voice clearer.

He finished off the shake, putting the empty bottle on the nightstand. Cyrus scratched the back of his head and nodded.

"I wanted to be prepared ... In case I ever had to feed off you. Or lost control..."

"Next time, get me coffee flavor," he said wryly.

The euphoria of the bite was working its way out of his system. Cyrus fidgeted a bit, biting his lower lip.

"You've never had someone sleep over, have you..." Killian's voice was teasing, already knowing the answer.

"No..." Cyrus huffed, standing and looking around the room. "I can give you a pair of sweats?"

"I doubt they'd fit. I know you're all big and tall, but I've got thick thighs and a fluffy tummy. How about we forego clothes?" Killian asked, sitting up more on the bed, eyes clear now. "I don't usually sleep with them on."

He raised his eyebrow suggestively. Cyrus shook his head, going to his dresser to pull out a pair of shorts.

"Oh no. *You* need rest. You lost a lot of blood," Cyrus said, sobering the moment. "Try these." He tossed the shorts over to him.

Killian moved gingerly but shook his head when Cyrus took a step forward.

"No, I'm fine. Just sore." He sighed as he undressed and shimmied into the shorts. "Oh ... They fit?" He raised an eyebrow as he looked up at him.

"Yeah," Cyrus mumbled.

"Did you get clothes for me?" Killian asked with surprise.

Cyrus' face warmed, and he grabbed his sweats and rushed to his bathroom. As he changed, he replayed the night through his mind. So much happened in such a short time. He was overwhelmed, and while Killian helped calm his bloodlust, he knew it wouldn't last. He could hold off overnight, maybe even through mid-evening, but after that ... He wasn't so sure.

He opened the door slowly to find Killian staring out the window. From the penthouse, all of Malagado could be seen. Ithea and the moon both shone in the clear, dark indigo sky.

What was it about this man that made him weak in the knees? He felt things he never did before. It vastly differed from what he felt for Bex, though both were as strong. His chest ached as he looked at his man's profile. Soaking in every detail, he looked at how his nose curved, the pout of his lower lip, his kohl-lined emerald eyes, and the chipped black nail polish. The thick man's tattoos reached from shoulders to wrists.

"Take a picture; it'll last longer," Killian said teasingly, turning his intense gaze to Cyrus. Those eyes slowly raked down Cyrus' shirtless body, stopping at his low-slung sweats.

"Oh, Daddy, you can't wear those." He clicked his tongue. "How do I go to bed knowing all that sexy goodness is next to me?"

Though his tone was playful, his eyes told a different story. He was exhausted, whether he wanted to admit it or not. Cyrus wasn't the only one who went through an emotional whirlwind.

"Your libido can wait, Pet," Cyrus chuckled, sliding into the bed beside him. Killian placed a gentle hand on Cyrus' shoulder when he lay down.

"This is new," he remarked, curiosity filling his gaze as he looked at Cyrus. His fingers hovered over the bite mark Bex left.

"You can touch it," Cyrus breathed, shuddering softly when Killian touched the scar. "It's Bex's mark…" his voice trailed off, wondering how Killian would take the information.

"Makes sense," his man said, smirking.

"How so?" Cyrus took his hand, turning his wrist up to kiss.

"They have you so wrapped around their slender little finger," Killian sighed playfully, a low gasp escaping him when Cyrus let his tongue glide along his scars. "It's okay. I'm glad it's them. Who else is better than my bestie? Cyrus, stop. You said no sex, and your tongue isn't helping."

Cyrus chuckled, releasing the man's hand.

As they lay down, he wrapped his arm around Killian,

spooning him. It was wild how well they fit together. His soft body fit perfectly in the curve of Cyrus'.

"Boo, I hoped you'd continue anyway," Killian breathed tiredly. He pulled up the covers and rested his hand on top of Cyrus' over his waist. Their fingers intertwined together, Cyrus nuzzling the man's neck. "Cyrus?"

"Mhmm," he mumbled into Killian's crook.

"Can I tell you something and you not be upset?" his voice was soft and vulnerable.

Cyrus held Killian's hand a little tighter.

"Go ahead..." He had a feeling he knew what Killian had to say, his heart pounding in his chest.

He wasn't ready...

"Now you don't have to say it back ... I don't expect you to."

He wasn't ready...

"But, Cy ... I love you."

Fuck. He. Wasn't. Ready.

Even if he felt the same.

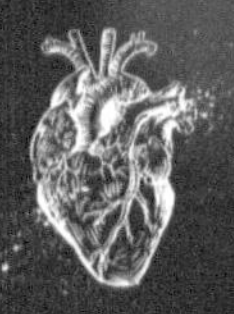

CHAPTER 24

BITTERSWEET APOLOGIES

SLEEP DIDN'T COME EASILY for Cyrus, whereas Killian fell into a deep slumber as soon as he said those three words.

I.

Love.

You.

What did he do with that? It was like his throat closed up, nothing going in or out. Words escaped him, replaced by the feeling of drowning. No one had uttered those words to him since his family died. Was he even sure he knew what it meant? Was that what he'd been feeling this whole time?

Duh, motherfucker.

Cyrus clenched his jaw, shifting in the bed. His erection brushed against Killian's ass, and he had to bite back a moan. The man yawned, arching his back in a stretch that pressed him further into Cyrus.

"Good evening, Cy," Killian's sleepy voice was rough.*

"How are you feeling, baby?" he asked, kissing his shoulder.

Killian stretched again, and Cyrus knew he was doing it on purpose.

"A lot better." He took Cyrus' hand and slid it down the front of his body to cup his erection.

Cyrus ground his hips into Killian, bringing out a soft moan.

"I have apologizing to do," Cyrus said as he pushed Killian's shorts down to his thighs. He held his hand in front of him. "Spit." As soon as Killian did, he wrapped his fist around the man's cock.

"Oh shit," Killian whimpered, back arching again. He turned his head to kiss Cyrus, rocking to fuck Cyrus' fist. Their tongues

---

* "No High" by David Kushner

clashed, Killian's piercing sending jolts of pleasure down his body.

"I'm sorry, Killian," he said softly against Killian's lips, speeding up his strokes. His man reached between them, rubbing Cyrus' cock.

He groaned when Killian sought to push his sweats down. Cyrus let go of Killian to pull out his aching erection. Without being asked, Killian grabbed the lube from the nightstand, holding it out for Cyrus.

"Prove it. Tell me why you're sorry, Cyrus," Killian panted.

He cried out when Cyrus pushed a slick finger into his hole. Cyrus pumped a few times, adding a second and scissoring them while thrusting in and out.

"You want me on my knees for you?" he whispered, watching as goosebumps raised along the man's skin. He covered his fingers in more lube to add a third.

"Oh!" Killian moaned, hips rocking so he could penetrate himself on the digits. "First, I want you inside me. Fuck me, Daddy."

"Anything for you," Cyrus growled, removing his fingers and covering his length with lube. He teased Killian's hole with the head of his thick cock. "I'm sorry," he said again as he pushed inside him.

"Say it again," Killian panted, ass clenching around Cyrus.

He slid his arm under Killian's, hooking it and grabbing the man's shoulder. He held tight as he languidly rotated his hips.

"I'm sorry. I fucked up," Cyrus moaned. "I took you for granted. Your heart. Your anima." He ground slowly, fucking Killian with a tenderness he'd never held in the past. His lips found Killian's shoulder, moving to his chin and then his cheek. "You know I'm no good with words," he breathed.

"Tell me why you're sorry," Killian repeated, gripping Cyrus' forearm.

"I'm sorry because I should've never fucked Aida ... Even after knowing what she did. I should've been stronger."

"No. It's not about strength," Killian said, spreading his legs to place his foot on top of Cyrus' calf. "Fuck me harder." He let out a loud moan when Cyrus did as he asked. He snapped his hips, rutting into Killian's hole. "We all make mistakes, Cy."

"I'm sorry for denying what I feel about you," he finally admitted.

Killian tugged on Cyrus' forearm.

"Touch me more, please," he begged, rocking with each rough thrust. He slicked more lube in his hand and wrapped his hand around Killian's hard cock. "Shit. Fuck," his man whimpered, back arched, pre-cum leaking through Cyrus' fist.

"I…" Cyrus' throat started to close up again, so he fucked Killian harder. The rough slapping of their bodies meeting was loud in the otherwise quiet space.

"You don't have to say anything," Killian blurted quickly, dick thickening in Cyrus' hand. "Just show me. Promise to show me."

"I promise," Cyrus moaned, quickly pulling out to flip Killian onto his back. After removing their pants, Cyrus drove into him with a rough snap of his hips. Their gazes met, and he took in his man's flushed face and swollen lips. "You're mine, Killian. Your smile, your humor. Your sadness, your darkness. Everything that you are is mine." He thrust hard. "This hole is mine. Mine to fuck and have. To fill with my cum." He slammed into him, their sex turning frenzied.

"You're mine. Your sarcasm, your intelligence. Your blood, your violence. All of it is mine," Killian replied, wrapping his legs around Cyrus' waist. "Your dick is mine. Mine to use and make me come." Killian's back arched, lifting his hips into each thrust. "Your heart is mine, Cyrus." The emotion in his voice was thick as he pulled Cyrus close by sliding his arms under his.

"My heart is yours," he whispered against the flesh of his throat, his bloodlust nowhere to be found. Cyrus could feel himself getting closer to his edge, so he rested on one hand to reach between them and pump Killian's dick.

"Louder," Killian panted, digging his heels into Cyrus' ass and allowing Cyrus to fuck him deeper. More pre-cum leaked all over his hand as he jerked the man off quickly.

"My heart is yours, Killian," he said more clearly. "Everything that I am is yours. Yours and Bex's."

"I love you, Cyrus, even if you can't say it back," Killian said as his tight hole clenched around Cyrus.

"Come for me, Killian," Cyrus said as he tried to stave off his orgasm.

With a shout, Killian's body bowed as he came on their stomachs. Cyrus pumped a few more times and pulled out to come on Killian's ass and balls.

"F-fuck," his man whimpered as Cyrus slid down to clean up his mess, sucking on one of his balls and then the other. He licked up and swiped the cum with his tongue.

"My heart is yours," Cyrus said as he moved back up, continuing his cleaning and licking Killian's cum from his soft stomach. On his trek to Killian's mouth, Cyrus trailed kisses along the man's chest, sucking on one of his nipples and finally arriving at his destination. Cyrus kissed his man deeply as if he was his last breath of air. "Go to the Ball with me," he breathed against his mouth.

"The Ball? Axton's Eve Ball?" he asked, his voice rough. His emerald eyes widened, and his plump lips parted in surprise.

"Yeah, what other one is there?" Cyrus joked, brushing sweaty hair from Killian's forehead. The man's already flushed cheeks deepened, redness creeping up his neck.

"Wow, you must be *really* sorry," he said as he looked away.

Cyrus gripped Killian's chin gently, making him meet his gaze.

"That is not why I'm asking you." He refused to let his gaze leave Killian's. "I planned on asking you before last night blew up."

Killian bit his lower lip, and Cyrus could tell he was having difficulty maintaining eye contact.

"Is it…" Killian squeezed his eyes shut, a tear leaking down his temple.

Cyrus kissed him on the forehead. "Yes. It is just for you. I wanted to invite you and you only, Killian."

"Really? I mean, I know it wouldn't be Bex's speed, but—"

"Whether it is or not … This is something I want to share with *you.*" Cyrus shifted his hips, brushing against Killian's cock, which was awakening.

"A-all right," Killian breathed when Cyrus ground his hips to rub their now hard erections against one another. "But Cyrus?"

"Mhmm?" he murmured, kissing Killian.

The man gripped Cyrus' shoulders, pushing him away.

"Keep apologizing." Killian arched a brow. "You said something about being on your knees for me?"

Cyrus grinned, letting Killian have his power play.

"Yes, Pet."

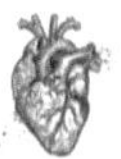

CYRUS' BREATH CLOUDED AROUND him as he stood outside Aida's apartment door. It was a colder than usual night, and while he didn't normally mind the cold, he also didn't want to stand around in it. He'd rather be home, enjoying a tequila by the fire.

It'd been nearly a week since the blow-up at his penthouse. He didn't know how much time for space he could give Bex, his growing anxiety eating him up inside. He wasn't even sure they'd be at Aida's, but seeing that the woman wouldn't answer his pings ... Well, here he was.

"What are you doing here?" came Aida's angry voice after opening the door. She glowered at him, crossing her exposed muscular arms over her sweaty sports bra, her coils in a hair wrap.

"Have you seen Bex?" he asked, scanning the space behind her. The scent of rubber and sweat traveled to him, and he knew he'd interrupted Aida's workout.

"I haven't," she answered quickly.

Cyrus narrowed his eyes at her.

"Aida..." he growled, vision hazy with red.

After waiting for nights, his bloodlust rushed forward. The thought that Bex was avoiding him had him acting irrationally. He *should've* fed, but he couldn't focus. There was no one to interrogate, which left him with no other option. He knew that with his lack of focus, he'd kill whoever he fed off of—violently.

"Don't growl at me. They aren't—"

"Mamita?" Bex's husky alto instantly filled him with relief. They turned a corner and froze when they saw him, eyes widening in surprise. In their hand was one of those little wolf plushies he saw back in their cabin. "Cyrus…"

Relief quickly shifted to anger as he pushed himself inside the apartment, kicking the door closed with his foot. He wrapped a hand around Aida's throat and slammed her against the wall.

"You don't know where they are?" he snarled, baring his fangs. Aida had the nerve to smirk as she gripped his wrist. He slid her up the wall, lifting her feet from the floor. "Are you *trying* to make me kill you?"

"C-can't," she bit out. "C-can't answer." She slapped at his wrist again.

"Cyrus! Put her down!" Bex yelled.

He snapped his gaze to them, but they stood firm, furious.

"Fuck!" he growled, letting the doctor go, not giving a fuck when she crumpled to the ground. He stalked up to Bex, who looked as pissed off as he felt.

"Where have you been?" he seethed. "Why haven't you pinged me? You needed space, and I didn't reach out, but it's been nearly a week, Bex." Unwanted desperation echoed in his voice.

"Me? Me!" they snarked, closing the distance between them. Their spiced scent wrapped around him, their hazel eyes clear and sober for once. "I lost my comm and asked Aida to ping you." Bex jabbed their finger into his chest. "But *you* didn't want to talk to me."

"What?!" he barked, glaring at the small woman who had steadily gotten to her feet. "Is that why you've been ignoring me? Keeping Bex from me?" His vision went so red it was almost black. "Are you suicidal?!"

His fangs ached with the need to tear flesh, and it took all his restraint to keep his feet planted.

"A few nights! That's all I wanted!" Aida yelled back,

throwing him for a loop. The raw emotion in her voice and stance was not what he expected.

"Okay, wait," Bex said, their voice raised, breaking through his haze. They pushed themself between Cyrus and Aida. The wolf looked at Aida. "You told me he didn't want to talk to me. You lied to me! Why?" The pain was evident in their voice.

"Because I wanted you to myself … For just a few nights," Aida said hoarsely, rubbing her neck. "I know it was sel—"

"Do *not* tell me how selfish it was!" Bex snapped, eyes turning neon in their anger. They pointed at Cyrus, who was still trying to wrangle his bloodlust. "I am tired. So tired of hearing how selfish you both are."

They nodded to the door with their chin. "Take off your shoes." They didn't say anything more as they stormed away, leading the pair into the living room. Their bare feet barely made a sound as they crossed the carpet and pointed to the couch. "Sit."

Neither Aida nor Cyrus disagreed, sitting as far away from each other as they could. Bex clicked their tongue, running a hand through their hair, turning those neon eyes on them. Anger lit them up, their wolf rising to cause their chest to vibrate with a growl.

"Do you think because I am a sub in the bedroom, you can walk all over me?" Bex seethed, four fangs extended. "That I am incapable of saying 'Fuck. You.' And leaving?" They scoffed. "Selfish … You both are beyond selfish. How did I manage to get caught between dom and domme?" The last question was more to themself.

"I am fucking pissed. I am tired of being used as leverage. I may play a toy, but I am *not* a toy!" Power thickened the air, the scent of spiced apples rising as Bex reined in their wolf.

Gone was the sultry, sexy vixen. They were replaced with a powerful, and intelligent werewolf. A reminder that Bex was just as dangerous as they were.

"I am messy. I am an addict. I am far from fucking perfect." After inhaling, they blew it out harshly through their mouth. The air lightened, their hands shaking as they placed them on their hips. "But I can't keep going with this. I don't need you both being besties. But I need there to be honesty. If you both can't do that, I can't do this."

"No, Bex—" Aida started but snapped her mouth closed when Bex glared at her.

"You want a few nights? Just communicate it with us," Bex said sharply. "He's not in the position to say no."

Cyrus clenched his jaw. Bex was right, and he had no place to disagree.

"It's about how *I* feel too. If I need space from *both* of you, I will do exactly that. You don't own me, and you don't control me." They came around to sit on the coffee table in front of them, ignoring Aida's sound of protest. "No more lies, Mamita."

The admonishment was quiet but firm. Aida nodded with a near-pleading look in her eyes.

"I'm sorry," she said softly. "No more lies."

Bex's gaze connected with his, drifting down to his bouncing knee. They rested their hands on it, and their warm touch instantly sent relief.

"I'm sorry," Cyrus said softly, blinking the red from his eyes. It receded slowly, finally dissipating completely. He was full of apologies lately. "I never thought of you as a toy … outside of play, that is. I've told you this." He rubbed the back of his head, sighing. "But I'll admit that I've been a bigger asshole than usual."

He glared at Aida, who snorted. Bex's soft fingers glided along his chin, turning him to look back at them.

"Maybe a little bit," they said, pinching their forefinger and thumb close with their free hand. "Your possessiveness, while sexy most of the time, can be overwhelming," they chided. "I know you both don't like that I'm an addict." Bex sat back, pulling away their hand, and he instantly missed their touch.

"No—" both Aida and Cyrus started.

"Stop," Bex said sharply. "It's not something I will change. And don't you go saying, 'You're so strong' or 'I believe in you'. If that is something you can't accept, tell me now. Stop looking at me with pity and understand this is *my* decision."

Cyrus knew all too well where Bex was coming from, and he'd been a hypocrite. He sat forward, resting his elbows on his knees.

"So, what do you want, little wolf?" he asked, nervous about their answer.

"I want you both," they said simply. "Not at the same time, though." They all chuckled, the tension in the room draining slowly. "But no exclusivity. I'm … I'm not made for that."

"Neither am I," Cyrus responded, glad they were on the same page. They looked at Aida, who shrugged.

"Yeah, same," she said nonchalantly.

Cyrus had a feeling she did not, in fact, feel the same. But it wasn't for him to call her out on her bullshit. Another argument was the last thing he needed.

"Also…" Bex looked at him as they leaned back to rest their hands on the table. They crossed their legs, the top foot bobbing. "I quit."

"What?" Cyrus asked, confused.

Quit? Bex just stared at him, tongue playing with their lip ring. Realization slowly crept up in his mind.

"Are you giving me your resignation as the royal spy?" His brow arched as he tried not to be distracted by their mouth.

"Yeah. Conflict of interest and all that," Bex said, pointing their foot at him and Aida. "It's the responsible thing to do, right?"

"I mean … Yes, technically," Aida said, uncrossing and recrossing her legs as they settled under her once more.

"Are you sure?" Cyrus asked, the surprise of their request still lingering. "You've been a spy for over ten years. Did I—we—fuck this up for you?"

He was genuinely curious. Did he regret claiming them as his? No fucking way. Did he feel slightly guilty for drastically changing the course of their life? Maybe just a little.

"Eh, I'd been contemplating it for a while. Before I met either of you. I declined many jobs, and my seniority allowed me that option." A smirk grew on Bex's face as their eyes lit with a flash of neon. "But then I met a vampire who let me taste his cum..." Desire shot through him at their words. "And I simply had to know more."

They looked at Aida, a smirk remaining in place. "And then I was assigned to spy on a mad doctor. Went for the curiosity, stayed for the fucking."

"You're lucky I lo—" Cyrus cleared his throat, rubbing the back of his head when Bex's eyes widened slightly. "Erm ... You're lucky I *like* you because Kayne will have a conniption when I tell him. You were supposed to be the next Spymaster."

"Will you defend my honor, my Lord?" Bex asked with a grin, placing a hand over their chest for dramatic effect.

"Shut up," Cyrus snorted.

"I think you'll be fine," Aida chuckled. "Bex ... You might sit at my feet, but you rule my heart."

The soft words surprised Cyrus. He knew Aida had fallen for the wolf but never realized it was as hard—if not harder—than he had.

"I'm sorry for being dishonest. I'm sorry for putting you in near-impossible predicaments."

Bex moved from their seat, sinking to the floor to kneel in front of Aida. The woman brushed hair from Bex's forehead, only mussing it further.

"Actions speak louder than words, Mamita," Bex breathed as they connected their mouths.

Cyrus had to keep himself from fidgeting as arousal shot straight to his dick. Watching them make out—a mess of tongues, lips, and teeth—affected him more than he wanted it to. Thankfully, Bex broke the kiss first and smiled at Aida.

"I will see you in a few nights, okay?"

"What—" she started but clenched her jaw to shut herself up.

Cyrus remained where he was, hoping to hide the rush of relief that flooded through him. Aida sighed, nodding. Bex stood and held their hand out.

"I think we need to talk with Killian, too..." they said,

wriggling their fingers.

He snorted, taking their hand as he got to his feet. Bex grunted in surprise when he tugged them close and slammed his mouth against theirs.

Fuck.

All it took was a few nights of not seeing them to nearly flip his world upside down. Bex moaned, melting into him as their tongues rubbed against each other. He pulled on their piercing with his teeth, sucking on their lower lip. It took every ounce of his will to pull away. He would've had them on their knees if they'd been elsewhere.

"All right, don't rub it in," Aida grumbled as she stood. I'd like to get back to my workout," she said, motioning toward the door.

While still holding his hand, Bex leaned down to give Aida another peck on her lips.

"I'll see you in a few nights," Aida reminded them.

"Mhmm." Bex grinned. "I promise."

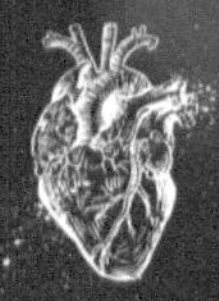

CHAPTER 25

LITTLE WOLF, LITTLE WOLF

THE SMELL OF FRESHLY ground coffee reached Cyrus when the penthouse lift doors opened. Bex hummed in approval, duffle bag slung across their back. He watched as they walked ahead of him. Back at Aida's, he didn't get to appreciate them like he wanted.

Their athletic shorts rested just above mid-thigh, their crop top exposing their midriff. Sliding out of their sneakers, Bex left them by the door next to his own. The two of them followed the scent of espresso to the kitchen. Killian bounced on the balls of his feet, dancing in a pair of shorts Cyrus got him. The man still couldn't dance, but damn, it was enjoyable to watch him smile.

"Hey, Kill-man. Working for free?" Bex's alto carried through the kitchen.

Killian nearly dropped the pour over he was preparing to skid to a halt. He placed it down gently and bolted around the kitchen island to tackle Bex in a bear hug.

"Bexie!" he yelped. "Deities, I was so worried."

His words were muffled as he stuffed his face in their chest. The wolf smiled, small canines glinting in the light as they hugged the shorter man.

"I'm good. I'm good," they chuckled as their embrace parted.

Killian returned their smile, giving them a soft peck on the cheek. His man turned those emerald eyes on Cyrus, and suddenly, his heart was in his throat.

"Hey, Daddy," he said huskily, trusting that Cyrus would catch him when he jumped up and wrapped his legs around his waist. He gripped Killian's ass as Killian locked his hands around

Cyrus' neck.

"Hey, baby," Cyrus whispered against Killian's mouth, devouring him in a kiss. The man melted into him, tongue ring playing along Cyrus' tongue.

A soft growl vibrated his chest as he sucked on Killian's lower lip until it was red and pouting. He walked to the island, placing his man on it, and reluctantly pulled away. Killian let out a protesting sound, gripping Cyrus' shirt to pull him in for a few more gentle, sweet kisses.

"Sorry," Killian said, looking at Bex, cheeks flushing red. He plopped his forehead onto Cyrus' shoulder, legs still wrapped around him.

Bex smirked, waving him off as they leaned against the island beside him.

"Don't apologize. I like seeing you happy," they said, pushing some dark hair from his forehead. "Watching you kiss was just a bonus." The way they warmly looked at Killian spoke volumes of their friendship.

"Too bad I'm gay, or I'd give you a bonus, too," Killian joked, wriggling his eyebrows.

"That's all right, I can make up for it." Cyrus' voice was hoarse as he cupped the back of Bex's neck and tugged them toward him.

"Oh really?" Bex smirked, tongue playing with their lip ring.

Cyrus answered with his mouth on theirs, enjoying the whimper that escaped them. Bex held his shirt for balance, opening for Cyrus to thrust his tongue into their mouth. A groan traveled up his throat when Killian bit and sucked on his neck. His free hand gripped Killian's ass making the man gasp. Killian trailed kisses up to Cyrus' earlobe, which he nipped and sucked on.

"Fuck," Cyrus panted, facing Killian to kiss.

It was Bex's turn to glide their tongue up the column of his throat, sharp canines running across the sensitive flesh. He couldn't fight the shudder that ran through him when he remembered he bore their mark on his shoulder. Killian and Bex's hands ran all over his body until they met at his erection.

"Shit, wait," he breathed, reluctantly breaking from his kiss with Killian. He nearly laughed at both their pouting looks.

"That word doesn't exist in my vocabulary. You should know that by now, Cy," Killian snickered, leaning back to rest on his hands. He let his feet drop from around Cyrus' waist, swaying them on either side of Cyrus' legs.

"So bratty," Cyrus chuckled. "Maybe I should gag that mouth of yours?"

"You wish," Killian grumbled, though the bright red of his cheeks told Cyrus he'd enjoy it.

"I don't know, Kill-man. Cy is pretty good at gagging folks," Bex said with a sultry smirk. "*You* might be wishing for it instead."

"Well, now I'm curious," Killian joked.

"Hey, don't talk about me as if I'm some sex toy you can use…" Cyrus grumbled playfully.

"I mean … Aren't you?" came Killian's smart-ass reply.

"I think so?" Bex shrugged.

"Oh?" Cyrus growled, noticing how the hairs on both of them rose to attention. He took each of them by the throat. Just tight enough that their eyes nearly glazed in submission. "What were you saying?"

"I don't remember," Killian breathed.

Bex made a sound of agreement.

"That's what I thought," he chuckled, letting them go. Cyrus stepped back from the island and helped Killian down. "Let's talk."

The three of them walked into his living room, and with a sigh, he sank into his couch. As if they were a perfect puzzle, Killian curled into one side while Bex curled into the other. Cyrus put an arm around each of them, chest tightening as he held the two. He wondered if they had an inkling of how much he cared about them.

Well, no, because you refuse to say it.

Cyrus shut up his inner voice as he idly played with Bex and Killian's hair. He wasn't sure how long they sat there as he tried to form words. He leaned his head onto the back of the couch to stare up at the ceiling.

Worlds were colliding, emotions threatening to burn him up from the inside out. How'd he get here? The past few months passed like a blur, and nothing prepared him for being on this couch with two people who held parts of his black heart.

"So…" Cyrus started as he sat up. His breath caught when they both shifted to look up at him. "Stop, don't look at me like that," he chuckled, making them grin.

"So…" Killian prompted.

"Well, here we are," Cyrus said as if that made all the sense in the world.

"For someone who is the Cortesano of the King and probably one of the most well-spoken men in Potroyan history … You sure are bad at words," Bex teased.

"I have said this. Repeatedly." Cyrus mussed up Bex's hair, laughing at their squawk of surprise.

"Okay, so here we are," Killian said, sitting up to look at Cyrus better.

"I spoke with Aida…" Cyrus fought not to roll his eyes. Bex and Cyrus filled Killian in on their conversation. "I know what Bex wants. What do you want, Killian?"

"I swear I melt every time you say my name," the man responded breathlessly as if Cyrus had kissed him instead. Killian cleared his throat, absentmindedly rubbing his wrists. "I agree with no exclusivity," he said with a nod. "Communication makes the world go round. I think we should be okay as long as we do that."

Killian reached across Cyrus to take Bex's hand. He smiled at his friend warmly, which Bex returned. "I don't mind kissing and forming a sexy little Cyrus sandwich…"

"I am *not* little," Cyrus interrupted.

"I know. I've got a sore ass to prove it," Killian quickly quipped back.

Bex let out a surprised snort, scratching the back of their neck.

"It's been forever since I've had a sore throat," they said, grinning when Cyrus' nose flared. These two were going to be the death of him.

"Okay. On the serious, I don't mind a make-out sesh. It's hot, I love it. I don't mind a puppy pile and all of us cuddling! But when having sex, I'd prefer to have just men and other dick-bearers," Killian said honestly.

"I understand, Kill-man." Bex gripped the man's hand. "You know I'd never leave you in an uncomfortable spot."

"Yeah, I know, Bexie."

"You two make me sick," Cyrus joked. He chuckled when they both simultaneously smacked him in the chest. "How do I handle the both of you in one space?" he shook his head.

"Look, if we both end up here on the same night, I don't mind not one bit if you and Killian want to go fuck or whatever. We can pass you back and forth, no problem." A playful smirk played on Bex's mouth.

"Is this how you feel?" Cyrus asked, half joking. He didn't mind it but at the same time, wondered if it made Bex uncomfortable. "That Aida and I just pass you back and forth?"

The wolf gripped his hand, using their free one to gently scratch the back of their neck.

"Yes and no. For a while there, I thought sex was my only useful feature." Bex shook their head to keep Cyrus from saying something. "But I know it's not. That I'm respected despite all my mess. As long as you keep reminding me, outside of play, that I am so much more than a toy, I don't mind being treated like one when it matters most."

"I want, no need, something else from you, Cyrus," Killian started, "When we're together, and you need to feed, you need to tell me. For my safety and your sanity. You're the only vampire to have bitten me before." The man rubbed his neck where the puncture marks still scarred the skin. "I didn't mind. It was hot as fuck. But I also don't want to be turned into a vampire … no offense," he said, face going red.

"I understand, pet," Cyrus said softly, hoping to ease the anxiety winding the man's shoulders up to his ears. "Though I'd have to exchange blood with you for that to happen, I'll make sure to say something."

"We all know I already struggle with living a normal human lifespan." Though he hid it with a smirk, Cyrus could see the haunted look in Killian's emerald gaze. "I am simply not built for immortality. Please promise never to turn me."

"I promise," Cyrus said, kissing him for additional comfort.

"Thank you," his man said softly.

Cyrus sat up, removing his arms around them to rest his elbows on his knees. "I need you both to understand that I can't always tell you what I'm up to, where I'm going, or what I'm doing. As the Cortesano of the King, I have responsibilities. Sometimes, those responsibilities can pull me away for nights or weeks. And a lot of the time, without notice. You'll have to be okay with that fact. I should also mention that being with me also puts a target on you both." He sighed, wondering why he hadn't thought about this already.

"We're aware of that. We're not innocent little cherubs who know nothing," Bex responded, Killian nodding in agreement.

"It's just that … I don't … I just…" He cleared his throat, gaze shifting from Bex to Killian and back. "Ah … Um, I care greatly about you both…" Cyrus managed to get the words out, and they both looked at him in shock. "Words. Me. Not good!"

"This is completely endearing," Killian leaned in to kiss Cyrus' cheek. He was sure the fire in his cheeks would've made him red if he hadn't been so dark-skinned.

"Yeah … Well…" Was Cyrus flustered? He cleared his throat again. "Anyway … I think this sums up a lot, right?" When they both nodded, Cyrus shot to his feet, pulling them up to stand. He turned to Killian, giving him a long kiss. "I'm going to give your sore hole a break and make their throat feel the same."

"Mhmm," Killian breathed, flushed. "Okay, Daddy." He looked to Bex and gave them a wink, turning to return to the kitchen.

"Fresh coffee and muffins will be left for you both," were the last words spoken as Killian sauntered out of sight.

"Tsk," Cyrus sucked his teeth, walking into Bex's space. His finger dragged along Bex's fuchsia collar. "Bad little wolf. You should be wearing *my* collar. Go to the bedroom and change into it and wear *only* it."

"Yes, my Lord," Bex whispered, eyelids closing halfway.

They grabbed their duffle bag, and he tilted his head to the side as he watched them walk down the hall to his room and slink inside. Slowly, he followed them, taking his time, heart hammering in his chest. Bex had a fist full of the organ and didn't even know it. A few nights. That was all it took to drive him mad with need.*

As Cyrus entered his room, he found Bex on their knees at the foot of the bed, wearing nothing but his red and black collar as he demanded. They watched him hungrily as he stripped his shirt off, exposing his ebony, muscled body.

"Look at you, an eager little cum slut," he growled as he stopped in front of them. "Tell me. Tell me that you're *my* eager little cum slut."

"I'm your eager little cum slut, my Lord," Bex rushed to say. They whimpered and opened their mouth, sticking their tongue out.

"Just filthy." His cock thickened as he spat in their mouth, their delighted moan sending arousal to flush through him. Cyrus unbuckled his belt and undid his fly as he looked down at them.

"Please," they whimpered as he pulled his aching length out. Cyrus sank his fingers into their thick hair. He smacked the head of his cock along their lips.

"Desperate for a throat fucking, aren't you?"

"Yes, so desperate," they moaned. Bex kept their mouth open, waiting not so patiently for him.

Using his grip on their hair, he shoved them toward him, thrusting his dick deep into their mouth. "Fuck!" he groaned, slowly thrusting in and out.

Cupping their throat, he felt it when they swallowed and took him further. Bex's hands flew up to grip his ass as his pace increased. They gagged, they drooled, they were utterly messy. They stared up at him, mascara leaving dark streams down their

---

* "Lose Control" by Teddy Swims

cheeks as tears fell. He pulled out suddenly, allowing them to gulp down air.

"On the bed and on your back. Head off the edge," he said with a growl. He removed the remainder of his clothes as Bex settled into position. They opened their mouth, tongue out as they waited. "Such a whore for my dick." He leaned over them, thrusting in once more. The new position allowed him to get deeper.

Bex garbled an agreeing sound, gripping onto the backs of his thighs.

"Tap my legs if you need me to stop," he groaned, leaning over to glide his fingers through their slick arousal. A sound of surprise was gagged by his cock, Bex's legs spreading wider for access. "So wet for me. You love a good face fucking, don't you." He collected their arousal and rubbed circles around their clit. With each swipe, he rotated his hips, enjoying their muffled whimpers.

A quick few taps on his legs had him pulling out of Bex's mouth quickly. He kneeled, cupping the back of their head to lift it as they panted. They looked at him with glassy eyes, swollen lips, and sweat coating their body.

"Are you all right?" he whispered, gently massaging their head. Bex gave him a hazy smile, nodding.

"Just needed a moment," they croaked, face flushed.

"Take as long as you need, little wolf."

Cyrus cradled their head, carefully watching them as they found their equilibrium. He lifted them to lay them in the middle of the bed, ignoring their yelp of protest.

"Wait—"

Their words were cut off by his lips on theirs. Bex melted under him, the head of his erection gently rubbing against their clit. They whimpered as he broke the kiss.

"I'm hungry, Bex," he growled. He bit and sucked on their neck, making them writhe. "But not for blood." He kept his gaze connected with theirs as he moved down their body. He tugged at their navel ring, enjoying their gasping sounds. "I want this greedy, soaking wet pussy."

"But I want your cum," they breathed, back arching when his tongue played with their hood piercing. "Please."

"I want yours more, little wolf," he said, groaning when he took a long, languid lick up their slit. He slid his hands up the back of Bex's thighs to push their knees toward their chest. "You'll get my cum when I say you will."

All protesting died on Bex's lips when he dove in like the starving man he claimed to be. Bex tried to squirm, their pussy gushing over his lips. He tightened his grip, knowing he'd leave bruises. The thought made him feral as he lashed and sucked at their clit faster.

"Oh … shit. Fuck!"

Their cries filled the room, along with the wet sounds of his mouth on them. They reached between their legs to grip the back of his head. If they wanted to smother him, he'd happily die with a face full of pussy. Cyrus bit their hood piercing, pulling it to give them that sharp pain they loved.

"Oh, Deities!"

"Tsk, naughty wolf," he growled as he pulled away just enough to brush his lips against their pussy. "My name is the only one you call out when you're with me."

"Cyrus!" they cried out as he used the flat of his tongue to rub against their clit. His name fell from their lips as a mantra, their grip on the back of his head tightening. He groaned when they dug their sharp nails into his scalp. "I'm going to come," Bex whimpered.

Cyrus doubled down on his ministrations, pushing their knees further apart to open them wider. With a scream, they came, flooding his mouth with their sweet arousal. He lapped at it, drinking their cum as if he were parched.

"Oh!" Bex moaned as he pushed past their orgasm to give them a second and, shortly after, a third.

"I can go at this all evening," Cyrus said, grinning as he let their legs go. Their wetness dripped from his chin. He swiped it with the palm of his hand, slowly licking it off.

"Oh my ... Damnit, Cy," Bex panted, looking at him as if he were a new person.

Maybe he was. Who knew? He had evolved and was still trying to figure out his new norm.

Cyrus rose to his knees, running his hand through Bex's arousal to use as a lubricant while he stroked his aching cock. Bex followed, staring at him while their nails glided down his abs. He hissed, making them flex under their fingertips.

"Can I have your cum now, my Lord?" they asked, kissing the mark they left on his shoulder.

A whole-body shudder rocked him at the light touch. He sank his free hand into their hair, pulling their head back.

"Eager, eager, little cum slut," he groaned, kissing them deeply.

They took over, stroking him, their thumb rubbing over the sensitive head. Bex broke the kiss with a gasp.

"Please?" they begged. "I need it. I need you."

"Open your mouth," he growled. As soon as they did, he let his saliva drip from his tongue to theirs. "Such an obedient little wolf."

Using his grip on their hair, he pushed them to rest their ass on the heels of their feet. A bead of pre-cum dripped onto their tongue as he only gave them the head of his dick.

"You want my cum so badly, don't you?" Bex whimpered when he pulled away. "How badly do you want it?"

"I want to feel you buried down my throat. Make me filthy and sore," they begged.

Cyrus grinned, enjoying their pleas but enjoying giving them what they wanted more.

"Choke on my dick," he bit out, thrusting deep into their mouth.

Bex gagged before relaxing their throat. Hot delicious pain trailed down his ass to his thighs as they scratched with their sharpened nails, encouraging him to pump harder. He pulled back enough for them to catch their breath, saliva pouring from their mouth before he thrust back in.

"Fuck, I will never get over throat fucking you," he groaned as he held onto their hair to keep them still. They swallowed, bringing his pelvis to meet their nose. "Greedy whore, taking this dick all the way down."

Already so close to the edge, he thrust a few more times, pulling out to come on their face. Bex kept their mouth open, tasting his cum with a look of pure satisfaction.

"Thank you for your cum," they rasped, collecting it and sucking it off their fingers.

Cyrus loosened his grip on their hair, which became a gentle massage. A low growl vibrated from them as he scooped them up in his arms. He walked them to his ensuite and put them on the bench so he could fill the tub. The scent of whiskey and oak floated from the water as he added calming bath oils.

They remained in comfortable silence while he washed them, rubbing the oils into their skin. As he looked them over, his chest felt tight, and his throat was thick. Their eyes had slid closed, and the peace on their face brought him a sense of guilt he had never encountered. Wrangling his emotions and figuring out how to voice them left him in a mental whirlwind.

Cyrus should've taken better care of them. Both of Bex and Killian. He should've been honest and more outspoken about ... everything. They deserved better. Someone with a more stable mind. Someone who wasn't such a danger. Someone who could express themselves.

"Are you all right?" came Bex's concerned but warm voice.

It pulled him from his spiral, and he realized the room was red, his breathing erratic. Their face came into view as they straddled his thighs.

"Where'd you go?" They trailed their fingers along his jawline, moving to his neck and collarbone.

"I'm sorry," he whispered. Bex looked at him in confusion. "For being a hypocrite. For not taking better care of you. Or Killian. I've hurt you both."

"Cy—"

"I, of all people, should understand boundaries. I should

understand the needs of an addict because I am one myself. I fucked up. I never meant to make you feel less than important to me." He sighed, everything tumbling out. "You're supposed to feel safe with me. I'm supposed to protect you and remind you of that … And I fucking failed."

Bex placed a finger on his mouth when he attempted to say something more.

"You never made me feel less than important. I distinctly remember you telling me never to tell you I was unimportant." A small smile remained on their lips. "You *do* take care of me. You take care of Killian, too."

Bex cupped his face, looking into his eyes deeply with an emotion he was sure was mutual. Realization dawned upon them, and they kissed him on the forehead, whispering, "Cy, I think you're experiencing a drop."

He looked at them incredulously. He had never experienced a drop. Was it because of how emotionally invested he was?

"W-what?" he stuttered, wrapping his arms around their waist and pulling them close. "I've never … Me?"

"Yes, papi. I'm almost certain." They buried their face into the crook of his neck and shoulder. "You're all right, Cy."

Their words made him hold on tighter. Bex ran circles on the back of his head, whispering soothing words to bring him out of the deep. His vision cleared, allowing him to lean back and admire all the colors of life Bex brought—from their hazel eyes to their navy hair, flushed skin, and eye-catching piercings. Everything.

"Whew, fuck," he gave a breathy laugh, rubbing a hand over his face. "Thank you," he said softly.

Bex gave him a sweet kiss.

"How about we get Killian and have a puppy pile tonight?" Bex asked with a smirk.

Cyrus chuckled, feeling lighter than he had previously.

"Yeah, yeah. You just want to make a Cyrus sandwich again."

"Nothing wrong with that. You're delicious."

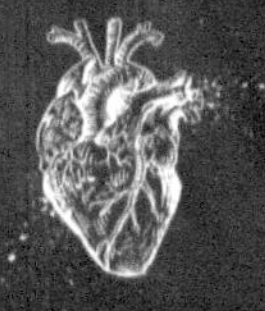

CHAPTER 26

MASQUERADE

CYRUS BLEW OUT A long breath as he looked at his reflection. A few months ago, anyone who knew him would've said he was incapable of attachment. There was no way the Lord of The Den would settle down. Well, maybe 'settle down' was a strong statement. More that the Lord of The Den would feel actual emotions.

What even were emotions?

"Are you nervous?" Bex asked from where they sat on the bathroom floor. They fiddled with a nasal inhaler, tapping it against their palm. "Haven't you been to a party before?"

"This isn't just a party, Bex," Cyrus said as he adjusted his brown tie for the umpteenth time. "This is diplomatic." He looked down at them in time to catch their scrunched face. "What?"

"Only you would use 'diplomacy' as a reason you're acting so fidgety." They tsked, rolling the inhaler back and forth between their forefinger and thumb. "Maybe I need to tell Killian to top you for once. To get that stick out of your ass."

Cyrus knelt in front of Bex, and their eyes widened at his sudden proximity. He wrapped a hand around their throat, grinning at how languid their body went.

"Should I make an example out of you? Ask Aida to keep you gagged until I see you again?" His leather shoes creaked gently as he waited for their answer.

"I'm sorry," they whimpered, wetting their lower lip with their tongue.

He smiled brightly, tugging them close by their collar. "Good," he said, giving them a quick kiss. They returned his smile as he stood to fix his tie again.

"Can I just say? Your tie is perfect." Bex snickered, pulling up one knee to hug. They absentmindedly tapped their inhaler against it as they spoke with him.

"Go ahead," he said softly, without judgment.

"'Go ahead' what?" they asked, pausing their fidgeting.

"Use the inhaler." He ran a hand down the burnt orange vest he wore over his white button-up. "You don't have to wait until I leave…"

"Okay, but—"

"I told you that I won't judge you for it. I meant it." He turned from the mirror to lean on the sink, crossing one ankle over the other. "Do you want me to leave? I won't hover either."

"Thank you," Bex said as they put the inhaler to their nostril and pushed a puff of air through it.

They inhaled deeply, holding it briefly before releasing it through their mouth. They did it three more times, equaling two puffs per nostril. He said nothing about the fact that most people only did one or two puffs. Their eyes went hazy almost instantly, a smile of relief crossing their lips.

"Fuuuuck," they groaned, leaning against the wall. "That first hit…"

"Always slaps," Cyrus snorted, holding his hand out to them. They took it, standing up with a bounce. "You good?"

"Oh, absolutely," Bex said with a wink. They sniffed briefly, using the back of their hand to rub the tip of their nose. "You should totally fuck me with this on one evening."

They grinned, letting their fingers trail his amber metallic mask. The design was intricate, etched with checkers, black obsidian adornments at his forehead, above his eyes, and temples. It was in the shape of an owl, framing his yellow eyes.

"Oh really," he purred, pulling them close by the waist. "Do you like the idea of being bound and left for the Lord to use as he pleases?"

He pulled their wrists around to rest at the base of their spine. His lips coasted over theirs, and he smirked at their whimper.

"Yes," they breathed, closing the small space to kiss him.

The sound of the penthouse bell made Cyrus' stomach nearly drop out of his ass. He gave them another kiss, stepping back. He cleared his throat, reaching for his suit jacket, but missed. Almost falling over, he stumbled till he snatched the damn thing.

"Oh, you're so cute," Bex laughed, running from the room with a yelp when he swiped at them. "Kill-man! You look amazing!"

Bex's squeal was followed by more laughter.

Cyrus looked at himself in the mirror one more time, pushing out an exhale. He wouldn't admit it out loud, but Bex was right. He was most definitely nervous. His shoes clicked down the hall, and his steps faltered when he saw Killian standing in the middle of his living room. Bex sat on a recliner, grinning like a wild cat.

Killian looked glorious. A wonderous black suit jacket covered his thick body, the coattails falling to the floor to form a train. Underneath was a sheer, floral lace, high-neck button-up that was the same burnt orange as Cyrus' suit. Black, loose-fitting velvet slacks draped over burnt orange shoes. Cyrus' mouth popped open as he realized Killian matched him. He continued his perusal, moving from bottom to top and landing on his man's face.

If Cyrus thought his mask was intricate, Killian's was outstanding. The mask was molded to Killian's forehead, so straps were not needed to keep it in place. Crimson floral etchings were subtle but eye-catching, nonetheless. On the sides, the mask's beaded fringe framed his full lips. True to Killian's fashion, his hair was tamed, but just barely so, with strands falling over the forehead of the mask. Kohl-lined green eyes peered at him with a heat that matched his own.

Fuck, his man was stunning.

Cyrus took slow, calculated steps toward him, a smile tugging up his lips at how Killian's breathing increased. Cyrus cupped the man's jaw when he stopped, taking every part of him in, committing it all to memory.

"Deities, Cyrus, close your mouth," Killian breathed, red creeping over the skin Cyrus could see.

He leaned in, tilting the man's chin up. "What if I don't want to? What if I want to get on my knees and worship your dick with it instead?" he asked against Killian's mouth.

"Now or later, Daddy?" he replied, voice sultry.

"Later," Cyrus smirked, giving him a too-quick kiss. "I have something for you. You'll need it."

He held his hand out for Killian, who took it, lips turning up in a smile. Cyrus led his man to his bedroom, nodding to the gifts he left on the lush bed.

"Oh..." Killian breathed, fingers gliding along the large butt plug. "You don't mean..."

"I do," Cyrus growled, coming up behind the man to press his erection against his ass. He slid Killian's jacket off, placing it safely on a nearby chair.

"And this too?" Killian squeaked, clearly eyeing the cock cage beside the plug, lube, a packet of sanitizing wipes, and a towel. Cyrus reached around his man's soft waist, unbuckling his pants and sliding his hand inside to cup Killian's length.

"Mhmm," Cyrus spoke into his neck, tongue gliding along his sweet pulse.

"Ah, for how long?" Killian moaned, rocking his hips into Cyrus.

He pulled his man's cock out, stroking it slowly. Cyrus held out his free hand, and Killian passed him the plug, wipes, and lube. He gently pushed Killian's back to bend him over the edge of the bed. Cyrus pushed Killian's pants down, smacking his ass when the man complained.

"For as long as I want," he breathed, pouring lube on his fingers. "I want you to beg for me, Killian." Cyrus pushed one and then two fingers into his man's ass.

"Oh, fuck," Killian whimpered. "But what if I don't want to beg?" He looked over his shoulder at Cyrus, a devious smirk on his plump lips.

"Hmm, you sure you want to be a brat tonight?" He pumped his fingers, scissoring them. When he thrust a third one in, Killian cried out.

"Maybe? Don't you love a challenge?" His man wriggled

his ass.

Cyrus chuckled, removing his fingers to use sanitizing wipes on them and the plug. After pouring an ample amount of lube on the toy, he edged Killian once more.

"Killian, this will be a challenge you'll lose," he growled, pumping the plug, working it deeper with each thrust. Cyrus reached around and stroked Killian's length in time with the toy.

"I doubt that," his stubborn man panted, soft moans escaping him as Cyrus continued to fuck him. Soon, the plug was fully in place, and Cyrus smacked his ass, jostling the toy. "Oh fuck!"

"You're going to come for me like a good boy. And then you'll wear this cage until I'm ready to let you out." Cyrus stroked him faster, his man's back arching as he cried out.

"Daddy, I'm close," he panted.

Cyrus quickly grabbed the towel, covering Killian's erection right as he came. He kept pumping, Killian's body jolting as Cyrus wrung out every last drop.

"Cage…" Without question, Killian tossed it to Cyrus. "Look at you, such a good boy."

"Stoooop," Killian groaned.

"I thought you wanted a challenge?" he purred. Cyrus chuckled at his man's whimper.

As soon as Killian was soft, Cyrus carefully put the cage on, ensuring it didn't pinch or hurt.

"Feel good?" he asked as he buckled it up.

"Y-yes. This is a first for me," Killian breathed as Cyrus helped him pull his pants up. "This … Wow."

"Do you like the way it feels? Does it bother you?" Cyrus asked.

"It's different. It doesn't bother me, though," Killian said, voice hoarse with need.

"Great." Cyrus grinned, lifting his sleeve to reveal his comm watch. He tapped it and nearly laughed when Killian let out a choked gasp.

"Oh no! Fuuuuck," Killian whimpered, gripping Cyrus' arms.

"Did I mention the plug vibrates?"

"Oh, you asshole," he breathed when Cyrus let up.

He pulled out another wrist comm, handing it to Killian. His heart pounded as the man took it with questioning eyes. He'd never given anyone the amount of control he was about to provide Killian with.

"It would be an unfair challenge if you were the only one suffering," he said softly. "I've got a cock ring on."

"What? Oh…" Realization dawned on Killian as he quickly put the comm on. "So, you mean…" he bit his lip as he tapped the device.

Instantly, pleasure lit up Cyrus' spine, the vibration around his dick making his eyes roll.

"Shit!" Cyrus groaned. It was his turn to grip Killian's arms, his hips rolling as the vibration slowly stopped.

"This is going to be fun…" Killian giggled.

"Did you just—"

"Shh. We don't talk about that, remember?"

"Are you up for the challenge, pet?"

Before Killian could respond, Cyrus' mouth crashed against his man's, making Killian moan. Cyrus ate his every sound, tongue thrusting in to fight against Killian's. The man's piercing rubbed along his tongue, and Cyrus groaned, gripping Killian's ass. Cyrus sucked in Killian's lower lip, using his teeth to graze and bite it until it was red and pouting.

"You-who," Bex sang, garnering the attention of both men from the doorway. Their grin told him they'd only just appeared and hadn't been eavesdropping.

Killian panted as they broke the kiss, giving Cyrus soft kisses along his jawline.

"One more minute," the man mumbled, licking the sweet spot under Cyrus' ear. He gripped the man's ass tighter, groaning when Killian bit the soft flesh.

"A minute has more than passed, gentlemen." The humor and warmth in Bex's voice made Cyrus grin as he gave Killian one more chaste kiss. "I don't think the King would like it if you're late.

Especially you, Cy."

"You're right…" Cyrus grumbled, adjusting himself, and the aching erection pushed against the front of his pants.

"Let me explain some things about the Ball first." Killian nodded for him to continue. "I have to sit with the King for the start. Once I have permission, I'll find you. But the Ball is more than it seems, and that's all I can say. Be mindful of how you use that power I gave you … Do you understand?"

"Yeah. Just don't forget about me," Killian said with a small smile.

"I could never."

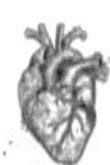

CYRUS NEARLY GROANED AS he sat in the throne-like chair next to Jacinto. The vampire was grumbling about part of the Asherite team being late, and Cyrus had to agree. He wouldn't feed into his Sire's energy, though.

"I mean, it's disrespectful. Who makes a King wait?" Jacinto groused.

He slouched in his chair, his black button-up shirt stretching around his body. He adjusted the white mask covering the entire left side of his face. His gaze kept shifting to the table of Demons next to them. It then slid to the Asherite delegation, which was missing three members. The goal was to keep all parties in sight. Times were turbulent, and it was driving Cyrus mad.

The Masquerade was in full swing, with drinks clinking and people laughing filling the space. The music was a thrum in the background. The ballroom was decked out in cosmic color, with magenta, dark teal, and plum drapes covering the walls. Lights that mimicked stars shone from the ceiling, giving the impression that the ballroom was in outer space. Dancing bodies filled the massive dance floor in the center of the room.

"Clearly, they do," Cyrus snapped.

Jacinto looked over at him with a smirk.

"I told you, go to your human."

"His name is Killian." Cyrus sighed, shaking his head. A hiss almost escaped his lips when a soft vibration started around his dick. He cleared his throat and spoke with his King with a surprisingly steady voice. "No, it doesn't look good for them to see the King without his Cortesano on the dais."

He nearly slumped when the vibration stopped. Damn, at least the man used the lower setting.

"You're right." Jacinto ran a hand through his long brown hair. "Where the fuck are they?" he growled.

"Siéntate derecho," Cyrus scolded.

For a King over five thousand years old, he could be immature. The thought made Cyrus snort, earning a glare from his Sire. Cyrus tapped his wrist comm, wondering where Killian was but reminding the man he hadn't forgotten about him. In response, his ring vibrated, and a soft groan passed his lips.

"Fuck…" he whispered, adjusting himself in his seat.

Pleasure traveled through him, the desire to roll his hips strong. The King gave him a sidelong glance, eyebrow quirking but saying nothing. The vibration stopped, and thankfully, a sound from the front covered the gasp of relief that blew through his mouth. Quickly, he tapped his comm, shutting off Killian's vibrator.

The entrance doors opened, and that's when he saw the remaining three Asherites walking in. Two men entered first. One was the color of storm, in grey and navy, dark brown skin glowing under the faux starlight. The other was the color of deep fire, wearing a plum so rich, it made his burnt sienna eyes nearly crimson. As they parted, a woman stepped through in an elegant gown of purple, turquoise, and fuchsia. The three were eye-catching, and it was apparent they were a polycule.

"I assume they wanted to make an entrance?" Cyrus mused.

Jacinto stood immediately and, without a word, left to meet them halfway.

"Well, goodbye to you too," Cyrus mumbled to himself. He kept his eyes on them momentarily, ensuring his King was all set before leaving the dais himself.

Cyrus scanned the ballroom, freezing to place a hand on a column as the ring vibrated again. This time, the intensity notched up, making him groan. He waved away the concerned looks of the servers.

"Fine. Everything is fine," he growled.

His dick ached, his need for relief increasing with the intensity of the vibration. He rested his back against the column, smirking as he tapped his comm. He could hear Killian's gasp from across the room, Cyrus' attention homing in on him by the bar.

Their gazes connected, and Killian's stunning smile and flushed face made his heart stutter. The man's hands were behind his back, keeping them out of Cyrus' view. Killian's lips parted, his panting clear. The challenge was in the set of his jaw, making Cyrus grin as he tapped his comm once more. Killian's eyes flared, chest heaving as he tried to keep his composure intact. His man didn't know the cage had a vibrator, and the thought made Cyrus' smile tug higher.

"Asshole," Killian mouthed, biting his lower lip.

Just as Cyrus chuckled, it was cut off with a groan when the vibration around his cock increased. He swore if he didn't get to Killian, he was going to come in his pants. He refused to lose this challenge. With two taps, he watched Killian's body slump. The man returned the favor by cutting off the vibrator.

Cyrus made his way to him, tugging him close by the waist. No words were shared because Cyrus didn't give Killian the chance to say anything when he captured his mouth in a fiery kiss.

"Hey, Pet," Cyrus breathed, running his thumb along Killian's lower lip.

The man brought it into his mouth, sucking on it gently. It sent desire straight to his cock. He ground against Killian to let him know how hard he was, and he felt Killian's cage as he did so. The King's parties often tended to lean toward exhibitionism and the like. People already separated themselves into the many comfortable alcoves.

"You're putting up quite the challenge."

"Have you come in your pants yet?" Killian chuckled after popping off Cyrus' thumb.

"Close. You were real close," Cyrus admitted. "Too bad you can't with this lovely gift around your dick." He reached between them to cup the cage.

A sultry grin pulled Killian's lips up. Quickly, the man tapped his wrist comm, making Cyrus hiss.

"Fuck..." he groaned, Killian now rubbing his erection.

"What's wrong, Daddy? Want to come?" Killian cooed.

Cyrus growled, wrapping his fingers around Killian's throat to pull him close. He took the man's lips in a kiss, thrusting his tongue in while removing his hand from Killian's cage to tap his wrist comm.

"Oh! Not faiiir," Killian whimpered, breaking the kiss with a gasp. His back arched, eyes nearly rolling.

"If you make me come in this suit..." Cyrus breathed, the vibration around his cock sending a constant pulsing of pleasure throughout his body.

"Y-you'll do what? Spank me?"

"Maybe." Cyrus slipped his hands beneath Killian's jacket to squeeze his ass, pressing the plug through his pants.

"Mmmm." Killian gripped Cyrus' lapels, breathing heavily. He could feel an orgasm nearing, and holding off was proving near impossible. "Okay. Okay!"

Killian tapped his wrist comm, allowing Cyrus to breathe a sigh of relief. He latched onto the man's lower lip, sucking on it until it was pouting.

"Those sounds you make are so delicious," he growled, tapping his comm.

"Fucking Orcus, Cy..." Killian gave him a megawatt smile. His face flushed with desire.

"Let's dance," Killian said suddenly. "I mean, if you can dance. You don't seem like the type to—"*

The man yelped when Cyrus spun him and turned them into the throng of dancing people. He only had eyes for the man

* "Skin and Bones – MEDUZA REMIX" by David Kushner, MEDUZA

before him as he took Killian's hand and wrapped the other under his suit jacket to pull him close. Killian wasn't the best dancer, but the fact he always did it anyway was endearing. Cyrus more than made up for it, leading him through the dance.

"Surprised?" Cyrus asked, turning Killian smoothly, the man's coat train never getting stuck around his feet. His man laughed as he was pulled in once more.

"Surprised is an understatement!" Killian brought Cyrus' hand to his chest, placing the opposite one on his hip. He stared deeply into Cyrus' eyes, depthless emotion filling them. "I love you." Cyrus gripped Killian's hand, trying to be mindful of his fragile fingers.

"My heart is yours," he responded, unable to say what he truly wanted to say.

If he hadn't been looking at him, he would've missed the slight twinge of disappointment in his man's eyes. Cyrus brought Killian's knuckles to his lips, kissing them softly.

"I'm sorry." Their foreheads connected, the masks making it hard for him to kiss Killian the way he wanted.

"I … I understand," Killian said, voice raw with feeling.

"Killian, I want you to know that what I feel for you can't be put into words," Cyrus said candidly. "But I made a promise. I promised to show you how I feel with my actions." He kissed his man sweetly. "Move in with me."

"W-what?" Killian stuttered, pulling back to stare up at him in shock.

The song shifted, and they moved off the dance floor. Cyrus locked his hand with Killian's, leading him toward one of the alcoves. It was thankfully empty and dimly lit.

Letting go of his hand, Killian removed his jacket, carefully placing it on one of the couches. It left him in just his lace shirt, nipples perking in the air. Cyrus had to hold himself back as he removed his jacket and sat down while Killian stood with his hands on his hips and paced.

"I know we're not exclusive," Cyrus started. "But waking up to you dancing in the kitchen, making coffee and pastries, is something I'd like. Waking up to your soft body next to mine and the smile on your face." Killian stopped his pacing, eyes wide. "Baby, I want your scent in every room of the penthouse. Have the place full of all the plants you like to care for."

"You noticed that?" Killian asked softly, allowing Cyrus to pull him down to the couch and sit.

Cyrus gently removed Killian's mask and his own. He brushed Killian's hair from his forehead, kissing it. The man's body shuddered as he gripped Cyrus' lapels.

"Of course," Cyrus whispered, trailing kisses down his face until he found the sweet spot under the man's ear. His fingers deftly unbuttoned Killian's the top of Killian's shirt, allowing him to pull down the high collar. He nipped and sucked at the newly exposed skin.

"I know you enjoy racing. Coffee isn't just a hustle but a passion. You care for your employees a great deal." Killian moaned, back arching as Cyrus let his hand glide over his tight nipples through his shirt. "You live life wholeheartedly, even when it gets hard."

It took all of Cyrus' restraint not to rip Killian's shirt off. Instead, he continued unbuttoning it until his skin was exposed. He kissed down the man's chest, slowly getting to his knees and nestling himself between Killian's thighs. He took the man's hands, kissing his wrists softly.

"I'm glad you're still here, Killian."

"F-fuck," his man whimpered, rolling his hips.

Cyrus sucked on one of his nipples before moving to the other.

"Those sounds you make. I want more. I want them all the time," Cyrus growled, undoing Killian's belt and nearly ripping off the fly.

A sense of urgency took over him. The need to please his man was strong and left him aching. He pulled down Killian's slacks and briefs to his ankles. His man's cock was red and dripping, blocked by the cage. Cyrus tapped his wrist comm, making Killian cry out as the plug vibrated in his hole.

"Cy, fucking Orcus!"

"Hmmm. Beg harder, Pet." Cyrus grinned when Killian's eyes widened.

"No," the brat said with a smirk. That was when he noticed the wrist comm in Killian's hand.

"Killian…"

"Oops!" his man tapped the comm, promptly tossing it out of reach. Cyrus' eyes rolled, hips bucking involuntarily.

"Fuck!" The ring vibrated at its highest intensity, filling him with pleasure in waves.

"Daddy, I want to see you come for me," Killian cooed. Cyrus' eyes popped open as he stared up at his man from his kneeled position. "What was it you told me? 'Your orgasm is mine'."

Cyrus shot up, leaning into Killian, grinding his dick against the man's cage. He stole the gasp from Killian's mouth with a thrust of his tongue. There was only one other person in his life he had ever let speak to him like this. Only one other person who he owed his orgasm to, and that was his King. But in this moment, with Killian, Cyrus wanted to give him so much more. Not just control over his body but his heart as well.*

"F-fuck, Killian," Cyrus moaned, unraveling by the moment. If he didn't show some restraint, he was going to… "Fuck!"

He let out a loud groan as he came so hard he thought he'd pass out. Wetness seeped into his slacks as cum covered his briefs. He panted, dropping his forehead to Killian's.

"Did I ruin you?" his man asked with a smirk, the ring still sending jolting vibrations up Cyrus' spine. Killian gasped when Cyrus reached between his legs to push the plug deeper.

"Well, you certainly ruined these pants," Cyrus chuckled, blindly finding the comm and shutting it off. His body nearly fell on top of Killian. "You won," he breathed, kissing his way back down Killian's body. The man moaned when Cyrus finally freed his cock from the cage.

"A-and what do I win?" Killian panted. Cyrus kept his gaze on his man as he let saliva drip from his mouth to the head of

---

* "Love Is Going To Kill Us" by David Kushner

his cock. He used it as lubricant to stroke it, making Killian groan. "Cyrus, please," he begged, lifting his hips to fuck Cyrus' fist.

"Didn't I say I wanted to get on my knees for you? That I'd use my mouth to worship you?" He licked the underside of his man's dick, moving up to swipe his tongue over the bead of pre-cum that dripped from his slit.

"Stop talking, please just suck my dick, Daddy." Killian gripped Cyrus' shoulders.

"Anything for you, Pet."

Cyrus took Killian's hard length in his mouth, reveling in the taste of his man. He growled as he bobbed, making Killian cry out and lift his hips. Cyrus gripped Killian's knees and spread them further apart. He cupped the man's balls as he sucked him down, massaging them and bringing out his favorite sounds.

"Cyrus!" Killian moaned when Cyrus pulled off for a moment. With one hand under Killian's ass to spread him, he pulled at the vibrating plug, slowly sliding it out. "Shit, shit," he panted, eyes rolling.

"Eyes on me, Pet. Watch me worship this dick of yours and fuck you with this toy," Cyrus said huskily.

The man's emerald eyes shot open, looking down at Cyrus. "Okay, Daddy," he whimpered.

Cyrus pushed the plug back into Killian at the same time he took his hard length back into his mouth. He held Cyrus' head to fuck his mouth, sliding down Cyrus' throat in the process. Killian shifted to the edge of the couch, allowing Cyrus to pump deeper. He gagged and made sloppy, crude sounds as he continued working Killian's length. Saliva pooled and covered Cyrus' hand, making it easier to fuck the man's ass.

"That feels so good. Keep doing that," Killian panted, hips continuing to rock as he let Cyrus come up for air.

"Lube," Cyrus croaked, nodding with his chin to the end table, which was always stocked in the event of spontaneous orgies. "Quickly, now."

Killian obliged, tossing it at Cyrus. He pulled the plug from Killian, making the man whimper. "Don't worry, I'm giving you more," he rasped, throat delightfully sore. "Bend over the couch."

Killian didn't waste a moment as he did what he was asked. Cyrus rushed to pull out his dripping, aching cock, needing to feel all of Killian around him. He removed the ring, tossing it to the side. After pouring the liquid onto his length, he plunged into his man's well stretched hole.

"Holy fuck!" Killian cried out, pushing back to meet each rough snap of Cyrus' hips.

He knew Killian wasn't far off from coming as he reached around to pump Killian's cock.

"You're mine, Killian. Everything that is you is mine," Cyrus whispered as he leaned over to fuck his man deeper. "My heart is yours."

"Your heart is mine, Cyrus," Killian moaned, reaching behind to cup Cyrus' head. He rushed to the edge of the cliff, knowing just how deep the fall was. It was deeper than he had ever fallen, and he wouldn't regret it.

"Come for Daddy, Pet," he growled, fucking him harder.

Killian let out a loud moan, and before he came, Cyrus had just enough sense left to grab a towel and cover his man's dick for him to come into. Cyrus quickly followed, filling his man to the brim. This time, Killian tossed him a towel, making Cyrus snort.

"Don't want to ruin these clothes any more than we have," Killian panted, plopping his forehead onto the couch.

After cleaning themselves up as best they could, they stood and watched the people dancing. Cyrus wrapped his arms around Killian from behind, resting his chin on his shoulder. Killian let out a contented sigh as they swayed to the music.

"I'd love to move in with you," Killian said with a smile.

"Thank fuck, I was worried I'd have to kidnap you," Cyrus chuckled.

Suddenly, his comm pinged. He stepped away from Killian to read Kayne's report. He ignored the wet spot that still covered the front of his pants, the work he had to do taking precedence.

"Fuck," he swore under his breath.

He looked up in time to find the group of Demons that he'd

been vaguely aware of standing from their table. The one in the middle, with the most obnoxious red and black harlequin mask, nodded to them, and they filed out.

"I have to go." He quickly kissed Killian's cheek, unable to give him a proper goodbye. He rushed to Jacinto, stepping up behind him.

"Cin. The spymaster left a report on Norrix." His urgent tone made Jacinto shift his gaze to him. "He's amassed a host of Demons on the outskirts of Malagado in Milagros. But we have another problem." Jacinto lifted an eyebrow and knew he would not like what he said next. "They plan to kidnap the bounty hunter."

The energy that flowed from his Sire made it hard to breathe. Cyrus wasn't sure of the connection between Jacinto and the bounty hunter, but he knew it ran deep.

"Not before I do." Jacinto hissed.

Cyrus raised an eyebrow in question.

"She's mine."

"We have to get with the Asherites and figure this shit out *now*," Cyrus said as they left the ballroom. He felt guilty leaving Killian as he did but knew his man would understand. "What are you planning?"

"I'm planning to destroy each and every Demon if I have to."

There was a glow in Jacinto's eyes that Cyrus had never seen before, but he didn't have time to question it. Right now, they had shit to handle, and it needed to be handled fast.

"Plan first, destroy shortly after," Cyrus said, needing to be the reasonable one. A crack of thunder shook the Palacio, making everyone in the halls gasp in fright. "I take it they didn't find her."

"I don't think so. Be prepared to go to war, hermano."

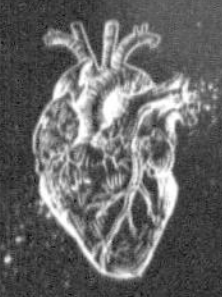

CHAPTER 27

BLOOD & TEARS

CYRUS GROANED AS HE made his way into the penthouse. He looked around, trying to figure out where to kick off his bloody boots, swiping at the disgusting gore on his face. He hissed, looking at his shoulder, which was burnt.

Fucking Demons. If he didn't get moving, he feared he'd drop to the ground and pass out right in the foyer. He unholstered the guns under his arms, at his hips and thighs, placing them on the table as if they were a set of keys. The tactical gear was shredded and covered in sticky, black blood. The sword on his back went next, clanging onto the floor.

"Cyrus!"

His gaze snapped up to see Bex running to him.

What were they still doing here? Where was Killian?

Cyrus fell to one knee, resting a hand on the floor. Keeping himself even halfway upright took all his energy. His vision shifted between red and black. How bad was his blood loss? After finding the bounty hunter, the warehouse exploded. He was barely patched up, and their after-battle meeting was brief. The Asherites lost a member, and they were not handling it well.

"Deities, what happened?" Bex asked, pushing themself under his arm and lifting.

He often forgot how strong the werewolf was and was amazed at their ability to help him up. He grunted as he allowed them to lead him to his bathroom. Their hands were steady despite the haze in their eyes, helping to remove his gear.

"Aida … I need Aida," he breathed.

They hesitated briefly before pushing off his shirt. He growled with a snap of his teeth at the pain in his side. Bex didn't flinch, simply moving their head to the side to avoid getting bit.

"Fuck!" he howled as they helped him sit down on the toilet.

Bex stood beside him, letting Cyrus rest his head on their hip as he caught his breath. He briefly heard them pinging the doctor.

"What the fuck do you mean he needs me?" he heard Aida scoff.

"Get your ass here. I have news about your brother," he said softly, hoping his voice traveled.

Her gasp and sudden click let him know that he'd been heard.

"What happened?" Bex asked again, grabbing a rag.

His eyes slid closed as he listened to the sloshing water. Fire lit up his side when they placed the warm cloth to clean it, making him hiss. He gritted his teeth as they continued cleaning him as best they could. Showering would be impossible without stitches first.

"Cyrus, why aren't you healing?" Their voice grew panicked while their hands remained steady.

"Demons," he breathed.

"Demons?" they halted, smacking his face. He growled, eyes popping open. "Stay with me. Demons?"

"That's … That's all I can say, Bex."

"Hmph." They returned to cleaning him up. "Your side won't stop bleeding."

They pushed a clean rag against it and held it, making him nearly bite his tongue off.

"F-fuck!" Beads of sweat formed on his forehead, and more dripped down his back. "Not that I mind you being here because I'm glad you are, but why *are* you here, and where's Killian? I thought you were going to Aida's?" he asked breathily, needing to get his mind off the pain of his entire. Fucking. Body.

"Well … I fell asleep, to be honest." Bex shrugged, kneeling next to him to better hold the towel against him. "Then, I decided just to stay here."

"Translation, you took another hit or two," Cyrus remarked,

trying to withhold his judgment. He needed to stop being a hypocrite.

Bex pushed the towel in, making him shout in pain.

"And? So what?" Bex snapped. "*Anyway* … Killian pinged me. You asked him to move in, eh?" They smiled, no hint of jealousy to be found. "He went to his place to grab some things."

"Makes sense," he sighed, readying to close his eyes again when his penthouse lift dinged.

Shortly after, Aida stormed into his bathroom. She dropped her med kit and nearly slipped on the bloody floor as she wasted not a moment to get him patched up.

"What happened?" she asked calmly while she worked.

He appreciated her professionalism, especially her steady hands as she cleaned and stitched him up, taking care not to make him hurt more than necessary. Was it surprising? Absolutely, but he was grateful nonetheless.

"Demons," both he and Bex said at the same time.

"Demons…" Aida trailed off as if expecting more.

"That's all I can say about that," he said, grimacing when she sprayed the new stitches with a medi-sealant that accelerated the healing and aided with wound care.

Slowly, the burn in his side subsided, the cooling sensation making his body slump in relief.

"Tell me about my brother," Aida said as she threw away the bloodied bandages and rags.

"I need you to sit for this," he breathed, body rigid again. He did not like what he had to tell her and would be heartless if he said he didn't feel empathy on her behalf.

"Tell me, Cyrus. Now!" Aida yelled.

Bex stepped behind her, placing hands on her shoulders. Their eyes connected with his, and he could tell they already knew and were prepared. He took a deep inhale and pushed it out between tight lips.

"Aida … Your brother was with us. The Asherite team," he started, standing and ignoring how his body wanted to protest.

She stepped back so she could look up at him.

"Okay?" Aida's eyes turned pleading. The realization of what he was about to say hit her. "No…" she shook her head. "No…"

"I'm so sorry," he croaked, feeling her pain. *Knowing* her pain.

"No, don't tell me that. Don't say you're sorry!" Aida screamed at him. She collapsed, Bex just barely catching her as they pulled her into their arms.

"Aida … There was nothing we could do. We tried. The King *tried*. We were overwhelmed." Cyrus didn't know what to do or say. The sorrow radiating off her nearly brought him to his knees.

"H-his body?" she asked, tears building in her eyes. Cyrus shook his head.

"We … we don't have him."

Aida shattered. Lightning cracked across the sky outside the window, clouds quickly forming to rain hail on the city below. She screamed and cried. Curling into herself, Bex held her tightly. She rocked back and forth, the storm growing outside. As tears fell from her eyes, they sparked like liquid lightning, making her silver eyes glow with their power. Electricity crackled around her, and Bex hissed but refused to let her go.

"I've got you, Mamita," Bex whispered against Aida's temple as she ran a comforting hand over her coils. They continued to whisper words of comfort, helping Aida regain her breath and control the electricity sparking like a live wire around her. "Let me take you home," they said softly as the storm outside died slowly.

They looked up at Cyrus, and he nodded, giving them space and limping into his bedroom. He gripped the edge of his large dresser so tightly it snapped under his hands. Keeping his composure was taking all of his lingering energy. He should've fed. He should've done better. Fuck! He should've done more!

A ping sounded from his comm, and he clenched his jaw when he read over the report. Fucking Orcus. He hated wars.

At the same time, he turned toward his ensuite, and Bex appeared with Aida in their arms. She was cradled against their chest, passed out, likely due to exhaustion.

"Stay here as long as you need," he said gently. "I am being called to Vascaria."

"Vascaria?" Bex whispered, motioning to his bed.

He pulled back the comforters and blankets, not caring if the blood on Aida's clothes transferred to the sheets. Bex placed the Wielder on the bed, resting her head on their lap. They ran a soothing hand over Aida's coils.

"Demons … I need to make sure our outpost is secure. I can't stay and wait—"

"I'll let him know."

"Thank you. Please let her know I tried. That I will find a way to help her find retribution."

"I will hold you to it," came Aida's raspy voice as she opened her swollen eyes to look at him. "You find a way to make these bitches burn and hand me the torch."

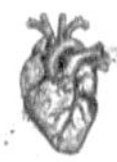

2 Weeks Later

CYRUS DROPPED HIS DUFFLE on the floor as he walked off his penthouse lift, staring at his living room in surprise. Plants with bioluminescent flowers were stylishly placed throughout. Sun lamps were lit over especially sensitive herbs. A small tree with teal leaves stood proudly in the corner by his ceiling-to-floor windows. Nearly overpowering the perfuming plants was the savory scent of burgers. Cyrus kicked off his combat boots in pursuit of it.

Killian hummed to himself, jazz playing softly as he flipped the burgers. His sweats did wonders for his ass, and Cyrus leaned against the doorframe with a grin.

While he'd been away, all he wanted was to get back. To get back to Killian, whom he had never had a chance to say goodbye to. To get back to Bex, and check up on Aida. Two weeks was a long time with no contact, and the next few months were not going to be any less stressful.

"Well, this is a delicious sight," Cyrus said playfully, spooking his man, who turned with his hand on his bare chest.

"Cy!" he yelped.

He stepped forward but held a finger to say 'Hold on' and returned to the burgers. He put them on a plate, moved the pan, and turned off the stove. He cleaned his hands with a towel, and once satisfied that there was no fire hazard, he bolted around the kitchen island to leap into Cyrus' arms. He chuckled as he caught him, hands under his thick ass while Killian wrapped his legs around his waist.

"I missed you too," Cyrus whispered against the man's lips, devouring him in a kiss. It was all tongues, lips, and teeth clinking against teeth. Killian matched his desperation. "Fuck, I missed you so much," he said again.

"I missed you too. It's been miserable."

"Is that why you decorated?" he asked with a soft chuckle.

Killian's face flushed as he smiled.

"Yes. I stress decorate … Or clean. Or both?" He shrugged, wriggling to be put down.

Reluctantly, Cyrus let him go, instantly missing Killian's soft body against his own.

"I've never seen you in your Guard uniform," he breathed, taking a few steps back to look Cyrus from head to toe. "Or a Guard uniform like that before," he said, motioning to the black-on-black military gear with a red Ayobaí emblem on the left pec.

"Sentry. I was a Sentry before I was promoted to Cortesano. The Guard wear crimson." Cyrus shrugged as if he didn't just let Killian know he was once part of an elite team of black ops.

"It's hot," Killian grinned.

"And I'm not allowed to have sex in it, so don't get any ideas," Cyrus said, returning Killian's grin.

"Oh, who will know, Daddy?" his man pouted.

"I will … Don't tempt me to punish you for pushing," he said with a sly grin. Arousal flashed in his man's eyes as he considered his options. "As much as I want to do whatever is going through your mind right now, I have to change and head back out."

He hated the fall of Killian's shoulders.*

"But you just got back," he said, nibbling on his thumb. Cyrus' eyes drew to the movement but caught onto something else.

"Killian..." Cyrus stepped forward, firmly but gently taking the man's wrist and exposing his forearm. New, fresh scars swiped across his skin, one dangerously close to his wrist again.

"Cyrus..." he grumbled, trying to take his hand back.

"Why?" Cyrus asked, refusing to let him go. Before Killian could react, he grabbed his other wrist to find the same. "Killian, what's going on?"

Tears welled up in his man's eyes, and it broke his fucking heart.

"I ... I was stressed. Not seeing you. Not hearing from you. I was worried. I thought the worst happened to you!" The tears fell in streams down his cheeks. "I didn't know how else to handle it. I don't like feeling abandoned."

"I didn't abandon you," Cyrus said, voice slightly raised. "Why would you think that?"

"I don't know! It makes no sense, but that's how I felt anyway." Killian sniffed, trying once more to take his hands back. "With everything that's happened, Bex has been with Aida. Helping her cope with what happened to her brother. I've been alone, spiraling."

"What about your brother?" Cyrus asked, tugging Killian close to raise his wrist to his lips. He kissed it softly, doing the same on the other.

"Oh, him? He went and eloped." Killian whimpered when Cyrus kissed his forearms. "Please, let me go." Cyrus complied, not wanting to make Killian more unstable.

"Killian, I'm sorry. I didn't abandon you. I just had no time to tell you where I was going. I was in a no-contact zone. When I told you this could happen, you said you understood," he said gently.

"Doesn't make it easy," Killian whispered, rubbing his wrists. "It's whatever. I'm fine now."

---

* "Dark Signs" by Sleep Token

Unease built in Cyrus' core as he looked his man over. *Truly* looking him over now that their reunion had passed. His eyes were mildly sunken as if he hadn't gotten much sleep. His hair was stringy, and it made Cyrus wonder when the last time he took a shower.

"When will you be back?" Killian's quiet question drew Cyrus out of his assessment.

"In a night or two. Killian, there's a lot I can't say, but I can say for sure that we're on the brink of war. The King is leaving the country and making me Regent."

"What?" Killian stared at Cyrus with wide eyes. "Does that mean—"

"Yes … I'll be ruling Ayobaí for the foreseeable future. It means my time will become extremely limited while we settle everything."

"Oh … Oh wow," Killian blanched, pacing over to the food he left on a plate. "I … Wow. Okay." Before Cyrus could stop him, the man tossed the food in the trash.

"Killian—"

"I think I need to just go home for a bit," he said softly, voice pained.

"What?" Cyrus asked, confused. "This *is* your home."

"No … I mean my place. My house. I wasn't planning on giving it up. I worked too hard for it." Killian brushed past him, Cyrus following in his wake.

"I didn't think you would. But—"

"I just need time to think about this!" Killian yelled, storming to the bedroom.

"About what, Killian? What is there to think about?" he snapped, snatching the duffle from Killian's hand.

"Give it back, Cyrus," Killian seethed.

Where the fuck was this anger coming from?

"Tell me what you need time for. Tell me what is going on in your head. I'm not a mind reader!" Cyrus refused to budge.

"How about this? Tell me how you feel, Cyrus. Tell me what is going on in that heart of yours. I'm not a mind reader!" he shot back. "You told me you'd show me and prove how you felt with your actions. But you're leaving again. And you are going to keep leaving now."

"It's my job! It is my duty. It is what I *must* do," Cyrus said, finding Killian's behavior irrational.

It *was* irrational, right? Fuck he wasn't sure. He let Killian take the duffle from him, and he stood watch as the man filled it with his essential items and clothing.

"That's the worst part! It was hard enough with you being the Cortesano. I knew what I was getting into being with you. Exclusivity or not, I knew you were a political figure. But Regent? I don't know how to handle that."

"As if I do? Do you think I *want* this?" Cyrus had to fight the urge to grip him by the shoulders and shake sense into him.

"Did you say no?" Killian asked as he threw on a sweater. Cyrus kept quiet, knowing that even if he could've, he wouldn't have. "Yeah. That's what I thought. You're the Cortesano; surely, you've been prepared for this." Killian shook his head. "I know I'm overreacting. But this is a lot to take in."

"Are you seriously going to walk out on me right now?" Cyrus asked, following close behind Killian as he approached the lift. "I tell you that I'm about to take on the biggest responsibility of my life, and your response is to leave? To quit on me?"

"No!" Killian spun on him, making Cyrus almost barge right into him. "I am *not* quitting on you. I just need time! What part don't you get?"

"The entire fucking thing!"

"Cyrus, you can't even tell me you love me and yet expect me to take this in stride?" Cyrus winced at the anger in his man's voice. "I can't do that. You made me fall. I told you I was hitting the bottom, that I was already there. These past two weeks have been torture. Has your attention spoiled me? Yes. Am I being selfish? For once, yes, the fuck I am. I am not in a position to tell you not to become Regent. I am smart enough to know it's important to you. But where do I fit in your life now?"

"Where you have been. Here. In my—*our*—home. I

wouldn't have asked you to move in if I didn't want you to have a permanent place in my life." Cyrus' world felt like it was blowing up, and he couldn't grasp the pieces falling through his fingers.

"I … I'm sorry."

Killian stepped into the lift. As the doors closed, he left Cyrus standing and staring blankly. Killian didn't know he took a piece of Cyrus' heart with him.

CHAPTER 28

WHAT EVEN IS A HEART?

IT HAD BEEN TWO nights since Cyrus last spoke with Killian. Two nights of wondering if his man left him for good. Two nights of wondering if he left him for wanting to do his job as the Cortesano.

He ran a hand over his face as he sat in his office, pouring over all the holoports on his desk. He underestimated how much work his Sire did, and while it intimidated him that it would now be his responsibility, he took it for what it was—his job.

"Hey, boss," came a familiar drawl at his door. Cyrus looked up to find Tristan with his arms crossed and leaning on the doorframe.

"Oh shit, hey man," Cyrus said as a smile formed on his face. As Tristan entered the office, he stood and met the man halfway to give him a handshake and half hug. "Damn, it's good to see you."

"Same. Hate the circumstances," Tristan said with a sigh. "I fucking hate war."

"I couldn't agree more," he groaned, motioning to his couch.

Tristan plopped down, leaning back to stretch out his long legs. Cyrus sat on the recliner and sat forward to rest his elbows on his knees.

"This whole thing is fucked."

"It truly is. But it was only a matter of time before the Asherite drama arrived here. The best we can do is try and find as many allies as possible and hope this doesn't end with Euhaven in ruins," the man said soberly.

Cyrus had never seen him so severe.

"Funny how we literally passed each other in Vascaria. You had arrived here right as I was leaving." Cyrus studied his hands. "And now you're leaving again with the team."

"Aw, did you miss me that much, buddy?" Tristan asked as if talking to a puppy.

Ah, there he was.

"Shut up," Cyrus snorted, looking back at him. "Seriously though, you have no clue how much my life has turned upside down since the last time I saw you."

For the next two hours, Cyrus told Tristan everything. It felt good to get it off his chest, to voice it all. While he had Jacinto to talk to about certain things, talking with Tristan, a man he considered a best friend—the only friend outside his Sire—was different. They sat there, bourbon in hand.

"Well damn, Cyrus, you've got yourself into a clusterfuck. Not necessarily the bad kind, but definitely the kind that I'd be worried about your dick."

"What..." Cyrus took a moment, trying to compose himself. "What does that even mean, Aries?"

"Well..." Tristan opened his mouth to answer but shut it. He shrugged. "I don't know." The Ice Wielder took a swig of his bourbon. "How's Sweets doing?" he asked softly.

"From what Bex told me the last time we spoke, she was coping. I let her have free reign as Interrogator, and it's been proving useful for her to let out her anger and grief." Cyrus sat back, rubbing his temple gently. "She's going to Asherai."

"What?" Tristan asked, placing his bourbon down. "Why?"

"The body that showed up weeks ago with the black eyes has been bothering her. After the exposure of Demons, the ferals, and now Deathstalkers, she thinks Asherai has the answers on what exactly they are and maybe how to eradicate them."

"How does she even plan to get that information?"

Tristan didn't seem too fond of the idea, and Cyrus wondered if the man had formed a kinship with the doctor. He for sure knew it wasn't romantic at all.

"How many times have you hung out?" Cyrus asked bluntly.

Tristan had been in the middle of picking up his bourbon when it clinked back on the table.

"What?" he nearly squeaked.

"You're awfully concerned about someone you only fucked once. Unless you two have been either hanging out or fucking." Cyrus shrugged, though he was a bit upset, if only because he felt protective of Tristan and didn't know what he would do if Aida tried to fuck with him.

"Okay, first things first. We haven't had sex since that night at the Den. Second, we hung out a few times. In the beginning, it was so I could get inside her head. Understand her and make sure she wasn't a risk. But then I found she wasn't so bad if you get past the arrogance." Cyrus snorted at that. "I mean, if I can worm myself into your life as a bestie … And you're arrogant as fuck."

"Hey," Cyrus grunted, tossing an ice cube at the man, which was the wrong move. Tristan Wielded it midair and thrust it back at him, letting it clink into his glass.

"Now I distinctly remember you telling me you'd have an answer about maybe finding love by the time I got back…" Tristan started, changing the subject.

"Tristan…" Cyrus groaned. "Really?"

"Yes, Cyrus, really." The man's voice pitched up like always when he was ready to get what he wanted. "Share with the class. After everything you've told me about the last few months… Where are you at?"

"Fuck if I know. Everything is a mess, remember?"

"Yes, but you should still know what's happening in that organ you call a heart."

"I know what I feel." Was all Cyrus could say.

"Okay, subject change," Tristan said, saving Cyrus from trying to explain the whirlwind in his heart. "I met someone."

"What?" Cyrus coughed on the bourbon he had been sipping.

"Eeyup," Tristan said with a grin. "Okay, well … I met her, but she doesn't acknowledge me much."

"Oh, Deities," Cyrus huffed, rolling his eyes. "Does she even know you exist?"

"Yes! You wanna know how?" Tristan asked as he sat up excitedly. He waited, staring at Cyrus.

Cyrus stared back at him for a beat.

"Well? How?"

"So glad you asked! Because I crashed her training sessions." Tristan beamed as if he was the best boy for doing so. "Now she has no choice but to spar with me."

"Tristan … it's not the Asherite assassin, is it?"

"Oh, sure is." The man bounced in his chair. "To be honest, I truly want to be her friend. More than anything, actually."

Cyrus relaxed in his seat.

"Oh. So, you met someone as in a new friend."

"Don't sound so bummed, boss!" Tristan got up only to forcefully park it next to Cyrus on the recliner.

Cyrus snorted, moving to allow the man to squeeze into the seat.

"Where we're going, I need a friend. And I have a feeling she does, too." He patted Cyrus' cheek. "Don't worry. You'll always be my number one bestie."

"I'm your *only* bestie," Cyrus quipped, snapping his mouth shut.

"Oh, so you admit! You admit we're besties." Tristan put an arm around Cyrus, getting mighty comfy. "I knew you liked me."

"Yeah, yeah. Just eat it all up while you can, Aries. You're leaving me for Deities knows how long…" Cyrus groused. "Before you ask … Yes, I'll miss you. I missed you all these damn months. You get back, and now you're leaving in a few weeks."

Oh, well, fuck did he sound needy.

"But I mean…" he coughed, clearing his throat. "I mean, I understand. It's cool."

"No, no. Don't do that," Tristan said, voice suddenly gentle. "It's okay to miss your friends, even if I'm one of the only ones you have." He squirmed, struggling to remove himself from the recliner. "I think I got us into a pickle…"

"Eh, I think I'm quite comfortable," Cyrus said, now wrestling with Tristan to keep him seated. They both fell into a fit of laughter.

"Despite everything, you want to know what I've noticed about you?" Tristan asked as he finally slid off the recliner to sit on the floor. He pulled his knees to his chest, his intuitive gaze connecting with Cyrus'.

"What's that, Aries?"

"You're more open. Well, at least with me. I know you've been going through Orcus these last few months, but something has shifted, and I can tell." Tristan rested his chin on his knees. "For the first time, I can see your heart, and I think it's wonderful."

"Oh … wow," Cyrus stuttered. "You can see all that?"

"I have my moments," the Ice Wielder shrugged with a wink. "It's not a bad thing even if things go belly up. It's not a bad thing to find a few people you can trust with that organ of yours."

"And what do you suggest I do with this knowledge you've just imparted upon me?"

"I think it's time for you to use your words."

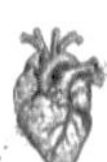

WHAT ARE YOU DOING here?" Aida murmured as she opened her door to look up at Cyrus. The evidence of her grief was written on her face. Tired eyes met his, rimmed with red. Behind her, the ordinarily neat apartment was a mess.

"Can I come in?" he asked, for once not feeling an ounce of anger or hatred toward her. "Please?"

Aida seemed to think on it momentarily, nodding and opening the door enough for him to walk in.

"They're not here if that's who you're looking for," Aida said softly, leading him to her eat-in kitchen and motioning to the breakfast bar to sit. "I promise I'm not lying."

"I believe you, but that's not why I'm here." He waited for her to sit, looking her over. "Have the interrogations helped?"

"Somewhat," she said candidly. She tapped her fingers

along the bar top. "It lets me get out of my head for a bit, but the thoughts return once I stop." She sighed, rubbing her eyes with her free hand.

"I heard you're going to Asherai." And for some reason, Cyrus wasn't too happy with that idea.

"I am. The answers we need about these ferals and Deathstalkers are there. I just know it." The look of determination on her face told him that no matter what he said, she would go.

"But by yourself? Are you sure this is the right idea?" he asked anyway. "How do you plan to get this information? You're no spy."

"I already got a job in the Monarch Tower," she said plainly.

"What?" he asked incredulously.

"Apparently, being a neurosurgeon and psychiatrist is in high demand." She shrugged, her tapping increasing.

He took her hand, surprising them both. His thumb ran gently over her knuckles making her let out a long shuddering exhale.

"I ... I have to do this," she whispered. "For my brother."

His chest tightened at the sadness in her voice.

"Can you at least travel with Jacinto?"

"Who knows how long that would take? Is he even going to Asherai? I know nothing of his role in this." She shook her head, shifting her hand to hold his. He wondered if she realized she did so but let her seek comfort wherever needed.

"You're right ... You're right." He swallowed a thick lump in his throat. "For some reason, I'm worried about you."

She gave him a slight smirk. "Don't tell me you've grown soft, sweet man."

"I can say the same about you, good doctor."

The two let out soft chuckles, settling into companionable silence.

"I have to tell you something," Aida said, breaking the quiet. She removed her hand from his and placed it in her lap.

"And what's that?" he asked, suddenly on edge.

"I'm not going alone." Aida bit her plump lower lip.

"You're not? Who..." His words died as he stared at her,

willing her to look up at him. When she did, he knew instantly who she meant.

"No." He stood so abruptly that he almost knocked the stool down. "Absolutely not."

"It's not your decision, Cyrus," she retorted, rising to her feet.

"So, you both made this decision without seeing how I felt?" he growled. Their brief moment of connection shattered around them. "Fuck me and my opinions?"

"We were going to tell you! Obviously. Bex just wanted to figure out how." Aida shook her head, pacing away from him to the living room.

He followed her and grabbed her elbow, spinning her to face him.

"Where is Bex?" he snapped.

"Getting their shit together," she snapped back, trying to remove her arm from his grip. "Let me fucking go."

"Getting their shit together where?" Cyrus refused to let her go until she answered all his questions.

"I don't know! They said they were grabbing gear, clothes, and … supplies."

The way she said 'supplies' and her accompanying wince had an uncomfortable pit forming in his stomach.

"Potions, you mean." Cyrus let her go, running a hand over his head. "You're letting them take fucking potions overseas? Do you realize you could get arrested at the Asherite border? Their laws are stricter than ours! It means death if they're caught. You included."

"Bex has it sorted out. I trust them to handle it because this isn't their first time leaving the continent. They're a spy, Cyrus. They're not stupid!" Aida yelled at him. "Am I happy about it? No! But we already agreed we wouldn't try to interfere, no matter how much we want to."

"I can't let them go … You don't know what you're asking of me," he bit out, walking away from Aida before he did something stupid like snap her neck.

"And you think I can go without them? Cyrus, you have Killian. I have no one!" Aida snapped her mouth shut as if she hadn't meant to say that last part.

He turned to face her, seeing the panic and tears welling in her eyes. Fuck.

"I ... I don't even know if I have Killian anymore," he whispered.

Aida stared at him, surprise lighting her up.

"What?" she asked, taking a few steps toward him. The anger they shared slowly drained as Cyrus leaned a hand against the wall.

"I'm taking over as King Regent, Aida."

"What!?" Aida exclaimed. "Fuck, Cyrus."

"It's too much for him. I promised to take care of him, and now I'll see him even less. He stormed out on me, and I have no clue if I'll ever see him again." Why he was telling her, he didn't know. Maybe it was his vulnerable state at the thought of Bex leaving. "My heart ... I don't think it could handle it if Bex leaves too."

"Cyrus ... I don't know what to say," she said softly, reaching out hesitantly to take his hand.

He allowed it, gripping it tighter than he wanted to.

"Stay. Just stay. Don't go."

"Cyrus, I can't do that, and you know it."

He knew she was right. She was so fucking right it made him angry. He dropped her hand to cup her jaw. Her eyes fluttered as she looked up at him in both a state of confusion and longing.

"In another life, I wouldn't let you go, do you know that?" he whispered. "I'd make you stay. Maybe I would've made you mine." He shook his head, wondering where his mind was at.

"You're just saying this because you're emotional. Because you don't want Bex to go," she breathed. "Don't fuck with me to get what you want."

When she tried to pull away, he gripped the back of her head, tangling his fingers in her hair.

"I'm *not* fucking with you," he bit out. "I agree ... I'm

emotional, and I hate it. But I long let go of my hatred of you. Especially after knowing how much you care about Bex."

"So, what are you telling me?" she breathed, her small body swaying under his as he pushed her against the wall, leaning his face to hers.

"That I'm letting you go. That I'm trusting you to take care of Bex. That … I don't even fucking know…"

It was then that he kissed her. Kissing Aida was not in his plans. Whatever fucked up, shitty plans he had for his life. But here he was, her soft lips against his own. Lips that were plump and delicious. He teased them until she opened for him and allowed his tongue to thrust in and rub against hers. Soft whimpers escaped from her into his mouth, his own groan rising in response. Slowly, he broke the kiss, still close enough to feel her breath against his lips.

"You better make sure you find me before you leave." Cyrus let go of her hair to trail his fingers along her jaw.

"I will. I promise," she responded softly. Tentatively, she rose to her toes to give him a chaste kiss. "In another life … I would agree with you. Find Killian, Cyrus. Tell him how you feel before it's too late."

Cyrus nodded, stepping away from her and the other life he could see clearly now. He left the apartment, face flushed, body thrumming with anxiety.

What in the fuck was he doing?

Life was so fucked up it wasn't even funny.

Once again, he was sacrificing everything.

Everything for his King. For his people. For his country.

Did he regret it? No.

Did it hurt? Absolutely.

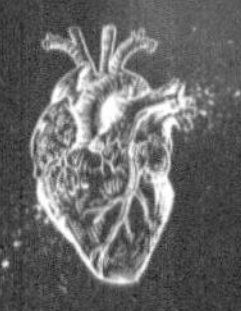

CHAPTER 29

WHEN THE BOUGH BREAKS

"**Y**OU CAN'T BE SERIOUS,** Jacinto," Cyrus groaned, pacing the King's office, frustration suffusing every pore of his being. "You're moving forward with Rodon?"

"I understand you dislike the vampire, but keeping him close is better than letting him continue to run around with his antics." His Sire was unphased by Cyrus' frustration, and it pissed him off even more. Jacinto crossed his ankle over his knee as he sat behind his large, ebony desk. "You know, before all of this shit with Aida and your human, the Den, and all of that, Rodon was on my radar as your replacement."

"I know, but—"

"Don't let your personal shit fuck this up. You *have* to work with him whether you want to or not." The commanding and authoritative tone was one Jacinto rarely took with Cyrus. "As Regent, you will understand that difficult decisions have to be made for the betterment of the Kingdom. I may be your friend and Sire. But I am also your King, and you will respect me as such."

"I'm sorry," Cyrus quickly said, letting out a long and frustrated exhale. "Truly. I meant no disrespect." He adjusted his tie, smoothing his hands down his navy vest.

"I know. Remember, responsibilities first, personal shit later. I am setting up a meeting in two weeks. We have to get on the same page before I leave. We still have so much preparation to do, and it'll be much easier if you work with me instead of against me."

"I'm not trying to work against you, Cin," he said sincerely. "However, if Rodon fucks up while you are gone, I can't promise I won't remove him from his seat."

"I understand. Don't give him the space to do so." Jacinto stood, motioning for Cyrus to do the same. "Venga, we have to go through the finances, and I have to take you to the treasury."

"Oh, joy. I hate math," Cyrus said with a groan.

"That is why we have a Treasurer, hermano. Grow up," Jacinto snapped.

"Oh, how the tables have turned," Cyrus groaned, making his King snort. "All right. All right. I'll get my head on right."

"Bueno." Jacinto stood still for a moment as if contemplating something.

"Ask it," Cyrus sighed.

"Have you spoken with your human?" Jacinto asked immediately.

"*Killian.* No, I haven't." His best friend grabbed his forearm when Cyrus attempted to drop it and leave.

"¿Por que?" Jacinto genuinely looked concerned, and Cyrus wasn't sure if it was a good or bad thing.

"I don't know what to say? He's ignoring my pings? We're falling apart?" Cyrus shrugged.

"When we're done tonight, go to him. I don't care if he's been ignoring you. No more excuses." Jacinto let Cyrus go. "I can't stand seeing you like this."

"I'm sorry…" he whispered.

"Stop telling me you're sorry." Jacinto sighed. "You need to learn how to use your words. I see the gears working, and I can see how you feel. You're always stuck in tu cabeza, and you're wearing your emotions as clearly as the moon on your sleeve. Just tell him."

"You're the third person in two days to tell me this…" Cyrus rubbed his face.

"Then you should follow our advice. Clearly, we are wiser than you."

Cyrus nudged Jacinto's shoulder.

"Yeah, yeah. I'll find him later. I just hope he'll hear me out." Cyrus sniffed, trying to keep himself controlled.

"Make sure you feed first. And then find him. Tell him. And

don't let him go. When you have something as precious as love…" Jacinto's eyes briefly went vacant as if reliving a memory before he shook his head. "Don't let it go."

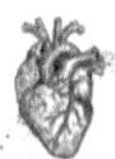

CYRUS' HOVERCAR HUMMED AS he drove to Killian's house. He tapped his fingers on the steering wheel, rehearsing his speech in his head. All the things he'd been having a hard time expressing, he would finally say aloud. His palms were clammy, his heart stuck in his throat.

Would Killian be upset that he showed up unannounced? Or would he be happy? Cyrus hoped to the Deities it was the latter.

The hovercar buzzed with energy as he pulled off the freeway. Anxiety gripped him by the throat. A ping alerting him to a hologram message pulled him from his spiral.

"Killian?" he asked before he realized it was a recording. He put the hovercar on autopilot and watched the hologram, his heart pounding.*

"Hey, Daddy. I'm sorry it took so long to send this message." Killian's green eyes looked tired, his hair messy as if he'd repeatedly run his hand through it. "I miss you. I didn't know how to handle the news of you being Regent. I was scared and thought … I don't know what I thought." Cyrus' heart ached when his man sniffed. "I never told you the story of my fourth suicide attempt."

"What…" Cyrus whispered to himself.

Why was Killian telling him this in a message and not to his face? His stomach sank, tapping a button on his dash to increase the speed on his autopilot. He wasn't far from Killian's and could've just taken over the car, but he couldn't look away from the hologram, even if he wanted to.

"I didn't want to be alone anymore. I hated the feeling, and I just felt … Well, maybe it would be better to just leave. What

* "When the Bough Breaks" by Sleep Token

was the point? My heart had been broken several times. My mind shattered. Why stay here? And I know this is unreasonable to say, but … Cyrus, I feel lonely. So lonely. And you being Regent … I don't think I could handle that sort of loneliness." His man shook his head, tears falling down his cheeks. "I love you, you know? Even if you won't say it back. I wonder if you even feel the same…" Killian breathed a manic laugh, scratching his forehead. That's when he saw his bloodied hands.

"No!" Cyrus yelled, roughly grabbing the steering wheel to pull the car out of autopilot and allow him to speed through the streets.

He bobbed through the cars, ignoring the blares of horns left in his wake. He held his breath as he nearly slammed into a hovercycle, sharply taking a turn that put him on the sidewalk. Pedestrians screamed as he whizzed by, avoiding contact the entire way.

The hovercar whirred as he finally turned onto Killian's lone street, weaving its way into the woods and to the cliff his home sat on.

Maybe it wasn't too late.

The message had only been recorded shortly as he pulled off the freeway.

There had to be time!

Cyrus' breaths came out in short pants as he leaped from the hovercar as it put itself in park.

"Killian!" he shouted as he burst through the front door.

The strong scent of blood made his fangs ache, but he pushed it aside, running up the stairs. He slammed into Killian's bedroom door, finding it locked.

"Baby, please. Don't do this," Cyrus panted, his chest tightening to the point he wasn't sure how he could still breathe.

"Cyrus?" came Killian's sweet but thready voice.

Cyrus rammed his shoulder into the door until it finally splintered. The sight before him stopped him in his tracks.

Blood. There was so much blood, and in the middle was Killian, lying on the floor, wrists split open.

"No! Killian, no!" Cyrus slipped as he fell to his knees and crawled to his man. "Killian, why? Why?"

He was distantly aware of the raw pain in his voice as he spoke. He lifted Killian's head onto his lap, taking one of his wrists. Fuck, the wound was too deep for him to simply lick closed.

"I'm sorry," Killian whispered. "I was so weak. I couldn't … I couldn't…" Killian's voice was distant, eyes glassy.

"I came here to tell you everything. You have to stay here. You have to hear it, please, baby," Cyrus begged as he held Killian's limp body tighter. "I lo—"

"No," Killian rasped. "N-not while I'm dying." He coughed, eyes fluttering.

A sob broke through Cyrus, shattering his heart and mind.

"Please," Cyrus cried. "Don't live for me, live for yourself. Please," he begged.

Cyrus cradled Killian's head to his chest, feeling his pulse slow. Panic and urgency rushed through Cyrus, erasing all logical thought.

Save him.

Protect him.

Keep him alive.

Mine!

Acting on impulse, he brought Killian's neck to his mouth. He breathed in Killian's heady brown sugar and espresso scent, the surrounding blood only adding to it.

"No, don't," Killian whimpered. "I don't want that." His man was too weak to resist as Cyrus' body shook with sobs. "Please…"

"Love, I told you I'm a selfish man," he whispered through sobs. "You can't leave me. Not now. Not ever."

He sank his fangs into Killian's throat gently, pulling just enough to push his venom into the man's veins.

"Cyrus, please don't do this," Killian cried.

Cyrus knew what he was doing was wrong. It was blasphemous to turn a human without consent. It was outlawed centuries ago, long before Cyrus was even born. Jacinto was going to be pissed, but his sire's wrath was worth making sure

Killian lived. He couldn't let him go, not after finally voicing his love for his man. He'd let the fucking world burn if it meant Killian would live.

Killian's pulse was so thready that Cyrus was concerned he might be too late. He pulled away and bit into his wrist. He knew what he was risking by attempting to turn Killian. He could be creating another berserker, but Cyrus didn't care.

"I love you," Cyrus whispered, putting his bloodied wrist on Killian's, spreading the vampiric infection. "Killian, I love you too much to let you go." He placed his wrist to the man's mouth, knowing how quickly the infection spread and how difficult it was to resist the call of the blood.

Without any more words to share, Killian latched onto Cyrus' wrist. He groaned as he pulled the blood into his mouth, the sensation zinging through Cyrus' body. He continued to cradle Killian's head while he fed from him deeply.

When Killian pulled away with a gasp, Cyrus' heart ached as he writhed in pain. The infection worked quickly, reshaping his blood and very DNA. And it fucking hurt. He watched as the wounds on Killian's wrists healed themselves, blood no longer flowing.

Cyrus wasn't sure how long he sat there after Killian passed out from the change. He ran his hand over Killian's hair, rocking and whispering sweet words of encouragement. Killian's heart beat strong and loudly, a sound that Cyrus could listen to for the eternity he'd just bought them. The fact that it almost went away had rocked him to his core.

"I love you, Killian," Cyrus whispered once more, cupping his face and pressing a soft kiss on his forehead.

Love was an odd thing. It made him do crazy things. The feeling of losing control should've made him pause. He should've thought twice about his actions. But desperation and greed ruled him, and regret had no place here.

There were no lengths Cyrus wouldn't go to to protect what was his, even if it meant destroying himself in the process. Even if it meant burning the entire world down.

A soft exhale and full-body shudder drew him from his thoughts.

"Hey," Cyrus said as Killian stirred.

Killian's eyes fluttered open to stare up at Cyrus, and his heart faltered, a stone dropping in his stomach. They were nearly depthless black, and a ring of red around the pupil was the only color—the color of a berserker's eyes. A growl vibrated Killian's chest. The man was pissed. Cyrus expected it, but not to this magnitude.

With a quickness Cyrus was unprepared for, Killian pinned him to the ground, straddling his waist. What he said next wasn't anything Cyrus wanted to hear, which destroyed any semblance of control.

"I. Hate. You."*

Cyrus flipped them, snatching Killian's wrists to hold above his head.

"What?!" Cyrus snarled, shaking his head at the bloodlust that rose, matching Killian's.

"I fucking hate you. That's what I said!" the newly made vampire bucked Cyrus off him, once more gaining the upper hand and straddled Cyrus. "I wanted to die. How could you be so selfish?!"

"What did you expect, Killian? I warned you!" Cyrus growled, pushing Killian off him.

The vampire flew back but caught himself from slamming into the wall. Cyrus got to his feet, baring his teeth at his man. Fuck, was he even his anymore?

"You were going to leave me. You were going to shatter me, Killian! What was I supposed to do?"

"Let. Me. Go! You would've eventually healed. You would've moved on," Killian panted as he rounded Cyrus. "I didn't want to be a vampire, Cyrus!"

"You gave me no choice!" He grunted when Killian rushed him and grabbed him by his lapels. Cyrus' anger rose to meet

* "DAMAGED (feat Spencer Charnas)" by In This Moment, Ice Nine Kills, Spencer Charnas

Killian's, his vision blanketing the room in red. Fuck, he forgot how strong new vampires could be.

"You have every choice, and you took away mine!" Killian's nails dug into Cyrus' chest, his own heaving. "I don't want this!" Tears welled up in Killian's eyes, the red eerie as his anger deepened. "Why would you do this to me? This isn't love, Cyrus."

"I did this *because* I love you! I've never loved *anyone* before. I've never felt the way I do for anyone else. Killian, you're supposed to be my forever. How was that going to happen if you were dead? I'd rather you be mad at me than leave me."

"Too bad you're getting both," Killian snarled, tugging Cyrus toward him, his eyes drifting to the vein pulsing in Cyrus' throat. "I hate you," he said again, striking and digging his fangs deep.

He slammed Cyrus against the wall, causing picture frames and artwork to crash to the ground. Despite his short stature, Killian remained steadfast.

Cyrus groaned, palming Killian's ass to lift him, and spun to push his back against the hard surface. Killian's legs wrapped around his waist as he growled into Cyrus' throat.

"You don't mean that," Cyrus breathed, the feeding sending desire down his body. He could feel Killian's cock grow hard between them, his own doing the same in response. "Fuck." He groaned when Killian rolled his hips.

No. No! He had to push his arousal aside. Fucking Orcus, he had to try and rein in some of his control.

Killian showed better restraint than Cyrus expected when he pulled away with a gasp. Blood flowed down his chin as he licked his lips. "Yes, I do. Yes, I really fucking do." Killian suddenly pushed Cyrus away, landing on his feet when Cyrus let him go.

"Killian..." Cyrus growled as his man circled him.

"Cyrus, you know what I want?" he said, tapping his chin with his forefinger.

"What's that, Pet?"

"No, you don't get to call me that anymore," Killian snapped as he slowly prowled toward Cyrus.

Cyrus' heart slammed in his chest, not from fear but from realizing the damage he did—of what he had just created.

"I am not your man. Fuck, I'm not even human anymore." He chuckled darkly, eyes flaring. "I'm a berserker, aren't I?"

"Yes," Cyrus bit out, watching Killian closely.

"That explains this … this energy. This incessant need."

"You have to feed. Let me help you."

Killian laughed again, "I think I can figure it out." Suddenly, the man was in front of him again, gripping his shirt. "Cyrus, I want…" His voice was low and menacing.

Gone was the man he fell in love with.

Gone was the man who gave him sweet kisses and showed him what it meant to be loved.

In his place was a monster of his own creation.

In trying to save Killian, Cyrus destroyed the man he loved.

"What do you want, Killian?" Cyrus growled, Killian's berserker fueling his own.

"I want you to hate me," he growled back.

"You want me to hate you? Hmm?" Cyrus sank his hand into Killian's hair, pulling his head back and lifting his chin. "I could never hate you, Killian." His grip tightened when Killian struggled to move.

"You will when I go slaughter everyone on this side of Potroya," the man bit out, clenching his teeth.

"You wouldn't…" Cyrus threatened.

"I *will*. Why not be the monster you made me to be?" Killian grinned, knowing he had hit the sore spot he intended.

Cyrus' berserker roared within as his grip on the young vampire's hair tightened. "You want me to hate you? Make me."

He tossed him to the center of the room. The red halos of Killian's eyes lit as he snarled and ran at Cyrus. The two collided, with Cyrus ducking to wrap his arms around the man's waist and tackle him to the ground.

"Fuck you for what you did to me!" Killian howled, getting the upper hand and snapping his wrist out to slam into Cyrus' nose.

Killian lifted his hips, bucking Cyrus off and rushing to his feet.

He kicked, his foot connecting with Cyrus' abdomen. It temporarily knocked the wind out of him, but when Killian attempted another, Cyrus snatched his ankle and pulled. The younger vampire fell back with a grunt, fangs bared.

"You won't win this, Killian," Cyrus growled, voice guttural as he wrapped his hand around the man's throat and lifted him to stand.

Shifting his hand to Killian's hair, he violently tugged him close and sank his fangs into his throat. The need to tear it to pieces hummed through him as he snarled, drinking deeply.

"Hate me, Cyrus," came Killian's strangled voice before a sharp pain struck him in the stomach.

Roaring, he shoved the man back, his fangs leaving behind torn flesh. Killian cracked his neck as the rapidly closing wound healed. Cyrus looked down to find a large shard of glass sticking out of his abdomen.

"You fucking stabbed me," Cyrus snarled, pulling it out, blood spraying from the nicked arteries.

Quicker than he could react, Killian was on him, slamming him against the wall. It was then Cyrus realized berserkers had a distinct scent like coals on fire. It flared brightly as the young vampire tore into Cyrus' throat.

Cyrus floated, mind taking him elsewhere. His berserker presented itself to him, giving him a choice.

Die, kill, or give Killian what he wanted.

Cyrus was on the edge of surrendering complete control, but he knew if he did, Killian would die by his hands. He would never be able to live with himself if he went through with it. Not after everything he did to ensure he stayed on Euhaven.

Dying was not an option.

"Fine. You want me to hate you, then I will," Cyrus rasped, gripping Killian's hair to force him to break his connection with Cyrus' throat.

Despite the blood loss, power thrummed through him as he pulled from his berserker. He spun Killian and slammed his face into the wall. It stole the breath out of the man, who gasped.

"You go on a rampage, and it will be the end."

"It's already the end, Cy," Killian panted, managing to rear his head backward and ram it into Cyrus' nose.

He let him go with a shout, stumbling backward as more blood flowed down his face. Killian's ragged breathing was loud as they stared at each other.

"It's the end because you don't know how to fucking love. Because you're a selfish asshole who only thinks about yourself."

"Fuck you, Killian," Cyrus seethed.

Killian's words were like glass stabbing his heart. His very anima was being utterly destroyed as the man glared at him. Killian wiped the blood on his chin with the back of his hand. He stared down at it, clearly looking at his wrists.

"I hate you..." Killian's voice was lined with danger and violence. His thumbs ran over the area his scars would've been had he succeeded. "I hate what you did to me." His black and red eyes snapped up to Cyrus. "I hate that you turned me into a monster. Just. Like. You."

Cyrus' heart shattered, and he remembered why he never wanted to say those three fucking words. A man like him never loved. He didn't deserve the joys that came with such a precious emotion. Killian was right. Cyrus was a monster. A berserker who destroyed everything he touched.

Love had no place in his life, and he shouldn't have allowed it in. His love was toxic, an infection to those who came near. Killian was evidence of his disease.

"Well, what are you going to do now, *Sire*?" Killian gasped when Cyrus rushed to snatch his shirt and yank him close.

"You'll remember me. You'll never forget my dick. My love. My heart." Cyrus whispered against the man's exposed neck. "You may hate me now. You may never forgive me. But you *will* remember me." He sank his fangs into Killian's soft flesh, blood spurting into his mouth.

Killian cried out, gripping Cyrus by the arms. The man laughed breathlessly, heart beating wildly against Cyrus' chest.

"You'll remember me too, Cyrus. You'll remember what

you did to me. You'll see me and know you made me what I am." Killian stumbled back when Cyrus let him go abruptly. "And you know what else?"

He stepped close, breathing erratically. A dark grin pulled up his lips as he brought them close to Cyrus'.

"I'll never forgive you for this. And I will find a way to destroy not just your heart but your life. You'll regret ever making me a monster."

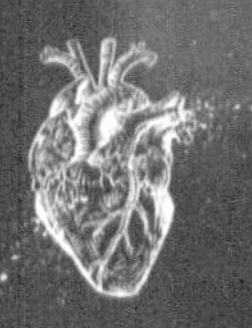

CHAPTER 30

HMMM

FUCK. THIS. SHIT.

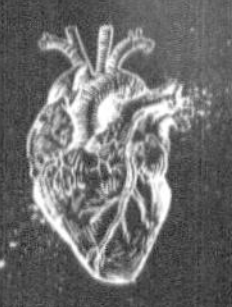

CHAPTER 31

SHATTERED & DESTROYED

THE HOUSE WAS QUIET as Cyrus sat on the edge of Killian's bed, staring at the pool of blood on the floor. Despite his threat, he didn't stop Killian from leaving. Part of him hoped he wouldn't try to follow through because Killian wouldn't stand a chance against Cyrus. He leaned forward to rest his elbows on his knees, rubbing his temples as a loud ringing sounded in his ears.*

Overwhelmed, Cyrus screamed. He screamed until his chest ached and his throat was raw. He roared until sound no longer passed through his lips. He panted, no longer truly seeing anything. Lightheadedness overcame him, and he was sure he was going to pass out if he kept holding his breath or screaming.

"…rus," came a muffled sound.

A voice?

Cyrus couldn't hear anything through the pounding and ringing in his ears. Urgent hands rocked his shoulders, slapping him sharply.

He growled, snapping his teeth at his assailant.

"Stop!" the voice yelled, becoming more apparent.

Cyrus focused on the man kneeling in front of him.

"J-Jacinto?" he rasped, staring into the eyes of his Sire. "I'm barely holding it together. I'm barely holding it together." He repeated over and over.

"What happened?" Jacinto asked, keeping his hands on Cyrus' shoulders. It was the only thing keeping him upright. "Where's Killian?"

"Oh, *now* you say his name!" Cyrus yelled. "Don't say it. Don't say it ever again." He shook his head, the pain in his chest

---

* "Bones" by Jared Benjamin

constricting his airway.

"Hermano, breathe," his Sire soothed, the gentle compulsion forcing him to comply, even if he didn't want to. His head cleared slowly with each breath. "Now tell me what happened?"

Cyrus told Jacinto everything with shaking hands and a bouncing foot. His body shook as he tried to contain his anguish. He would not shed any more tears.

"I want to kill him," Jacinto growled.

"Cin, don't," Cyrus pleaded. "Not after everything I went through to keep him alive." He gripped his own shirt, which was still covered in Killian's blood.

"Fuck, you're right," Jacinto sighed. "Venga, let's get out of here," Jacinto said as he stood and pulled Cyrus up with him. "Wait, you said he was a berserker, yet he didn't tear you apart or go on a rampage."

"He was extremely lucid and in complete control. I've never seen that, even with regular vampires. Do you think it's ... Because *I'm* not a regular vampire? What did I do? What the fuck did I create?"

"That might be the reason. We won't know until we talk to him. *If* we talk to him."

Cyrus grimaced. "I have a feeling we haven't seen the end of Killian Pierce..."

CYRUS GROANED AS HE turned in his bed. It'd been a few nights since his ordeal with Killian, and sleep had been practically nonexistent. Every time he shut his eyes, he saw Killian bleeding out in his arms one moment, only to morph into a vampire who hated him.

Pinging caught his attention, but he ignored it. He didn't have to be available for another few hours. Whoever it was could wait. As soon as it stopped, it started again. And again.

"Fuck," he mumbled, looking at his comm to see Aida was

trying to reach him. He sighed, sitting up against his headboard and answering, "Yup…"

"Bex knows what you did," the doctor said sharply. "Have you spoken with them?"

"Wait, slow down," Cyrus urged, fully awake now. "Bex knows?"

"Yes…" Aida said softly. "Killian contacted them. It was a mess, and Bex bolted like they always do when overwhelmed. Cyrus, he's so angry. I barely know him, but even I know it's unlike him. What happened? How?" Aida shook her head. "Sorry, that isn't my business."

"I honestly can't talk about it. I…" he sighed. "I just don't have the energy for it."

Cyrus was glad when Aida nodded and honored his boundary. If only he had done that for Killian. No! If he had, the man would be dead, and he couldn't accept that.

"I haven't heard from Bex. Not since they confirmed plans for the three of us to discuss Asherai." The worried look on Aida's face told him more than she probably wanted to admit. "Aida, what's wrong?"

"Bex pinged me while I was in surgery. Twice. They left a message that concerned me, so I pinged you immediately. Bex mentioned 'fucking up'. And that they 'didn't mean to'. The message went out before they could finish, and now I can't get them back on the comms. Can you find them? I am trying not to panic here…" Aida chewed on her lower lip, and a pit settled into his stomach.

What the fuck was happening here?

Why was his world imploding around him?

"I think I know a way to find them. Once I do, I'll let you know," Cyrus said, his calm tone belying how he truly felt. Anxious. Panicked. Everything in between.

"All right. Please tell me as soon as possible. Please, Cyrus," Aida pleaded.

"I promise. I swear to it," he responded.

After ending their connection, Cyrus pinged Kayne.

"My lord, is everything all right?" the Spymaster asked, long black hair tousled from sleep.

"Did Bex come in for their tracker removal at all?" He didn't want to waste time with pleasantries.

"No, not yet. They were supposed to last night, but they rescheduled to next week."

"Good. That's good. I need you to track their location." Cyrus stared at Kayne, who looked at him, perplexed. "No questions, Kayne. Do it now."

The Shadow Wielder nodded, moving off the hologram to do whatever he needed to find Bex's location.

"I've got it," Kayne said softly. "I'll send it to your comm."

"Thank you. Good work," Cyrus acknowledged, quickly closing the connection to review the address.

He quickly dressed, pulling on jeans and a hoodie. He strapped a gun to his lower back and left. As he traveled down the lift, he sent pings to Jacinto and Aida, giving them Bex's location. Aida was the furthest from the address, with Cyrus the closest. She wanted him to wait for her, but he refused. Unease was eating him up inside, and he wasn't going to wait for anyone.

Cyrus sped down the freeway, weaving in and out of cars on his hovercycle. Had it only been a few weeks since Bex showed him the deepest parts of who they were? Brought him to their cabin in the woods and let him in?

Cyrus jumped off the cycle, barely waiting to put it in park. He ripped off his helmet, dropped it to the ground, and ran up the steps. He slammed through the door, looking around the dark home.

"Bex?" he called out, déjà vu making his steps falter.

Were they passed out somewhere in the house? He hadn't been shown the rest of the place, and it was larger inside than it looked outside. He searched their bedroom, heart racing when he didn't find them.

As he walked back toward the living room, he took a deep inhale through his nose. All the different smells came to him at once. The plants from the garden outside, the paint strewn about the floor. But under that was the faint smell of spiced apples and … vomit.

"Bex?" he called out again, louder this time.

His feet moved faster than his brain could keep up. Doors opened and slammed as he searched every room he could find. The locator could only tell him Bex was at the cabin, but not their exact location. Finally, he reached a door that seemed to descend into a finished basement. Their scent was more potent, but so was the smell of vomit and other bodily fluids.

"No…" he whispered to himself.

Maybe he should've waited for Aida. Waited for Jacinto. His hands shook as he held the railing and slowly descended the stairs. Cyrus' heart pounded against his ribcage, the smell getting stronger. He flipped the light switch and froze.*

This couldn't be happening.

Not again.

Couldn't he get a break? Couldn't life just … stop!

"Bex…" he said softly, approaching their still body. They were sitting on the floor, leaning back on a couch. "Little wolf?" he asked, voice cracking.

He paused, afraid of what he would find when he reached them. Afraid of confirming what he already knew. Pain radiated up Cyrus' body as his knees hit the floor. He touched their cold hand, a sob catching in his throat.

"No … Not after everything," he whimpered. He kept his gaze averted, not wanting to see them.

Not yet.

The cool touch of Bex's hand in his own was enough to bring his entire world crashing down around him. It felt as if everything he built in his life was just a figment of his imagination. The last few months were a blur, a fuse burning through his life until it exploded. He gripped their hand, putting it to his lips, kissing their cold knuckles. Their potions inhaler dropped from their palm.

"I should've done more," he rasped. "I should've made you stop." A wetness seeped into his jeans as he slid to sit. He didn't

* "when the party's over" by Billie Eilish

want to think about what it was. "Little wolf..." he whimpered.

He sat there next to Bex and put an arm around their shoulders, pulling them to his chest. His heart shattered more when he noticed the painting across the room. *His* painting had been in their direct line of view.

"My little wolf," he whispered, pushing their hair from their cold forehead. He kept his eyes forward while he held them and rocked. Numbness crept up his body, his anima ... His heart. "I failed you, Bex. I told you I didn't mind the potions, but I did. I really fucking did, despite how hypocritical it was," he said softly, continuing to rock and pet their hair.

"You tried. But I should've made you try harder. Fuck what you said about not pushing you. I should've." Guilt wracked his body. A shuddering breath left him. "I'm so sorry. Please wake up. I'll make it up to you. Just please, wake up."

Cyrus' eyes were unseeing as he sat with them in his arms. He sat there for what could've been hours.

Was he in shock? Maybe he was. At least it felt better than being in pain. So much should've been said. Meaningful words he should have shared. But it had terrified him, and because of that, he didn't get the chance to say how he truly felt.

And now, he sat there knowing he'd never be able to.

Footsteps above barely registered in his consciousness. Rapid thuds made their way down the stairs, and he could do nothing but sit there as Aida's scream pierced the room.

"Bex!"

"No! If you value your life, do not move another step." Jacinto's voice filtered through the din.

It was then that he understood why the room was so dark. He was utterly lost to his berserker. Growling echoed in the space, and it took him a moment to realize it was coming from him. His hold on Bex tightened when Aida tried to take a step regardless of Jacinto's warning.

"No, please, please! I need to see them. Need to see if I can—" A sob cut off her voice. "Bex..." the whimper that escaped the doctor radiated through Cyrus' body.

"Cyrus," came Jacinto's soft and soothing voice. Trying and failing to pull him from the dark hole he buried himself in. His lips curled up in a snarl when Jacinto tried to approach, and he snapped at the man's hand like a rabid dog. "Lo siento. I am not trying to take them away from you."

Cyrus rocked still, petting Bex's hair. Their thick, messy hair. The hair he loved running his hands through. The hair he loved gripping to hear their little moans.

He held their body tightly with the opposite arm, trying to be mindful of how frail it was now. He brushed his lips over their forehead, hoping it was all a dream and that he'd be met with warm skin. Instead, his body shook when it was cold.

"Cyrus—" Jacinto started.

"No. Shush. You'll wake them," he whispered. "I tried waking them, but they're in too deep a sleep." Tears splashed onto Bex's hair, tears that he realized were falling from his face. Bleary-eyed, he looked up at his Sire, who looked at him with grief. He had never seen him cry before. "Why are you crying? Do you think they won't wake? Are they asleep forever?"

Cyrus was devolving. Any progress he'd made in the last few months was being stripped from him bit by bit. Delirium set in as his mind left him. He was tired of the pain. He couldn't take any more of it—especially all at once.

He shut down slowly, like the power going out after a long night, and the bulbs slowly went black. His body felt heavier as he tried to push it all away.

All the pain, all the heartbreak, all the sadness.

All the joy, all the happiness … all the love.

The further he shoved it, the more clarity returned to him. Enough for him to look at his Sire and say, "Take it away."

When Aida attempted to approach, Cyrus let her this time but refused to let Bex go.

"Bex, please," Aida cried.

Cyrus struggled but managed to shut out her sorrow. He barely had space for his own. Jacinto finally got to his knees beside Cyrus and cupped his face.

"Do you understand what you're asking of me?" he asked softly.

Cyrus shifted to open his arm and let Aida into the embrace he held with Bex. Her sobs rocked Bex's body, and Cyrus nodded.

"Yes. I can't do this. I can't. I can't." Tears fell down his face, and he forced his grief back. "I'll be no good to you. To this kingdom," he choked out. "Please," he begged.

Despite his words, he cradled Aida's head as she placed her forehead on Bex's shoulder. "Please," he whispered.

"All right," Jacinto breathed. He held Cyrus' face in his hands, making their eyes connect. "Cyrus. You are going to forget how you feel about Killian Pierce, Bex Lopez, and Aida Broderick. You will not forget your time with them. You will not forget these last few months. But those emotions, you will no longer feel."

Cyrus sighed softly, rubbing his nose to keep from sniffling. He let Aida say her goodbyes to Bex as he stood and sat on the stairs. They pinged emergency services, and soon, sirens could be heard. Everything moved fast, and he watched with dull eyes as they carefully put Bex on a stretcher. Numb, he watched as Aida left with them in a fit of tears and sobs.

"It's time to go," Jacinto said as he placed a hand on Cyrus' shoulder, making him jump. "Are you okay?" his Sire asked, assessing him.

"Yeah, I'm good," Cyrus muttered.

But it was a lie.

He *wasn't* good. He was far from it.

Because the compulsion didn't work, and that in itself was concerning. If his King's compulsion didn't work, what else would it fail to prevent?

Cyrus still felt everything. Felt it in painful detail. He quickly realized that their magnitude couldn't simply be erased. But he wouldn't let his Sire know. He wouldn't let anyone know. No one will know because he'd be numb. He'll continue to force everything into the very recesses of his anima until it was nothing but a blip in the history of his life, wearing a mask he would have to wear until it became his reality.

Because there was one thing Cyrus knew for sure. He would rather be numb than feel anything ever again.

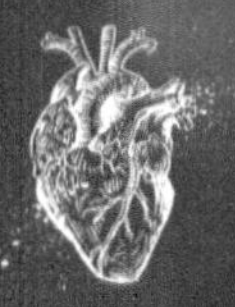

CHAPTER 32

RAINY NIGHTS

WHY DID IT RAIN during Pax-sending rituals? It was said that it meant the cosmos cleared the way for animas to make their way to Orcus. That it took a full seven nights to make its journey. For seven nights, people gathered and offered offerings to help the departed anima reach Pax, knowing they were loved.*

To the world, Cyrus seemed put together. He had locked himself away for seven nights, processing and practicing to keep his emotions in check. He forced on a mask he would wear for the rest of his immortal life. But tonight, his mind raged.

Earlier in the evening Cyrus had found himself on his knees, screaming his sorrow. With his hands gripping his head and his body curled into a ball, he had sobbed. All the work he had done went out the window as soon as it dawned upon him that Bex's Pax-sending was tonight. Would they find peace? Did he screw up by not admitting how he felt, and now they'd find themself in Cassus? The guilt wore him down, and he almost decided not to attend.

But he couldn't do that. Because if he didn't show up, Jacinto would know the compulsion failed. That was the last thing they needed. So, he reined himself in once more. The wall went up brick by brick, and his body shut down. Yes, his mind raged, but he was stoic and void to the world.

Cyrus stood by the open mausoleum that held Bex's coffin. Everything about it was as bright as they were in life. Inside were flowers and plants of all sorts left by Killian. Throughout were small wolf plushies and gifts from Aida. He arrived early, knowing others

---

* "The Night Does Not Belong To God" by Sleep Token

would show up for the closing of the doors. Once they were sealed … Well, that was it.

Cyrus gripped his offering so tightly that the leather groaned. He took deep breaths, placed a hand on the coffin, and tried to keep his composure. Under the slab was his little wolf—the one who had turned his world upside down in the best ways and now in the worst.

"I miss you, Bex," he whispered. He slipped his offering into his inner jacket, deciding he would place it right before the closure.

"It looks like I didn't have to destroy your life," came a bitter voice from behind.

Cyrus turned slowly, jaw clenched as he took in Killian. Messy straight hair fell over his brow as if he ran his hand through it several times. He wore a loose-fitting black turtleneck, one of his tattooed hands stuffed into the pocket of his black jeans. Kohl lined eyes a yellow so deep it was almost golden, with red around the pupils.

Killian wriggled his ring-covered fingers at Cyrus, anger radiating off him in waves. "You did that all by yourself, *sire*."

"Fuck you, Killian," Cyrus snapped. "Now isn't the time." He rounded the coffin opposite the younger vampire.

"Do you know how pissed Bex was when they found out what you did to me?" he asked, leaning on one of the window ledges. He crossed his ankle over the other while picking up one of the bright magenta flowers. His focus remained on the plant as he spoke. "They couldn't believe it." Killian wrapped his hand around the flower. "That you would turn me against my will."

He growled as he crushed the delicate petals in his fist. The flower emitted a sweet, almost sickly scent, and deep navy nectar flowed like blood through Killian's fingers. His eyes, now the color of crimson, met Cyrus'.

"You know what they said? The last thing they said about you?" Killian pulled a handkerchief from his pocket, cleaning his hands as he waited for Cyrus to respond.

Cyrus knew he shouldn't allow himself to be baited. He

knew that whatever Killian had to say was to get a rise out of him and find any cracks in his now rock-solid exterior. And yet…

"And what's that, little boy," Cyrus said, landing his mark when the man winced.

"*Don't* call me that!" he snarled suddenly before Cyrus. The scent of espresso mixed with lit coals assaulted him, making his nose flare. "Bex told me you were a disappointment. That they were so angry at you!" Killian took a few steps back, swiping at the tears that formed in the corner of his eyes.

"You broke your promise." He jabbed his forefinger at him. "And it sent them into a spiral." The vampire grabbed another flower, this time gripping the thorny stem.

Cyrus growled at the scent of his blood. His initial reaction was to keep the man from harming himself, but he stopped himself in time. No. This wasn't his fucking problem anymore.

"This isn't the time," Cyrus said again. The way he wanted to rage against Killian was a strong visceral pull he had to fight to ignore.

"It's your fault, you know?" Killian seethed, dropping the bloodied flower.

Cyrus froze, watching as a smug smile pulled up Killian's full lips. The vampire's demeanor shifted before his eyes, arrogance exuding from his very being. His steel-toed boots thudded as he approached Cyrus, and the shoes gave him extra height. Any sign of sadness was quickly erased, transforming his once lover into someone else … a monster.

"What is?" Cyrus asked as he looked down at Killian.

"Hmm, all of this," he swirled his forefingers around. "You destroy lives, Cyrus. You take them and crush them." Killian leaned in as if telling a secret. "Imagine if you had just … Not sucked us into your orbit. I'd still be a human."

"Or dead," Cyrus bit.

"Bex would still be alive. Your drama wouldn't have made them spiral, and they wouldn't have overdosed." Killian continued, ignoring Cyrus. "Aida … Well, she probably would've been arrested for her fucked up mind."

"Why are you telling me this?" he asked, annoyed.

Killian scoffed, rolling his eyes. His fingers walked from Cyrus' shoulder to his jaw. "You think I don't know?" he whispered, gripping Cyrus' chin to tilt it down and putting their faces within kissing distance.

Cyrus didn't respond, not feeding into Killian's attempt at seduction. His very good attempt, but a failure, nonetheless.

"Rumor has it the King compelled you to forget all those ugly emotions." Cyrus tried to jerk away, but Killian's grip tightened. "I think he failed." He let his lips coast over Cyrus'. "And I think you know you fucked up."

Cyrus glided his hands up Killian's arms until one wrapped around the man's throat. He held him still as he bit Killian's lower lip sharply. It was Cyrus' turn to grin darkly when Killian's breath faltered.

"You have a lot of learning to do, little boy," he growled. "I think you still love me. But hey, what do I know about love?" He let the vampire go, who quickly took a step back and adjusted his sweater.

"That's the question, isn't it? When you ask yourself that, think about Bex. Remember that it's your fault that they're dead. It's your fault they spiraled. That it's your fucking fault for all of this!" Killian yelled, turning to storm out of the mausoleum.

"Is it really all my fault for their spiral, or are you just projecting?" Cyrus snapped, making the man falter in his steps.

"What?" Killian faced Cyrus, a haunted emotion passing through his eyes so quickly that Cyrus would've missed it if he hadn't been looking.

"I turned you, yes. But *you* told them in your anger. You told them before I could explain *anything*. And who knows what the fuck you said?" Cyrus' anger rose as he took a menacing step toward Killian, who smartly took one back.

"I needed my best friend. They were my friend first before we ever met you! How fucking dare you put this on me!" Killian's façade faltered, that haunting emotion passing once more. He shook his head, running a hand through his hair.

"Right. As if you didn't know what you were doing…"

"It wasn't my intention!" Killian narrowed his kohl-lined eyes at Cyrus. "You are *not* putting this on me. You were the first domino in this massive fuck-up. Like Bex said, you're a disappointment." With that, Killian exited the mausoleum.

Cyrus let out a shuddering exhale as he leaned on the coffin. He knew this was going to be hard. But fuck.

"He's a liar."

He stood up straight at the sound of Aida's voice. She was breathtaking in a lavender dress that fell mid-calf. It brought out the silver of her eyes and complimented her dark brown skin. An oversized, black leather jacket draped over her shoulders, and he realized it was Bex's. The sight shot a pang through his chest.

"It's not your fault…" she said softly, a handful of plushies in her hands. "They made their decisions … And fuck, it's hard to accept." She looked so young in her sadness.

"It is. Want help?" he asked, offering to take some stuffed animals.

"Sure." Aida passed him a few, and in the quiet, they placed them in the few empty spots left on the ledges. As they did their lap, they ended up in front of each other.

"This might be a stupid question, but how are you? So much has happened."

"You're right. That is a very stupid question." She huffed, swiping at a few tears that broke from her lashes. "I'm angry."

"When aren't you?" Cyrus asked playfully in the hopes of making her smile. It worked as she nudged his shoulder.

"Speak for yourself," she said. "My anger is my fuel. It's going to get me through this next part of my journey. I *will* find the answers I need, and I will find a way to get revenge. I don't have to feel anything else if I stay angry."

"I understand that." Cyrus nodded, rubbing the side of his jacket that held his offering. "When do you leave?"

"This evening," Aida murmured. "I needed this closure." She looked up at him with lightning-bright silver eyes. "Be well, Cyrus. Things are only going to get harder from here."

"I am fully aware," he said with a sigh. "Travel safe, good doctor." He snorted when she punched his stomach.

"Don't call me that," she groaned despite the smile on her face. She sobered when she looked at the coffin. "I loved them, you know? I told them right before Killian blew up the night about what happened with you both."

"Fuck, I'm sorry," he said softly.

"Don't be. Everything overwhelmed Bex. We can all try to take the blame or place it on others. But ultimately, their decision was theirs," Aida repeated.

Cyrus knew it was for his benefit. He wondered if she knew Jacinto's compulsion had failed. He wouldn't be surprised.

"Bex knew you felt the same. Whether you said it or not, it was obvious."

"Yeah. I guess," Cyrus said, trying to brush off how those words made him feel. *Fuck* emotions.

"Right. I'll leave you be," Aida said softly. She bent over the coffin, kissing the smooth marble surface. "I love you, Bex."

Before she could leave, Cyrus gently took her wrist and pulled her close. She blinked, staring up at him with wide eyes.

"Please be safe," he said softly, his large hand cupping her face. His thumb brushed a tear that traveled down her cheek.

"I will." Their gazes held, and she gripped his hand. "Cyrus … I *will*."

"You better. And you better stay in contact. Anything you need, it's within my power to provide you with." He paused, letting her truly soak in what he was saying.

"T-thank you," she whispered. He leaned in and gave her a soft and unexpectedly sweet kiss.

"Thank me by finding revenge. Rage, Aida. Burn it all, the fuck, down."

Aida nodded, sighing as she stepped away from him.

"In another life…" she started.

"It would be different. But here we are."

"Here we are," she agreed. "Be well."

Cyrus' hands shook the moment he was alone. He told

Jacinto to focus on finishing up his remaining loose ends. To not worry. His Sire wasn't too sure about it but ultimately agreed.

"Life is pretty fucked up, isn't it?" Cyrus sighed, reaching into his coat jacket to grab his offering. "There will never be someone like you, do you know that?" He thumbed the smooth leather. "Maybe you can hear me wherever you are. I hope so." His breath hitched. "I love you, Bex. And I hate I never got the chance to tell you."

A soft clinking rang when he lifted the red and black collar in his hand. When Aida was given Bex's personal effects, they had been wearing his collar. That piece of information sought to break all the new binds he put on his heart. It was a battle to keep it all contained. To be able to breathe without pain searing through his chest.

As he placed the collar at the head of the coffin, Cyrus let a tear cascade down his cheek. The last tear he'll ever let fall. His body straightened as it settled once more. He gently rubbed the spot on his shoulder that still bore their mark as he walked out of the mausoleum, wiping the tear from his face. Grabbing the handles, he took one last look at the black and red collar on top of the coffin.

As the doors closed, he whispered for the last time, "I love you, little wolf."

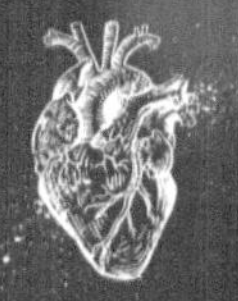

EPILOGUE

FOUR MONTHS LATER

CYRUS' JAW CLENCHED AS he took in the body on the coroner's exam table. The victim's throat had been nearly torn apart, with pieces of their deltoid chewed through as well. The significant blood loss told him exactly who was behind it.

"We found this one in Aludam. But another two were found in Seeker's Pointe," Lynn, the coroner remarked, nibbling on her pen cap as she assessed the body.

"What is the current body count?" Cyrus asked, crossing his arms and lifting his hand to rest his chin on.

"One hundred…"

"Fuck!"

Cyrus resisted the urge to lash out lest he accidentally hurt the werewolf. He paced the room instead, looking at the atlas that hovered over a desk. Along the east coast of Potroya were dozens of markings. Each represented a body with its throat brutally torn and drained of blood.

"Killian…" he whispered to himself.

As King Regent, he felt as if he were failing. If he couldn't get this under control, what else would slip through his hands? He knew Killian was making a statement, and it was working. It fucking hit him every time a body popped up.

"Cyrus?" Lynn's voice drew him from his spiral.

"Are we any closer to finding him?" he asked softly, reining in his frustration. His emotions banged on their cage, begging him to rage, but he locked it down.

"No. But if anything changes, I'll tell you immediately." The werewolf approached him slowly. "We're doing everything we can."

"Do more." Was all he said, ignoring her wince as he left.

Cyrus let out a frustrated growl as he made his way home. The lift that brought him to his penthouse felt slower than usual, like moving through sludge.

As he entered his living room, an incoming ping drew his attention to his comm. Seeing it was Aida, he accepted it. Her beautiful face filtered into the space, eyes lit with excitement.

"You're looking good, Aida," he said with a smile, his mood lifting instantly. Their communications were something he found himself enjoying. When he couldn't speak to Jacinto or Tristan, he could rely on Aida.

"He's alive!" she blurted.

"What?" he asked, brows raised.

"My brother. He's alive. And I wanted to say thank you."

"Me? Why?" he asked, taking a seat as he processed what she just told him.

"He was compelled, and because of our experiments, I was able to break it and get him back."

Tears filled her eyes. His own widened as he ran a hand down his face.

"Where are you?" he asked.

"We're in Asherai. But we are moving out to Silvermoon Harbor. I don't know all the details on the why. I just know there's a lot happening." A muffled voice caught her attention, and she nodded a few times in response. "I'll reach out again as soon as I can."

Before he could respond, the connection cut off. His comm rang again, this time being his King.

"Perfect timing," Cyrus said with a downturn of his lips, taking in Jacinto's tired look.

"Oh? Why's that?" he asked, a smirk playing on his mouth despite the exhaustion.

"Another body was found." He sighed, sinking into his chair more. "Please tell me you're on your way back," he said sarcastically.

"I wish, hermano. I wish." Jacinto looked him over.

Something glinted in his eyes that Cyrus nearly missed.

"What's wrong?" Cyrus asked, sitting up.

"Nothing. You know, we're going to war," Jacinto said softly, running a hand through his long hair. "This next leg of this mission is going to be dangerous. We've learned new information and are waiting on supplies before we make the next move."

"Hey, don't forget your promise, okay?" Cyrus said, making Jacinto look at him thoroughly. "You make it back here in one piece, Cin."

"I will." A softness in his tone and eyes left Cyrus longing for his touch. Just for some stability after months of numb fucking. "I have to go. I just wanted to check in before our formal meeting in a few days. I hope you're taking care of yourself…"

"As best I can," Cyrus said, brushing him off.

Jacinto just smirked, clicking the comm off.

Cyrus stood slowly, walking to the stunning piece of art that hung from the wall. His fingers glided over the canvas, feeling the soft grooves of the paint, the brush strokes, the passion. A panther stared out at him, eyes black with red-rimmed pupils. His eyes. It was half shrouded in foliage made of greys and whites, dahlias standing out the most. The blood that dripped from the leaves perfectly summed up who he was: death and destruction wrapped in a handsome package.

Did Bex really view him with such wonder? When he decided to put the artwork up, he knew it would challenge his steel exterior. It was a constant reminder, but he needed it.

What could Cyrus say about the last year of his life? It had been tumultuous. Before, he had no fucks to give. No commitments to make or keep. All he had to do was focus on his King and kingdom. Do his duty and call it a night.

But life had a funny way of interrupting his normal, throwing everything into disarray. Love was never in his plans. His plans were usually meticulous, and everything went out the window. Riding the coattails of bittersweet love was tragedy. He knew all good things had to end. He just thought he would've had more time.

Time was an odd thing. Cyrus always thought he had both

too much and too little. It was relevant and never felt the same at any given time. He often wondered where he'd be if he only had more time. But he shut those thoughts down as soon as they appeared.

Regrets, longing, memories … he couldn't focus on those things. He had a commitment to his kingdom. He could never lose sight of that—no more distractions.

The easiest way to do that was never to love again.

To never let his heart bleed for another.

To never feel them die in his arms when he eventually fucked up.

Love had no place in his life. He'd tried and failed. After four long months, he had found peace.

No, love wasn't meant for Cyrus.

And that was okay … right?*

* "Popular Monster" by Falling in Reverse

THE END...

FOR NOW.

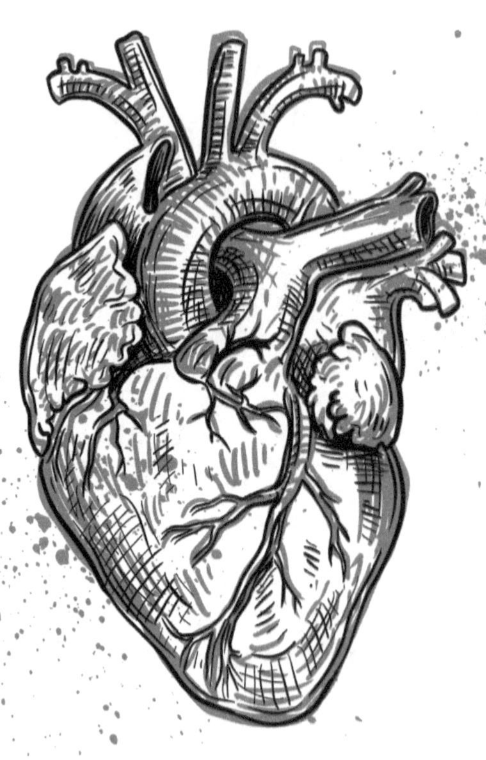

ACKNOWLEDGEMENTS

There's a lot to be said about writing "Cyrus". I knew I was taking a risk writing such a tragic story. One that was dark, gritty, raw, and messy. I was scared and nervous. I almost said "nope" and quit. But my strong author and reader communities encouraged me to continue. To write the story that needed to be told, no matter how risky it would be.

Many thanks to Cynthia! Your encouragement is what drove me the most. You are so familiar and intimate with my characters and often knew what they would do before I did! You pushed me to write this story and you pushed HARD. And I am forever grateful for your friendship and feedback!

Barbosa... CAPTAIN!!! Thank you for not only editing, but helping me develop this story further. You helped me see things within the story that I wouldn't have thought about otherwise. Your wisdom is why it shaped up the way it did in the end. You'll always be the Spongebob to my Patrick!

Many thanks to my beta readers. Your feedback truly meant a lot. You have no idea! Being able to hear from a reader's perspective helped me see ways I could improve. Y'all stuck with me and had patience when I floundered. THANK YOU!

Bri, you are awesome and amazing for creating such a vividly dark cover for this book. You saw my vision and didn't hesitate to deliver!

B. (Flash Fryed), you brought my characters to life! It was like you dug into my brain and pulled them out. Thank you!

To my ARCs, readers, and book community, I will forever be grateful for your support! Your DMs and reactions to all of my stories mean the world to me. Thank you for believing in me!

Cyrus WILL be back next year (2026) with the continuation and ending of his story.

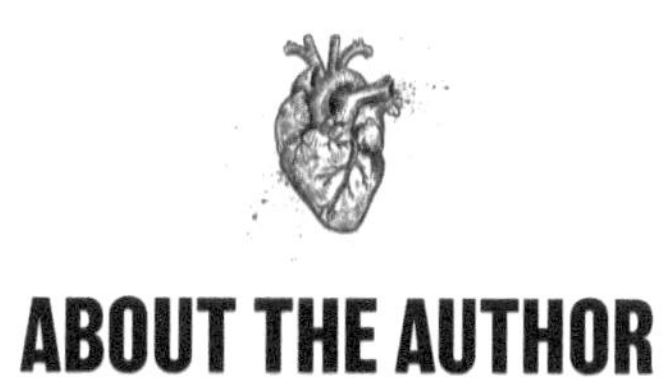

ABOUT THE AUTHOR

A.E. Cosby is a Puerto Rican and indigenous person obsessed with the dark and arcane. They are a bruja who honors their Ancestors and the path that have been put before them. They believe with their whole chest that they lived on another planet in another life. Being an Aquarius, this is not a surprise! Having vivid dreams of this world, they invite you to experience this planet through their dark urban fantasy novels. They share the darkest parts of their soul through their work.

A.E. is a neurospicy comic book nerd, enjoys sci-fi and fantasy, and tattoos. Ask them how many they have. (Hint: 14+). They have three chaos gremlins and a husband who supports their dream.

You can connect with them through their website and social media channels.

hello@anissacosby.com

https://linktr.ee/anissacosby

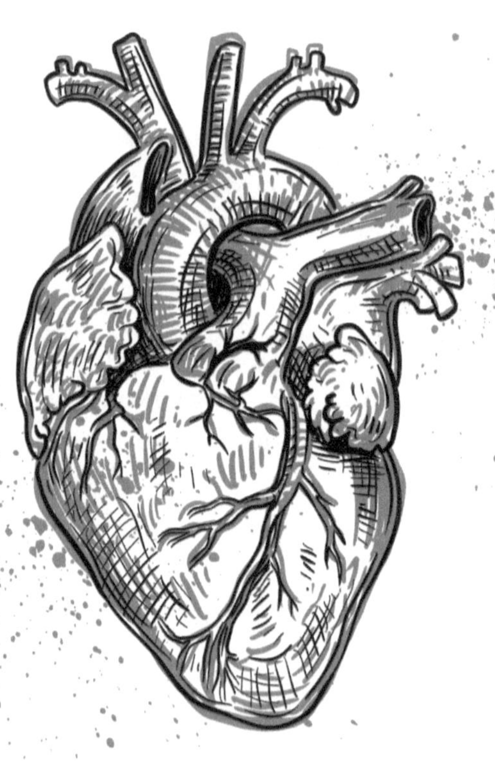

OTHER WORKS BY A.E. COSBY

THE CHAOS SERIES

The Chaos Wielder
Wrath's Daughter
Death & Shadow (companion novella)

BLOOD & HEARTS DUOLOGY

Cyrus

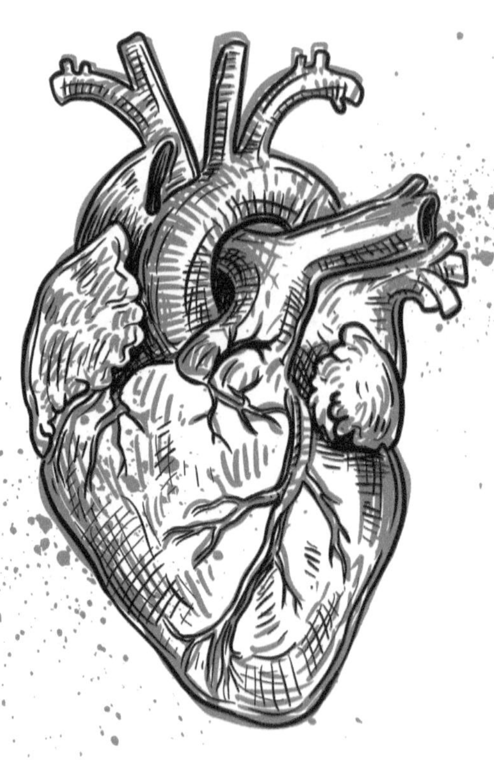